Praise

The RECESSIONISTAS

"Smart... Wall Street financial whiz Alexandra Lebenthal has first-hand experience with these characters in real life." —*Cosmopolitan*

"Hilarious... provides a glimpse into the lives of the ladies who lunch."
—*New York Post*

"A tightly plotted mystery narrated by a cast of wives, assistants, and mistresses—but it's packed with information... The book is centered on real-life events, from the firesale of Bear Stearns to the Bergdorf Goodman–Manolo Blahnik lunch event that one character—the spendthrift wife of a Lehman bond salesman—attends on the day of that firm's collapse." —*New York Magazine*

"Timely, trendy, and sassy. Enjoy the book and don't be surprised if a film version of it follows in the near future."
—Associated Content

"A read that you can't put down... it's extraordinary... No one knows better than Alexandra what happened to the city when the markets started falling apart... every character I met in this book I felt I knew, every single one of them."
—Joan Hamburg,
The Joan Hamburg Show, WOR Radio (NY)

"*Gossip Girl* with grown-ups!" —*Star Magazine*

"Fun and sassy...delivers satisfying poetic justice in its depiction of the hubris and sense of entitlement that led to the economic downfall of many wealthy New Yorkers."

—*Library Journal*

"Fabulous...humorous."

—Parker Ladd, *Palm Beach Daily News*

"A romp of a book. It is fun and funny, devilish and decadent, wry and witty. It is also a razor-edged portrait of that *sui generis* creature known as the Manhattan Upper East Sider, oh so painfully learning that life is not always a billion-dollar hedge fund."

—Buzz Bissinger, author of *Friday Night Lights*
and contributing editor, *Vanity Fair*

"Told in the fashion of good, solid gossip...a yes yes to a reader who is curious to know 'what' it/they was/were like."

—NewYorkSocialDiary.com

"No one but Alexandra Lebenthal—part financial wizardess, part keen social observer—could write this unflinching portrait of New York's neo-gilded age, pre- and post–Wall Street apocalypse."

—Jill Kargman,
author of *The Ex-Mrs. Hedgefund*

"A fabulous read." —*Complete Woman*

"Lebenthal's book is about a world I know well and she knows better: very rich people in Manhattan and the Hamptons...a book Balzac would have enjoyed."

—Jesse Kornbluth, HuffingtonPost.com

"As only she could do so well—given her platinum pedigree and Wall Street cred—Alexandra Lebenthal has written a smart, sassy novel that peers into a world of wealth and privilege turned on its crazy head. This is a dishy, divine first novel."

—William Cohan, *New York Times* bestselling author of *House of Cards*

"A good, dishy book... rich detailing... like a *Gossip Girl* for grown-ups... But readers be warned, this isn't just a name-dropping, more-fabulous-than-thou fluff read, Lebenthal also spins quite a good financial tale as well. For every fashion name dropped, there's a financial one too... It's clear that Lebenthal knows her subject matter intimately."

—Luxist.com

"A rollicking debut by an author who clearly knows the secrets of the boom—and the bust."

—Mark Seal, contributing editor, *Vanity Fair*

The RECESSIONISTAS

Alexandra Lebenthal

NEW YORK BOSTON

This book is a work of fiction. Names, characters, places, and incidents are the product of the author's imagination or are used fictitiously. Any resemblance to actual events, locales, or persons, living or dead, is coincidental.

Grand Central Publishing
Hachette Book Group
237 Park Avenue
New York, NY 10017

www.HachetteBookGroup.com

Printed in the United States of America

Originally published in hardcover by Grand Central Publishing

First Trade Edition: August 2011
10 9 8 7 6 5 4 3 2 1

Grand Central Publishing is a division of Hachette Book Group, Inc.
The Grand Central Publishing name and logo is a trademark of Hachette Book Group, Inc.

The publisher is not responsible for websites (or their content) that are not owned by the publisher.

The Library of Congress has cataloged the hardcover edition as follows:

Lebenthal, Alexandra.
The recessionistas / Alexandra Lebenthal. 1st ed.
p. cm.
ISBN 978-0-446-56367-3
1. Socialites–Fiction. 2. Rich people–New York (State)–New York–Fiction. 3. Recessions–Social aspects–New York (State)–New York–Fiction. 4. Upper East Side (New York, N.Y.)–Fiction. 5. Chick lit. I. Title.
PS3612.E247R43 2010
813'.6–dc22

2010001139

ISBN 978-0-446-56368-0 (pbk.)

For my mother
Jacqueline Beymer Lebenthal

Acknowledgments

There were a tremendous number of people who helped me in the process of writing this book and I owe them all heartfelt thanks for their assistance.

First and foremost, my agent Richard Curtis, who contacted me several years ago and asked if I'd like to write a book. After a few years I said yes. Richard's faith in me, and as important, his faith in my characters, helped this story take shape and come alive.

It is is difficult to publish without a publisher and a book certainly won't be nearly as good without an editor to guide it, so to everyone at Grand Central Publishing, I am deeply grateful for all the tremendous enthusiasm shown *The Recessionistas* from day one. Above all, deepest of thanks to my editor, Karen Kosztolnyik, who loved my ideas from the start, giving me gentle yet firm guidance throughout the process.

There were many people who I relied on for information about the various worlds I wrote about, so in no particular order but with the same level of appreciation, great thanks are due for filling in the blanks that have made this story that much better: Lydia Fenet, "Aunt Mary's nephew," Doug Millett, Michelle Smith, Frederick Anderson, Somers Farkas, Sheila Parham, Odette Cabrera, Bruce Pask, Judy Poller, Roger "Raj" Meltzer, Allison Aston, Jessica Stark, Howard Read, Lisa Podos, Richelle Grant, Sue Conroy Frith, Jon and Andrew Tisch, Rae Bianco, Jeff Hirsh, Gillian Miniter, Charlie Ayres, and Matt Moneypenney. A special note of thanks to Dr. R. H. Rees Pritchett, Dr. Patricia

Kavanagh, Dr. Barry Stein, and Dr. John Golfinos for their medical knowledge, which wasn't quite what I wanted to hear. Thank goodness this is fiction.

Thanks also to my cousin Buzz Bissinger for a few insights into the publishing world, which I knew so little about.

I give very special and heartfelt thanks to David Patrick Columbia, who showed me that I had a voice, silent all those years, but waiting to come out. He encouraged it and gave it life on www.NewYorkSocialDiary.com. I will be ever grateful to him for his support and will continue to be in awe of his writing and profound social observations.

Special appreciation to my family: my sister, Claudia, my brother, Jimmy, and of course, my inimitable, creative, supportive (and great writer himself) dad, Jim.

Thank you to my children, Ben, Charlotte, and Ellie, who embody only the best of the Silver children, well, most of the time. I love you dearly. Thank you for your ideas and encouragement throughout.

And especially, and above all, to my husband and love of my life, Jay Diamond. Without your support, suggestions, and editing assistance, these pages would all be blank.

The RECESSIONISTAS

CHAPTER ONE

A Perfect Life

The Tuesday after Labor Day in New York City is the definitive sign that summer is over. In certain neighborhoods, and frankly nowhere more so than the Upper East Side of Manhattan, streets that only the week before had been veritable ghost towns suddenly are full of life with Razor scooters, towheaded children, shrieking teenagers who haven't seen one another all summer...and above all, the mothers. These are women of a certain social and economic status who somehow manage to take up most of the already narrow walking area on Madison Avenue. As they get caught up in conversation, good luck to anyone on the street needing to get around them, for in some bizarre showing of animal behavior, these women manage to take up the entire width of the block with dogs on expandable leashes, shopping bags, and long, toned legs, usually outfitted in workout garb, as they mark their territory.

Grigsby Somerset was one of those mothers. On most days from September until early June, she could be found between 8:00 and 9:00 a.m. on the corner of 92nd Street and Madison Avenue at Yura, the gourmet coffee, muffin, and meeting place at the epicenter of Carnegie Hill, a stone's throw from a handful of the top schools in the city. Grigsby was a queen bee and was almost always surrounded by others who aspired to be like her. She had been the alpha girl even as a child in Darien and had a certain level of confidence that made others deferential toward her. Often, one of her friends getting a second cup of coffee as they sat in the window seats would say, "Latte, extra foam—right, Grigsby?" Knowing Grigsby's coffee order signified their status in her inner circle.

When Grigsby left Yura, it usually involved another ten minutes on the street outside, further cementing her dominance of the neighborhood. But not this morning. Today she was situated firmly in her apartment on Park Avenue with important work to do. The long and luxurious Southampton summer was clearly over, and as she pulled her blond locks into a messy bun and then grabbed her list and bottle of water, she was not looking forward to the task that loomed ahead. For the Tuesday after Labor Day is the dreaded application day for ongoing and nursery schools. Grigsby, however, was ready. She had the list of schools that needed to be called for her four-year-old daughter, Bitten: Spence, Chapin, Brearley, Nightingale, and Sacred Heart, with Hewitt and Marymount as "safeties" already loaded into her speed dial.

Spencer, eight, and William, six, were at Buckley, and while she was a firm believer in single-sex education, at least until boarding school, Grigsby did wish for a moment that she had sent them to coed Trinity, Dalton, or Horace Mann so Bitten would have sibling preference, thereby making today not quite as crucial. The process was so competitive, however, that there were even some horror stories of younger brothers or sisters having to go to P.S. 6 because they hadn't gotten into their sibling's school. More than one family had been known to suddenly announce they were moving to Greenwich, which coincidentally came right after school notification dates in mid-February. But Grigsby knew that once you moved to Greenwich, even though the public schools were terrific, everyone ended up wanting to be at Greenwich Academy or Brunswick, which meant ultimately encountering the same application nightmare there. The fact is that some people would gladly pay $30,000 a year to have their kids at the right schools with the right people rather than get an equally good free education at a public school.

Grigsby really would be happy with any of the schools, although she had her heart set on Spence. She pictured Bitten on her first day of school next fall in her green plaid tunic outside 93rd Street and Madison, where Spence's lower school was located in the former Smithers Mansion, renovated with the proceeds of a successful capital campaign. Chapin was her second choice, although there would be logistical issues getting from their apartment on 92nd and Park to Buckley on 73rd and "Lex," to East End Avenue and 84th Street. Even with Sheldon driving them in the Range Rover, it would be tough going every morning and barely give her time to get to Yura to meet her friends. The congestion of limos on Oscar night had nothing on drop-off at private schools in New York City.

While she had her preferences, each school had its own reputation that had stood the test of decades, though the city itself had changed enormously during that time. The school a child went to could end up defining both the child and his or her family. Spence had *the* right mix of parents with whom Grigsby wanted to be associated. The education, of course, would be top-notch there, as it would at all the schools to which she was applying. Chapin still retained the old money feel that it had for generations, going back to when a young Jacqueline Bouvier had been a student. Everyone said Nightingale was "wonderfully nurturing" and had produced its own set of notable alumnae, from designer Shoshanna Lonstein Gruss, to Democratic strategist Mandy Grunwald, to Cecily von Ziegesar, author of the *Gossip Girl* books. And while she and Blake were not Catholic, she knew several families that were quite pleased with Sacred Heart and Marymount—and what's wrong with a little religion class to instill moral values in children? Of course, that Sacred Heart uniform with its red gingham pinafore was just too adorable. Brearley was located down the street from Chapin and was excellent, but she always felt the more "bohemian" families ended up there. She also remembered with dismay that the Brearley girls she went to college with were often serial Grateful Dead followers and quoted Camille Paglia a bit too often. It was a little much for her. And because it was close to Chapin, she would have the same location issues. Then there was Hewitt, which unlike the others had changed a great deal. Years before, it tended to be the school for girls who were not as strong academically (at least according to their ERB scores), but in the last decade, with the private school competition as intense as it was, Hewitt's boat had risen along with the tide of fortunes in the city. All in all, she had many wonderful choices—but first she needed to get the application process completed!

Before Blake left for work that morning, Grigsby made sure that he had the list of schools to call and instructions that he and his assistant needed to follow. It was critical that all calls be made that morning, not just for her daughter's future academic career, but because Grigsby had an incredibly busy first day back ahead of her and she didn't have time to chase Blake down to make sure he had completed everything. She had a 12:30 lunch at Bergdorf, followed by a fitting in the couture department on four for the gown she was planning to wear to the New Yorkers for Children Gala in two weeks. Then (desperately needed) highlights at Blandi at 3:00 and hopefully some downtime to get herself back on her city schedule before she met Blake, his half brother, Chip, and his new wife, Chessy, for dinner at Swifty's at 7:00.

After spending the whole summer away, Grigsby knew things would be a complete madhouse. Thankfully, Donita had agreed to come back to work on Labor Day, so with any luck, by later today most of the laundry would be done and put away. But there was still so much to organize before she could even allow herself one second to relax. The boys had their first day of school on Wednesday, and Bitten would start nursery school gradually that week, starting with an hour on Thursday and two hours on Friday. Schools were concerned that after summer vacation four-year-olds might encounter the same separation anxiety they had in their first year of nursery school, so they started with a gradual schedule over the course of several days, asking that a parent start out in the classroom, then move just outside, and then be in the neighborhood, with the ultimate goal of separating entirely. Most children entered the room and barely glanced at their mother. It usually wasn't the children who needed the proximity, however, and once in a while an overly protective and attentive mother had to be told gently that her child would be fine and asked to leave.

This was not the case with Grigsby, who found that getting back to normal, seeing all her friends, and gearing up for her social calendar made for a hectic first week back. Having to be tied to school made that more difficult. It was really too much for her. It would be terrific to have her own assistant, and she had started mentioning casually to Blake what a time-saver it would be. She knew eventually she would get it, because eventually she got everything she wanted.

Grigsby was also irritated that Blake seemed distracted when he left at 7:15 that morning, just as she came in from her four-mile run in Central Park with her trainer. She repeated the instructions she had given him and was astonished that he did not remember the same drill they'd gone through for nursery school two years before or for the boys when they'd applied to ongoing schools. She couldn't be expected to take care of all these things herself. It was hard enough to keep their home as chicly appointed as it was, manage their Southampton house, take care of their social schedule, plan vacations, do her charity work, keep the children well dressed, and of course always look as good (not to mention toned) as she did without having another project thrown on top of it. Each school to which they applied would require three visits: the tour, the parent interview, and then the child interview. Multiply that by six schools and it was on the order of eighteen different appointments. Of course, applications would have to be filled out, and more important, lists of all the boards of trustees would have to be studied to determine whom they might approach for recommendations, because as everyone knew, anything that you needed in the city could be made possible by connections with the right people.

Frankly, though, Blake had seemed detached for the last several weeks. For the first time since they had been going to Southampton, he hadn't even made it out for all of the final two weeks of the summer. He had finally come out on the Jitney on Wednesday night of the last week, but for most of Thursday and Friday he was pacing the long lawn in front of their house leading down to the bay while on his cell phone. More than once he had approached her wide-eyed and angry, pantomiming at her to take the kids away from him so he could finish his call. Welcome to life with children. It wasn't as if she hadn't spent all summer trying to deal with them.

Grigsby knew she probably should pay more attention to what was going on in the financial world, but in general it was all too complicated and boring. She had to admit that even for her, this year had certainly had its share of drama. Her friend Winter "Winnie" Smith's husband ran one of the derivatives desks at Bear Stearns. In March, when Bear Stearns was "acquired" by JPMorgan at a fire sale price, she and her husband had lost almost everything, although he did end up getting hired by JPMorgan. Grigsby hadn't seen her much over the summer, and when she had, Winnie had seemed harried and drawn. She even thought she'd noticed Winnie look away on the beach a few times and was sure she had crossed the street when Grigsby saw her on Jobs Lane. What was even more shocking, the Smiths hadn't come to the Somersets' annual clambake on the beach, an event people usually rearranged schedules to attend.

But thankfully Blake worked at Lehman Brothers, not Bear Stearns, so Grigsby really wasn't all that concerned about their situation. Anyway, everyone said that Bear always skated too close to the edge. Lehman Brothers had much more stability. At least that was what Blake told her and what she had picked up from conversations between him and his friends from business school, most of whom also worked on Wall Street.

"The Spence School admissions department, may I help you?"

Grigsby snapped back to attention from her thoughts as the voice answered on the other end.

She went through the list of questions, giving her and Blake's name and their address, along with Bitten's date of birth and nursery school. She set the date for their tour, Monday, September 15, at 9:30 a.m. Fantastic. One down, six to go!

Thankfully, by 10:00 that morning she had reached all but two of the schools and e-mailed Blake for the third time to check on his progress. With still no answer, she finally called his office and reached his assistant, Andrea.

"It's Mrs. Somerset calling. Please put my husband on." She always said the same thing and never bothered to ask Andrea how she was or even said hello. Andrea had long ago stopped trying to say or do anything other than to get Blake on the phone, since it was clear Grigsby didn't really care, let alone even know who was answering the phone on the other end.

"Yes. Hello, Mrs. Somerset. I'm sorry, but Bla...er, Mr. Somerset has been out of the office all morning, and I'm afraid I can't reach him."

"What??" Grigsby shouted, making no effort to conceal her anger. "Hasn't he been making calls for schools? I made it absolutely clear that was project *numero uno* today! Out of the office??!! I cannot believe him. I simply cannot believe him. Doesn't he get what is going on today?!"

Andrea rolled her eyes at the phone and wondered if Grigsby had managed to read any papers in the last several months. Wall Street and the economy were melting down, and it wasn't just in *The Wall Street Journal*, but in the mainstream media. Somehow Marie Antoinette, as Andrea liked to refer to her, hadn't gotten the memo.

Before Andrea could respond, however, Grigsby said brusquely, "Ugh...never mind. I'll do everything myself—as I always do. Just tell him to call me as soon as he gets out...and that the only schools we still need to speak to are Hewitt and Marymount... but I'm not going to be here past eleven because I have lunch and a lot of other appointments... so call my cell or send me an e-mail or text... but I don't know if I will be able to respond then... so if not, I'll see him at dinner... which he better not have forgotten about either... It's at seven p.m. at Swifty's with Chip and Chessy." Grigsby slammed the phone down, as usual without bothering even to say good-bye to Andrea.

Andrea could hardly contain a snort as she listened to Grigsby's account of her "busy day." Try getting up at 5:00 to take the bus in from East Brunswick to Port Authority and then get up to Seventh and 49th Street and be lucky to get back home by 8:00 p.m., with no time for errands except on weekends. Shaking her head, she dutifully wrote Grigsby's message on Blake's memo pad of calls, which was already quite long.

But the truth was that while Blake had left that morning with his list of schools to call, he had no intention of making any calls. He had a meeting that he couldn't miss, couldn't be interrupted from, and had been instructed under no uncertain terms was highly confidential.

CHAPTER TWO

Back to Work

As Grigsby was starting her stressful day, several other "back to regular life" stories were unfolding across the city. A few blocks away on 88th and Fifth, Sasha Silver was waking up to her own living hell. When the alarm went off for the first time at 6:30 a.m., she covered her head with the pillow, as if it were a helmet that would protect her from the perils of the morning—at least for the next nine minutes, until the snooze button went off. She knew from experience she could give it one additional push until she would have to face the day.

Sasha always took off the last two weeks of the summer, and she looked forward to it all year long. It was a time when most of the city was away, so she missed little—and there was less of a chance for things to run amuck at work. She was ecstatic when her vacation finally arrived, though it also signaled the end of the summer. For Sasha, nothing on earth compared with being at her beach house in Quogue, from the minute she woke up in the morning and took a leisurely walk down the driveway to get the papers that she actually had time to read, as opposed to the rest of the year when she rushed through, barely reading them. From walking by the ocean with her children collecting shells, to running every day, to consuming bottles of Chardonnay at dinner parties nearly every evening with close friends, this was one of the periods of time when she allowed herself the unusual luxury of contentment. Unfortunately, the joy and elation of the Friday night that started those two weeks were equally matched by desperate agony as they ended. Her depression usually set in on Friday of Labor Day weekend, when even the September light seemed to taunt her that summer was over. By Monday she was usually close to tears, truly despondent that the next day she would have to go back to work and deal with her horrible situation.

And today she was even more upset and uneasy than in past years.

This situation was, to a certain extent, of her own making. In 2005, when she and her partners were approached to sell Silver Asset Management Partners Inc. (SAMCO, as it was known), she was the one who had pushed for the deal, and as majority shareholder she had the final decision. At the time, she knew deep down, frankly even not so deep down, that BridgeVest Financial was not the right company to sell to, but Sasha had made an art form of assuming that once she got to the other side, she would be able to take care of any problems that arose. That was the way she had always dealt with things. She was a caretaker and unfortunately gave little thought to how much she might need or want to be taken care of herself.

Ultimately her partners had agreed to the deal, but they all retired within a year when it became clear that their new friends in Springfield, Massachusetts, were not going to leave them alone. Feeling that she had made her bed so now she'd better sleep in it, Sasha stayed on, and while she told all her friends and family that she would leave when her contract was up at the end of 2010, she didn't know how she could desert all the employees who had been loyal to the company and to her for all those years.

To be fair, there was one great benefit: the money. It was hard to turn that down. After a career of working as long and hard as she had, finally having enough money to spend was intoxicating. She and her husband, Adam, upgraded their apartment to one overlooking Central Park, bought a boat, started taking more expensive vacations, increased their charitable giving, and still managed to put away a sizable amount. For Sasha, the fun part was being able to make some venture investments. She loved hearing about a new business idea and plans for expansion. Some worked out and some didn't, but these investments allowed Sasha to feel she was still an entrepreneur instead of stuck in a corporate box with no room to move or stretch.

The universal thing about having money, however, is that no matter how much you have, it isn't enough. Credit cards still have a balance due—only larger; someone else next door always seems to have more; the dinner party at someone's apartment or beach house is always that much larger and nicer; the jewelry is always that much more opulent. Someone else always seems to have the perfect life in terms of the material possessions they have and others covet. Sasha was no different. She wondered at times if she might have been able to get more if she hadn't sold when she did. She was irritated at the number of people who had ten times what she had but certainly weren't ten times smarter (if at all).

SAMCO oversaw the assets of high-net-worth investors and focused on fixed income. Their goal was to preserve their clients' wealth, not make huge gains. That was a hard strategy to maintain when other, riskier investments were in vogue. People were always willing to bet it all on red, or Internet stocks, or subprime mortgages, in a bull market. She'd seen it all over twenty years of working.

BridgeVest particularly liked SAMCO because it complemented their own business. SAMCO had a terrific reputation of being honest and ethical and was a pristine name, something few companies could boast of, particularly as time went on. BridgeVest itself had been owned for several years by Empire Bank, a New York–based commercial bank.

Sasha was good at what she did. She had a great perspective on strategy, a unique ability to execute any plan, and she was liked by both clients and many of her colleagues, especially other women. There weren't a lot of prominent women in her firm on Wall Street, for that matter. As a result, she was their champion. She also had four children in three different schools on the Upper East Side and an active philanthropic social life in New York. It might appear that Sasha burned the candle at both ends, but in reality she was the type of person who was most fulfilled when she was busy and found that everything she did was connected to everything else. She'd been given great opportunities by being involved in so many different things, so it drove her to do more.

Unfortunately, while Sasha was still seen by clients and employees as the CEO, the reality was that she worked for BridgeVest and was essentially a puppet who did what they wanted, when they wanted. She had no control.

Some of her male colleagues at BridgeVest went out of their way to derail her at work. She was a threat to them, so they dealt with it by a full court press of political warfare against her. She'd observed more than once that men, once they'd left school and couldn't hit one another with bats and balls, turned into the biggest bunch of backstabbing, cliquish, petty high school girls she'd ever seen. It was indeed their sport. From what she could tell, it wasn't having the talent that got you to the top of a company with these men, it was the political gamesmanship.

What made matters worse, ironically, was that several months prior, Kirk McNeal, CEO of Empire Bank, had sent word down that Sasha be given a meaningful leadership role in the firm. She was made vice chair, but rather than continue to oversee clients as she had in the past, she was given what she referred to jokingly as the girly staff stuff—overseeing HR and communications. Her co–vice chair was given all the "line" businesses, those that generated revenues, on top of the businesses he already oversaw.

Through 2008, as assets declined, revenues and profits became all the more critical. Sasha was frequently told she needed to present plans for downsizing staff and was then usually expected to execute them alone. Terminating person after person, some of whom reported to her male counterpart (without his being at the meetings to share the burden), was draining and dreadful. She often wept after, although she never let the guys see—caring was a sign of weakness to them. Unfortunately, while she was taking care of this, Harry Mullaugh, the CEO of BridgeVest, always seemed to schedule strategy and business development meetings, frequently with the senior executives at the bank. Frankly, it was Harry who caused her the most grief and allowed the other men to torture her as they did.

As much as Sasha was miserable, there was always a little spark inside that still made her excited about the possibilities ahead. And as much as she was tortured, she also had an innate sense that good people would win in the end and somehow she would be rescued. Every day was a battle Sasha could win, either as a damsel in distress expecting to see a white horse at any moment or as a fighter who could hit back when she needed to.

This morning, she clearly felt like the damsel as she dragged herself out of bed. At least she felt a tiny bit encouraged that she had a new red Dior suit—and that it was a size four. She was glad that dress-down or casual dress or whatever it was called had gone out of style after the last market crash a few years ago. To Sasha, dressing well translated into success and gave her a little extra confidence wherever she went. Slim and petite at five feet three, Sasha knew the right clothing made her stand out more.

Accessories were her armor. If she had a meeting with anyone she felt might intimidate her, she broke out chunky Chanel cuffs or a vintage Miriam Haskell pearl choker. She knew that how she dressed also irritated the guys at her parent company, and each time she had to schlep up to the home office, she made sure to pick something a little more fabulous than her last visit. She figured if they were going to talk about her, she might as well give them more fuel for their fire. Truth be told, it wasn't easy transferring from Metro-North in New Haven to the Amtrak connection to Springfield in five-inch Louboutins with minutes to spare, but damn, she looked good getting there!

Before she could start her workday, Sasha had to get her house up and running. Adam, who ran his own fund with two other partners, needed to be on the desk early. Adam was deeply involved in what was going on in the credit markets meltdown and had been on edge for some time, not just the summer. Last night before they went to bed, he said, "Sasha, it's going to be a shit show this week," a phrase that always filled her with a bit of excitement and a little fear. As if this year hadn't already been one long shit show. God, what was going to be next?

Most of the time, Adam was a phenomenal husband, but when it came to the kids, he unfortunately left her to take care of almost everything, which was one more thing to deal with in addition to her already tough schedule. This morning after two weeks of vacation the apartment would likely be a madhouse within minutes, and Sasha wasn't sure she had the strength to deal with it today.

Sasha loved her kids dearly, but at times they could try her patience. They also could be a bit wild, and Sasha did not have a great ability to control them. Three-year-old Samantha, a curly-headed imp, had a way of talking that was most likely picked up from watching too many Disney programs with her older sisters. This involved rolling her eyes and periodically saying, "What-*ever*," or, "Say whaat?" Seven-year-old Josh was usually creating some havoc at school and bothering his sisters at home in whatever way possible. Lily and Coco were the sweetest twelve-year-old twins, although their lives were always wrapped up in some "tween" self-created drama. Keeping them grounded while living in a pampered world wasn't always easy either.

Sasha did her best to make sure that they didn't see how unhappy she was, but like the twins, she had a bad poker face, so they had more than a sense of what was going on than she would have liked. Once in a while, Lily or Coco would come up and hug her and say, "It will all be okay, Mama. Don't worry." It made her even sadder that they knew she was not happy.

Amazingly, a working mom with a high-powered job living on the Upper East Side was still somewhat of an anomaly even in 2008, and Sasha knew that even some of her close friends probably criticized her behind her back for still working. For many women, it just wasn't worth the salary they could make when their husbands made so much more. What was the point of making $200,000 when her spouse could be making $10 million? Balancing became a guilt trip where nothing could be done perfectly and it was easier to live off the fruits of their husbands' labor. Sasha's life did require a fair amount of balancing, and there had been more than one time when she found herself desperately running up the street to find a taxi so she could get to a school play on time when she was already late. The classic moment came when she needed to supply the ruby slippers for Coco as Dorothy in *The Wizard of Oz* in fifth grade (a little more advance notice than that same morning might have been good) and had to slide them across the stage five minutes into the play.

But this was the way Sasha wanted it. She liked being identified as a smart person in the working world. At times she envied the "mothers" like her friend Grigsby Somerset, who had time for coffee and workouts in the mornings after drop-off, but she knew that it would grow thin for her after a few weeks.

When she came out of her bedroom at 7:45, much to her wonderful surprise, Maura, the children's nanny, had already come in. She loved her Jamaican nanny but often joked that "island time" meant coming in anywhere from fifteen to thirty minutes after she was supposed to be there. But thankfully, Maura did seem inherently to realize that the day after vacation was bound to be busy and had already started breakfast, which would be real eggs instead of cold cereal. Surprisingly, though, the kids were all still asleep, their schools not starting until later in the week.

So before she left, she checked in with Maura. "Hi! If you can believe it, the kids are all still sleeping, so I'm going to sneak out before they wake up. Otherwise it's going to take me another half hour to get out of here. How was your vacation?" she asked.

"Oh, good, I went to Toronto to visit my family."

"Great. Well, everyone missed you. Listen, I think that Samantha may have taken a lollipop to bed. I thought I'd seen her with it earlier in the evening and then realized in the middle of the night that I hadn't done anything about it. So can you please check in her bed and make her brush her teeth extra hard? I'm so terrible. One day my kids will have no teeth and I'll be hauled away by the dental police. Also, can you please make sure that Josh does not watch TV all day? Try to get him out to the park at some point. I will meet you at East Side Kids for shoes at five forty-five. That should be enough time to get everyone shoes for school. If I'm running late, which I probably will be, I'll text you. And please sign our name on the list if you get there first. There will probably be a line to the West Side."

"Okay, good morning. No problem."

Sasha loved the way Maura always said, "No problem," even though there were always many problems.

Sasha was glad to sneak out but at the same time sad not to hear the cacophony of the children's voices. She peeked into each of their bedrooms and stroked their cheeks and kissed them all (and did manage to pull a sticky cherry lollipop from Samantha's clenched fist) before she headed to the front door, picked up her Prada bag, *Wall Street Journal*, and *New York Times*, and walked out.

Sasha usually spent the first morning back at the office going through mail, internal reports, and getting the hang of being back, but yesterday afternoon, just as they began the drive home from the beach, she had received an e-mail from Harry Mullaugh, the CEO of BridgeVest, asking her to meet him for breakfast. It was unusual that he would be in New York City to begin with, and her stomach flip-flopped when she saw his e-mail. She responded by asking if they could meet for lunch instead, but he had answered back, "No. It can't wait that long." Needless to say, she had been churning with apprehension ever since. She was able to make a reservation at the Regency Hotel, which at least was her own turf. As she left the house, she took a deep breath, squinted at the Tuesday morning sunlight, and firmly put her foot forward, wondering whether her own "shit show" was about to get worse.

CHAPTER THREE

It's My Money

"You are not getting one more FUCKING penny of MY money. It's MY money, not yours, not ours, MINE. I made it—you only lay there. Can you get that through your Botoxed head, you fucking bitch!?"

And with that, John Cutter rather calmly slammed the phone down on Mimi, his soon-to-be, though not soon enough, ex-wife, once-upon-a-time college sweetheart, and mother of his child.

John Cutter was used to dealing with people in whatever way he chose to, which usually meant cursing, screaming, or, on occasion, throwing things at them. This morning, he was in no mood to be even remotely charitable. Mimi had made it her life's goal over the last eighteen months to suck out of him whatever money she hadn't already spent during their marriage, and the financial crisis had been keeping in step with her. Both had turned up the heat over the summer without a break. John, who'd always had a knack of finding his way out of trouble, felt as if he were fresh out of rabbits this time.

He had hoped the last two weeks of the summer would give him time to relax. In earlier years, it would have been a quiet time, but for the second summer in a row, it was anything but. When he wasn't on the phone or his BlackBerry dealing with work, he was doing the same with his divorce lawyer.

Under the terms of the separation agreement, Mimi had the use of their twelve-thousand-square-foot home on Fordune Drive in Water Mill, Long Island. Fordune was a gated enclave with a limited number of mansions created from the 235-acre former estate of Henry Ford II, each with its own deeded ocean access. The Cutters had bought the house in 2000 and named it Casa de Cutter. Mimi had insisted on living there while the divorce was going on, and John, with no strong feelings about being in the house, gave in on that one. For that matter, he thought it would be better to be in a different town altogether, so this year he was in a three-bedroom summer rental in Southampton, for which he hadn't thought twice about paying $175,000.

In reality, he wasn't likely to see her around anyway. Since their separation, he had happily left their "domestic" life behind. No more dinner parties with three or four couples where the conversation was inevitably dominated by the women talking about spending their husbands' money. No more Saturday night benefits for God knows what cause held at oversize mansions where numerous photographers were waiting to document their every drink. And thankfully, no more of what he detested most, the interminable cocktail parties in *stores*, where somehow Mimi always ended up spontaneously buying something unnecessary that usually cost thousands of dollars.

This summer, however, John was in a spiral of partying at night, followed by golf during the day. He usually took a helicopter late on Friday afternoons (Thursday night if he could), arriving from the city in less than thirty minutes, and headed right out to one of the clubs like the Pink Elephant in Southampton, where he hooked up with some of his hedge fund buddies who were also "between wives" or had never married.

Usually within a few minutes of arriving, they were able to find several women looking for men rich enough to shell out $1,000 for table service. These women were fully prepared to return the favor with whatever was desired at the end of the night. It wasn't a problem with John, because at forty-eight, unlike other men who had passed into middle age, he was still intensely good-looking: blond hair, piercing blue eyes that made most women's stomachs do a little flip-flop when he looked directly at them, an amazing smile that curved up on one side, and a body that had benefited from years of the most expensive and sought-after personal trainers from Radu to David Kirsch.

Aside from his physical good looks, John also had *the* most important feature of all—he looked rich, from his Tod's driving shoes, Paul Smith shirts, Hermès belts, and APC jeans faded just so, to his Patek Philippe watch that cost $96,000. It was something you couldn't put your finger on but was noticed immediately, especially by women on the lookout, who were instantly drawn to him.

He often came to the next morning, the sun streaming into the bedroom, his jeans, a pair of Jimmy Choos, and lingerie strewn about the bedroom—and someone lying next to him. One Saturday morning, there were even two women in his bed with him. (He hoped that together they might equal his age.) They hadn't even gotten back to the house until 2:00 a.m. and then done lines until 4:00. He woke up at 11:40, remembering that Mimi was due to drop their five-year-old, Annabella, for her Saturday visit in twenty minutes. Luckily, he was able to get the "ladies" out a few minutes before she drove up. That would have been a bitch to explain and would have caused no small amount of yelling and additional conversations with his attorneys the next week, which probably would have cost him thousands in legal bills. Mimi and her lawyer seemed to specialize in Friday morning motions, which ruined his weekend and cost ridiculous amounts of money to deal with. Starting a new issue on Monday would take more stamina than he had. Lucille Smith, John's matrimonial attorney, was one of the best at fighting back, but she charged through the nose for every strike.

In the midst of his divorce woes, the reality was that John was more than content when it came to his current romantic activities. He wasn't looking for anything more than a good fuck, end of story. Thinking of this reminded him to be sure that Richie had taken care of getting rid of Amanda while he was out last week. Their affair had been fun, but he really didn't need her moping about the office, pining to be the next Mrs. Cutter. It was also safe to say that even if the markets had been better, Amanda was clearly more focused on him than on marketing his fund to investors. He was going to be on his own for a long time, perhaps forever—and that was fine with him.

John's weekends at least partially took his mind off his financial issues, but come Monday morning—or rather, Sunday evening, the new start to the Wall Street week, for government actions were usually announced before Asian markets opened—he was back in a Sisyphean effort of trying to keep his fund's assets from draining away.

While a life on Wall Street, by its very nature, had a level of stress most people would never understand, this was well more than he'd expected at this stage of the game. Sometime over the last decade, the Wall Street he had grown up in had changed drastically. When John started at Salomon Brothers in the early 1980s, joining the then relatively new world of mortgage-backed securities, it was the analysts, associates, and junior traders in their twenties who took on the bulk of the work in the evenings and weekends. It was a heady time at "Solly," and John soon became a protégé of the legendary Lewis Ranieri. He ultimately became one of the most skilled traders in the business. It is an elusive thing to be a great trader. Everyone looks at the same screens and sees the same movement, but just as an artist can look at two colors and instantly know they go together, a great trader intuitively feels when it's time to buy or sell.

After Sandy Weill acquired Salomon in 1997 through the "merger" with Smith Barney, John stayed on at the newly merged company. He'd almost considered joining Long-Term Capital Management run by John Meriwether a few months prior, but he didn't want to commute to Greenwich. Mimi had refused to move out of the city and become a "Greenwich tennis lady," as she derogatorily described it. Thank God, because later that summer LTCM had imploded and he would have lost a fortune. But John truly longed to run his own show. He loved what he did, and the guys who worked for him were incredible, but he hated the unnecessary corporate politics, operating committee meetings, and mergers or deals that he had nothing to do with but that ended up affecting his department or, worse, his annual compensation.

So in 1999 he launched his own fund, Flying Point Capital, named after the beach they frequented in Water Mill, Long Island. With John's prowess and reputation, Flying Point (FPC) took off, quickly becoming one of the hottest new funds around, drawing assets from other firms on the Street, state pension funds, and the newly desirable and wealthy Middle Eastern sovereign funds. By early 2007, FPC had nearly $12 billion in assets.

FPC was a "long short fund that specialized in big macro calls." Mimi rolled her eyes whenever she tried to describe what "long short" was; she usually just said, "He doesn't always have the balls to stick with what he wants to buy, so he buys some of what he doesn't like, too, and agrees to sell some of what he likes if he screws that up. It usually works out, or at least doesn't make him look dumb, and we make lots of money no matter what!" The funny thing is, her friends usually got what she was saying and would giggle in unison. But if she said that at a party with men around, John shot her what she called his "SITFU" look (code for "Shut the fuck up!"), which did shut her up, at least in public.

And they did make a lot of money. They certainly hadn't slouched before, pulling in anywhere from $5 million to $10 million, but John's fund, like most others, had a "2 and 20" structure, so he earned a 2 percent management fee and on top of that a performance bonus of 20 percent of the annual profit he was able to generate. With assets of $12 billion, revenues were over $3 billion, and while John compensated his twenty employees handsomely, his own take was in the hundreds of millions. What he and Mimi didn't spend, he kept in the fund.

Suffice it to say, though they spent a lot of money on themselves—their Tribeca loft and the one they bought next door; Casa de Cutter;

vacations; clothes; jewelry; and, of course, art, including the twenty-foot-tall Keith Haring yellow barking dog sculpture that was outside the Casa house. Mimi had spent her early years in the city, before she had children, working for an art gallery so she knew who all the great artists were. The Cutters were always at the contemporary art auctions at Christie's and Sotheby's, and Mimi never missed Art Basel in Miami every December.

John had always worked long hours, but he and Mimi still managed to spend a lot of time together. She would often meet him for a late dinner, even after their child was born, since they always had a live-in nanny.

Somewhere along the way, however, things began to change. Neither of them ever spoke of it or even acknowledged it. Sometimes he looked at her and wasn't quite sure how they'd ended up together or whether she was the same person he had known in college. Sensing his distance, and reflecting her need to look different from everyone else, she had developed a habit of "enhancing herself" through whatever plastic surgery and procedures were in vogue.

Then one night after a closing dinner at Nobu for an FPC private placement, John and a few of his traders ended up with the women at the table next to them. Whereas John had always looked, that evening he touched. The next time became easier, as did the time after that, and after that. It wasn't long before John was well versed in telling Mimi that he had a work event while he was really with another woman. Then Amanda Belden had started work as head of marketing at FPC. It wasn't long before they ended up having sex in his office, which led to a regular room at one of several hotels near the office.

Mimi was no saint, either, but John was careless about his transgressions, and one night it all came to a head when Mimi threw him out. From that point on, it was a race to hire the best attorneys and start the war of who would end up with what.

So that was what got these two people to September 2, 2008. As he got in the chauffeured Mercedes, John could already see that the European markets were having a rotten day, following on the tail of yet another disastrous Asian market, which had closed down nearly 2 percent. His BlackBerry was buzzing every thirty seconds with a mix of market updates, problems that his staff needed him to deal with, and questions from angry investors. Reading *The Wall Street Journal*, *FT*, and *New York Times* on the way uptown was like reading a report of casualties from the front lines of a war being fought on several fronts. At least the Yankees had won 13–9 on Labor Day.

He arrived at Flying Point Capital's offices at 9 West 57th Street. He'd been able to secure space with a view of Central Park in 2005 for the "cheap price" of $150 per square foot. With fifteen thousand square feet of space, that equated to $2.25 million per year, a staggering sum for most companies but only a pittance for him. The inside wasn't spared any expense, either; from the custom kitchen stocked with specialty snacks to the billiards room with the cigar vent that whisked away smoke, it was a testament to what money could buy. What's more, John had developed his own taste for modern art and had begun collecting Jeff Koons's balloon works; there were twelve of the balloon dogs lining the walls of the conference room.

Shit! He remembered as he walked by the giant orange 9 outside the building that his new assistant was starting today. He couldn't even remember her name. He never bothered to interview them, just took Richie's word that she would be adequate. They were all the same, anyway, and wouldn't last more than a month or two at most; yet another bimbo who wouldn't know how to get shit done and would probably disconnect calls when she wasn't on the phone with her friends or reading *Cosmo*. Man, today was going to suck.

He got off on the thirty-ninth floor and opened the double glass doors etched with the Flying Point Capital sea-spray-and-seagull logo.

As he walked toward his office, a tall black woman he didn't recognize approached him.

"Good morning, Mr. Cutter, I'm Renee Parker, your new executive assistant. I've already gotten your venti dry half-caf cappuccino, and I have a list of messages for you when you're ready to go over them."

John was stunned. This was the first time this had ever happened. Usually there was a woman flipping through a magazine at her desk who barely seemed to notice as he walked up. Someone who knew his coffee order and had already sorted through his calls!? Someone who was also drop-dead gorgeous?

"Um...I...ah...sure." He grabbed the coffee and recovered his game face quickly. "I don't stand on ceremony, so you shouldn't, either. It's John. Mr. Cutter is my father. Give me five minutes and then bring it all in. What was your name again?"

"Renee. Of course. And there's one other thing I wanted to mention to you that seemed important. A man called several times and was most agitated and anxious to speak with you. He wouldn't say his name, but his number was on caller ID, so I wrote it down and was able to trace it. It was a Mr. Blake Somerset from Lehman Brothers. Would you like me to try and get him on the line for you?"

And upon hearing that name, John Cutter knew his day was not going to get any better.

CHAPTER FOUR

The World According to Ms. Renee Parker

As it turned out, Renee Parker was familiar with the name Blake Somerset and his wife, Grigsby. Her mother, Donita, had been their maid for the last five years.

What John didn't realize was that Renee neither came from nor was going to the same place as his other assistants, who as soon as they walked in at 8:31 a.m. were counting the minutes until 4:59 p.m., when they could put on their flip-flops or sneakers and walk out to Staten Island, Queens, New Jersey, or Long Island, where their real lives resided.

But Renee Parker, daughter of Donita and William Parker, had been raised in Harlem and taught to keep her head high and reach for whatever she could, so she would be one rung closer to the next opportunity. Donita had emigrated from Jamaica and had been a maid for most of her adult life. She didn't mind. It was part of her own American dream, to give her family the next step to something better. No matter how tough things might be financially raising a family in New York City, she still managed to send money home each month to take care of her family in Kingston.

William Parker's family had been in the United States for many generations, but their "emigration" had been involuntary. (His family traced its genetic lineage to the infamous South Carolina slave owner and Confederate stalwart Colonel Russell T. Parker.) William had spent the last four decades as a bus driver for the Metropolitan

Transportation Authority, driving the M4 route, which took him through many of the city neighborhoods. Every day he started at the Cloisters, just below Inwood, drove down the once Jewish, now Latino, neighborhood of Washington Heights until he reached Broadway, then curved around Central Park North at 110th Street. It was the only street on the perimeter of Central Park without coveted real estate—at least until the last decade, when even Harlem fell prey to the inexorable ascension of real estate prices. He always felt a lift when he reached Fifth Avenue and traveled down the boulevard from the Central Park Conservatory Garden on 106th Street (especially on the day of the Central Park Conservancy "Hat Lunch," as dozens of women milled about in colorful hats with feathers and flowers), to the regal apartment buildings on Fifth Avenue, and on to the office buildings and stores in midtown, before winding around Herald Square. On the route back uptown, the bus traveled by the high-end boutiques on Madison Avenue and then into the no-man's-land of East Harlem, just past the outpost of civilization known as Mount Sinai Hospital before heading back to upper Broadway by the "college town" of Columbia University and Barnard College.

Every day, as he took commuters, schoolchildren, and the quirky assortment that represents New York through these varied neighborhoods, he had a great sense of pride about his contribution to their city. He liked to say, "The city couldn't move without me!" Renee would respond, "Daddy, then they'll just take another bus!" He would say, "But no other driver takes care of them like I do, sweet cookie."

Both he and Donita tried to fill their four daughters with a sense of how important it was to assist people, no matter how menial others might think their role was. They never let them feel sorry for themselves. It filled both parents with great pride that all of their children had gotten scholarships to good colleges after graduating at the top of their classes in high school.

Renee, though, was special. She was the baby of the family. She was doted on by her older sisters, who were nine, eleven, and thirteen when she was born. As she grew up, she was clearly the smartest of the girls, though their parents loved and appreciated them all dearly.

Perhaps because she was born into a ready-made family, Renee learned early on to "hold her audience," as her father used to say. And so she did. Like her older sisters, Renee was a part of Prep for Prep, which identified kids from public schools whose families would neither have been aware of the private schools in the city nor known how to get their children admitted and gave them the tools and skills to do so. The schools themselves were only too happy to have a ready source of diversity. Thus, like her sisters before her, in 1992 Renee entered the Spence School as a sixth grader.

Whereas the other Prep for Prep girls with whom she matriculated tended to stick together, Renee, with the encouragement of her sisters, figured that as long as she was in this strange place so unlike her own world, she might as well explore it to the fullest. There was something about her effervescent personality that drew other girls toward her, and it wasn't long before she was having after-school get-togethers and sleepovers in some of those same Fifth Avenue buildings that her father drove by and in which her mother toiled.

No matter how confident and popular their daughter seemed to be, because of the distance of their world from the one farther downtown, William and Donita tried to ensure that Renee was aware of the dangers of getting too close to the wealthy. They also encouraged her to focus on her own strengths: her brain and winning personality. It also was worth noting that she was beautiful, which was evident even in grade school. For the most part, their concerns were unfounded. Many of the Park Avenue mothers couldn't help but remark that Renee Parker had qualities they wished their own daughters shared, although it was often in a backhanded way, such as, "And you know what her parents do, don't you? Isn't it wonderful that we can bring girls like this into our schools?"

As she made her way through high school, Renee's popularity grew. She was often the center of parties and, much to her parents' surprise, would bring kids home to their cramped apartment, where there was always something in the kitchen that Donita had made: meat patties, chicken curry, or her famous banana bread. Renee was proud of her heritage, not to mention cuisine! Her family used to joke that Renee must have had curry in her baby bottle, she loved it so much. Both Parkers were proud of their daughter's confidence yet at the same time a little dismayed. They intended for Renee to move out of their world, not bring people into it, but parents sometimes learn from their children, too.

There was one girl, though, who went out of her way to discredit and hurt Renee. Amanda Belden, a "queen bee in training," had been at Spence since kindergarten. She was from a wealthy, socially prominent family. Frankly, they didn't have the nicest reputation in the city, although few people would admit it. Amanda despised Renee's popularity and constantly tried to pit the other girls against her. Once, in ninth grade, Amanda accused Renee of stealing her credit card when it was missing. Renee's friends told her not to be bothered by Amanda, but she was devastated and cried for a week, until the card was discovered behind some books in the library. Amanda didn't even bother to apologize and was overheard to say, "Well, why wouldn't I think it was her?" Usually, Renee had little patience with Amanda's silly games, but this one hurt more than she admitted. The memory of it never left her.

In part because of this hurt, Renee came to value her family's love and values and grew even closer to them. When she graduated from Spence, although she could have gone to any Ivy League institution, she chose Barnard, the women's college on her father's bus route adjacent to Columbia. Renee had come to appreciate the value of single-sex education during her years at Spence and felt that being at a women's college would be beneficial for her.

She spent the four years of college living in Barnard housing, ever conscious of the fact that her parents lived in very different circumstances a few blocks away in Harlem.

As in high school, Renee was just one of those people who fit in wherever she was. It didn't matter if she was rich or poor. And William and Donita got used to her bringing a new group of friends home to Harlem when Renee wasn't busy exploring the city and its neighborhoods and nightlife. They came to appreciate that she was so confident in herself and her family heritage, she wanted her friends to share in it.

When Renee graduated from college, she wasn't quite sure what she wanted to do. But, like many of her classmates, she was magnetically pulled to Wall Street. The work was exciting and the pay was much better than in any other industry. Without knowing much more than that, Renee interviewed at several firms, not in the analyst programs many gravitated to automatically, but in more creative areas. She accepted a position at Merrill Lynch in the marketing department, where all of the print and electronic ads and brochures were produced. Renee worked in the group that assisted the retail financial advisors with client communication and was tremendously well liked by her colleagues as well as by the financial advisors she assisted across the country. More than once, one of them sent an e-mail to her bosses telling them how helpful she was and that she understood the advisors' need to get information to their clients—yesterday.

It wasn't long before she was taken under the wing of one of the senior people in the department. After her first year, she was invited to work on one of the recognition trips for the financial advisors who had generated significant commissions over the prior year. Regardless of the fact that she was there to work, three days in Miami at the Ritz-Carlton Key Biscayne was the nicest trip she had ever taken (except for the time a classmate at Spence had taken her on the family's jet to Anguilla).

When she'd started in 2002, times only seemed to be getting better. But the blue skies of the first half of the decade were taken over by a tornado that started in 2007, leaving little unscathed—even venerable Merrill Lynch. When Charlie Merrill and Edmund Lynch founded the firm in 1915, they set out to make buying stocks and bonds within the reach of average Americans. As with so many Wall Street firms, however, the addiction of greater profits pushed the company into areas that gave it even greater profits than dealing with individual customers in the retail brokerage business. Leveraging their own capital was the way to make that happen, and nowhere more so than at Merrill when it was led by E. Stanley O'Neal. The firm pushed the envelope in the commercial and mortgage-backed securities arena in an effort to compete against firms like Goldman Sachs and Morgan Stanley. Risking the company's capital worked well on the upside, but as the financial crisis took hold, Merrill began losing billions each quarter from its ill-timed bets. "Stan," as he was known, was finally ousted after weeks of speculation at the end of 2007 (after having written off $8.4 billion that quarter alone).

It was widely expected that a legend would come in to return the firm to its prior glory. And so John Thain, who'd had an elegant and successful career on Wall Street as president of Goldman Sachs, and then as savior of the New York Stock Exchange, took on the thankless task of righting the good ship "Mother Merrill." Internally, however, people also knew that he was going to look at every expense item on the firm's books. This meant only one thing to the sixty thousand employees worldwide: cuts, layoffs, or—the proper business term—"reductions in force," better known as RIFs.

Thus, Renee Parker, on a dazzlingly beautiful day at the end of August 2008, was tapped on the shoulder by someone from human resources there to announce the layoffs that day, told that her position was being eliminated, and given a separation agreement to sign. While surprising and upsetting, it wasn't disastrous for her at age twenty-eight, as it was for older colleagues who had families to take care of. She would get one week of pay for every year she had been at the firm—two, if she agreed not to pursue any actions against Merrill—as well as benefits through the end of the year. She signed the agreement and pocketed twelve weeks of pay representing her six years of work.

Because Renee was so widely beloved, Annette Sambucci, one of the longtime executive assistants in the department, pulled her aside as she was leaving and said, "Listen, hon, it's probably not what you want to be doing, but my cousin Richie runs the office at a hedge fund, Flying Point Capital. The chief honcho at the place needs a new assistant. The guy's apparently a real prick, and going through a big divorce from his society wife, too, from what I see on 'Page Six,' but you might as well give it a try. It pays pretty well, too, from what I hear. There ain't a lot of jobs out there, and it's gonna get worse. I feel like the five forty-seven to Ronkonkoma is getting emptier each day. Here's the number if you want to give it a try. Let me know if it works out for you, and please keep in touch with the girls here. You got a lot of talent, sweetie, and people love you. That doesn't happen too often. Don't waste it, okay? Good luck, cookie."

Renee thanked her and said, "Annette, all I can do is try to do my best and hope it will be good enough. Life is tougher for a lot of people than for me being laid off. I'm only twenty-eight. I'll make it just fine."

It was worth a try, even though it was a step back in position. She had spent summer vacations and Fridays during Barnard working as a temp, so she actually had a fair amount of experience working as an assistant.

Renee also had two reasons why finding a new position as quickly as possible would be in her best interest. Her father had recently started dialysis, and she was helping financially with the treatments. If she could find a new position right away, she could put aside a big chunk so that her parents wouldn't have to worry any more than they already did about making ends meet. Her sisters were married and had their own family obligations, so the burden to help was squarely on Renee's shoulders.

The other was a more selfish reason. Over the years, Renee had—ironically, given her background—become fairly active on the social scene, even though she was from the "wrong side of the subway tracks," as she liked to joke. It evolved from jury duty, of all places, when she started talking to a woman who asked if she could borrow her copy of *Vogue*. They immediately hit it off, and by the end of the week, after sitting in room H-49 on Centre Street, the woman asked her to join her at her table at a benefit. Subsequently, they became great friends. Renee was transfixed by this world, and after attending a few more benefits, she started going out quite frequently. She was soon asked to join the junior committee of certain organizations, but while those tickets were priced lower than the "grown-up" ones, she still needed money to pay for them. She was lucky enough to be able to borrow dresses from designers who knew that due to her striking beauty, not to mention dark skin, an unusual sight at benefits, she would be photographed in them, which in turn would be good PR for the designers. She also found great vintage pieces online, so no one knew how little she actually spent. Her parents would never have understood, but her picture had been in the "Style" section of *The New York Times* several times. When she proudly produced it for them, they didn't realize she had paid to go and were more caught up in the idea that their daughter was in the society pages, of all places.

Renee called Annette's cousin Richie that afternoon, and he asked if she could come in the next day, the Thursday before Labor Day, for an interview. As she entered the lobby at 9 West 57th Street, she stopped at the security desk to get her pass for upstairs, stared obligingly into the tiny camera, but gave it a look as if to say, "Well, here I am now," collected her ID pass, and rode the elevator up to the offices of Flying Point Capital. She approached the receptionist.

"Good morning. I'm here to see Mr. Richard Sambucci. I have a nine a.m. appointment."

The receptionist dialed an extension and said, "Richie, your nine o'clock is here." She looked Renee up and down with what Renee thought was a pitying look.

A few minutes later, Richie Sambucci came out to greet her. Richie had seen it all in his thirty-two years on the Street. Interviewing assistants was definitely way at the bottom of his list of priorities. But he was startled to see this tall, elegant black woman, dressed impeccably, before him. He didn't know women's clothing that well, but he didn't think her outfit came from the same places where his wife and daughters shopped.

"Hey there, Ms. Parker. Nice to meet you. My cousin Annette tells me you're the best. Thanks for coming in on such short notice." He was equally surprised when she extended her hand and, with the firmest handshake he'd had from man or woman, flashed her winning smile, saying:

"Absolutely, Mr. Sambucci, my pleasure."

Richie led Renee to an office down the hall. She looked avidly from side to side, amazed at the art on the walls. She had majored in art history at Barnard and had done her senior thesis on how graffiti art had moved from the street to the gallery and become a commercial success in the early 1980s. She'd been hooked on contemporary art ever since. She always got a copy of Christie's and Sotheby's contemporary art catalogs and tracked the results on Artnet.com. Now, to see that some of those pieces ended up hanging on these very walls was mind-blowing.

They sat down and Richie said, "Look, Ms. Parker, I'm gonna give it to you straight. This is a tough job. John Cutter runs this fund, and he is very, very particular about the way he likes things done. He has a pretty big temper, and it's not easy right now given the market. Assistants don't usually last a long time with him, but if you can stick it out for a year, there are other opportunities here. We pay pretty well, and it could be a good opportunity."

"Mr. Sambucci, from what I have read online about Mr. Cutter, he created a tremendous success and should have high expectations of those around him. One of the things that I try to do is anticipate the needs of those I encounter. I think that I am very well suited for the position."

As the interview went on, Richie felt a wave of relief. In the last three days, he had interviewed fifteen women and two gay men, all of whom he knew John would chew up and spit out within a few days, not even leaving a trace of bones. He couldn't even imagine the harassment actions the men would have been able to file had one of them worked for John. Richie had enough to do with the market right now and needed to get back to his real job of making sure that the office functioned smoothly. Interviewing people knowing he would be back in the same position in a few weeks was not going to make that easier. He had long ago stopped bringing in seasoned executive assistants and at this point focused just on getting someone good-looking. "Form over function" was his motto.

Richie had tried several times over the years to get John to be a bit easier on his assistants, but it was an exercise in futility. "Fuck these moronic bimbos, Richie. I'm the one who has to do the hard work. How fucking hard could it be to answer my fucking calls, get my fucking coffee order right, make sure my fucking schedule is managed, and open the fucking mail?"

What John didn't realize was that calling women with limited skill sets names or throwing an empty Starbucks cup at their heads wasn't helpful. Richie would have one of the other assistants tell him the first time John's latest was found weeping in the bathroom, because a week later, either she would quit or John would tell Richie, "Don't ever let me see her fucking ugly face again, got it?"

Richie had given the "There Are Opportunities Here If You Can Last" speech many times before, but it was usually just part of the routine. No one had ever actually lasted long enough to make it that far, let alone the six months until they could be included in the company 401(k).

Normally, Richie would have said, "Let me give some thought to our conversation and I'll let you know later today what my decision is, all right?" It was a way to see how anxious and interested someone was. But because she was so terrific, and in part because he needed to have the position filled by the time the day opened on Tuesday, he found himself saying, "Ms. Parker, I'd like to offer you the position right now. I think you can handle it, and we really need someone who can start right away. Can you start at the beginning of next week right after the holiday? The compensation is one hundred thousand dollars per year."

Renee was staggered—$100,000! She had been making only $72,000 at Merrill. This way, she would have more money and be able to give her parents her severance. She also could buy her ticket to the New Yorkers for Children Gala that she wanted to go to in two weeks. She responded quickly, "Yes, absolutely, and since you mentioned Mr. Cutter is out on vacation until Tuesday, it would be great if I could come in tomorrow and get myself situated a bit and find out where things are and the like. That way, when Mr. Cutter returns it will be one less thing for him to have to deal with. You don't have to start my pay until Tuesday."

Richie could barely suppress a "Thank you, God" for this angel who had just offered to come in the Friday before Labor Day and work without pay. He almost felt bad that she had accepted. He made a mental note to pick up a box of cannoli at Del Fiore's Italian Pork Store in Patchogue as a thank-you for Annette to bring to her annual Labor Day barbecue this weekend. As it was, most of the office would be out all day, and certainly by 1:00 in the afternoon almost everyone would be long gone to spend the last unofficial weekend of the summer out of the city. In fact, Richie was taking a much needed day off himself. He'd deal with that other "problem" on Tuesday before John came into the office.

Thus, on Friday, August 29, 2008, rather than spending the day on a blanket in Central Park's Sheep Meadow, Ms. Renee Parker of 145th Street in Harlem began learning as much as she could about Flying Point Capital and how things worked, especially John Cutter's specific coffee order, which so many others before her had usually remembered only as the cup hit them squarely on the head.

On Tuesday, September 2, Renee awoke early and dressed simply but elegantly in a Tory Burch dress, Lia Sophia necklace, and the Chanel ballet flats she'd bought NIB (new in box) on eBay for half price. She stopped at Starbucks to get John's coffee. As she walked into the office, however, she froze in her tracks. Of all people, who should be coming toward her, tears streaming down her face, but her childhood tormentor, Amanda Belden, followed by a red-faced Richie Sambucci.

CHAPTER FIVE

The Evolution of Mimi

Somewhere along the line, Mimi Cutter became a clown.

She was born Margaret Del Grucci but was always known as Mimi. She was a fun, smart, naturally beautiful girl who grew up on the south shore of Long Island. Her mother was a special ed teacher in the Sayville School District, and her father was a contractor. During the summers, for extra money, Mimi's mother would take the ferry from Sayville over to the Pines on Fire Island to clean houses.

The Pines was a well-known gay summer community, and by the time Mimi was in high school, she would go along to help her mom out. She would see the most incredible art (among other things) in those houses. She would flip through the art books on the tables when she was supposed to be dusting and became mesmerized by the works inside. The people who summered there also befriended her. They were sophisticated, funny, outrageous, and cultured. For her, the gay community in the Pines was a window to the outside world.

From that time on, Mimi wanted nothing more than to get out of Sayville as soon as possible. She couldn't see a life there holding much more for her than what her parents' and friends' lives offered, and she wanted none of it. A local job or commuting to Melville or Riverhead to work in a branch of a big company as an assistant had zero appeal for her. Life was going to bring her more than that. She graduated at the top of her class at Sayville High and was able to get a financial aid package to Harvard, where she met John Cutter. He was three years ahead of her, started on the varsity soccer team, and was a catch. Mimi noticed him the day she arrived and was moving into her dorm. John was on the prowl for hot freshmen women, and they hooked up that first weekend. Their relationship was volatile, to say the least. They must have broken up once a month when she got jealous at some girl throwing herself at John. They always got back together and promised never to fight again, but that usually lasted until the next weekend. Somehow, though, after John graduated and moved to New York City to start working on Wall Street, their relationship became more stable, maybe because they weren't in constant contact where they could push each other's buttons. Mimi visited every other weekend, and whatever the two of them did on the alternate weekend wasn't admitted to each other. It seemed to work out fine.

After senior year, Mimi, too, moved to New York and, still fascinated by the art scene, started work at Mary Boone's gallery. It was the early eighties, and the art scene was booming. Basquiat, Keith Haring, and street graffiti art were all must-haves for the then hip and rich with money to spend.

She and John were the perfect couple. They moved easily between the parties that John's Wall Street colleagues were throwing and the art events that Mimi needed to attend for work. People naturally gravitated to them, as they were young, cool, and an incredibly attractive couple.

Mimi always managed to look stylish whether she had money or not. While working at the gallery, she would always make sure she had one fabulous piece of clothing or jewelry so that everything else would look expensive. She scoured a range of cutting-edge stores and designers like Fiorucci and Stephen Sprouse for the perfect item that she could afford and would make her outfit stand out. She could always count on that sweet Marc Jacobs, who worked at Charivari, to help her find the right piece.

She always knew what the hottest trends were and what was coming next. When she and John got married in 1991, Vera Wang had just opened and she bought her dress there. No one who knew her was shocked that her dress was bright red. As John moved up the ranks, it was a fantasy come true for Mimi to finally have money to spend. She started spending more and more time at her "three B's"—Barneys, Bendel's, and Bergdorf's.

Perhaps it was because she was left alone much of the time or because she was bored that Mimi got to the point where she wasn't really that much fun any longer and seemed to have lost that inner confidence. The great girl from Sayville was now just another hedge fund wife with no real friends, too much time, and too much money.

She also developed a sad side effect of the excessively wealthy, which was a need to be the most bedecked in any place. The more successful John became, the more divorced she became from reality, taste, and sensibility. Every piece she wore had to be the most expensive and over the top, and she had to wear many of them at the same time. She started to favor the avant-garde designers, like Yohji Yamamoto, Comme des Garçons, and Vivienne Westwood.

So distanced was she from who she was that Mimi always thought she looked wonderful, and none of her friends, salespeople at stores, or her personal stylist, Flamenco, whom she began using for major events, told her otherwise. As her fashion sense became more extreme, she also developed an obsessive need to make her body perfect. A personal trainer came to the house every day for a two-hour workout, but that wasn't enough. She started out innocently enough. She'd always hated the bump on her nose, so the nose job was first. When eyebrow shaping was all the rage, she started a biweekly regime and then had them stenciled in. Next came collagen injections to plump up her lips. Botox was a dream come true for her, especially when she turned forty. But the cheek implants were just about the last straw for John. And that was just her face. She also had a tummy tuck, breast enhancement, and liposuction. Mimi became more like a fembot than a woman.

Jewelry was another story. Mimi had a cortisone deficiency and thus always wore her MedicAlert medallion. Rather than the simple bracelet most people wore, Mimi had literally dozens of custom-designed MedicAlert necklaces that she coordinated with every outfit she had. There was one in all diamonds, there were some in quartz, there was even one that was macramèd with African elephant hair and gold from a gold mine she had visited on an Abercrombie & Kent Tanzanian safari.

When she went to galas and parties, people loved to talk behind her back. Once or twice she was even in the "What Were They Thinking" column of *W* magazine. Mimi didn't care. Her look was a way for her to show that she could buy whatever she wanted, but also that she mattered, stood out, and was more than "Mrs. John Cutter," although having that name on her credit cards certainly mattered a great deal.

She also used John's money as a way to get what she wanted in terms of attention and social prominence. She knew that most organizations were perennially on the hunt for donors, contemplating, launching, or nearly finishing a capital campaign. The Cutters had a virtually unlimited checkbook, so all she had to do was express an interest in being involved, and soon the board chair and executive director would call to ask her out for lunch or coffee to discuss their plans. She usually chaired a major gala at least once a year. Due to her name, money, and clothing, she was well known. Photographers would leap like fish jumping out of a pond at a dragonfly to shoot her, and she was equally drawn as soon as she saw the cameras go up the minute she walked in. She felt an incredible rush as she turned and posed for each of them. It was also one of the few times when she, not John, was the center of attention.

While it is true in New York City that the path to social acceptance can come from money, power, or prestige, one is generally expected to conform to the same sensibility or style as everyone else. Being too front and center is considered déclassé. Thus, not everyone thought Mimi was so fabulous. The long established social women thought her tacky and obviously out only for social status, which she clearly (to them) appeared to be trying to buy. They clucked like hens behind her back at her ridiculous sense of style, before events, at events, and the day after events.

When Mimi and John's marriage reached the point of no return, Mimi was certainly not prepared to give up the life to which she had become accustomed. She was well aware of John's dalliances and expected him to fully pay her for those as well. He had humiliated her, and she did not expect that she would give up her social life or her financial life.

John's indiscretions had come to light in the most basic way, when one of his bimbo assistants had called Mimi thinking she was the person he was going to be with that night. Mimi would never forget the call:

"Amanda, Mr. Cutter wanted to let you know that dinner this evening will be at Per Se, and the key to the hotel room will be waiting at the desk." When Mimi said, "Excuse me, this is Mrs. Cutter," the assistant simply said, "Oh," and quickly hung up. When John finally came home at 3:00 in the morning, Mimi said, "Did you fuck Amanda at the Mandarin before dinner at Per Se or after?" John looked totally shocked. "Tell your assistant next time to make sure she's calling the right person. Oh, on second thought, tell your assistant I'm divorcing you."

She went right out and hired the city's best-known divorce attorney, Roland Deitrich, who was famous for managing his own PR as well as, or better than, the divorce he was handling. His clients often didn't realize that the way those items found their way to "Page Six" came directly from his own office. The day Mimi walked in, she sat down and said, "I want that fucker to give me everything he has. Everything! And I'm not settling for much less." Words like that were music to Roland's ears.

Roland was used to women like this and he knew how to control them. The truth was that even the women who said they didn't hate their husbands, who started out saying they wanted to be fair, still wanted everything. It was also true that many of these women still loved their husbands, and getting everything was the next best thing to getting him back. It was women who were as well known as Mimi, as angry as Mimi, and as rich as Mimi who were the best clients for him to have. He would throw motions wherever he could to beat the other side into submission. When it came close to trial, he would start feeding salacious details of the marriage to the press, generally the *New York Post*. It didn't really matter who looked bad, his client or his client's spouse. It was all a part of getting to a settlement, or at least getting his billable hours as high as possible.

What Roland should have been trying to find out was the reality of John's net worth, so he could figure out what more than twenty years of marriage and one child would give Mimi. After all those years, and John's infidelity, she had a right to maintain her lifestyle, no matter how excessive it might seem. Rather than feeding his own desire for press, Roland should have been demanding copies of all the various investments John had made. He should have been tracing funds to figure out if John had been buying his girlfriends jewelry. He should have been doing a lifestyle analysis to determine realistically how much money Mimi would need for spousal and child support until their daughter emancipated or she remarried. But Roland could barely understand a simple bank statement; thus, John's spreadsheets of this partnership or that grant of stock options (if John even gave them all) might as well have been Greek to him. What's more, Roland didn't really want Mimi knowing that he didn't quite know how to understand John's net worth, but frankly, the longer it took the better it was for him. It wouldn't be unusual in a case like this for Roland's firm to bill seven figures in fees, and that was if it settled. If it went to trial, it was party time. He would pat her hand and keep her comforted as much as possible, knowing that she would still end up with a pile of money at the end and he could add another notch to his belt and count on luring more high-profile, wealthy clients. Of course, every case only added to the sales of his current best seller, *The Beginning of the End of the Marriage: Learn How to Maximize Your Divorce Outcome BEFORE the Love Ends.*

Mimi, however, wanted it over as soon as possible. She didn't understand why John wouldn't just agree to give her everything. He was the one who had cheated. He was the one who had been such a jerk. It was all his fault.

What John's fund did was so complex that she didn't understand that it had been performing badly and that much of the fund and John's wealth was illiquid to begin with, so it couldn't easily be turned into cash. There was also something that neither she nor Roland would ever be able to figure out, which was that hundreds of millions of dollars had been siphoned offshore for years, to accounts in the Cayman Islands that only John knew about.

CHAPTER SIX

Breakfast at the Regency

Sasha got a cab going down Park Avenue, a feat that would be next to impossible the day after tomorrow, once school started. After dropping off their kids, and already late to work, throngs of parents would be clustered at each corner, arms outstretched wildly, hoping to get a taxi downtown. She slid into the backseat and said, "The Regency Hotel, 540 Park at Sixty-second Street, please," and sat back to skim the headlines of *The Wall Street Journal.*

Sasha could remember when she read every article of the *Journal,* but now she barely skimmed the headlines above the fold, her eyes only darting about for words or phrases that were of interest to her. Maybe it was because she got so much news from the Internet or Bloomberg, or maybe it was because after all these years of markets moving up and down and back again, she had lost interest to a certain extent. Whatever the case, today she really had to struggle, but more so because she was nervous about what Harry was going to discuss with her.

The cab pulled up to the hotel and she paid the fare, saying hello to the doorman on the way in. There was something about the Regency Hotel that was comfortable and homey and yet at the same time emitted a feeling of power and prestige. Sasha had been going there for years and had worked her way up from a small table in the side room to being welcomed warmly and given one of the prime tables in the main room.

As she walked in, she saw Rae, the maître d' who had been there for years and was one of the most powerful people in the city, although not everyone realized it. Some attempted to try to sit without being seated, complained about their table, or, worse, were arrogant to her. They soon found that was the wrong approach, as she graciously yet firmly put them in their place, not always where they thought they should be.

"Sasha. Good morning. Your guest is here."

Sasha was disappointed to see that Harry Mullaugh was already at the table. This bothered her for two reasons. One was that she liked to sit facing the door so she could see who was coming and going, get her bearings, place her BlackBerry on the table, and start reading the *New York Post*, which she picked up from the neatly organized piles of complimentary papers on the way in. The other reason was that she usually knew a number of people there and liked to stop at various tables to say hello, and especially to greet whatever members of the Tisch family (who owned the hotel) were there. It was a bit awkward when someone was waiting for her. As it was, people usually commented during breakfast, "Is there anyone you don't know, Sasha?"

Harry Mullaugh was a different story. He was the son of a New York City fireman, which wouldn't have held him back professionally or socially. In fact, half the traders on Wall Street had family working for New York's Bravest or Finest. One child chose those professions, while another went to Wall Street, though usually the rough-and-tumble side of trading and sales rather than investment banking. Sasha could picture half the guys on any trading desk in uniform. Harry, however, had spent most of his career working outside of New York City, and as such he lacked the insider status of most of the men Sasha knew. It was an unspoken source of discomfort between them. It wasn't good to be more connected than the boss, especially as a woman.

Harry had an unpolished look about him. He wasn't unattractive, but he was a little past his prime, and Sasha could tell his suits didn't come from Paul Stuart or Brooks Brothers. She always suspected that wherever he bought one, he got one free too. Frankly, she was always a little embarrassed to be with him when she was in her own environment. And today, as it turned out, he was sitting in *her* seat at the table.

She attempted to suppress whatever feelings she had, walked up cheerily, and said, "Hi, Harry. How are you?"

"Hey, kiddo. How was vacation?"

Why? Why did he insist on calling her kiddo? It reminded her of the sexual harassment commercial years ago where a woman literally shrank as her boss told her to dress better and look prettier. Each time Harry said "kiddo," she could feel herself turning back into a college kid, light-years away from the accomplished forty-three-year-old woman she was. And for the record, Harry was only fifty, so it wasn't as if she were even that much younger than him.

"Great. Everyone had a terrific time. Ended too soon," she responded while thinking, You have no idea how soon it ended, buddy.

"Well, you were missed. We had some strategy meetings last week, and we sure could have used your focus. Sorry you couldn't join us."

If there had been a red button between her stomach and her throat with a label that read, "Press in times of clear danger!" it would have been firmly pressed and flares would now be shooting from her body. For as much as Sasha wished that she could react calmly when she knew she was being manipulated or something didn't feel right, she felt her stomach turn, and all of a sudden a million thoughts were rushing through her head.

Why were there strategy meetings without me? Shouldn't I have been told and asked to come in? Did they do this on purpose? I am a vice chairman of the company. Should I not have gone on vacation? Who has an important meeting the week before Labor Day anyway? What would happen if I just start screaming in the middle of the Regency right now and throw my coffee across the room? Would I still get a good table the next time I come? Would someone call "Page Six" and report a blind item? "What social business lady was so agitated, she threw a cup of coffee and nearly missed Al Sharpton sitting nearby? People were complaining so much, we hear they've asked her to post a 'bond' the next time she eats there."

"So anyway, kiddo, we want to be aggressive about where we stand right now and are going to be moving in some new directions."

She forced herself back to attention and hoped that Harry couldn't tell that she had been thrown off-kilter by his comment.

"You know you have done a great job in the past several months, and I know it hasn't been easy," he continued. "I really appreciate everything that you have done for the firm."

The discomfort of not being in control of the situation and not sure what he was going to say next made her mouth feel a little dry. She reached for her glass of water but had a hard time steadying her hand.

"Anyway, at our meeting last week Kirk came and met with me and the rest of the team. He was sorry he didn't get a chance to see you. I'm sure he really would have appreciated your thoughtful insight."

Now Sasha truly was about to flip out, hearing that the chairman of Empire Bank was at the meeting. Kirk had a very busy schedule. This meeting had to have been arranged with a fair amount of advance notice, which meant that Harry had purposely not told her about it. Her antennae were up even more now.

But before she was able to learn what had happened, the waiter arrived to take their order. Sasha, with little appetite at this point, ordered some dry toast, but Harry took full advantage of the menu and ordered an omelet with extra cheese, sausage, orange juice, and an English muffin, the opposite of what powerful men usually ordered. They generally ate sparingly, fruit or an egg white omelet if they were feeling adventuresome. After the menus had been collected, Harry continued.

"So as I was saying, Kirk has decided that he wants to spin us off from the parent company, as he thinks the premium he can get will be attractive and allow them to focus on their core banking business and put additional capital back on their balance sheet. I wanted to make sure you and I had a chance to meet first thing, in case word gets out. I'm also here to see the corporate development people at headquarters to discuss the presentation. Of course, SAMCO is really important in the transaction, and so are you. It's really critical to show that we have breadth of talent, products, and, ah, well, the diversity doesn't hurt, either, if you know what I mean." Harry chuckled as he said that, which really irked Sasha.

HOLY FUCK!! she wanted to scream. HOLY FUCKING FUCK!

Sasha's mouth was completely dry, but she knew if she reached for her water glass, her hand would shake uncontrollably. She tried to breathe deeply and started to speak.

"Harry, I really don't know what to say. About the potential transaction, of course, but more so how this meeting could have been held without me, given my role at the company."

"Well, kiddo, it was only because you were on vacation and you've been working so hard all year that I just struggled with the thought of taking you away from your family. That's why I wanted to meet with you as soon as possible. You couldn't be left out, even if we wanted to!" Sasha was slightly puzzled when he said that. "You know how important you are to the company."

She didn't know what to say. On the one hand his response made sense, but on the other hand she knew that it wasn't the truth. If she pushed the issue, she would run the risk of being perceived as thinking only of herself rather than about the whole company. She also knew that serious things were about to unfold. Selling the company at a time when the markets were in turmoil certainly wasn't going to be easy. Furthermore, as she knew from the past, a sale would bring tremendous upheaval and anxiety. And while deals were always good for buyers (at least at the beginning) and sellers, they usually were not universally good for one group, the employees, who became targets for "achieving savings." There had already been massive layoffs in the first eight months of this year from the mortgage market implosion—thousands alone from

Bear Stearns. Sasha would likely be the one who would have to oversee that, not to mention that she would be indirectly responsible for the second sale the SAMCO employees would have to go through in three years. She was smart enough to know that she would not have control and some of her most loyal employees might lose their jobs. It was hard enough when they sold to BridgeVest, and at least her partners had been there then to assist with the process.

"Harry, I'm a bit staggered by this. I'm sure you can imagine how surprised I am. Of course, I understand Kirk's need to shore up his balance sheet now, but I really didn't see this coming. That's baseball, I guess," she said, trying to sound tougher than she felt. "So what do you need me to do?"

"Well, we need you to focus on keeping the team and employees intact for the time being. I'm sure as things unfold I'll ask you to be more involved, especially in meeting some of our potential new partners."

One of the things that drove Sasha crazy about Harry, and many other men on Wall Street, for that matter, was the need to refer to people as "partners" when they clearly were not. When someone buys your firm, they own you. They are not your partner. Sasha thought it was made up to give the guys a false sense of equality. It also had a passive-aggressive component of letting people believe they were on an equal plane when in fact they were not.

"Okay, well, I assume you will want me to be involved in the presentation, certainly the SAMCO component," she said, fishing to get a sense of how much Harry planned to involve her, especially since, as he said, "she was so important to the company."

"Of course you'll see it, Sasha! Look, don't get ahead of yourself here, okay? This is all very new, and we need to let the corporate development guys get things going." He then added, so smoothly that she felt even more uncomfortable, "I'm sure Kirk will want to talk to you at some point. He thinks the world of you." Harry always threw out the prospect of talking to Kirk to mollify her. Not surprisingly, those meetings rarely, if ever, came to fruition. She was left to find ways to connect with Kirk on her own, making sure that Harry didn't find out about those occasions.

Just then, James Ullman, a noted investor and financier in her industry, whom she knew from her social activities, walked up to the table. "Sasha. Hey, how are you? Ginny just showed me a great picture of you in *Town and Country* magazine, from the ballet. I swear I don't know how you get out as much as you do. Do you ever go to work?!"

She laughed nervously. "Well, you know how it is, burning the candle at both ends. But I get everything I need to and more done, even in the evening." Her eyes darted toward Harry, who looked a little annoyed that their conversation had been interrupted to discuss Sasha's active social life and presence in society magazines. She also recalled it had been that very evening that she had been seated next to the head of a corporate pension fund, which led to a $50 million bond account for the company.

"James Ullman, meet Harry Mullaugh. He is the CEO of BridgeVest, which owns SAMCO."

Harry put out his hand. "Nice to meet you, James, but Sasha got it wrong. She is my partner."

Sasha felt like throwing up.

"Oh, hi, Harry, it's nice to meet you. Sorry I didn't know who you were. I didn't even realize BridgeVest was still around."

Harry's brow furrowed, and Sasha felt like crawling under a rock, but she quickly cut in.

"Harry, James runs a fund that acquires asset management companies. He has done a few transactions already this year, even in this market."

It certainly was not her place to convey to James what Harry had just told her, but she knew James should definitely be on the short list of buyers. She assumed Harry would pick up on what she had just said and suggest a meeting.

He responded, "Great. Nice to meet you. Let me know if you see Sasha out too much." With that, Harry turned back to Sasha as James waved good-bye and walked toward the door.

Sasha was dumbfounded. Harry didn't seem the slightest bit interested in talking with James. Was it because of her connection to him? If so, that further confused and concerned her.

As James walked away, Sasha said, "Harry, James's company could be someone we would like to speak with. Would you like me to set up a meeting?"

"No, we don't need to home in on anyone today."

"Um, okay, it's just that his company should be on the list, and I'm sure he would be interested in speaking with us, so if you want, I could—"

"Sasha, I said not yet. Okay? Just stop for now. I am the CEO here, aren't I?"

She could see Harry starting to get red and knew she had better stop. "Okay, not a problem. I am here to support you however you need."

The rest of breakfast was awkward at best, making idle conversation about the markets, the weather, and trying to act nonchalant. But Sasha was anxious and desperate for more details. She also was nauseated by the gobs of ketchup Harry doused his eggs with, not to mention the way he wolfed his food down. He wiped his mouth, just missing the piece of egg still on the side of his lip, and said, "Great. So listen, not a word, of course, but I'll be in touch as soon as I have something to fill you in on, kiddo." And with that, he looked at his watch nervously and asked Sasha if she minded taking care of the check. She would just expense it anyway, but she was always shocked by his lack of decorum in sticking her with the bill.

Afterward, as Sasha headed to her office, she was perplexed and upset. For whatever reason, Harry wasn't going to include her in the way that she wanted, deserved, and needed to be. Sadly, for Sasha this was a familiar routine. And as always, because it was in her nature to do so, she would be as helpful as possible, in the hope that at some point her hard work would be recognized, her opinion would matter, and her talent would be appreciated. If she did just a little bit more, maybe Harry would change his mind and include her. Maybe they would get sold to a firm where she would have a more active role, not just be a figurehead. Maybe there was a possibility SAMCO could get sold separately from BridgeVest and she could be independent once again. Maybe she should go see James Ullman by herself to get a sense of whether that might be possible with his firm or anywhere else. All her socializing had given her a Rolodex that could be invaluable right now. She wanted to feel that tiny sliver of hope but for the time being could only feel a great sense of worry about what the coming weeks and months would bring.

CHAPTER SEVEN

Getting Ready for John

Renee didn't know what to say as Amanda walked by. She had seen her briefly at their fifth reunion from Spence, but Amanda hadn't been at their tenth last spring, not that Renee would have gone out of her way to say hello.

As Amanda walked toward Renee, she suddenly noticed her through her tears and said, "Renee Parker! Oh, my God, what are *you* doing here?"

"Amanda. What a surprise to see you as well. I am actually starting here today, working for John Cutter."

"You're working for John! Well, isn't that just perfect. I'm sure you two will be very happy together. Richie, you couldn't have picked a better one this time. Renee, did you lie to get this job like you lied all through high school?"

Renee was staggered and almost dropped the two coffees she was holding. Richie looked a little startled but quickly cut in. "Renee, why don't you go into the conference room. I'll be with you in a second. Amanda, I'm sorry things are ending this way, but they are. Let's not make this any more difficult. I'll make sure that your things are delivered to your home by the end of the day. If there is anything you need, please call me."

Amanda sniffed and said, "Richie, I am *absolutely* sure there isn't anything I could possibly need from you or anyone else here. Do make sure John knows that if I were him, I would be very careful. He doesn't know how powerful my family is, and don't forget, I know a lot about what's gone on here—and it's not all good."

Richie reddened a bit. He didn't like people making distinctions of their power, or their family's power, for that matter. In *his* world, one thing mattered: money. And he certainly didn't like the threat Amanda was making, whatever she meant by it. He assumed it was just a jealous ex-girlfriend trying to make herself heard. Man, why couldn't John keep it in his pants, or at least not do it with women in the office? "Amanda, we need to say good-bye now."

Meanwhile, as Renee was waiting in the conference room, she had a moment to collect herself. She could not believe that on this day, of all people, she had seen the one person who had always managed to make her feel inferior. She assumed Richie would want to talk about what Amanda had just said, although clearly it appeared she wasn't leaving on the best of terms and Richie hadn't seemed to pay it much attention. What was Amanda talking about with John Cutter and the company? There certainly was a lot of drama at this place, whatever it was.

While she was wondering, she also was able to look around. Supple leather chairs surrounded a black-lacquered board table that was just about as long as her dad's bus. Leather holders held notepads and cups of fountain pens. Every kind of drink from FIJI Water to IZZE clementine sparkling juice was lined up against the counter in the back next to crystal glasses etched with the Flying Point logo. There were twelve Jeff Koons balloon dogs lined up along the window, which framed a magnificent view of Central Park in its late summer glory. It looked as if they were taking a surreal walk in the park. Everything about the room screamed money and power.

"Renee, I'm really sorry that happened," Richie said as he entered the room.

"Umm, it's no problem. I went to school with Amanda Belden, but I haven't seen her in some time. She and I weren't the best of friends, to say the least. I'm sure you would like me to explain what she meant by that comment—"

"Renee," Richie interrupted her, "I know enough about you so far, and I know exactly all I need to ever know about Amanda Belden and people like her. Let's forget this happened. I already have. Now, let's get you started and make sure you know where everything is."

Renee breathed a sigh of relief, but at the same time, she wondered what Amanda meant by knowing what was going on at Flying Point. And what did she mean by her and John being very happy together? While Richie said it didn't matter, she was still unnerved and felt some of those same feelings from the incident in school rushing back. Today of all days, this was the last thing she wanted. She did not want anything to jeopardize this opportunity and six-figure salary. She resolved to put it aside as best she could and made her way with Richie down the office hallway. Since she had been in on Friday, she knew where her desk was but hadn't met most of the people, given the holiday weekend. As Richie introduced her, she noticed that most people rolled their eyes or didn't do much more than grunt a quick hi. They'd seen too many assistants before to invest a lot of time exchanging pleasantries.

As they got to her desk, Richie said, "Renee, I think you have a great shot here, and I know you were able to get your bearings on Friday, but just be tough. Try and anticipate as much as you can and I think you will be in good shape. That's the best lesson I could give anyone on Wall Street. Let me know if there is anything I can do for you, okay?"

"Okay, Richie. Don't worry. I'll be fine."

"And Renee," he said, "nice touch with the coffee." He gave her a wink as he walked away.

Renee smiled, put down her bag at her desk, and went into John Cutter's office to make sure everything was organized. On her way though she heard the phone ring and rushed to pick it up.

"This is John Cutter's office, may I help you?"

"Yes, put him on right away, please?"

"I'm sorry but he isn't in yet. May I take a message, sir?"

"Shit! I thought he'd be in by now! Ahh. No, uh, I'll call back." And she heard a click on the other end of the phone.

Renee didn't think much of it until about ten minutes later when the same man called back. Again, she tried to ask if she could take a message, but even though he seemed more agitated than before, the man still would not leave his name. When it happened a third time about five minutes later, she wrote down the number that showed up on caller ID: 212-555-5412. She recognized the 555 exchange as being from Lehman Brothers. She had a good friend from college who worked there, so she dialed her number.

"Jen, it's Renee. Hey, I just started a new job at Flying Point Capital... Yeah, I'm a 'hedgie' now! But I need a favor. Someone called a few times and I can tell it's a Lehman number by the exchange. Can you tell me who it is? I don't want to call directly. It's 5412."

"Sure. Let me look at the online directory. Umm, 5412, looks like it's Blake Somerset, a real player in the financial products group."

Blake Somerset! Renee was stunned as she hung up with Jen. Her mother had worked for Blake and Grigsby Somerset for the last five years! Donita never talked about the Somersets, but once or twice she had made comments about them. They went out a great deal, didn't spend much time with their children, spent a tremendous amount of money, and as far as Donita could tell seemed to be two people living separate lives together. It was a far cry from what Renee had experienced with her family growing up.

Renee thought it was odd that Blake had called but didn't want to leave a message. She was used to people identifying themselves right away, especially on business calls. Why wouldn't he want to say who he was? And why did he sound so distressed? She'd make sure to let Mr. Cutter know as soon as he got in. Hopefully, he would be pleased that she was able to get the information for him.

Renee spent the next few minutes making sure her own desk was ready to go. She hoped John would get there before his coffee was cold, but Richie had assured her he came in at 8:30 on the dot. Sure enough, when she saw him approaching, it had just struck that time.

As he came toward her, Renee thought he certainly didn't look like the terrifying monster she had imagined he might be; in fact, he was downright good-looking! Even better than the pictures she had seen online when she'd researched him and the firm. When she presented him with the messages from Blake Somerset, he didn't blink an eye. He went into his office and gathered himself, then called out to her, "Okay, let's start the day off with a bang, shall we? Get Somerset on the line ASAP."

Renee went out to her desk and dialed the number. "Please hold for Mr. John Cutter." John shut the door, but she heard him say, "Blake, I hear you've been calling all morning... Yeah, don't tell me how the fuck I know, I fucking know, okay? Listen, I'm expecting to see your ass here for our meeting, which as I recall was about three minutes ago, so I'm not really sure what the frantic calls are about. I thought everything was happening on schedule!... Good. Okay, later."

John slammed down the phone and yelled out to Renee, "Okay, listen, Blake Somerset will be here in a few minutes. I'll meet with him in here. *No interruptions no matter what!* Got that?"

A short while later, reception buzzed back that Blake Somerset had arrived. Renee went up front to get him and led him back to John's office. After getting him a cup of coffee, she shut the door and left them to talk. From time to time, she could hear heated voices coming from the office and at one point she heard John yell, "You created this fucking crap that is now worth shit! You walk away with your bonus and I'm fucking screwed. This plan of yours better work."

While they were meeting, an assortment of calls came in, but nothing that Renee was unable to handle. After about an hour, however, the phone rang, and when Renee answered, the person on the other end said, "Good day, this is Mr. Alistair Smythe, managing director, calling from First National Cayman. Unfortunately, the wiring instructions we have on file for Mr. Cutter aren't working, and if the funds are to be sent, I must have correct wiring instructions before ten thirty a.m. If not, we will not be able to make the distributions in time. Could you please give them to me."

Renee was not sure what to do. It was currently 10:20. Should she wait, look through files in her desk, or interrupt John? His words, *No interruptions no matter what! Got that?* rang in her ears. She responded, "I'm sorry, Mr. Smythe, I've just started today and Mr. Cutter is behind closed doors. Let me see if I can quickly find anything in the files that might relate to this."

"Very well, my dear, but I must have them as soon as possible. Couldn't you put Mr. Cutter on the phone for me?"

"No, I'm sorry, he is not to be disturbed."

As Renee riffled frantically through the desk, there wasn't much hope of finding anything. What files there were didn't seem to relate at all to bank accounts or to anything about the business, for that matter—a testament, she supposed, to the fleeting tenure of John's previous assistants.

"Mr. Smythe, is there any way the wire can be delayed?" she asked, although knowing a small amount about banking, she guessed it was not likely. The banking system usually had inviolable rules on wiring deadlines so that money could flow from institution to institution smoothly.

"Oh, my dear child, would that were so. No, I'm afraid not."

It was now 10:23. Clearly those instructions were not anywhere that she could find them. Renee knew if John had instructions, he would probably need a moment to find them and then the bank would need to input them into their system. She had no choice. She gathered her courage and knocked on John's office door.

"What the FUCK are you doing?" John, not so calmly, yelled in her face. "I told you NO FUCKING interruptions! GODDAMN IT, YOU MORON!" Renee could see Blake Somerset in the background, looking red and angry.

"Yes, I know, sir, but there's a Mr. Smythe from First National Cayman on the phone and he needs new wiring instructions within the next seven minutes or he won't be able to take care of your distributions. I looked in my desk, but there aren't any files related to any accounts, and I don't want you to miss the deadline at ten thirty."

"Oh shit," John said. "I'll take it in my private conference room." He stepped into a room to the side of his office and shut the door.

Renee went back to her desk and sat down. She had made the right decision, but she was not thrilled that she'd had to endure being yelled at by John like that so soon on her first day. She hoped it would be the last time, but she also guessed that it wouldn't be. John clearly shot first, then aimed. She would do what she could to stay out of the line of fire.

After the call, John must have gone back to Blake, because they emerged together about an hour later. Blake had an odd look about him, but John seemed calm, bordering on emotionless.

When he came back to his office, he said not a word to Renee about the meeting or the phone call from Alistair Smythe. She figured John Cutter wasn't the type to apologize for yelling.

Thankfully, the rest of the day passed without incident, although she was pretty shocked by how much, how loudly, and how extravagantly John cursed. Richie came by a few times to see if everything was going all right and seemed relieved to see her still there, and generally composed, for that matter. At 5:30, Renee started to get ready to leave. She knocked on John's door, which was shut, as it had been for much of the day, and peered in. "John, is there anything else I can do for you this evening? I'm happy to stay as late as you need me to."

"Holy shit! Still here? I figured you would have been out of here at four fifty-nine."

"I usually like to make sure everything I have is done, and if there's something that's needed, I'll stay as late as I have to," she responded.

"Ah, okay. Well, I am glad to hear that. I haven't had much luck with assistants. I usually get the bottom of the barrel. I'm fine for the evening, so you can go."

"Okay, well, here is my cell phone number if you need anything during the evening or tomorrow before work. If not, I will see you tomorrow."

"Right. Oh shit, I actually will be in late tomorrow. I have something I have to take care of out of the office. So I'll see you at eleven or so."

"Is there anything you need me to arrange for you? I'd be happy to—"

"No, I said I'd be in around eleven. That's all you need to know."

Renee couldn't figure out this man. Certainly one day wasn't enough, but she knew one thing: There were indeed some dramatic elements going on around here. She assumed as the days and weeks unfolded, she would learn what those were.

CHAPTER EIGHT

Dinner at 7:00

As Grigsby got in the Range Rover to go to dinner, she checked her BlackBerry. She saw a new message had come in from Blake: "Running late. Should be there by 7:30 at latest. B."

"Ugh," she said out loud to herself, but really to her driver, Sheldon, as well. "I don't see why he cannot be on time. It's really annoying. Now I have to sit and make conversation with them."

Sheldon had long ago learned how to not listen to Mrs. Somerset's mindless muttering. He wondered how women like this came into existence. Were they born like that, or did something happen along the way to make them such irritating, self-important chatterbugs? Come to think of it, having driven her and her mother together once or twice, he guessed that in her case it was inherited.

Sheldon didn't mind Mr. Somerset. He was a nice guy. Nothing to write home about, but always pleasant and cordial. He usually only drove him to work in the morning. Mrs. Somerset usually had him running around for the rest of the day and into the evening to whatever events they had on their schedule. Mr. Somerset was lucky if he got a ride to those, though, because they were coming from opposite directions. He usually met the Mrs. by cab.

Sheldon's job was easy, but it also wasn't. He basically sat in a car all day. If he wasn't driving, he was waiting. The driving was what you would expect: annoying city traffic, taxi drivers who didn't know there were directional signals on their cars, jaywalkers oblivious to lights and cars, reckless pedicabs and cops usually trying to tell him he couldn't stop where he wanted to. The waiting was also what you would expect: a lot of sitting around. Mrs. Somerset never came out when she said she would, but he had learned to deal with it. He read a lot and had bought a mini–DVD player and watched movies, a lot of movies. He also took a lot of naps. Anyway, the job paid the rent and monthly trips to Foxwoods and the Mohegan Sun, so he was content.

Mrs. Somerset was generally cordial to Sheldon, but he always noticed a distinct air of snobbishness in everything she said to him. That was fine with him, too. People could act like they wanted. As long as he got paid, what did he care?

"Sheldon, I am going to Swifty's on Seventy-third and Lexington and am supposed to be there in five minutes, so I would appreciate your figuring out the best route to get us there."

"Sure thing, Mrs. Somerset." He didn't bother to explain that they were on Park Avenue, and aside from going south on that street, which was absolutely wide open, the only other option was to take Lexington. They were going only nineteen blocks, so the idea of a clever "route" wasn't really necessary.

They arrived at Swifty's in exactly three minutes.

"Here you go, Mrs. Somerset. Record time."

"Thank you, Sheldon. I was expecting Mr. Somerset to be here on time, but apparently he is late so you might want to see if there's time for you to get him."

As Sheldon drove off, Grigsby checked her phone one more time but didn't see any more messages. She walked inside.

Swifty's was the heir to a well-known restaurant, at least in certain circles, called Mortimer's, which in its heyday was *the* "ladies who lunch" spot in town. Glenn Bernbaum, the proprietor, was notorious for seating "his ladies" while turning away those he didn't know or care for. Invariably, in those days the window table would feature the likes of Nan Kempner (who was "outseated" only by

Brooke Astor), usually dining with other luminaries like Pat Buckley, Bill Blass, and Kenneth Jay Lane. Lunch, for the most part, consisted of a few leaves of lettuce, for it was in those days that the well-known truism emerged, "You can be neither too rich nor too thin." So lettuce it was. When Glenn Bernbaum died, two of his longtime key staff opened Swifty's, naming the restaurant after his dog and continuing the tradition of a seemingly casual restaurant where people go to see and be seen.

As Grigsby walked in the narrow entryway, she spied several people she knew, some of whom she hadn't seen since last spring, since they summered in Nantucket, Newport, Locust Valley, or Litchfield County, and as such they had not seen one another for three months. It was like the first day of high school.

"Steffi. Hiiii. How arrrre you?!" she purred as she did a double air kiss with platinum blond hair that was set off against deeply tanned skin.

"Great, Grigs. How are you? How was your summer? My God, you look fabulous," Steffi responded with a deep voice that oozed money and privilege.

"It was marvelous, but hectic. So much running around, and the traffic in the Hamptons has gotten insane. Beyond insane! Sometimes I feel like we need a new place. How was Newport? I really should try that one year."

"It was fabulous, darling. Simply fabulous. The boys were at sailing camp all day long, so I finally got a chance to RE-lax! But now I'm back to my hellish existence."

"Oh, don't I know it. I had school calls to make all morning."

"School calls!! There is nothing worse. Oh, my dear, I truly ache for you. I spent the morning on the phone with our landscaper in Palm Beach. We have had absolutely debilitating saltwater damage to our lawn, and as a result, the bulkhead has collapsed! It's just ghastly. He doesn't know if it's going to be done in time for our annual Christmas party, and I'm going to scream. I just do not know what I am going to do. As if I have time to deal with that!"

"Steffi! That is dreadful! Your Christmas party is always the highlight of the season!"

"Yes, I know, but ever since he started doing the Madoffs' landscaping, he's gotten all high and mighty. He keeps talking about that fund of Madoff's that he's now invested in. At least that's what Peter tells me. I just find it irritating. I mean, he is a landscaper, for heaven's sake. Anyway, Peter says he would never invest with *someone like that.*"

In fact, Grigsby actually had no idea what Steffi was talking about, but she nodded in agreement nonetheless, especially if Peter said that. She was more horrified at the idea of Steffi's Christmas party being in jeopardy. She simply loved that party. She already had a dress for it.

"And on top of that," Steffi continued, "my real task of the day was to make our Christmas, and Washington's birthday, *and* spring vacation airline reservations," she said, pausing dramatically in between each holiday. "I tell you, it is just too much for me at times. And it's not as if Peter would give me one second of appreciation, and God forbid his assistant should do it. I mean, she's got the time, doesn't she?"

"Oh, I know. Well, I am hoping that I can get my own assistant this year to help with so many of the things that I have going on. How is Peter, anyway?"

"He is fabulous. Thank God he left Bear Stearns three months before they went under and Lehman took him out of his Bear stock as an enticement to leave. That's twenty-five million I would not have appreciated losing. He is doing really well at Lehman. I'm thinking Verdura under the Christmas tree for me this year! Do he and Blake ever see one another? I think they are in the same department."

"Oh, I don't know. Blake never tells me anything that goes on there, not that I would even understand what he talks about. It's all CDO this and MBS that. Anyway, Blake is on his way, or so I hope. God, wouldn't it be nice if these men managed to ever make it on time?"

"Well, let's definitely get together for lunch soon. Or maybe the four of us can get together for dinner. I would *looove* to catch up."

"Yes, darling, me, too. Let's talk later this week when we have both had a chance to get settled."

And with another double blond, double air kiss, they parted ways. Lunch or dinner would be arranged, at which there would be many more exchanges of how many impossible tasks there were and not enough hours in the day to complete them, not to mention the lack of appreciation by their husbands of what it took to maintain a perfect life.

Grigsby saw Chip and Chessy already seated, so she waved hello to several other people and once or twice said, "Hello, darling! So good to see you. Yura, Thursday after drop-off? I *cannot* believe it's that time already!"

She went over to the table and kissed her brother- and sister-in-law. Chip and Chessy were quite a few years younger than her and Blake. Chip was actually Blake's half brother—same mother, different father, born when Blake was ten, and much less further along in his career. In fact, he and Chessy had gotten married only about eighteen months before and were still in the "love is a many-splendored thing" phase. They'd had a glorious Greenwich wedding not unlike her own, where everything from the guest list to the weather on a June Saturday was perfect. Chip was an investment banker at Merrill Lynch, and Chessy also worked at Merrill, as an institutional saleswoman on the equity desk.

While Grigsby had no particular like or dislike for Chip and Chessy, she usually found herself bored to tears by conversations with them, as they were focused on the markets, deals, and whatever was in *The Wall Street Journal* that day. Chessy didn't have a care, or flair, for that matter, for fashion, and she usually dressed in gray or black pantsuits and plain-colored shirts from Banana Republic. Grigsby found herself completely bored by Chessy's blandness in personality and clothing. She gathered her energy and said with excessive, bordering on fake, cheeriness, "Hi. How *are* you guys? Blake is running a bit late, so let's order some cocktails while we wait. Shall we?"

While they were saying hello back to her, Grigsby was already waving the waiter over to order drinks. Dealing with boring and irritating situations was made a little easier by a glass of Pinot Grigio. Summer evenings while dealing with the kids were made a little easier by a glass of Domaine Ott. Listening to Blake drone on and on about whatever was made a little easier by a gin and tonic in Palm Beach. Like many women of her mother's generation and social status, Grisby was starting to drink every evening, or sometimes in the late afternoon, to take the edge off, be more comfortable, or just feel less bored.

While waiting for Blake, Grigsby went through the laundry list of questions: How was their summer; how was the apartment; were they thinking of moving to the suburbs. She was about to ask them the obligatory "And when are you going to have children?" when Blake finally came in, looking unkempt and a bit distracted.

"Hi, guys, good to see you!" He gave Grigsby an obligatory peck as she obligingly, if halfheartedly, put out her cheek to receive it. "Sorry I'm late. Things have been crazy today, first day back and all."

As Chip and Chessy brushed off his tardiness, Grigsby said, "Yes, Blake, it really would be nice if you could keep the schedule straight. It takes a lot of arranging."

Chessy and Chip gave each other the newlywed look that said, "We will never be like that," while at the same time smiling lovingly at each other.

"Darling, let's get you a cocktail," Grigsby continued. "I was just asking Chip and Chessy when they were going to have children."

Chip paused and then said, "Well, actually, we do have some news for you. Chessy is pregnant with twins! She is due in March. We just passed the three-month mark."

"Hey, man that's great! Awesome! Congrats, guys," Blake said.

"How absolutely wonderful," Grigsby said. "Now you can quit your job!"

Chessy reddened and said, "Oh, no, I'm not quitting. I'll take three months off, make sure my accounts are covered by other salespeople, and then go back to work next June."

Grigsby looked absolutely horrified. "You're not going to leave your job?! But why would you want to keep working?"

"Well, um, I actually like working. I love the markets, I love the accounts I deal with, and I work with great people."

"Oh, well, I'm sure everything is lovely, but you will definitely change your mind once you've had a few months off. And if you are going back to work, why go back in June? I'd take the summer off—"

"Hon," Blake interrupted, "you can't really take six months off and expect to walk back in. It's hard enough as it is. Six months and everyone will have forgotten about her."

"Well, if you ask me, it's all just crazy. I don't even understand what you all are talking about half the time. Oh, look, there are Sarah and Bobby! Hello, darlings! Oh, look at that cute Milly dress Sarah has on. Don't you love it, Chessy?"

"Oh, yes. It's lovely," Chessy said, still not over Grigsby's admonition to her. Frankly, Blake's comment about no one remembering her in six months made her concerned about how she'd fare after three months. Boy, these two were a piece of work.

Grigsby was ready to order dinner, and especially a bottle of wine for the table. She always seemed to take control, and even though she asked what everyone was eating to determine what wine they should order, as usual, it ended up being exactly what Grigsby wanted.

During dinner, Chip talked about how things were at Merrill. Since new leadership had come in, there was definitely a feeling that the firm was going to come out of this crisis, but his department, mergers and acquisitions, had seen business drop off a good percentage from the prior year. With only four months of the year left and things as seemingly unsettled as they were, everyone was worried about bonuses at year-end. In a good year, Chip could expect to take home $1 million in bonus, but this year who knew? Chessy's compensation was much more dependable; she worked on commission, so she was paid 30 percent of the gross revenue she generated. Last year she had made $575,000. There had been lots of cuts at Merrill already that year, and they were both bracing for another round, hoping they'd make it through unscathed.

Grigsby got up twice during dinner to say hello to various people, which was fine with everyone else, as they were engrossed in conversation about what was going to happen next in the financial world.

Dinner ended at 9:30. Grigsby told Chessy they should get together and insisted on having a baby shower for her. They got in the car, where Sheldon had been waiting for the two hours they'd been inside. While it certainly would have been easy for the Somersets to offer Chip and Chessy a ride home to their apartment on 73rd and York, it would never have occurred to Grigsby to do so. After all it *was* in the opposite direction. Meanwhile, Blake was busy wondering to himself why they couldn't send Sheldon home after he dropped them off for dinner. Why not take a cab for $7 instead of paying him an extra $100 in overtime? He knew if he brought it up to Grigsby, she would tell him that one simply did not do such a thing. Come to think of it, it was worth $100 not to hear her tell him what everyone else was or wasn't doing.

CHAPTER NINE

Try to Remember, It's September

When Sasha got back to her office, she was in a stupor. She went through all the usual greetings and comments about how relaxed she looked. Funny, the usual dread of the end of vacation she'd felt yesterday was now overshadowed by a deeper discomfort at the news she had received this morning. She looked at all her employees as she walked through the office and wondered if she would have any control over their lives in the future. There was Sam, the receptionist, who had gone back to work after her husband lost his job. Would anyone care that they had a mortgage to pay? Or what about Pat, the messenger who was mentally disabled but knew the city subway system with uncanny precision and, as she had told him, would always have a job as long as she was around. Would a buyer feel the same way? His salary of $28,000 plus the health care benefits, which were an additional 17 percent on top of his compensation, could easily be eliminated. How many of them would be able to keep their jobs? How many would be asked to come into a conference room and given the news that their jobs were being terminated? Sasha had observed over the years that while many people didn't like having to go to work every day, and complained about their bosses and colleagues, they expected their daily routine to be dependable until *they* chose to change it.

Sasha had called Adam after she'd left the Regency, but he had been in a meeting. He returned her call a short time after she'd arrived at work.

"Hey, hon, how was breakfast? What was the big mystery?"

"You won't believe it. BridgeVest is going to be sold. Apparently Kirk wants his balance sheet to be freed up and it's a good strategic move, blah blah blah."

"Wow, I can't believe it, although it does make sense. Empire's stock hasn't been doing well. Kirk must be getting nervous he could be a target or that his own position might be in jeopardy." (Leave it to Adam to look at the facts of everything.) "So how are you doing?"

"Wait, there's more. Apparently there was some meeting last week up there and Kirk *came* to it. That's where the sale was discussed. You know how busy Kirk is, so you have to know the meeting was arranged several weeks beforehand. Harry gave me some BS about not wanting to bother me on vacation, but I know there's something else going on. Then James Ullman happened to be at the Regency and I introduced him to Harry assuming he would want to talk to him because he would be a natural buyer and—"

"Sweetie, I gotta run. Call I need to take. Can we talk later? I really want to hear more about it. Love you. Bye."

And as he was so often, Adam was gone in an instant.

This only increased Sasha's irritation. She knew Adam had a lot going on. His business was so much more tactical than hers. He needed constantly to be watching and reacting in a way that she didn't. Her focus was on long-term issues and strategy and dealing with clients. At the same time, it was always hard to have him rush off when she was in the middle of telling him something, especially when it was really important and she needed his advice or at least needed a shoulder on which to lean. It made her feel alone and unsure. There wasn't anyone else she could speak to about this, and there was so much that she wanted to pour out to him right now.

She look a quick look at BridgeVest's revenues for year-to-date. So far, they had generated $150 million. SAMCO's business was about 25 percent of that. She didn't know if it was good or bad that they were such a large percentage. When she had first sold the company, it was only 10 percent. She was actually quite proud that they'd grown that much in less than three years. Was a buyer going to see that as an indicator of how *meaningful* SAMCO was? Were they going to see how meaningful she was?

She spent the morning alternately going through materials, e-mails, and messages that she hadn't dealt with while she was away and thinking more and more about what the sale was going to mean for her and everyone.

At noon, she had her regularly scheduled weekly management team meeting. It was usually a bellyaching session of how irritating, nonstrategic, and generally just plain dumb the BridgeVest people were, punctuated with, "If only we were independent again, we could..." It was difficult for Sasha to keep her distance in conversations like these. As much as she agreed 100 percent, she knew that it was bad form to do so and only added fuel to the fire. If it was okay for the CEO to do it, that would spread through the ranks. As much as they neither liked nor respected BridgeVest, that's where the paychecks came from every two weeks. It also made her feel guilty that she had led them down this path in the first place. Today's meeting was no exception, and all the more so as two weeks had passed without her, during which additional frustration had built up.

"Sasha, you have got to get them to listen to us," Bill Conrad, the chief operating officer, said to her. "They completely misunderstand our business and the way it works. We are constantly in danger of damaging very significant client relationships, not to mention our reputation itself! We have always had such a premier position in the marketplace and it's devastating to hear 'Ever since you people sold to that outfit' every day from clients. Especially now when it's hard enough to keep the clients we do have, let alone get more business from them. Isn't there anything you can do?"

Sasha had noted well before she sold the firm that any business relationship one company had with another tended to have its fair share of miscommunication, mistrust, and even dislike of the other side. Why was it that generally one group always thought that their own people were smart while the others were the screwups? However, in this case it really was true! The BridgeVest management team brought incompetence to a new level. She attributed that to Harry and his lack of leadership. Sadly, there were a few hidden gems in the company who were never given the opportunity to shine. She actually felt worse for them than she did for herself.

"I hear what you're saying, but I need some specifics on what the issues are—I can't just say 'You are damaging our brand' without getting my rear handed to me. And that, by the way, only furthers the impression that already exists up there that we don't listen and we should because they own us. So who wants to give me a thoughtful and organized memo which includes solutions on what we need to have happen?"

"Okay, sure, I can do that," Bill responded, "but I need to mention that it was really ridiculous for them to ask us to provide all that information two weeks ago and then a whole additional set last week. It took us a lot of time to get that together, and we were really short-staffed with everyone out on vacation. It was ridiculous!"

Sasha's radar went up again. What information was requested? All of a sudden, she had an even more disturbing feeling. She didn't want her team to notice, though.

"Forgive me. I guess two weeks away and my brain has cobwebs in it. Remind me of what you are talking about?"

"Sasha, you really must have forgotten. When Harry's office called, they said that it had been discussed with you right before you went away. You know, it was all the details on the company asset and revenue growth since the sale. And news flash! They own us! Shouldn't they have that information somewhere?"

She tried quickly to pretend that she knew exactly what they were talking about. "Oh! Sorry, they're doing a big industry comparison for that regional managers meeting and wanted to show our growth versus acquisitions at competing companies." She was really concerned now. There had been no such discussion with her. Why would they have told her people that she had approved something when she didn't know anything about it? It was as if they'd suspected that a request of this nature would immediately bring questions if her people thought she wasn't aware of it. One of her people would have gone right to her. In turn, Sasha would have immediately called Harry. But why would they have asked for information without involving her? And to ask for it twice? That was certainly odd as well, although knowing them, she assumed they had probably lost the first set. Whatever the reason, she knew it obviously was tied to the meeting with Kirk.

"Let me just say this again. I know that it's hard to deal with them, and I am not minimizing the frustration at all, but we have to understand we are not an independent company, as much as some may wish that we were. We have to respond to their requests and, unfortunately, find ways to work with them or around them. I know you all wish we were independent again, but there are some benefits that come along with it, too. We don't have many of the risks we used to, and we have access to more resources as part of a bigger company."

As Sasha was speaking, every bone in her body was yelling to her, "You big huge liar. You don't believe one word of what you are saying! You desperately long for the risks that you used to have. Screw bigger companies! They are just people stuffed in boxes not able to do anything without someone telling them to get back in their box. Ha! 'Think outside the box' must have been made up by some sadomasochist CEO!"

She managed to make it through the rest of the day and was only twenty minutes late to East Side Kids, although there were still four people ahead of them by the time she got there. She marveled at the price of leather Mary Jane party shoes for a three-year-old, only $82. Samantha didn't like the color Sasha picked out, exclaiming,

"Barnacles!" her favorite line from *SpongeBob*. Sasha then explained to the twins that even though *everyone* was going to be wearing the boots that cost $189, that didn't mean they had to also. Somehow they managed to get out of the store with a bill of only $675 among the four children, which, all things considered, wasn't too terrible. If the twins had had their way, they each would have gotten $400 worth of shoes, the vast majority of which would have been worn once before they were dismissed with a disdainful, "I don't like them."

Adam called to say he was on the way home, and when he walked in, he looked exhausted. After he had cut her off that morning, they hadn't spoken for the rest of the day.

He gave her a big kiss. "Honey, sorry I wasn't able to talk today. I do want to hear about what you were telling me. Did you find out anything else?"

"Not really. Only that apparently they ask—"

"*Mom!* Josh took my Barbie!" Samantha wailed with a scream that shook the foundations of the apartment.

Sasha knew that there was little chance of having a conversation with the interruptions that were likely to take place until the kids were asleep. "Okay, honey. I'll make him give it back. Joshua Gerard Silver, hand that back to her *this* instant or plan on no Wii for the rest of the week. Adam, we need to wait until later to talk. You know how I can't stand to be interrupted, or maybe I should just send you an e-mail?! But I want to hear about your day. What were things like? Tell me in ten seconds or less!"

"More of the same. Feels like there's something really bad on the way. Credit default swaps widening on a bunch of names. It doesn't feel good."

Sasha didn't have a lot to do with the more complex components of the market like Adam, but she'd always found credit default swaps intriguing and somewhat perverse. While originally used to protect one's own position should an investment go belly-up, in the last few years they had become a tool for speculation by others. Sasha had once described credit default swaps to a friend as being like taking out an insurance policy on a house you didn't own and hoping that someone would then burn the house down. The widening Adam was talking about meant that people were preparing for, or possibly even assisting in, the creation of bad news. Credit default swaps had been the portent of Bear's demise earlier that year; it was hard to imagine others hadn't helped to create the company's end through the use of these products, although this was never proven. The prime suspects were Bear's competitors and some of the largest hedge funds.

"Gosh, what do you think is going to happen?"

"What do I think? I think we are in for a big, fucking, scary time. I think Bear Stearns is going to look like a tea party. And I think the government is going to find itself rushing to put out more fires than it ever dreamed of, using a garden hose that has a kink in it. The last eight years of easy credit and little to no regulation is going to give us a hangover like we haven't seen since the thirties. That's what I think."

"Oh, come on! What are you saying? That there will be a crash of that magnitude followed by another Great Depression?"

"Yes, I am. Even with the problems of this year, we have been in an insane bull market for several years. And over what? The assumption that housing prices will go up forever. Sasha, you know as well as I do, markets can go down as fast and furiously as they went up."

"Yes, of course I do. But you always see things so negatively. I'm just not convinced that things will unravel like that. Not that I don't think you are the smartest man I know."

"We will see, Sasha. I just call 'em as I see 'em. I could be wrong. But I'm not!"

Sasha chuckled and went to put Samantha in the tub. As she sat there, she checked her BlackBerry. There was an e-mail from Bruce Smith, the CEO of a company in which she had made an investment:

"Sasha, can we get together in the next couple days? Need some advice on some things that have come up."

"Sure," she typed back as she checked her schedule. "How @ Thurs or Fri aft?"

She always got a little excited when she heard from one of "her" companies. Their issues were so unique, their businesses were new, fresh, and unencumbered by the political issues she faced day in and day out. It made her feel entrepreneurial again.

"Friday is great. 5:30 Ok?"

"Sure," she responded, and put aside her BlackBerry as it just missed getting drenched by Samantha pretending to be a mermaid and flipping her tail. Before the evening ended she would somehow find ten minutes to fill Adam in on the rest of her day, and the disturbing meeting with Harry.

On Friday, Sasha was able to get out of the office early enough to meet Bruce Smith, the owner of That Old Black Magic. She had met him a year ago in a random encounter, as she had a number of people in her life. She had overheard him while he was meeting with someone at the table next to hers at the Regency one morning. Black Magic, as she called it, specialized in taking vintage jewelry and attaching it to hats and bags. Since Sasha was herself a collector of vintage costume pieces, she thought it was a terrific concept. She'd waited until his guest had gotten up to leave and then she'd leaned over and said, "Excuse me. I hope you don't mind my listening in to your conversation, but I think that is one of the best ideas I have heard in a while. I would really like to talk to you more about it."

Needless to say, Bruce was thrilled. They'd made arrangements to meet at his studio. Sasha went through his business plan and saw all of his sketches and creations. She was hooked! His plans were relatively modest. He needed working capital to acquire inventory and hire two people to work in production, and he also needed a modest amount for

PR, to get some buzz for the products. Sasha knew from every handbag, hat, clothing, and jewelry line out there that even with PR there was still a lot of competition to make sure the right people wore the pieces to the right events. She could help him with that in addition to making an investment.

She ended up investing the full $150,000 that he needed, in return for a 30 percent stake in his business. This was her money alone. She loved what he was doing and wanted to see him succeed. If she ended up making three, four, or five times her money back, it would be tremendous. If the business failed, it wouldn't be enough to devastate her. She liked Bruce because he never took no for an answer, was creative and passionate about his company. He had already had a tough time trying to get a traditional bank loan and just didn't know enough about finance to get what he needed. Sasha was a dream come true for Bruce, too. She gave him money, access, and a clearer understanding of his needs.

She wore a hat of his to the Central Park Conservancy lunch in the spring of 2008. He had taken an oversize green straw hat and attached several jeweled butterflies, dragonflies, and flowers to it. Some were on the hat itself, while he had attached others about a quarter inch above with wire, which made it look as if they were in the process of landing on a luscious green lawn. The hat was by far the hit of the lunch, although one woman remarked when Sasha brushed by her by accident, as the hat was so large, "That woman needs to learn to control her hat!" (As if that were easy in a crowd of several hundred women, the vast majority of them wearing similarly sized chapeaus.) For the most part, she was besieged with "*That* is the best hat of the day!" and "Where did you get that? It's fantastic! Simply fantastic! I have got to get one for next year." By the end of the lunch, at least five women had asked to see Bruce's things. It was tremendously rewarding to her to be able to make that kind of connection for him. She'd e-mailed him right after she left and the photographers had taken one last shot of her at the gates to the garden: "Bruce!! Huge. HUGE response. Orders on the way... so happy. YAY!!!"

She spoke to Bruce at least once a month and they met every quarter to go over his numbers. Since she had made the investment, his sales had gone up 20 percent. She was happy with the numbers, of course, but the reality was that she was even happier to have this wonderful outlet into which she could pour some of her pent-up creativity. It actually helped her to lose some of the unhappiness she had in her own work situation.

They met at the Bryant Park Grill, which they both loved because the park was so peaceful and beautiful in the middle of the chaos of midtown. As soon as she sat down, she could tell he was distressed.

"Hi, Bruce, what's going on?"

"Well, I am really in a dither, and I don't know what to do."

"Why? Tell me what is wrong."

She was already running through all the possibilities in her head. He had lost his entire inventory. An employee stole something. He was deathly ill. She was sick to her stomach with the possibilities.

"I got a call a few days ago from someone who had seen my things and wanted to talk to me about buying the business."

"Well, that's not terrible at all. Did you meet with them?"

"Yes, I did. I had a long talk with them. It's Cheim Chebah. You know, from one of the Syrian Jewish families that are in the garment business? He wants to expand my line into a number of stores in the country."

"Wow. Yes. He certainly knows what he is doing. He did that big deal with Wal-Mart last year, as I recall. Has he discussed a number with you yet?"

"Well, generally, but I told him that you are a thirty percent owner and he needs to speak with you. He said it would be for a multiple of the current revenues, though."

"Okay, Bruce, I'm still waiting for the bad part."

"Well, the thing is it might be great, but for some reason every time

I think of it I feel this overwhelming sense of sadness. He started talking about how the jewelry can just be bought from China to significantly lower costs. Part of the allure of what I do is making sure that quality isn't sacrificed for profits."

Sasha looked at him. She could see his confusion and concern. "Bruce, do you want to sell the business? Do you like what he is suggesting?"

"Well, yes, I mean, I don't know. I feel like I'm supposed to, but I'm just not sure if this is the right thing to do now. But it's money, and as you know, everything I have is in this. And as I said, I just keep getting this feeling, but then I wonder if it's just cold feet or something."

"Bruce. If you don't want to sell it, don't sell it."

He looked surprised. "But what about your investment?"

"What about my investment?"

"Well, isn't this why you put money in, so you could make it back?"

"Bruce, let me tell you something. I have been in your shoes, and I did exactly the wrong thing. I sold the company and have been miserable ever since. You will know when the right time has come, or you will sell when it is enough money to walk away and be happy, or you will want to stay to see the business grow. I invested in your company to help you in any way I could, and that means helping you make the decision that is right for you. You are the one who has to live with this company every day."

"I don't. I don't want to sell it. Ugh, I am so relieved to be able to say that."

"Then there's your answer. See, that was easy!"

They talked for a while more about the current state of the business and whether it would be worth it to spend $5,000 to sponsor the after-party for the junior committee at an upcoming gala. It would be good exposure, but Sasha wasn't sure that would translate into sales. She was pleased that Bruce seemed calmer and wished as she finished her glass of wine that she had listened to her own internal voice several years earlier.

CHAPTER TEN

The Weekend the World Ended

Friday, September 12

As Blake left for work on Friday, Grigsby said, "What time do you want to leave for Southampton this evening?" There were only one or two more weekends in the country before their social life would shift to the city until late the following spring. They would continue to go to Southampton here and there, but trips would invariably be replaced by children's soccer games, weekend dinner parties, and periodic jaunts to Palm Beach to visit Grigsby's parents.

"Grigsby, I really don't know what is going to happen today," he responded. "They've asked everyone in a senior capacity in my group to stand by because of the potential deal with Barclays or Bank of America, so I probably will be spending the weekend at the office. We are going to have to stay here and keep the weekend open."

Grigsby responded with exasperation, "Are you kidding me? Can't the management of the firm work things out? I told the Donaldsons last weekend we would have dinner with them tomorrow night at Red Star."

With everything on his mind, Blake was finding it harder to deal with Grigsby's complete lack of appreciation for the seriousness that current events held for them. It was like talking to a child sometimes. He couldn't deal with this now.

"Grigs, I can't discuss this on the fly and I'm going to be late for my meeting. I'll call you later, okay?" he said, deciding it would be better to deal with it by phone this afternoon, when he could just say, "We aren't going, period!" than to get into a discussion now. Grigsby, for her part, was always ready to put off a discussion, because in her mind it meant she had won.

In fact, there was a great deal weighing on Blake's mind that was tied directly to the future of Lehman Brothers. On Thursday, the stock had closed at $4.22 per share, down almost half in one day alone, and amazingly, it was likely to go down more today unless a deal to sell the company was announced before the market closed. Blake almost couldn't believe that as recently as June, the stock had traded at nearly $35 per share. It had dropped like a rock since he came back from vacation, if you could call it that. If the financial crisis had shown one thing, it was how fast and far a once healthy blue-chip stock could fall. It was one thing in 2001 when Internet companies went from 100 to 1. They had no revenues! But these were companies that generated billions of dollars a year. They were the foundation of the financial system. It was crazy.

Nine months ago, Blake Somerset had been worth nearly $55 million, but today that number was $4 million—$4 million! He almost laughed. He hadn't had that little in years!

There was no way the Somersets could afford their very expensive lifestyle without their Lehman holdings. Every year, a portion of Blake's annual bonus was paid in stock, and even if he'd wanted to sell, which he didn't, it would have been impossible to do so. Employees were actually prohibited for five years from selling new shares received as part of an annual bonus—and he had gotten most of what he had in the last five years. If he and Grigsby had to live solely on his base salary of $250,000, they couldn't begin to survive. So they lived bonus to bonus.

But while he wasn't allowed to sell the stock, he was able to borrow against it, which he did constantly. Every year, he would pay off the loan in January with the cash portion of his bonus—but by the next month, he would start borrowing all over again. He really felt like Sisyphus. Somehow he could never manage to get the rock all the way up the hill—and get it to stay there. He hoped he would reach that point someday, but Grigsby also seemed to have her own agenda. Invariably, she came up with some additional "necessary" thing they absolutely needed to have. The house on the bay had been a tough nut for them. Yes, it was a gorgeous house, and he loved being there, but it cost a lot to buy, and it cost a lot to maintain with the pool, landscaping, boat, and caretaker. Now she was angling for a house on the ocean and had started dropping a few hints about a house or condo in Aspen. Her latest thing was talking about how she needed her own assistant. He actually laughed at the thought. Her own assistant! For what, making hair appointments? What the hell did she actually do all day? There was no way any of these things would happen for a long, long time. With the stock this low, he just hoped he would be able to keep what they had now. He could only have a loan that was 50 percent of what his shares were worth, and he'd already sold most of his other investments. He still had an outstanding loan of $2 million. Right now, he could just barely make it.

If Lehman announced they were being sold today, it would be a relief, and it was pretty much common knowledge that it would be either Bank of America or Barclays. Just like Bear Stearns six months before, Lehman sported a great big invisible bull's-eye on its back, and the firm's leadership could do nothing to escape the bullets coming directly their way. A sale was the only hope right now.

The last week had been critical. For several months, it was well known that the firm had been having conversations with Korea's investment arm to make a sizable investment in the firm. If that happened, hopefully it would be enough to at least stabilize the stock price. It had worked so far for other companies that had been trying to raise capital. Tuesday, however, there was an announcement that discussions had ended. Boom. That was it. Over and done with. At that point, everyone could tell as soon as they walked into the building in the morning that there was a mad scramble on "thirty-one," the executive floor, to try to figure out a solution. Outside, sharks were circling, and thus the decline in the stock price in the last two days.

The next morning, Lehman's management decided to hold its second quarter earnings call early. They announced staggering losses of nearly $4 billion, but also that they would be spinning off some assets. Lehman's chairman, Dick Fuld, who was one of the longest-serving CEOs on the Street and also a great trader who knew when to hold out for the winning trade, said on the call, "This firm has a history of facing adversity and delivering. We have a long track record of pulling together when times are tough and then taking advantage of global opportunities."

In any other time that would have been a great rallying cry, reminding people internally and externally that this was a great firm that had been through a lot in its 150 years. However, 2008 was different from any other tough time or crisis. Ironically, words of encouragement and perseverance were now interpreted by everyone as meaning that the end was near. Internally, it was like a deathwatch for most of Wednesday and Thursday, with despondency being the main emotion, along with a healthy dose of Wall Street gallows humor.

Even with all the uncertainty and anxiety in the air, Blake hoped (and expected) that if the worst happened and no other company wanted to buy them, at least the government would intervene. Lehman was too integral to the world financial markets. If the Federal Reserve and the Treasury Department had shown anything over the last several weeks, it was that they were willing to step in and prevent an outright collapse of the financial system. They wouldn't just let Lehman fail.

No way.

Grigsby had a busy day ahead of her. She was almost done with all of the school applications, and she had a committee meeting for the museum benefit coming up. After that, she was going to Bergdorf Goodman for "The Blue Shoe Has Arrived," a celebration of the sumptuous blue satin Manolo Blahnik evening pump with the rhinestone buckle made famous in the *Sex and the City* movie. What was more, Mr. Blahnik himself was going to be making an appearance! It was as if God Himself were going to be parked in the second-floor shoe salon. Because Grigsby was such a good client at Bergdorf's she was usually invited to events they held there. But it was going to be tough to make it on time. One would think that simply running a few errands and going to lunch would leave most of the day free, but in fact it was just the opposite. Fitting in her workouts, child drop-off, and pickups was very tough logistically. What was worse was that Fifth and Park between the hours of 10:00 and 3:00 were always a tangle of vans and trucks delivering furniture, flowers, and supplies for parties, not to mention contractors, glaziers, painters, and a host of other laborers working on the perennial renovations of the multimillion-dollar apartments that lined the avenues. As a result, it could take Grigsby nearly twice as long as normal to get from Park and 93rd Street to Fifth and 57th Street.

Life could be very hard at times.

When Sasha got to work on Friday, she was startled to see a message that Harry had called. Great, of course he calls the day that I'm at a parent-teacher coffee, she thought. She dialed his office, and his assistant, Jacqueline, answered.

"Hi, it's Sasha. I'm returning Harry's call. Is he there?"

"Oh, hi, Sasha. Gee, he's in a meeting with the guys. I'd better not interrupt him. He said only if someone important called."

Sasha suppressed, as much as she could, the extreme desire to yell, "*Listen, you stupid bimbo! Who exactly would you qualify as someone important?*" But instead, as usual, she said nicely, "Oh, well, he called earlier, so I'm returning his call," hoping that mentioning this was a return call would inspire Jacqueline to decide Sasha was "important," or at the very least that Harry might want to talk to her. She also wondered what he was meeting with the "guys" about. She imagined it was something about the deal, and that made her even more irritated.

She knew she was crazy to worry about why she wasn't important to the Jacquelines of the world, but clearly if she was important enough to Harry, it would have been made clear to his assistant as well. Given how high-profile Sasha was in her own world, it was hard for her to accept.

Sasha had a very bad habit of assuming there was something wrong when someone called. She always felt that she was in trouble or that something bad had happened and she was the one responsible. She didn't know why she always had that sense, but it was worse with Harry, perhaps because he called her only when there was a problem.

When Renee got to work at 8:15, she was surprised to see John already in his office, his coffee in hand. He never got his own coffee! She stuck her head in and asked if he needed her for anything, but he was on the phone. Between telling someone to "go fuck yourself" and asking them "why the fuck should he care what they thought," he waved her off in a way that told her she had about five (fucking) seconds to get out of there. She quietly set down the coffee she'd brought at his desk and left the room.

She assumed that the market decline was affecting John's fund significantly and that was the reason John was in early and why he had been increasingly rude to everyone (even for him) over the last several days.

Saturday, September 13

Blake had come in late Friday night, so thankfully he didn't have to endure Grigsby's whining about staying in town. Somehow, with a great deal of patience Saturday morning, he finally got Grigsby to understand that he, too, would rather be in Southampton having dinner with

Steve and Suzanne, and he attempted to explain to her what the likely outcome would be for Lehman. He was fairly certain at that point that a deal would be announced Saturday or Sunday. It had to be announced by then, as the Asian markets opened Sunday evening New York time. He assumed there would be some premium paid for the stock, though not much. Maybe $6 if they were lucky. At least that would be a finger in the dike that would stop the flood of their personal assets. The stock had closed Friday down another 25 percent, so he was skating even closer to the edge than he had on Thursday. Whoever bought Lehman would be in a better financial state and hopefully would be able to do well over time, especially with the Lehman franchise.

He'd also heard that apparently a bunch of bigwigs at all the major firms, including the CEOs (except Dick Fuld of Lehman), had been called down to the New York Federal Reserve Bank to figure out solutions for Lehman. Blake thought it was a little like inviting a group of vultures to see how they could help save a cow lost in the desert that hadn't had water in days. He pictured all of them salivating over the possibility of Lehman's end. But regardless of what they came up with, Blake knew at this point that Lehman as an independent company was dead, no question.

Sunday, September 14

Blake's cell phone rang, and he saw it was John Cutter. "Hey, I was just about to call you. What's up?"

"What a coincidence! Just about to fucking call me! You tell me what's up. What's going on with Lehman?"

"I don't know, man. It doesn't look good. I'm hearing that both deals have fallen through. Apparently the meeting at the Fed yesterday was more about how to divide the spoils than trying to figure out a solution. And now the word is B of A is actually going to buy Merrill Lynch."

"Merrill! What the fuck? I can't believe it. Shit, I should have shorted the sucker."

"Yeah, dude, I'm a little freaked by it. If nothing comes through, I think we go Chapter 11 tonight."

"Well," John said, "what the fuck happens to my assets now?"

Of course, Blake knew that the only reason for John's call would have been his assets. It wasn't surprising. Everyone was out for themselves right now, but he wondered if John realized that Blake's world was also crashing down.

"I'm not sure right now. We are all just waiting for any information we can get."

"Okay, well, call me as soon as you know anything, and I mean anything. If you hear Dick Fuld went out to take a piss, you call me. Got it? I don't want to read about this in the *Post* tomorrow morning."

Sasha went for her weekly manicure at Peachy Nails on Sunday afternoon. She'd been following the news all day on her BlackBerry to see who was going to buy Lehman. Not only did she have a lot of friends who worked there, but she knew that the financial system needed stability. It was deeply disconcerting that yet another large player in the market might disappear, the second time this year, but if Lehman could be removed as a concern and absorbed by a stronger company, that would be a good signal for the markets. As she was sitting in the chair and had just said, "Ballet Slippers," her usual color, to the manicurist, she got an e-mail from Adam: "S — Hrng BST gave a DK to LEH!! BAC buying ML... Sh*t show Mon!!"

"Oh my God!!" she said out loud to no one in particular. When people looked up, she felt the need to explain herself and said to the assorted women, "My husband just e-mailed me. It looks like Barclays isn't buying Lehman, and neither is Bank of America. They are buying Merrill Lynch!"

There were shocked looks and gasps. One woman started saying,

"Oh no, oh no, oh no," and two women got up in a hurry to leave, one with paper towels still coiled around her wet toenails while the salon staff clucked behind her, saying, "Not dry. Not dry! Two more minute!"

Kimmy, the proprietress, said in broken English, "What this mean, Mommy?" Sasha couldn't help but smile, even now, that she was always referred to as "Mommy," as were many other women who had been coming in with their daughters since they could sit still and hold out their tiny digits for bright pink nails with green flowers painted on them. It was probably the same at every other Korean manicure salon on the tiny island of Manhattan.

"Well, Kimmy, it's not very good. Not good at all. There is a company on Wall Street which handles investments, you know, stocks and bonds. It is called Lehman Brothers, and like many other companies, it made some very bad decisions. So now, as a result, it is in very bad shape. Everyone thought they would be bought by one or two other companies, but those deals appear to have fallen through, and now they may have to declare bankruptcy. It is very bad for them, the stock market, and the economy." And probably not so good for your nail salon, Kimmy, she thought.

To her surprise, Kimmy erupted with, "Oh no! Just like the Bear company! Not good. I own the Lehman stock!" And she started cursing in Korean (or so Sasha assumed).

If Sasha could have called a market top, the moment it hit its high point, it probably would have been the day that Kimmy instructed her broker to go long Lehman.

About the same time that Sasha was discussing the news in the salon, John dialed Blake's cell phone again. His voice mail picked up, so John left him a message: "Get your ass into your goddamn office before they lock the place up and get my fucking files out of there. And delete your e-mails."

* * *

Renee turned on the television and wasn't all that surprised to see special programming was running to comment on the historic turn of events. Sunday night for CNBC was usually reruns of special programs, but now the anchors, who were normally on during the trading day and an hour or two after the close, were reporting live. They were uncharacteristically somber, looking out of place, and turning to their European and Asian counterparts for reports on the disastrous losses already occurring there. Renee knew this was very bad and wondered what would happen the next day when she got to work. With the sound of the TV in the background she fell asleep around 12:30 but slept fitfully. If she had been watching at one point, she would have seen footage of Lehman employees walking out of 745 Seventh Avenue with boxes of files and belongings, worried that the doors would be immediately padlocked as a result of the bankruptcy filing. Among the many men in jeans and Lehman baseball caps, she would have clearly seen Blake Somerset carrying two boxes. But by that time, she was already dreaming that Amanda Belden was chasing her with a venti Starbucks cup, while Richie Sambucci lay red-faced in the corner with Jeff Koons's balloon dogs on top of him, licking his face with gigantic blue chrome tongues.

Monday, September 15

"You have got to be kidding me. You actually think I am going to go to an interview for kindergarten?! Today! After what's just happened? Don'tcha think that maybe I should be at my office today to see what's going to happen? Do you not get that the world we lived in last week isn't here anymore?"

Blake would have laughed had it not been terribly tragic and a sign that the woman to whom he had been married for ten years had very little understanding of the real world. In any case, Blake wanted to be at the office as soon as possible to be sure there wasn't anything else he needed to do regarding his situation with John.

"Blake, how can I call them and say that we need to reschedule? I might as well just call and say, 'Reject us, please.'"

"Grigsby, I guarantee you that across this city right now there are people canceling school interviews, decorator appointments, vacation plans, house closings, you name it. Everything has changed, do you understand? Everything!"

"Well, then I am going without you so it's not a total loss."

"Do what you want, Grigsby, but just remember that private school costs thirty thousand dollars. We have two other children, which means that next year's tuition bill is almost a hundred thousand dollars. I'm not even sure if I will have a job by the end of the year, or even by the end of this week, and we are going to have margin calls on our stock *today*. I don't even know if we'll be able to stay in the city. There is going to have to be some serious reduction in expenditures around here until I can figure out where things stand with our assets and liabilities."

At this point, Grigsby turned an odd shade of red. "Listen to me, Blake Somerset. Don't you dare talk to me in all these technical terms. It's *your* job to make sure we have enough money to live *our* life. So I will continue living as we have and will expect the bills to be paid."

Blake was rendered utterly and totally speechless by his wife's lunacy. Technical terms? Maybe she would like him to describe the hedging strategy of using total return swaps on the equity tranche of a collateralized debt obligation? She was utterly clueless about the fact that their former net worth of over $50 million would now most likely be in the negative million or two once he spoke with his private banker and determined the extent of the damage.

He just looked at her and said, "Grigs, you can say whatever the hell you want and live in your own demented, imaginary world. I'm going to figure out what's left of us."

He couldn't believe that, as he left, he heard her call after him, "And don't forget tomorrow evening is New Yorkers for Children, so you had better hope your tuxedo still fits after this summer."

Grigsby furrowed her brow. She didn't understand what Blake was talking about. They really couldn't be in such dire financial shape, could they? He had made so much money over the last few years. They had a beautiful ten-room Park Avenue apartment, a house on the bay in Southampton, vacations in Palm Beach and Aspen; whatever she wanted, she got. She was hoping that next year they could think about buying a house in Aspen or at least a condo at the St. Regis so she wouldn't have to deal with reservations and hotels every time. She also had her eye on an oceanfront house in Southampton. She was definitely ready to upgrade from the bay. She and Blake were supposed to be part of the lucky group whose fortunes only went up. Blake worked for one of the most established firms on Wall Street. She had married him in part because he represented everything she wanted. It just didn't make sense that things would ever go in the opposite direction for them. That only happened to people she talked about, not to her.

She picked up *The New York Times* and tried to understand the articles. It didn't make much sense to her, though. Why didn't any other company want to buy Lehman? Why didn't the government do something? Hadn't they already done this for everyone else who was in trouble? So what if they had filed for bankruptcy. Couldn't the government change its mind and do something after all? This just didn't seem fair.

But one thing she was certain of was that she had no intention of canceling that Spence interview. As she was so adept at doing, she pushed any worrisome thoughts out of her blond head and put on the Herrera shift dress that she'd bought especially with school interviews in mind, absentmindedly ripped off the $2,790 price tag, and selected a pair of Manolo "Caroline" slingbacks from her closet. She decided the Seaman Schepps earrings she'd bought in Palm Beach last spring vacation were the ideal understated yet elegant accessory, along with her Cartier love bracelet. She looked like the perfect Upper East Side wealthy mother. Rachel Zoe herself couldn't have styled her better!

As she walked up to Spence's lower school building on 93rd Street off Madison, she imagined herself dropping Bitten off next year before her morning coffee and workout. It would be the perfect addition to everything she'd achieved for them already. If Blake's absence put that in jeopardy, she didn't know what she would do.

She announced herself as "Mrs. Blake Somerset" to the receptionist, who made a phone call to admissions and then asked Grigsby to take a seat. A few minutes later, a young woman emerged and said, "Good morning, Mrs. Somerset. I am Alexandra Lennon, senior admissions associate. It's lovely to have you here this morning."

"Thank you, it's a pleasure to meet you as well," Grigsby responded. Then, summoning her courage, she said, "I'm afraid my husband won't be able to join us this morning, however. I'm terribly sorry about it, but you see, he works in the financial services business, and I assume you saw the news about what's been going on. So, unfortunately, he couldn't come this morning..." She practically blanched with mortification as she eked out the words and surprised herself that she couldn't even say "Lehman Brothers."

"Oh, yes, I have. As a matter of fact, we have had some cancellations today. I'm terribly sorry. We completely understand, though. It must be terrible for you. I see on your application that your husband is at Lehman. I'm so sorry. Why don't we talk for a while and then I'll take you on a tour. It is perfectly fine if we can get Mr. Somerset to come in and meet in a few weeks. So shall we talk about your daughter a little bit?"

Grigsby felt both deflated and relieved. Maybe things wouldn't be so terrible after all.

Sasha laughed as Adam uttered the usual "It's gonna be a real shit show today" while he was getting ready to leave for work. "Hon," she responded, "I think you can stop saying that. Pretty much every day is a shit show."

"You're right. Let's come up with a new term. How about pile of poo? Dungfest? Bring your pooper-scooper today? Wear your waders?"

They both laughed at the ideas. It was one of the reasons they got along so well. They understood the big-picture things that were going on in the world, but they still could laugh like third graders at immature things. Then Adam said, "So, are you going to speak to Harry today?"

Sasha stopped laughing. It certainly wasn't Adam's fault for bringing it up. She hadn't heard from Harry all day Friday, even though she'd sat by the phone like a teenage girl waiting for the guy who said he would call but never did. True to form, Harry never did call either. She'd left another message with Jacqueline, who'd made her feel even worse by saying, "I gave him your message, but he left early for his son's football game. He's starting varsity this year, you know." Clearly she wasn't that important, and that desperately hurt her ego. It was obvious, though, that in the two weeks since Harry had told her about the impending deal, he'd had little intention of including her in the sale process. Frankly, she really didn't know what to do.

"Well, apparently Harry has other things to do than call me, doesn't he?" she said to Adam. "I just hope I can find out whatever is going on sometime before this deal gets done. Meanwhile," she said, changing the subject, "how are things going to be with you guys today?"

"I really don't know. As far as I can tell, our credit lines are in pretty good shape and our leverage is pretty low. I've been betting that bank stocks would go down since July Fourth—and shorted the index that represents those companies. So if things continue the way they have, those should go through the roof. But the scary thing about right now is that anything could happen today, anything at all. Every day we make it through is a day we have made it through. I really feel like the world is coming to an end, and I'm just hoping that we can hold on tight while it does and then be able to crawl out of the rubble after."

This definitely did not make Sasha feel any better. She liked to know that when her world was so unsettled, Adam's was secure. She needed a foundation to hold on to. But she'd somehow push those concerns out of her head until she needed to face them.

"Okay, well, don't forget we have that second-grade parents' night at five thirty. Shall I meet you there or pick you up on the way?"

"Sasha, you know I can't commit to anything until I see how the day turns out. I'll let you know later, but don't count on me."

"Adam, it's really frustrating that I have to do all this stuff myself. I know you're in the thick of things, but it's not like I don't have a big job, too. We both need to be there."

"Well, unless Harry calls you back and involves you in what's going on, it doesn't seem like you're that busy. You've spent all weekend whining about how you are shut out of what is going on, so you *can* be there, whereas I *can't* predict what's going to happen in five minutes."

"Wow, Adam, that was a really low blow, on top of you probably—oops, *possibly*—not being able to be there. Thanks a lot." And she turned away from him and walked into the bathroom.

"Sasha..." Adam followed after her. "That came out wrong. I'm sorry. You know I support you totally. I will do what I can, okay? I promise. I'm just uptight about what the day is going to be like. You know, dungfest and all?" And he smiled in that cute way he had to try to get himself out of trouble.

She wasn't about to give in that easily. Still angry, she shrugged and said, "Right. Just call me later, okay? I'm sure I'll have more than enough time to talk to you."

The reality was that whether a woman worked or didn't work, the responsibility for the kids' doctors, dentists, clothes, schools, and activities was still the mother's. Sasha sighed and resigned herself to the fact that she likely would be alone later this evening, but she'd still hold out hope that she would be pleasantly surprised.

She grabbed the new green Oscar skirt that went with the brown-and-gold embroidered cardigan hanging in the closet, paired the cardigan with a Gap white T-shirt, added vintage Kenneth Jay Lane chandelier earrings, a giant ring, and a pair of platform shoes, and went downstairs to make sure the kids were in good shape for the day.

John knew today was going to be ugly. By the time he woke up at 5:30, Asian and Euro markets were in a free fall. The Lehman news was being viewed as a sign of a potential world meltdown, and Flying Point would be right in the center of it. What was worse was the e-mail he got saying that all assets prime brokered at Lehman were to be frozen in a bankruptcy. He would be unable to access his fund assets. Richie had already e-mailed him that he was on the case, but John suspected it would be days, if not weeks, before they had any information. He just hoped they could continue to trade. Great. One more fucking nightmare to deal with. He only hoped that Blake had gotten those files out last night.

CHAPTER ELEVEN

Party Like It's 1999

In New York society, there were about a dozen galas through the course of the year that were must-attend events. They covered a range of causes from the ballet to museums to opera and to organizations devoted to the poor, sick, or hungry. Often, there were both fall and spring galas so as to attract people as they were about to leave for their summer homes and vacations or when they had just returned from their summer homes and vacations. Aside from the museums or Lincoln Center, they were held mostly at the handful of elegant venues that can seat a few hundred guests: the Plaza, the Waldorf, the Pierre, and Cipriani's 42nd Street. Once in a while, in an effort to save money, a group decided to go to the less preferable Cipriani's Wall Street location. There was much complaining about the inconvenience of having to go all the way downtown, and attendance suffered as a result.

There was always palpable excitement as the car or taxi approached the party. It was as if every event were a high school prom that held the pregnant pause of what possibilities lay beyond the doors: business, love, dancing, and drinks or just a great photo op.

New Yorkers for Children was one such event. The September gala was scheduled for the third Tuesday after Labor Day at Cipriani's. A red carpet that stretched the length of the room was lined with dozens of photographers, several of whom were well known to the attendees. They were as much a part of the scene as the partygoers themselves, and without them an event lacked the right buzz: blond surfer Steve Eichner from *W*; elegant former model Julie Skarratt, whose photos appeared mostly in *Town & Country*; aristocratic Mary Hilliard, whose work was frequently in *Vogue* and NewYorkSocialDiary.com; and Sherly Rabbani and Josephine Solimene, whose photos were featured on Style.com. Then there were the McMullan guys, starting with the inimitable and gregarious Patrick McMullan himself, and the many terrific staff photographers who worked for him. And finally there was the most sublime of all, Bill Cunningham.

It is difficult to fully explain the feeling of being photographed by Bill Cunningham, whose pictures for the "Style" section of *The New York Times* "On the Street" and "Evening Hours" columns have appeared in the Sunday paper for decades. He simply didn't take pictures of anyone or anything he didn't find personally interesting or that didn't appeal to his own impeccable sense of style.

When his eye was caught by something interesting, or beautiful, or at times bizarre, it was as if time were suspended. The camera was like a frog that could catch a bug in a split second as it captured the shot and then went back down again. He was so old school, his camera held only real film, requiring him to pause periodically to reload.

Waking up to look at the paper the following Sunday or two when the pictures ran was always exciting for Sasha and Renee, who happened to be two of his regular subjects. It certainly didn't match their professional and personal accomplishments, but it was nice to be recognized for being stylish in the eyes of someone who knew style, plain and simple. He was one of the few people who appreciated Mimi's unique look and featured her often, but interestingly enough, he had never taken Grigsby's photo, much to her annoyance and dismay.

Getting ready for one of these evenings was another event in and of itself. New dresses had to be picked up, borrowed jewels had to be signed for, and car services had to be ordered for those without their own car and driver. Hair and makeup appointments began in the early afternoon, either at the salon or preferably at home. It could take hours to truly be ready. For working women, however, prep time was reduced to rushing home and scrambling into a dress, bringing makeup into the car, and barely making it on time. Men, for the most part, could get ready anywhere and often brought their tuxedo to work, changed in the bathroom, and left their suit at the office until the next day, as their colleagues made fun of them for wearing a penguin suit so often.

Grigsby spent the morning of Tuesday, September 16, in shock. After his rant about the Spence interview, Blake was even more adamant about not going to the gala with her that evening, telling her, "You had better get your priorities in order. There isn't going to be money to do silly things like this in the future." Silly things? This was her life!

Luckily, she had been able to reach Thruce Cogson, who was free to "walk her." Some women could not fathom the idea of going to an event on their own, as if rules of decorum from the antebellum South or Victorian England still existed. It was women like Grigsby for whom Thruce existed.

Thruce Cogson had been around forever and was ubiquitous on the social scene. At first glance, he seemed elegant and erudite, while in fact he was quite the opposite. He was not particularly well liked by most and was called "Thrice" behind his back, as his father was rumored to be gay; thus, as the third child of his parents, the general joke was that they'd had sex only three times. Thruce's own sexuality was a small question mark. While he was usually seen only with women, certain reliable gay men on the social scene told tales of him pulling them aside at a benefit and asking in a whisper if they'd like to see how well-endowed he was. (The offer was universally declined.)

Thruce's daily activities were questionable at best. In the early 1980s, after Studio 54 had passed its prime upon the incarceration of its founders and ceased to be a place for Bianca, Calvin, and Liza to party, his name became ubiquitous on invitations to the club for elite private school kids who were always on the quest for a more glamorous party locale than Upper East Side school dances or their parents' apartments. As time went on, Thruce dabbled as a publicist, wrote a party column here and there, and at one point created a line of very expensive men's cuff links, which quickly faded by the wayside. Mostly, though, Thruce lived off his family money, which, while extensive, was meted out parsimoniously by his mother from her perches in Southampton, Palm Beach, and Fifth Avenue, even into his mid-forties. Thruce surrounded himself with people like himself, who didn't take kindly to those who didn't come from the same background. He was, in the very old-fashioned sense of the word, a snob.

Grigsby was one of half a dozen women he regularly squired around town when their husbands were on business trips, had left them, or, more frequently, just didn't like going out. He wasn't bogged down by traditional working hours, business trips, or meetings and always had a clean tuxedo or set of tails ready to go. It also worked out quite well for Thruce, as he loved attending events but was cheap and hated buying tickets himself. He attended for free, while espousing what a "wonderful cause" they were supporting. So much for the philanthropic spirit.

Like Grigsby, Thruce had another aspect to his personality that neither of them would ever admit: He was a photo whore. As soon as he saw out of the corner of his eye the flash of a camera, he made a beeline for the area. He would feign agitation at having to pose, pausing begrudgingly in his conversation to put on a smile with his "date" for the evening, but secretly he was thrilled. He even had a signature "pose," arms folded and head turned to the side.

The doorman buzzed Grigsby's apartment to let her know that her hair and makeup people were on the way up. Grigsby had long ago stopped getting ready on her own. She really photographed so much better when she had professional assistance. It took about ninety minutes and was definitely worth the $500 to have it done at the house rather than

$250 at the salon. Besides, it was one less thing to have to rush around doing on the afternoon of a big event.

She had the television on as they were working on her and flipped by the evening news.

"More big news from Wall Street just in. The federal government has announced it is putting eighty-five billion dollars—yes, folks, that's billion—into insurance giant AIG. The largest company yet to crumble under the weight of the massive financial crisis is in receivership. For more on this story, we go now to our financial correspondent."

The story ended with, "These are certainly unprecedented times. Starting with the Bear Stearns fire sale to JPMorgan earlier this year, to today's actions, which essentially puts AIG under government control. And those are only the first and last of a long laundry list: Mortgage giants Fannie Mae and Freddie Mac were placed in government conservatorship just last week, and Merrill Lynch, once considered the proudest 'thundering herd' on Wall Street, was pushed into a hastily arranged wedding with Bank of America this past weekend. Lehman Brothers' bankruptcy filing yesterday, which ironically has been the only situation so far in which the government has said 'not my job,' certainly has a lot of shareholders and employees crying foul. What's more, many expect there to be even more fallout in the days ahead. Amazing to think it could get even worse than this. Back to you, Sue."

Grigsby flipped the channel, but even through her veil of self-absorption she thought that something wasn't right about what had happened. She did wonder if the things Blake was ranting about were true. Should she be worried?

But as she got into her gown, a Kim Hicks couture confection that cost $17,000, she looked at herself in the mirror and was quite pleased. This dress was going to get a lot of attention. She could hardly wait to get to the party. She knew she would be one of the best dressed there. Perhaps this was the night she would finally get photographed by Bill Cunningham.

She called to Donita that she was leaving and that Mr. Somerset would be home later. She usually tried to slip out so the children wouldn't get dirt on her dress or mess up her makeup, and because they usually cried when she left, so seeing them really wasn't a help to anyone, least of all her. She went downstairs to the waiting car and got inside.

Mimi was at the loft and in a fashion quandary. She always liked having two people there to help her get ready. One was her daughter, Annabella, and the other was her personal stylist, Flamenco. Mimi had been very close to her own mother growing up, but their relationship had been based on helping her mother with chores. She wanted to be able to share a better life with her own daughter. Mimi also intended for Annabella to inherit her dress collection one day. She envisioned Annabella as a woman herself, recalling the evenings all those years before when Mimi first wore them.

Flamenco was another story. Raised in the slums of São Paulo, he had made his way to America in his late teens, and through a roundabout series of relationships with much older men, he'd ended up on the club scene in the early 1990s with many of the "club kids," like Michael Alig, who frequented places like the Limelight, Club USA, and the Tunnel. Mimi, who had spent some time herself there in those days, ran into Flamenco a few years later as he was struggling to build his own fashion collection, especially since his former club pals Richie Rich and Traver Rains had created a sensation with Heatherette. Mimi wanted to back Flamenco, but John snorted, "Why the fuck would anyone want to wear dresses that look like fucking soda can tops sewn together with yarn? No fucking way, Mimi, no fucking way."

Flamenco ultimately became a personal stylist, with Mimi as one of his top clients. She probably dropped about $150,000 a year for his "assistance." This evening, he was also attending the gala as Mimi's escort. He had arrived at 4:00 with several garment bags for Mimi and was garbed himself in a gold leather suit, matching Stetson, and red patent-leather cowboy boots.

"*Chica*, I have three ensembles for you. You will be sexy. You will be smoky. You will be gorgeous." Flamenco had a strong Latin accent, so it came out as "Chu will be sexy. Chu will be smoky. Chu will be gorgeous."

"Ooh, I can't wait to see," Mimi said with anticipation.

With great drama, Flamenco laid out the garment bags in the dressing room and took each ensemble out, swirling it around on the hanger in front of her.

The first was a Rodarte. While the majority of that collection is flowing, long, and impeccably designed, this one was a short, mostly white dress, with what appeared to be black ink staining the front. The bust was covered with a see-through plasticine gauze, and the torso was completely diaphanous. The dress was paired with knit white tights that looked like gigantic spiderwebs and white platform lace-up sandals.

The second was also a short dress, this one by the Italian label Etro, normally known for luscious knits and vibrant colors. This piece, however, was a black minidress that appeared to be a modernized version of the classic French maid available at Ricky's costume shop for $49.95 around Halloween. The skirt barely covered the top of Mimi's thighs, but thankfully, or not, that would not be noticed. Instead, the eye would be drawn to a wimple-like collar with large white spikes coming out of the neck, which had the effect of making her appear to be a human chrysanthemum. Thick black tights went along with the dress and were topped, or bottomed, off by white peep-toe slingbacks à la a 1940s pinup girl.

The third gown was by the talented British designer known simply as Giles. Mimi had been to his fall show six months prior when she was on a trip to London, and she remembered this outfit. It was a long red dress with a crochet top that transitioned to a red satin skirt embellished with large pieces protruding, which made it appear as if a giant wing were growing out of it. When he presented it to her, Flamenco said simply, "The only accessory, chu wear black lipstick," snapping his fingers to emphasize how perfect a look it would be.

"They're all so unique," Mimi said, and started stripping down to her underwear. Annabella was used to this and continued drawing in the coloring book she had with her.

Mimi tried each on in the order in which Flamenco had presented them. Her body, given all the work she did and had done to maintain herself, was a perfect mannequin, but to the average person, each dress would have looked more ridiculous than the previous one. Flamenco oohed and ahhed over each one. Mimi, however, was unsure.

"I don't know, Flamenco. Maybe they aren't right. What do you think?"

"No! Chu are to be the best one there. These are all couture! Couture! No one else will look as special as chu. No one."

"Well, I guess you are right. You wouldn't steer me wrong, would you?"

Flamenco looked hurt that Mimi could even think such a thing, saying, "Mimi, chu and me, we are together so long. No one but Flamenco knows how to dress chu. How can chu say such a thing?" He seemed devastated.

"Oh, please, I didn't mean to hurt your feelings, Flamenco. Of course I love everything you've done for me. You are one of my closest friends. Which do you think I should wear?"

"The Giles. Ees the best."

"Annabella, sweetness, which do you think Mama should wear?" Mimi always liked to get Annabella's opinion.

Annabella looked up from her coloring book. She glanced at all three dresses, looked at Flamenco and her mother, and then turned the book toward Mimi and said, "This one."

It was a picture of Cinderella in her classic light blue crystal ball gown, complete with crown and glass slippers. It was the perfect little girl's vision of what a woman should wear when going to a ball.

"Oh, sweetie," Mimi said, hugging Annabella, "I love you so much. Mama will wear one like that next time, okay?"

Flamenco seemed completely perplexed by Annabella's choice, but he held his tongue. He would hopefully have time to help shape Annabella as she grew up, to ensure that her style would become more like Mimi's and to also be sure that he had an ongoing source of income from the Cutters.

As she put on the long red gown with the gigantic wing springing out of the side, Mimi did have one more pang that perhaps this wasn't perfect, then remembered that if it wasn't right, Flamenco would never have selected it.

Flamenco was wrong about one thing, however: her accessories. In addition to the black lipstick, she needed to select the MedicAlert necklace she would wear that evening. She went to the vault in her closet and entered the combination. Inside was an amazing assortment of materials and gemstones. She pulled out several: the black onyx, the African rubies, the Robert Lee Morris, and a few other pieces she'd gotten designers to make for her. Just then she remembered, and she rummaged around in the vault until she found it. It was red feathers with black yarn around it. It couldn't be more perfect. As she tied it on and looked at herself, she was complete.

Before she and Flamenco left to go uptown, she tucked Annabella into bed. "Good night, my darling. I will see you in the morning. Have a good night's sleep."

"Mama, will I marry a prince just like Cinderella?"

Mimi, knowing that life was not like a fairy tale when it came to love, or living happily ever after, felt another pang. A five-year-old girl didn't need to know the truth, however, so Mimi responded, "Yes. Yes, you will."

And with that, she made sure her black lipstick was evenly applied and went down to the waiting car with Flamenco and his gold-bedecked self.

Sasha had planned to leave the office at 4:00 so she could get her hair and makeup done. It gave her a little bit of time to relax and transition from the workday to the evening. She would be able to respond to messages on her BlackBerry, except when her eyes were being done, although frankly she was so good at it, she could type with them closed. She was in the car on the way up to the appointment, however, when Fern, her assistant, called and said, "Sasha, I have Harry Mullaugh on the phone. He says he needs you right now. I'm transferring him, okay?"

"Shit! Now he calls! Just when I'm on my way to my appointment. Okay, put him through," she said. Fern connected them.

"Hi, Harry," she said, trying to sound cheerful. "What's going on?"

"Hi, kiddo." (Groan.) "Sorry we didn't get a chance to talk last week. I was in meetings all afternoon Friday." Sasha rolled her eyes as he said that, since Jacqueline had obviously let it slip that Harry had left for a high school football game. "Anyway. I called because I need you to come up to Springfield."

"Okay, sure. When?"

"Right now."

She would have laughed had she not been so flabbergasted. "Now? Harry, Springfield is three hours away. I can't be there before eight p.m. at the earliest. What do you need me there for?" Needless to say, she was also exceedingly distressed because she did not want to miss the gala.

"Well, we need to do a run-through for the presentation tomorrow morning."

"What presentation tomorrow morning? With whom?"

"Oh, with a private equity fund located up here. They called last week to arrange it. Didn't Jacqueline tell you about it?"

"No, Harry. She did not. I got a message that you called on Friday. I called you back and didn't hear back from you. She said nothing about this whatsoever." Sasha's initial annoyance with Jacqueline was now pure rage at the botched message, if Harry really did tell her to convey that.

"Oh, well, she's been so busy lately, poor kid, she must have gotten confused. In any case, no worries, but you do need to be here."

She took a deep breath. What was she going to do? If there was even a train to catch this evening, who knew when it might arrive. If she took a car, she still had to go home and get clothes and then make it up 95 in rush-hour traffic. And damn, she really didn't want to miss the benefit. She felt like crying.

"Um, let me see what I can arrange. Is there anything you need me to work on during the ride up?"

"No, I don't think so," he responded. "Oh, actually, can you do a brief piece about the SAMCO strategy?"

Holy shit. "Sure, Harry," she said. "Anything in particular you want me to emphasize?"

"No, just do what you always do so well. You are terrific on your feet, kiddo. I don't need to tell you that."

"Okay, I'm going to have to see if I can still get a train up there or take a car service. What time is the presentation tomorrow?"

"It's at ten thirty."

After she hung up, she called Fern back and told her to cancel the hair and makeup appointment and see what travel could be arranged. She called Adam to tell him what was happening, but he was in a meeting. She got home and was putting some things in a bag when Adam called.

"What's up, babe?"

She couldn't contain herself any longer and started sobbing. Somehow she got the story out. She knew what had transpired in the world that day was certainly worse than the torturous existence she lived, but not to her. Adam was the one person in her life with whom she could have a meltdown. He didn't judge her but rather just let her wail.

After a few minutes of her crying and him attempting to comfort her, she heard the beep that signified another call coming through on her cell phone. She looked and saw that it was Harry's office again.

"Shit, Adam, it's that fucker on the phone again. What the hell does he want now?"

"I'll hold. Can you make it sound like you haven't been crying?"

"I think so." She cleared her throat. "How do I sound now?" she said, talking in a loud, clear voice.

"Good."

"Yes, Harry," she said as she clicked onto her other line.

"Hi, Sasha. It's not Harry, it's Jacqueline."

"Oh, hi," she said, even more irritated, hating every bone in Jacqueline's body that she didn't already hate.

"Harry said to tell you never mind. He doesn't need you after all. He promises he will call you first thing after the meeting."

If Sasha had a gun in her hand right now, she would have placed it clearly on the mouthpiece of the phone and shot it, hoping that the bullet would travel directly to Springfield and somehow hit both Harry and Jacqueline.

"Okaaay. Umm, did he say why?"

"Nope. Just said not to bother."

She clicked back over to Adam, who was still on the line. "Adam, you will not fucking believe it now. Just guess. Just guess what that was about!"

"I don't know."

"That was Harry's bimbiotic assistant. Harry told her to tell me never mind. I don't need to come after all." And she actually started crying again.

"Oh man, Sasha. I hate these guys for you. I really do. I wish I could go up there and kneecap 'em for you. And you know I would, too. Just say the word. You have got to take control of yourself and your life, sweetie. They are going to keep doing this shit to you."

"I would like you to beat them up. But I can't do anything now. I just have to hang in there. If I do, everything will work out the way it is supposed to." As she said it, a fresh round of tears started. "Now I missed my hair appointment, too!"

Somehow she managed to get herself together and look halfway decent, although as she was doing her makeup she could see her eyes were still red. She wondered if she should just take an early train up and surprise them at the meeting, but then she realized that any private equity firm headquartered in Springfield, Massachusetts, probably wouldn't be worth the trip.

Adam actually made it home early and got into his tux. They left amid a whirl of children screaming and carrying on, especially Coco and Lily, who were oohing and ahhing over Sasha's gown. Sasha loved leaving for an evening with all the kids waving good-bye and nodding their approval. She hoped that when they returned that night, everyone would have made it to bed on time.

Sasha's cell phone rang just as they left. Great, now what?

A familiar voice spoke: "Hey, girl! It's Renee!"

Sasha smiled. She'd randomly met Renee Parker when they had sat next to each other at jury duty several years ago. Sasha had run out of reading material and noticed the new issue of *Vogue* sitting on Renee's lap. She had asked to borrow it, and they'd ended up spending the next hour going through the magazine together. Sasha had invited Renee to sit with them at a benefit, and from that point on, they had become good friends. Sasha was fifteen years older, but there was something about Renee that made her an old soul. Sasha also loved seeing how Renee had taken to the benefit circuit, and she was always a welcome addition on committees and at events. "Hey, you, back! How are you? How's the new job? I can't wait to hear about it and see you. We are just leaving and will swing by and pick you up if that works."

"That would be great. I'm sure you will look gorgeous. You always do. I'll tell you about the job when I see you. Text me before you get to my house and I'll come downstairs."

When Renee joined them in the car, there would be more fabric than anything else. At least Renee favored long slim dresses by J. Mendel, the furrier turned couturier, so hers wouldn't take up as much room as Sasha's, which was a cream puff of taffeta and lace, not to mention the tulle lining underneath.

"Move over, guys. I'm coming in," she said cheerfully. "Hi, Adam, good to see you. How are you?"

"Hey, Renee, I'm okay. Definitely not a great night to be going out with everything going on, but I'm looking forward to a drink... or four. I hear you have a new job! Flying Point Capital is a pretty big deal. John Cutter's got a lot on his plate given where the markets are right now. I hear he can be a handful to deal with. You handling it okay so far?"

"Well, he's certainly an intense guy, but I'm learning a lot and it's actually been kind of fun only two weeks into it. Kind of neat to be in the middle of everything that's going on. Some things don't quite make sense to me, but I'm sure I'll get there over time."

"Well, I'm happy to help explain anything if you ever need it, and I know Sasha will, too."

Sasha chimed in, "Of course, Renee. Anytime."

"Thanks, guys. I would actually love it, because of course I know the basics, but there's still a lot I need filling in on. John's been through a lot of assistants, and I'd like to try and be the one that makes it. They say that there are a lot of opportunities there, and frankly, the pay is pretty good, too."

"Okay, maybe if we still feel like doing something after the party, we can go out for a drink?" Sasha suggested.

Adam groaned, but Renee said, "I'm always up for the after-party, even if it's to learn about the markets!"

At that moment, they pulled up to Cipriani's and took a few minutes to extricate themselves from the car. Adam held out a hand for each lady, and they walked in the door. Cipriani's is in a tall Italian Renaissance–style former bank building on 42nd Street right across from Grand Central Terminal. Just past the entrance several young women, who were working the event and, in contrast to most of the partygoers, dressed in simple, inexpensive long black dresses, were sitting at a table with clipboards of the evening's guests' names. Just after that was the red carpet, the sides of which were strewn with photographers.

They walked down the aisle. Unless a photographer requested a picture of him with Sasha as a couple, Adam always tended to hang back, knowing that his tux was hardly as desirable as the froth of Sasha's gown or Renee's statuesque column. Renee and Sasha knew how to pose and make eye contact with each photographer. They made a good shot together, and Adam knew better than to throw it off balance.

As they made their way to the end of the line, they entered the cocktail area, at which point Sasha spied Grigsby Somerset. "Grigsby, hi! I haven't seen you in forever. How *are* you? How is Blake? I have been thinking about you guys the last couple of days."

Grigsby gave Sasha a double kiss. "Hello, dear. It's lovely to see you. Blake couldn't make it this evening. There is a lot going on, needless to say, but everything is fine. You know Thruce, don't you? He was nice enough to bring me this evening."

"Of course I do. Hello, Thruce," Sasha said, giving him a kiss, actually a double kiss, as that was Thruce's style. Sasha was always thrown off by double kissers. It was hard to know who was one and who wasn't. Invariably, she got stuck somewhere in the middle of someone's face. "I'd like you both to meet my friend Renee Parker. I don't know if you have ever met."

Thruce was cordial in a very formal, almost rude way and barely offered his hand to her.

Grigsby tentatively put out her hand to shake Renee's. "No, we haven't met, but I have actually seen your picture in 'Sunday Styles' a number of times." (Grigsby kept track of who was in the paper each week.)

"Well, it is a pleasure to meet you, but I actually know who you are. My mother, Donita, works for you."

It was just like Renee to be perfectly up front about her background and parents' line of work, but this was not the case with Grigsby (or Thruce, for that matter, who could barely contain a sound that was akin to a gasp, scream, and snicker all at once). On social occasions such as this one simply did not meet people who were connected to one's staff. Grigsby was speechless for a moment, then managed to regain some sense of composure and responded with, "Oh, my, yes... Well...ah...What a surprise. Your mother is quite wonderful."

Renee smiled back. "Yes, she and my dad are terrific, hardworking people, and my sisters and I have reaped the benefits of it our entire lives. If not for them, I don't know how I could have survived Barnard, or Spence, for that matter."

Again Grigsby was rendered speechless, but she managed to stammer out, "S-S-p-pence? You went to Spence? The one on the Upper East Side?"

Sasha, who was somewhat enjoying the moment, having already been aware of both Grigsby's snobbishness and how wonderfully honest Renee could be, decided she should help smooth the way. She said, "Grigsby, aren't you doing applications for your daughter this year? She must be just that age."

"Oh, yes," she responded. "It's awful and seems to be all the more so in light of everything going on right now. Blake's schedule is a little bit hard to predict or plan around."

"I'm sure, but you aren't the only ones in that situation, so the schools must understand. Which ones are your top choices?"

"Well, I am very committed to the single-sex education model. I think it gives a girl such a solid foundation, confidence, and values that prepare her so well for later in life," Grigsby said, as if reciting from any one of the girls' school catalogs. "And how ironic, our first choice is Spence." She darted an eye at Renee nervously.

Renee jumped right in. "Really? I'd be happy to meet your daughter and talk to you and her about the school. I am on the alumnae board, so I certainly can be helpful."

Grigsby was flummoxed. She desperately wanted Bitten to go to Spence, and while it didn't seem that Blake's absence had hurt them yesterday, she didn't want anything to go awry. She had yet to find someone she knew well enough either on the board or meaningfully connected to the school who would write a letter for them. At the same time, she had never in her life needed something this important from someone who worked for her (well, the daughter of, in any case). But if Renee was on the alumnae board, that was a big deal, and Renee's "diversity" probably wouldn't hurt either.

"I would really appreciate that, Renee. Thanks so much. Perhaps Sasha can get me your number and we can get together in the next few weeks."

"Yes, of course, or I can always get to you through my mom," Renee responded helpfully.

"Um, well, I guess, yes, that would work, too." Clearly, Grigsby would rather leave Donita out of it. It was awkward enough to need help with something so important to her world from her maid's daughter. She would rather pretend that connection didn't exist.

At that moment, Thruce could bear no more to be witness to the conversation. "Grigsby, dear, I think I see Cap and Minnie over there. I've really got to catch up with them about the benefit next week. Let's head over there and get some champagne on the way, all right, dear?"

As they walked away, Sasha heard Thruce say, "My God, Grigsby, spare me the democratic leanings. I cannot *believe* what I just saw. Anything for the kids, I guess, but really you better be careful. Associating with the *help*!? Next you will tell me that you're going to vote for Obama!"

Unfortunately, as they walked away Thruce missed, although Grigsby caught out of the corner of her eye, Bill Cunningham snap a series of photos of Sasha and Renee, almost as if he'd waited until they were alone.

All of a sudden, one could sense a commotion at the red carpet as Mimi and Flamenco entered. The photographers went into a tizzy. The majority of the other guests tittered. Grigsby looked as if she were in shock. Thruce uttered one of his snorts. Renee wasn't there at the moment, as she'd gone to get another cocktail. Sasha was standing with Adam and couldn't help laughing. Adam, for his part, said, "Sasha, I think I'm going to get a gold suit like that for the next gala, all right?"

As Mimi and Flamenco entered the room, they didn't really talk to anyone, just kept to themselves and whispered to each other while photographers came up and took picture after picture. This was the way it usually was at events. Mimi didn't identify with the other women there anyway. She thought them to be snobbish and rude.

As cocktails came to an end, waiters gently asked people to take their seats. It was an act similar to sheepherders very nicely asking the sheep to move into the barn. Once one or two people made their way into the dining area, another three or four would go back out to get another drink or see someone else they knew. As people looked for their tables and found their place cards, there was a commotion of chairs squeaking, trains being stepped on, and evening purses being placed in the center of the table away from dripping candle wax. Renee, Sasha, and Adam found their seats and managed to sit down. As often happened, Sasha wished she had another chair for the excess fabric of her dress and resolved to wear simpler things in the future, while knowing deep down she wouldn't.

In general, Adam was a wonderful dinner partner. He was engaged and engaging and always managed to talk about Sasha and her business. Usually after an event, whatever woman he had been seated next to would say to Sasha, "Your husband is wonderful. I so enjoyed speaking with him, and good luck with the business. I really should come in and speak with you about my investments." Sasha loved that Adam was always looking out for her and that women enjoyed sitting next to him. He could make her crazy with all the times she was left to deal with household things, but he was a good man and she knew a lot of husbands who didn't treat their wives all that well. It wasn't as if any man, short of Thruce, lived to put on a tuxedo after a long day at the office. Most of them would rather put on sweats, drink a beer, and watch whatever was on ESPN. Sasha knew of more than one man who thought his wife's desire to attend these events annoying and would fabricate business dinners to get out of going. There were also one or two who used these events to scour the room for romantic opportunities. There was a dreadful story, although it might have been urban legend, of a husband discovered in a stall of the bathroom with one of the special events staff assigned to hand out gift bags at the end of the evening. He apparently received his early.

Tonight, however, Adam was not on his best behavior. Sasha glared at him several times throughout the evening as she saw him peeking at his BlackBerry under the table. At one point, she almost asked him to hand it over to her, like an elementary school teacher confiscating a comic book. At the same time, she knew it was an important evening and that repercussions from the last two days had already begun. What Hank Paulson did with AIG, but didn't do with Lehman only a day before, was going to set the tone for the next several days, if not weeks, months, or even years. Some of the men at cocktails were already starting to say the Treasury secretary, as a former CEO of Goldman Sachs, had a vendetta against Lehman and that he'd helped AIG only because it was good for Goldman. Sasha wasn't sure what she thought at that point. It could be true, except at the same time wasn't Paulson trying to make decisions in the middle of cataclysmic events without a lot of time to analyze everything? She was glad that he was in that position rather than the two guys President Bush had in place before him. She couldn't imagine how John Snow or Paul O'Neill would have reacted if someone told them that credit default swaps were widening to historic spreads. She suspected if Bush had done anything right in his two terms—and to her, that was a stretch—it was hiring a Wall Street leader to run Treasury.

It was ironic to be at an event such as this one, where women in $10,000 dresses were at seats that had cost $1,000 or more. There was to be a live auction after dinner, and Sasha wondered if evenings such as this would continue or become a relic of the past. My gosh, forget charity events! Would capitalism even survive? Where would they be a year from now? Would people be hawking belongings on eBay just as they sold apples on street corners in the Depression? Right now, she honestly wasn't sure and wondered if Russian nobility or French aristocracy had been conscious that their world was changing before their eyes or if they only awoke one day to an entirely different existence. There might be no return from the abyss.

Sasha realized that the main conversation at dinner was the financial system. That was unusual. Even women who normally didn't bother themselves with what their husbands did were asking her, "What do you think, Sasha? What should I do with my money?" She didn't know the answer.

Her thoughts were wrapped up in her own saga. She was still flustered and upset from Harry's earlier antics. She felt herself tearing up again at the thought of it and started fantasizing about what she would say to him if she ever let loose. She was so lost in her own thoughts that she wasn't paying attention to the speakers at the podium, until all of a sudden she saw a young woman stand up to receive an award from the organization that provided programs and self-esteem to underprivileged inner-city kids. She started listening and was so overwhelmed by the terrible childhood this woman described—her determination to succeed, and the gratitude that she had to the organization—that it knocked her out of her own self-pity. If someone with a much harder life than Sasha's could make it, she'd persevere too. When the silent auction took place later that evening, Sasha raised her hand to make an extra contribution, as she knew that in the coming months, charities like this were going to be sorely tested financially.

As dinner was ending, Sasha saw James Ullman across the room. She had long ago decided one ran into people at times and places for a reason, so she always took advantage of the moment. It wasn't a coincidence when she saw him at the Regency two weeks ago while she was with Harry, and it wasn't a coincidence now. Thus, when the plates had been cleared, she made her way over to his table.

"James. How are you?"

"Sasha. Good evening. You look terrific as usual. Thank God you make your own money. I'd be in the poorhouse if Ginny had as many dresses as you do."

"Ginny does have as many dresses as I do, James. And I think you're still fairly far away from the poorhouse, even after the last few days, I'd suspect." Sasha laughed as Ginny waved from across the table and rolled her eyes at James's comments. Sasha also noted that she was wearing the Marchesa dress she'd been eyeing at Bergdorf's that cost $9,750. She was always bemused by men who liked to feign poverty when their net worth had three commas in it. "James, I'd really love to get on your calendar about some things that are happening right now. I think it might be of some interest to you. At the very least, I certainly could use your advice."

"Sure, call my office in the morning and have Eileen set something up. I'm always happy to talk to you and help if I can. Look forward to hearing what's going on."

"Fantastic. I'll have Fern call in the morning."

As Sasha made her way back to the table, she felt that at least she had put her own wheels in motion. Harry could leave her out as much as he wanted, but at some point he was going to have to realize that Sasha could get to pretty much anyone in New York who was important in the world of finance. If he didn't plan to include her, it was time she took steps to do so herself.

CHAPTER TWELVE

The After-Party

It was only 10:00 p.m. when people started leaving the gala, so Sasha, Adam, and Renee discussed heading to Café Carlyle for a cocktail. "Please, Adam, just one drink?" Sasha pleaded.

"Ugh. I'm exhausted, and tomorrow's gonna be a total—"

"Yes, yes, I know. But so will the day after that and the day after that. Besides, if it's going to be so bad, you might as well still be drunk in the morning!"

"Sasha, only you would say that and actually be serious. Okay, just one. But if you girls decide to do anything after that, you're on your own," he said grudgingly. "Anyway, I wouldn't mind a snort of single malt to top the evening off."

They walked into the bar and could see that several people who had attended the gala were already there among the regular patrons. It made for an interesting scene, long gowns and tuxes at one table next to jeans and blue blazers at another.

Sasha could see Grigsby and Thruce across the room and waved while saying to Renee, "Well, that was certainly an interesting scene with you and Grigsby. That's so nice of you to help her with her daughter. I actually like her. I'm not sure why, because she sort of seeks out everything I find mildly ridiculous about this world, but she is actually a good person deep down. I feel a little sorry for her, too. She probably could have been successful if she took all the energy she puts into her social life and put it into something useful."

"I'm always happy to help people, you know that, Sasha. How did you meet her, anyway?"

"Oh, she and I chaired an event a few years ago. She actually worked her tail off getting people to come and brought in one big sponsor that gave a hundred and fifty thousand dollars. It wouldn't have happened without her. I'm still not sure if it was because she cared about the charity or because it would make her look good, but the event was more successful than it had ever been before, so end of story as far as I'm concerned."

"Sasha, she is a social-climbing, vapid ding-a-ling," Adam piped up. "I sat next to her at one event and almost chewed my leg off to get away," causing them all to chuckle, especially since Adam rarely complained about a dinner partner.

"Okay, she can be a bit much, but as I said, she brought in a lot of money, and there are people that all these organizations do help, so that's what I want to focus on. The woman who spoke tonight showed that more than anything. And look, we all know there are some people I like to call 'sociasites,' a combination of socialite and parasite, who just want the borrowed dresses and jewelry and don't even think they should have to buy a ticket! They're the ones we should be complaining about, not Grigsby. Okay, I'm off my soapbox. Renee, let's see if we can give you *Long-Short Hedge Fund Strategies for Dummies*. Maybe there's a book in this!" Sasha said. "So what do you need help understanding?"

"Well, it's not like I don't know a lot about the financial world, but remember my job at Merrill was assisting financial advisors with marketing. I wasn't exposed to the complexities of hedge funds. I'd just like to understand it a little more, or at least confirm what I have already picked up. And I know that John is this legendary trader and investor, so I'd like to understand more than I do now."

"Ah..." Adam perked up. "My favorite topic. The illusion of genius is part of the legend of hedge funds!"

Sasha smiled. She actually loved listening to Adam talk about this stuff. He had a way of making sense to the novice and sophisticated investor alike.

Adam continued, "A buddy of mine, Bill Brigogratz, just left Flying Point—he couldn't stand being called a 'fucking asshole' more than twice a day."

"Twice a day?" Renee said in disbelief. "He must have been John's favorite guy if it was only twice a day."

"Well, maybe, but he said it really started to grate on him. Anyway, he told me that from the time Cutter started in 1999 through the middle of 2007, he routinely cranked out returns that were thirty percent and more every year—and that's after fees. That's unbelievable!"

Renee interrupted, "Everyone is always saying 'two and twenty.' I'm not really sure what that means."

"Here's the one thing to remember: A hedge fund is a way for the manager to get paid. The fund charges two percent on assets—so on every million invested, that's twenty thousand dollars, okay?" When Renee nodded, Adam continued. "Okay. But it also takes twenty percent of the profits. Now, if John's getting returns of thirty percent a year, he had added three hundred thousand to that million-dollar investment. Twenty percent of that is sixty thousand. Add that to the twenty thousand charged on assets, and Cutter's made eighty thousand just on you and your measly little million bucks, and—"

"Actually," Renee said, "our minimum is five million!"

"Right," Adam continued. "So, we know the investment world is full of lemmings—meaning money chases performance—so the better Flying Point Capital did, the more money wanted in. Professional investors become insane with desire when they can't get in a fund."

"It's like trying to get into Butter," Sasha added, mentioning the downtown nightclub.

Their drinks arrived, and Adam took a sip of his Springbank single malt. "Ahh, it doesn't get better than that," he said.

"The list of Flying Point investors is pretty impressive. I think we have every state and large-city pension fund, not to mention dozens of countries around the world," said Renee.

"Allocating pension money to hedge funds became all the rage some time ago when David Swensen, the head of Yale University's endowment, became an institutional investment guru."

"His book is on the shelf in John's office," Renee said. "I started reading it. It's actually pretty interesting."

"Swensen's thesis is that endowments have long-term investment horizons and don't often make withdrawals, so return is incrementally less important," Adam said.

Sasha interrupted, "That means no one's gonna take their dough out regardless of performance. Speak English, Adam!"

"Okay, sorry," he said. "Anyway, I guess you already know that." Adam actually seemed somewhat disappointed that Renee knew of Swensen, but he continued, "Basically, a lot of hedge funds saw their investors' capital as permanent, despite the fact that they could cash out their holdings on a quarterly basis."

Renee nodded. "So I bet that if you don't think you need cash to redeem next quarter, you put money into longer-term investments. And so then you start feeling bulletproof even if investments don't pan out."

"I hate to be critical of the opposite sex," Sasha said, winking at Adam, "but a lot of these guys became quite enamored of their power and more than a little cocky. John Cutter is no exception. He has charm and dynamism that keeps investors happy. Have you seen his quarterly investment letters?"

"As a matter of fact, I have," Renee said. "He is quite an amusing writer. One is going out this week. He's got this line about what a great opportunity it is right now that says something like 'Smart investors run into burning buildings, and that time is now.' We will be buying mortgage-backed securities until our hands bleed because they can't go any lower."

"Yeah, he has a very good sense of humor and writing style, although his reports were always semiplagiarized," Adam said. "They always get passed around the Internet after they're published. He also is infamous for his cynical and profanity-laced investor conference calls. He knows the impact of a strategically placed f-bomb, particularly when dropped in front of the head of a teachers pension fund of some midwestern state. A large part of John's fund-raising success is his innate ability to make himself into the smartest guy in the room."

Renee added, "Well, I wouldn't necessarily say his f-bombs are 'strategic.' For him, saying 'fuck' is like breathing."

Both Sasha and Adam laughed.

"Yes, I guess there was a shortage of soap in John's house growing up to wash his mouth out, but in the end, it all came down to results. Flying Point's returns not only kept investors happy, they also helped them to overlook the amount of fees that were pulled out for John and, probably to a much lesser extent, his employees."

"Yeah, but still not bad, Adam," Sasha said. "Remember the surprise fortieth birthday Bill threw for Suri Brigogratz? Kanye performed with Beyoncé, and then Bill presented that Bulgari vintage necklace to her? That party alone was probably a few million. Renee, it was unbelievable."

"I remember reading about it in *Vogue*, or no, I think it was *Bazaar*. Didn't she wear a Lacroix haute couture dress that was rumored to cost a hundred and fifty thousand dollars?"

"It was a great party, and Bill wasn't at a loss to pay for it," Adam said quickly, since he knew this could fast turn into a minute-by-minute replay of that infamous event. "But anyway, one of the things that happens to these guys periodically is that they get asked how they regularly generate profits that are better than everyone else's. John's analysts would pull out reams of reports while he spouted various jargony concepts designed to throw them off, like alpha, beta, and gamma, market convergence, and statistical anomalies. Questioners would be inundated with so much information that it usually stopped them cold. 'Disclosure typhoon' is what Bill called it."

"Hi, guys, how are you?" They were interrupted by Lynn Fenestre, a well-known art consultant who attended many of the same events. There was always a good vibe around Lynn. Smart and cheerful, she knew and was known by everyone, including the three of them. What's more, she was just so genuinely nice that people couldn't help but be her friend.

"Hi, Lynn. Were you there this evening? I didn't see you," Sasha said.

"I got there late. I have some clients that have some big pieces about to go on the market, so I was in a meeting until seven with them."

"I'm sure it's an interesting time," Renee said. "How are you feeling about the art market with everything that's going on?"

"It's not pretty, but there are substantial works that will always find a home. If it's not the hedgies, it will be the Russians. If not the Russians, then the Chinese, and if not them, well, we can always go find some Martians that want to buy a Damien Hirst diamond-encrusted skull for a hundred and twenty-five mil, right? Some of the auction houses guaranteed some big prices, so I'm waiting to see if the prices in the fall sales match what the buyer was promised. If anyone asks me, there will be a big gap!"

"Oh, I can imagine," Renee said. "Any artists in particular that are going to be on the market?"

"Oh, a little of everything, I'm sure. It will depend on who is in the most distress, and some of those are going to be private sales because certain people won't want publicity that adds to the impression that they need money, and some of course do. Anyway, that's the state of things as of right now. Any of you guys up for a trip downtown? I'm meeting Mimi Cutter at the Gates for a late night drink."

"Mimi Cutter!" Renee, Sasha, and Adam all said in unison, looking at one another.

"Yes. Did I say something funny?"

"Oh, no. It's just that Renee works for John Cutter. Did you see her this evening?" Sasha said.

"Yes, I sat with her, as a matter of fact. Mimi is a client of mine. They have a pretty amazing collection. I don't know whose side it will end up on, but a few of their pieces will end up on the market," Lynn said.

"The artwork at the office is incredible. Probably fifty million right there!" Renee added.

"Anyway, we're just finishing up a drink," Sasha said. "We would love to join you downtown, but we all have early mornings. See you soon, Lynn."

After she left, they chuckled at the coincidence. Renee, who had missed Mimi's entrance, loved hearing Adam's description of what she was wearing, which he called "winged victory in red." Renee steered the conversation back to finance. "So, Adam, tell me how hedge funds actually make money. Is what they do so different from mutual funds or other money managers?"

"The answer is yes, and no. There are really only four ways that hedge funds make their magic: They can see macro trends before others; they bet against the market, or 'go short'; they rely on the momentum of buying what everyone else is buying or selling what everyone else is selling; or they massively borrow money, or leverage themselves, which enhances the return and the risks. Only the brave go short, because you can lose your entire investment. Most hedge fund managers rely on leverage and momentum. John Cutter is in that group."

"So who is in the first group, the ones who see the trends?" Renee said.

"The legends are George Soros, Michael Steinhardt, Julian Robertson, and today, John Paulson."

"I've been reading about him," Renee said. "He's the guy who saw the whole subprime mortgage thing coming and that, as a result, all the financials were way overvalued. He personally took home billions of dollars last year!"

"Yep, but he is one of the few and far between. Over the last few years, hedge funds have popped up like mosquitoes after a rainstorm and not because of a lot of brilliant soothsayers. Think of how many guys tried to pick you up telling you they ran their own hedge funds!"

"Oh please, I can't begin to count." Renee laughed. "If I had a nickel for every guy who told me he was a long short alpha macro micro tech, I'd be in John's fund myself by now. Sasha, remember that one guy we met at the Winter Wonderland Ball last year who referred to himself in the third person? 'Sweyn only invests when markets are clearly in his favor.'" They both started giggling at that.

"Man, you girls are going to have me here all night trying to get through this if you keep talking about other stuff," Adam said. "Anyway, Renee, there are just a couple of other things I'll share with you. John Cutter relies heavily on his own network of other fund managers who pretty much gossip all day long about what they are seeing in the markets. And then they basically gang up on a particular market or company to drive the price up or down. Sometimes they've even been a bit too aggressive and been sued by the companies they target. Some would argue their efforts also involve insider trading."

"Oh yeah, John gets calls from these guys all day long. I can hear snippets of the conversations." Renee started mimicking them in deep voices, throwing lots of terms around: "'Man, what do you think of GM at sixty?' 'Dude, I'm thinking the euro looks rich at these levels.' 'Didja hear about David Einhorn's speech on Allied Capital?' 'I think property REITs look like they've got room to run. Sweet!'"

"Exactly!" Adam said. "Renee, every time you hear one of those jargon-filled lines, you can bet that they have a specific trade on in one of those things. When the stock or bond has moved up or down to the price they want, they look to slower-moving investors to take them out of their position and—"

"What does that mean—'slower-moving investors'?"

"Oh, retail. Individual investors. The last ones on the food chain. They usually do this by chatting up a newspaper or television reporter. John is well known to be close buddies with Jed Crater—you know, the reporter with the stock-investing column for *Investors Weekly Market Review*."

"Yes! Crater is on his speed dial! He's so obnoxious, too. Incredibly rude when he calls. Plus I hear he makes passes at most of the female employees when he comes into the office. I've yet to meet him."

"Yup. So when you hear Crater say to buy something, it's usually because John and others like him are selling."

"Well, this has really filled in some gaps for me. Thank you both! Let me pick up the tab for this. Then I've got to get home and hit the sack or I'll be useless tomorrow and John will call me a mindless twit before I've even given him his coffee."

Sasha, who was barely keeping her own eyes open by this point, added, "Anytime. We didn't even get to leverage."

"Well, when's the next benefit? You can fill me in on it then."

Against their protestations, Renee paid the bill, and they walked out onto Madison Avenue, now empty except for a few cars and taxis cruising up the avenue. The air was cool and nice, but Sasha had that feeling that fall was coming and winter wasn't far behind. She dreaded the bitter cold that would inevitably arrive and also wondered what the coming months would bring for all of them.

They caught a taxi and were home in five minutes but gave Renee enough money to cover the rest of the fare up to her apartment, this time against her protests. As they came into the house, they could see the remnants of the evening. The twins appeared to have done their homework while watching television because the TV was still blaring an episode of *Hannah Montana* and their schoolbags were on the floor. Josh had set up his fighter planes in the kitchen, discovered by Adam when he stepped on one as soon as he'd taken off his shoes. Entering the bedroom, Sasha could see that Samantha was fast asleep in their bed and was wearing a pair of Sasha's Jimmy Choos, on the wrong feet. Adam carried her into her bedroom while Sasha got out of her gown and washed her face. Adam came back in and got out of his tux. As he got into bed, he said, "You know, Sasha, Renee's going to have an interesting time the next few days. I think John's got a bunch of wrong trades on, and I don't think even Jed Crater has the ability to help him now. I could see Flying Point completely blowing up."

"Really? That would be unbelievable. And it would be terrible for her, too. She's been able to help her family so much because of this new job. She's such an awesome person. I really hope that she ends up okay."

"Me too, honey, but I think that a lot of awesome people are going to be facing some tough times."

"Well, with that lovely thought, let's turn the lights out and get some sleep. It will be tomorrow before you know it."

CHAPTER THIRTEEN

Desperation Grows

Blake had just hung up with his private banker, who told him that no one at the company was getting any grace on margin calls just because they owned Lehman stock. He still had some room on the home equity loan that he'd taken out on the apartment, and he asked his banker to see what kind of line he could get on the house in Southampton. With the banks clamping down on credit, it was going to be tough. That would tide them over for the time being until he could figure something else out. Hopefully, Barclays was going to pay some kind of retention bonuses at year-end. Maybe they would even do it before that.

Grigsby had also put a packet of bills in his briefcase that morning that included $7,245.89 to Bergdorf Goodman and an invoice for $10,000 payable by check, credit card, or gifts of appreciated securities for a table they were taking at some event or other that he had zero desire to attend. Appreciated securities? Ha! That was a good one! And the second of four $25,000 installments of their kitchen renovation was due. He had told her he was going to have to let Sheldon go, and Donita at the very least would have to become part-time. He was in no mood to be yanked around by Grigsby, who as usual was telling him about someplace they had to be, otherwise everyone would think less of them. They had a terrible argument that morning over her spending.

"Grigsby, I don't give a shit. We have lost so much money, and we have a margin call that is basically going to wipe out all our liquid assets and then some. Meanwhile, you seem to think it's time to party like it's fucking New Year's Eve. I am cutting wherever we can, and you need to also. Even if I'm offered a permanent position at Barclays, it's going to take several years at least to rebuild what we have lost. Frankly, I'm not even sure we can."

"Well, the table has to be paid for. We can't back out on it. And what am I supposed to do, return the clothes I've bought?"

"Well . . . are the price tags still on them?"

"Some."

"Then get your ass down to Bergdorf's this morning and return them. I guarantee you won't be the only one."

Grigsby ran out of the room in tears.

When Blake wasn't despondent about how much he had lost, he and his colleagues spent a great deal of time building their conspiracy theory about Paulson and Goldman Sachs. It certainly seemed that way to every employee of Lehman Brothers, who wondered why they weren't saved. Why did their stock become worthless? Why did their net worth evaporate while AIG was taken under the government's wing? To be sure, AIG stock still fell to under a dollar, but at least it had a chance. Nothing like an $85 billion lifesaver to keep you afloat.

Even after her cocktail with Adam and Sasha, Renee was still trying to keep up with what was going on by reading as many papers as she could. As best as she could understand it, the situation was like looking at a knitted pattern that looked like separate images on one side, but on the other was pretty much a tangle of threads and colors all meshed together. After the night of the gala, it was clear that the Lehman bankruptcy was a disaster of unprecedented proportions. The ripples already running through the financial system turned into a tsunami. The default of Lehman's short-term paper and the unwinding of their trades throughout the financial system was the last straw. Midweek, a money market fund announced that it had "broken the buck," or fallen in value below a dollar a share. Plain and simple, it was like the Maginot Line. Almost overnight, there was a very real fear of a run on banks, which hadn't happened since the Depression. Only money held in U.S. Treasury bonds, or under mattresses, for that matter, was considered safe. Merrill had just barely escaped the same fate as Lehman, and now Morgan Stanley seemed to be next on the chopping block. Its stock plummeted 75 percent in a matter of days, even after it was announced that a Japanese bank was taking a huge ownership position in it. Even Goldman Sachs was starting to seem vulnerable, a sure sign that life as people knew it could come to an end.

Renee went over to her parents' apartment early the next week. As soon as she walked in, she could tell something was wrong.

"Mama, what is it? Is everything okay with Daddy?"

"Yes, cookie. Daddy is fine."

"Then what is it? I can tell something is wrong."

Donita sighed. "Mrs. Grigsby said she has to cut my hours back. Things are very bad there, and I don't know what to do. You know we need the money for Daddy's medical bills, especially because we don't know how long he will be able to work, given his health."

Knowing Grigsby the little that she did, Renee knew that things must indeed be very bad for her to cut back on that. It wasn't as if Grigsby knew how to mop floors and do laundry. She wondered who was doing the work at the apartment.

"Oh no! Don't worry, I will help with any bills. I'm doing well now. But did she say it was going to be temporary or permanent?"

"She said she doesn't know. She hopes it won't be permanent, but it isn't my place to ask."

"I can understand that, but she doesn't seem like the type that can get by without a full-time maid," said Renee.

"Dear, we can all take care of ourselves if we need to. We never know where we will find ourselves until we are there. God gave us two arms and two legs to work with and walk with."

Renee could hardly imagine Grigsby realizing that her two arms and legs were for anything but boots, shoes, rings, and bracelets, but she smiled at her mother's simple view of the world and human resiliency. That was the way Donita was.

She spent a few hours there. The good news was that when Donita was upset, she did extra cooking, so there was a fresh batch of vegetable patties and rice and beans. Renee filled herself up and took some extras with her when she left. She wondered how things would work out for her mom and worried about them both all the way home. With the responsibilities her sisters had for their families, she wouldn't expect them to help, even if they wanted to.

Later that evening, Grigsby picked up the phone and dialed Renee's number (which she'd gotten from Sasha, not Donita).

"Hello, Renee? It's Grigsby, Grigsby Somerset. How are you?"

"Grigsby!" Renee was shocked to hear her on the phone. "Hello. Um, how are you?"

"Fine. I wanted to follow up on our conversation about Spence, you know, regarding my daughter?"

Renee didn't know what to say. "Really. I'm surprised to hear that," she responded.

Grigsby had no idea why Renee would say that. "Well, you said that you would be happy to meet with my daughter and be helpful to us in regards to our Spence application," she said, trying not to sound irritated that she had to put her desperation out there.

"Well, yes, I did, but that was before you cut my mother's hours back. I'm really a little surprised that you would call me to ask a favor right after you did that."

Grigsby was flabbergasted. Frankly, it had never occurred to her that the two were related. "Oh, well, yes, but I really had no choice given what is going on right now. You see—"

"Yes, I am aware of what is going on in the world right now. What is also going on is that my father is ill, and my mother, who has been working her tail off for you for years, needs money to pay his bills. You, on the other hand, need to get your daughter into Spence. So until my mother's job is fully reinstated, I am afraid I can't be of any help to you."

Grigsby was speechless. Didn't anyone realize how hard things were on her right now? She didn't want to cut Donita back; in fact, Blake had told her she had to fire her altogether, but she'd put her foot down at that. She simply couldn't survive without anyone at all. Grigsby had also made it absolutely clear to Donita that she was terribly upset about having to do this. Now, to be told that her Spence dreams could be placed on hold when it was distasteful enough to be asking for a favor from the daughter of her maid? This was too much.

"Why doesn't anyone understand how hard this is?" She started to sob. "All I have ever done is try to be a good wife and mother and be a leader in the philanthropic community. All I *ever* do is take care of *everyone*. I rush from meeting to school pickup. I barely have time to get my hair done or exercise before I have to rush off to another event to help someone less fortunate. And now that things aren't going well for me, all of a sudden everyone and everything is coming down on me. I can't take it anymore." She sobbed uncontrollably.

Renee herself was now speechless, although she was also trying not to laugh. This poor demented woman's life was an endless series of parties, shopping, dinners, and vacations, along with a very healthy dose of working out and hair appointments. Yet at the same time, she felt a little sorry for Grigsby, who obviously really felt things were so hard for her. But Renee was not about to give up on the possibility of getting her mother's hours back. There had to be some way Grigsby could find the money. She then remembered the Merrill financial advisors telling her about a selling technique that she'd actually used herself called "Feel. Felt. Found."

"Oh, Grigsby, I can understand exactly how you must *feel*. Things are so tough right now, and with all you do it must be so difficult not to be able to help as many people as you want to. I *felt* exactly the same way when I was working on a charity event last year and just couldn't raise all the money I wanted for the event. What I *found*, however, is that when I am completely overwhelmed, sometimes if I can do just one small thing, it makes everything a bit easier." She paused to see how Grigsby would respond. She heard the weeping become more of a sniffle.

"What was the event you worked on?" she asked.

"Oh, it was Women in Need. The annual lunch."

"Oh, I was there!" Grigsby had now brightened considerably. "I think I wore my Lela Rose dress... no, it was the Douglas Hannant. It was so wonderful, wasn't it?"

At this point, Renee wasn't sure whether Grigsby was asking whether her outfit was wonderful or the lunch. "Yes, absolutely. It was so rewarding." Renee wanted to get the conversation back to Donita's hours. "I was so thankful after that lunch that I made an extra contribution because I felt like it would come back to me in other ways. That's something they instilled in us at Spence, you know, because we were all so privileged to be there." She hoped that would be a little hook, to get Grigsby back to the issue at hand.

"Oh, what wonderful values to teach in school. I try and teach that to my children, but reinforcing it at school is so critical to the health of a child." Grigsby was now back to sounding like the school catalogs. For her part, Renee was dubious that the Somerset children were getting a daily dose of values instruction.

Renee took another stab. "Well, how funny, because I also learned it from my parents. Even though we obviously did not have even close to what other families had, they always taught us how lucky we were, and that we should pay it forward to others. So you see, it's really because of my mother and Spence that I am where I am now. Being able to support others and having a wonderful job and being in a position to help so many people in different ways."

"Why, yes, I guess that is true," Grigsby responded.

Renee felt she could now close the deal, as her Merrill friends would have said. "So you know what I think would be so great? Don't you think you could maybe find a few dollars here and there to help my mother? It's probably only about a hundred and fifty a week. You would really be doing such a wonderful, *charitable* thing, and I will absolutely convey to the admissions department, the head of school, and the head of the board of trustees just how wonderful your family is. You seem to embody so many of the school values. I could see you chairing the annual benefit."

Grigsby could see at least one dream coming back into focus. She wanted Bitten at Spence, and the idea of herself running an event there was making visions dance in her head. Her mind raced as she thought about where she could get the extra money. She would just have to make sure that Blake didn't realize Donita was still working as much as she had been before. Come to think of it, that wouldn't be a problem. He wouldn't notice anyway. She knew exactly where she could get the money, too.

"Okay, Renee. I have your word?"

"Yes, you do," Renee replied. "Oh, and don't tell my mother I had anything to do with this," knowing that Donita would not have approved of her meddling or deal making one bit.

"Of course," Grigsby responded. She certainly didn't want the balance of power between employer and employee to be upset any more than it was going to be in her mind.

"Okay, I'm so glad this all worked out. I will start writing my letters to the school, but I really need to meet your daughter, too, just so I can describe her and say a few kind things about her. Shall we meet at Sarabeth's for breakfast this Saturday morning?"

"Oh, yes, that would be lovely. Let's do it early since it fills up and you can't make reservations. How is nine a.m.?"

"Perfect, Grigsby. I'll see you and Bitten on Saturday morning at nine. Bye."

As Renee hung up the phone, she breathed a sigh of relief. What she had really learned from her parents was to take care of your own. They need you, and you need them. She wondered if Bitten Somerset was ever going to get that from her mother and father. In any case, she was looking forward with some amusement to breakfast on Saturday and wondered if Grigsby would wear the Lela Rose or the Douglas Hannant.

Amid all of this, Sasha set up an appointment to meet with James Ullman at his office on September 22. She was anxious to discuss the situation but also was nervous. It was inappropriate, bordering on insubordination, for her to talk about the potential transaction or try to find other options for herself.

As she walked into his building at 375 Park Avenue, she thought about how many private equity firms, hedge funds, investment bank boutiques, and money management firms were tucked into this building, not to mention others up and down the avenue—or, for that matter, the entire radius that stretched from Sixth Avenue to Third and from 42nd up to Madison and 62nd. What were all these people doing in there? They were all like individual ants in their own ant farms, not realizing there were thousands of others just like them, scurrying about.

If midtown was ground zero, 375 Park was its epicenter. Built in 1958 by the famed architect Mies van der Rohe as the headquarters of the Seagram Company Ltd., it had been known ever since as "the Seagram Building." The building helped to define a twenty-five-block stretch of Park Avenue as the center of New York business. The most important tenant of all, the Four Seasons restaurant in the lobby, served as a cafeteria of sorts for the rich and powerful. From time to time, a gigantic white tent would arise on the plaza outside the building to host a party for one of the corporate titans in need of more space than the restaurant itself could provide.

Sasha took the elevator up to the twenty-second floor, where James's offices were. Walking in, she had the distinct feeling that everyone and everything in the place was dedicated to James. But unlike the Flying Point headquarters or those of some of the other large hedge funds and investment banks, these offices were decorated simply and reflected the personality of someone who was supremely rich but appreciated where he came from, his family, and his friends. Sasha was led into James's office in the corner, which had windows on two sides and gave him a full view of the other Park Avenue fortresses. She noted that most of the photos on the credenza were of James and his wife, children, and friends. Truth be told, it was a little difficult to see the photos clearly because James was almost always smoking a cigar in his office, which created a dense cloud. He didn't give a whit about smoking laws. It was his office and his company, so the stogies were going for most of the day.

"So, Sasha, tell me what is going on and how I can be of help."

"Well, James, first of all I am stepping out of line by being here, but I really need your advice."

"Sasha, if people didn't step out of line when they needed to, half the world wouldn't have gotten to where it has today, and the other half would be even more screwed up than they are now."

"Well, that's a good point, too, come to think of it."

"So what's going on? I think I might have annoyed your CEO the other day at breakfast."

"Probably, but don't worry about it. He needs that once in a while. But the situation is actually directly related to that breakfast. As you may recall, SAMCO and BridgeVest are both owned by Empire Bank."

"Right, Kirk McNeal. Good fellow. Belongs to the same club I do. We were on opposite teams at the member-guest tennis tournament this summer," he said, and started to chuckle.

"Oh, really!" She tucked away this piece of information for the time being. "Well, apparently Kirk wants to sell both companies and be a little more nimble in today's world. Of course, I can understand that, but that means my company and BridgeVest have to get a deal done, and of course there is the unknown of who the new parent might be in all of that."

"Right, right. What is the cash flow of both companies right now?" he asked as he checked some things on his Bloomberg.

"Two hundred million. SAMCO is twenty-five percent of that."

"Hmm. Tell me about the CEO. What's his name, Munroe?"

"Mullaugh, Harry Mullaugh." She felt a bit nervous not knowing whether she should throw him under the bus now—or later. "Harry is... well, let me put it another way—"

"Sasha, you don't need to say any more. If you liked him or at least thought he was competent, you would have started with that. From what I know, BridgeVest is a third-rate firm with weak leadership. I'm sure you must piss the hell out of them. You're smart, dynamic, and know how to hold your own in a man's world. EILEEN!"

James's assistant, Eileen, had been with him for seventeen years. She knew his business and life inside and out, and as a result, he was constantly bellowing out her name and asking her for something.

"Yes, James."

"Get me stats on Empire Bank, and BridgeVest, too. I also want to see the valuations of the last three transactions I've done."

"Sure thing."

She was about five feet away from his office. "EILEEN!"

"Yes, James."

"Call Ginny and ask her what time dinner is with the ambassador."

"It's at seven fifteen at Twenty-one," she said, winking at Sasha, since she was the one who had made the reservation. She made all the reservations, in fact.

He turned back to Sasha. "Okay, so who do you think buys you?"

"I don't know. I don't even know if a deal would be done for both companies together."

"No, they aren't going to buy a piece of crap without the one shining star. The price that Kirk would get wouldn't be worth it. Who's on the list and what's the asking price?"

Sasha felt a bit awkward but said, "Look, James, I'm going to be completely honest with you. For whatever reason, maybe it's Harry's competence or lack thereof, or perhaps it's as you say that I piss the hell out of them, I haven't been kept apprised of what's going on. Harry was telling me that day at breakfast when I saw you that I wasn't included in the meeting when it was discussed with the executive committee. When I introduced Harry to you, I assumed that he would immediately want to talk to you, but he cut me off and hasn't kept me aware of what's going on. I haven't seen a presentation and haven't seen a list of buyers."

James leaned forward, looked into her eyes, and said, "Sasha, why do you want to let yourself get fucked?"

She looked startled. "Excuse me?"

"I mean, seriously, the writing is on the wall. They don't want you around, and yet at the same time you should be important to the deal. If you want to, then go do what you need to do. Talk to Kirk, shop your company yourself."

"Well, but—"

"No 'well, buts.' Look, Sasha, this is Wall Street. No one takes care of anyone. You have no friends. It's every man for himself, and that goes for you girls, too. If I were you, I'd call Kirk directly. In fact, EILEEN!"

Eileen appeared.

"Get Kirk McNeal on the phone."

"Actually, James, I really appreciate it, but I'm not ready to do that."

James looked at her. "Are you sure? I can have him on the line in one minute."

"Yes, I'm sure. I can always call him directly. Let me just take a little bit of time to figure out exactly what I want to do."

"Okay, you will do something when you have nothing left to lose. For whatever reason, right now you still feel like you do."

As she left his office and went back outside, the corner of Park Avenue and 52nd Street was busy. Men in business suits scurried about as they usually do in the middle of the morning, on their way to meetings and closings, but at the same time, in late September 2008, there was a different aura to it all. The thing was, all of those ant farms in each building and each company had just been knocked over by a giant foot and were scrambling to figure out which end was up.

CHAPTER FOURTEEN

It's a Crime

As September turned into October, things continued to get worse for John, but his downturn had started well before that. Now, the combination of ill-timed moves and a reliance on lower-rated investments and leverage had all come home to roost for Flying Point Capital. What had been a constant stream of redemptions—cashing out of investments—turned into a flood. Some of his oldest clients wanted out, and the positions in the fund were deeply underwater. Selling was out of the question, especially when he factored in his leverage.

Leverage worked well when things went up. If John could make a profit, borrowing money would increase the profit exponentially. Instead of a three times return, it could be ten times, even after he paid back the borrowed money. In fact, he had done a levered trade with Google a few years ago that was so astronomical, Jed Crater did a special article on John's fearlessness as an investor. Flying Point sent out so many reprints that Richie Sambucci told his friends, "It was like confetti on Broadway during a parade for the Yankees!"

But leverage enhanced losses as well as gains. If a bet went wrong, his entire investment could be wiped out, and he would still have to pay back the loan. Now, it was happening all over his portfolio, weekly if not daily. The curses erupting from John's mouth were almost nonstop. He had no choice but to bar the gates and stop all redemptions so investors weren't able to take out their money. Every fund was now doing the same thing, but John's stress level was at an all-time high. "You and I are fucking tied at the hip, buddy, so you better deal with it," he shouted at the phone every day when irate investors called. Stop fund redemptions, he hoped, and he could buy time to make back some of what he'd lost.

Aside from the redemption freeze, John was counting on one other thing to save him, and it came out of the peculiar relationship between him and Blake Somerset. What had started as a salesman trying to sell some mortgage-backed bonds a few years ago had turned into a dangerous situation that could bring them both down. There were a million stories that would come out of the housing crisis, and Flying Point Capital was yet another.

The housing market bubble had been growing for years. In reality, it was also a debt bubble created by the free and easy availability of credit to virtually anyone with a pulse, aided by Wall Street's creation of a mortgage-backed securities machine and all the investors panting to buy the bonds.

Wall Street, John reflected, had always been known for taking a good idea and subverting it. Take mortgage-backed securities, which had long been a simple way of financing the housing market. But the subprime mortgage market was something new. It began when interest rates dropped after 9/11. One result was that virtually everyone in America refinanced their mortgage. And then they refinanced again, and again, and found, as a result, they could also take out a lot of equity to buy things. Then they started taking on mortgages to buy bigger houses, invest in second homes, vacation homes, and beach houses. Builders stepped up their building activity, new developments and condos sprouted up in hot markets like south Florida, Las Vegas, and San Diego, speculation in housing kept rising for the next several years, and housing values kept rising. What started as the American dream ultimately led to the American nightmare. What started as a couple of hot housing markets became a national obsession, and the culture began to reflect it with hit TV shows like *Flip This House* and infomercials that promised, "You, too, can get rich on real estate!"

It seemed that everybody made money during this buildup of the housing bubble. They say people who had been day-trading Internet stocks in the nineties were selling real estate in south Florida in 2005. Mortgage lenders generated enormous profits by giving mortgages to just about anybody. It was easy for them because they could get rid of their credit risk by selling them as the fodder for mortgage-backed securities, which Wall Street then packaged, creating slices, or, in Wall Street lingo, "tranches," within each, and each with its own level of risk. Then they created another derivative of that and called it a collateralized debt obligation, or CDO, putting even junkier mortgages into each one.

And of course, so-called smart investors like John Cutter kept buying them, especially the riskier pieces, forgetting the old adage that what goes up must always, inevitably, go down.

John also used leverage when buying these to generate profits that would keep his investors happy. It worked spectacularly well for a while. Home prices rose constantly. People continued to get mortgages even if they had little to no credit. It just kept going and going. And the music played on. But ultimately, the hundreds and hundreds of billions of dollars' worth of securities that had been created, all sitting on top of a much smaller pile of ever-worsening residential mortgages, were on the balance sheets of banks, insurance companies, sovereign wealth funds, and hedge funds.

Home prices finally stopped going up in the summer of 2006, but everyone involved in the mortgage machine wanted to keep the money flowing to more people who shouldn't have gotten mortgages, and it all seemed fine—on paper.

And then the unthinkable happened: The music stopped.

Housing prices started to fall, the economy turned south, and like hungry termites, credit problems in junky mortgages started to eat their way through not just the mortgage-backed bond market, but the entire financial system itself, which started to collapse under its own weight.

John Cutter got caught right in the eye of the storm, and Blake Somerset helped him get there. A few years before, when he was looking around for new investments, John finally returned Blake's call after several years of ignoring him. He actually knew Blake from Harvard but never liked him much. He thought he talked too much and was weak. He always drank too fast and ended up booting or passed out on the floor. He had the kinds of girlfriends who dated him because he was a good catch, not because they were into him; more than once, John would end an evening with one of Blake's girlfriends after he'd passed out. People turn out pretty much the way you think they will in college, and sure enough, Blake ended up marrying someone who loved his pedigree as a Lehman Brothers bond salesman in the structuring group. Much of his business was generated through golf outings, steak dinners, and strip clubs. John didn't need to play those games, although he was always up for a strip club, but Blake still constantly called him and e-mailed him, trying to get him to buy some structured note or derivative that John certainly would be the last to admit he didn't understand. In early 2005, when John was looking around for the next big trade, he called Blake back.

"John, good to hear from you. I've got a beautiful bond for you."

"Blake, there is no such thing as a beautiful bond, only beautiful prices."

"You're right, as always, John. I've got a beautifully *priced* bond for you."

"What is it? You know my return hurdle is pretty high, so I'm hard-pressed to think of anything you might have to sell me."

"This is different," Blake said, breaking into the kind of linguistic shorthand that he knew his friend would easily grasp. "It's the junior tranche of a Countrywide residential mortgage structure, and it's bulletproof. It will get you a fifteen percent return unleveraged, but our prime brokerage group will finance it for you to get the return to over forty percent."

What might sound like gibberish to the man on the street was part of the language of the bond market that John lived in, but the word *finance* made his ears prick up. If he could borrow, his returns would grow even more. But another thing Blake said made him pause. "What does bulletproof mean?"

"It means that if home prices appreciate just three percent a year over the life of the security, you won't lose a dollar of principal to credit losses."

"And what if they don't rise three percent a year?"

"That has never happened, John, and our models tell us that it is a virtual impossibility. In short, housing prices will always go up by at least that much."

"What do you get out of it?"

"I get my usual quarter point, but more than that, I can finally say that I sold John Cutter a bond."

"Fuck that shit. Just send over the docs so I can have my guys look at them, and I'll call you back by end of day."

"You got it. It'll be on your Bloomberg in five minutes. And John, if this works out, you should know that we are ready to do this trade over and over again, and do it in a big way. My structuring group has people lined up outside ready to do these deals."

Five minutes later, the offering memorandum came attached to Blake's Bloomberg message, which read, "John, here you go. Remember: bulletproof."

Funny thing about e-mails. Most people still have not learned their lesson. Never write things like "bulletproof."

And that was it. John bought $10 million of that first deal, and just as Blake said, it was bulletproof. John made some nice money on that trade. It was just a toe in the water for his fund, but John saw that he could do it again, even if he didn't quite understand the structure. After the fourth or fifth one, though, he had stopped reading the documents, and by the middle of 2007, Flying Point Capital had half its assets essentially in a one-way bet on the housing market continuing to go up.

Even though the returns to date had been terrific, John was getting concerned about how concentrated his fund was in these risky investments. He tried to sell some of the bonds, only to find that the market for these kinds of assets had started to get wobbly. The prices were starting to fall, and financing for them was getting very hard to find. John was getting desperate...

He started bullying Blake to find a buyer.

He started bullying Blake to keep up the financing.

And then he threatened to use Blake's "bulletproof" Bloomberg message against him (since, as it turned out, these securities were not bulletproof). Then, in late 2007, Blake came up with an actual idea one night when he got John to go out to Scores with a group of Lehman guys.

"We have to find a way to sell what you own," said Blake, "but at prices that are close to what you paid for them, not what they are worth now. Current market values are only a reflection of panic in the market, not their true value."

"No shit, Sherlock. How are we supposed to sell shit at a premium price?" asked John.

Again, Blake launched into one of his shorthand descriptions: "We use the structure that got us here in the first place. We will create a CDO using all of the securities you own, and chop it up to make senior and junior portions; you can get a higher price for the less volatile part. The only thing is that you don't actually have enough of these assets to make a CDO, so you have to buy some more."

John was pissed, though he knew Blake was right.

"Look," Blake continued, "I know this is the last thing you want to do, but I think you have to double down to pull yourself out of the hole you are in."

"All right. Get started. I fucking hate this, but do it."

John fended off concerned investors while Blake started to put the deal together in December 2007. There were some small redemptions in his fund, but John was able to meet them. Yet he was worried... existentially worried... and he was a good enough chess player to see how this was all going to play out. He was also increasingly agitated for other reasons, as his marriage to Mimi was on the rocks. He was out with other women and then exclusively with Amanda Belden—well, almost exclusively. So he started protecting himself. He had kept much of his wealth invested in Flying Point, but he secretly began funneling cash and securities into an offshore account in the Cayman Islands. Occasionally, he would meet redemptions from investors from this account, but mostly he was trying to shield assets from the coming implosion and his bitch of a wife. It was easy enough to do. He kept all the records himself and found a nice bank in the Caymans that didn't care where the money came from as long as it received it by 10:30 in the morning.

In February 2008, Blake told John that the new deal was going to happen. He had worked out an arrangement with Bear Stearns to sell half the senior debt to an Asian government fund, while Lehman would sell the other half to a German bank. John would hold on to the junior debt. The proceeds from the sale would pretty much cover John's original investment. It was beautiful. Once again, John seemed to have been one step ahead and was breathing a sigh of relief.

The deal was supposed to close on March 15, but then Bear happened and everything fell apart. Both foreign buyers dropped out, and John was left in an even worse financial position. And now the world knew about it. Forget "Page Six," the *New York Post* business section had a whole article about the divorce and his net worth plummeting. They even took a photo of Mimi and John from some long-ago event but substituted John's body for the Monopoly man holding his hands out in distress. Lehman started calling in the loan it had given him on the assets—because they had fallen so much in value.

John started bullying Blake again, called him a shithead for thinking this was going to work. "You sold me all this crap, and now it's worth twenty-five cents on the dollar! And your firm, the firm that I enriched and paid fees to, the firm that employs you, who bought an apartment and a house in the Hamptons on the commission you earned from me, your firm is now cutting off my financing! I will tear you several new assholes if you don't fix this! You and your goddamn 'bulletproof'!"

Blake didn't know what to do. The market for these assets was extremely volatile, and right now there were absolutely no buyers, at any price. He knew it would be impossible to get a deal done with all the crap that he had sold to John. The assets just weren't good enough to structure a deal that would get past the rating agencies, which after years of rating everything AAA—whether great or lousy—were starting to feel the heat as well.

What he should have done was man up and tell John that he was on his own. While he would always be terrified of and intimidated by John, deep down Blake knew that John was living proof of what Warren Buffett once said about bear markets: "It's only when the tide goes out that you learn who's been swimming naked."

John Cutter was naked.

Still, Blake was afraid of John the way a dog way back in the pack was afraid of the alpha male. John had the loudest bark, could probably tear him to shreds, and what's more, would enjoy doing it in front of others. Blake also knew that John had cuckolded him in college. Then there was the small detail about the e-mails Blake had sent to John over the years—he knew that he'd gone over the line in his salesmanship and been way overly promissory. "Bulletproof" was his biggest regret. He didn't know if John would do anything about it, but he didn't want to risk it. He had to come up with something.

On the Friday morning before Labor Day, Blake thought he might at least get in a quiet day, but his cell phone rang at 9:30, just as he was about to set out for a run on Meadow Lane during his truncated vacation.

"Asshole," began a stream of expletives. It meant one thing: John.

"I want to see you and your ass already sitting in my office Tuesday morning when I get there at eight thirty a.m. I have reached the point of no return with you and your fucking brilliant ideas. From what I can tell, about forty percent of my fund is in crap you sold me."

"Okay, John, sure. I'll be there."

"And as usual, I only want to see you. Those useless guys you think can help me are the ones who usually call in my credit lines. The only time I want to see anyone else from Lehman is when I turn you in or sue you."

There was the threat Blake had been dreading.

Just then, Blake heard Grigsby call, "Sweetie! I hope you aren't going to be gone for too long. The boys want you to take them body surfing and I am going into town with Bitten."

With that one phone call, his Labor Day weekend was ruined. All he could think about was what the meeting would be like. He was growing tired of being called asshole this and fucking that.

On Tuesday morning, though, Blake was sure that he had to tell John he was on his own. He couldn't help him. He tried to call a few times to say he wasn't coming, but John wasn't in yet. It would be much easier over the phone, and he really didn't want to have to see him face-to-face. But then, after John called, he had no choice but to go to his office and get a new one reamed, and he knew it would be impossible to extricate himself from this nightmare.

But Blake did have a solution. He'd been thinking of it for a while. It was dangerous, not to mention illegal, but it just might work. After John got off the call that Renee had interrupted their meeting with, he said, "John, I think I know a way out of this for you."

"It better be good."

"I think it is, but it will involve a little, um, paperwork. Your problem—"

"*My* problem?" John erupted. "*My* problem? Blakey Blake, this is *your* fucking problem right now. First you sold me shit, and then you sold me more shit to try to get the deal with Bear done, and now I'm stuck with a huge pile of shit. That *you* sold me! And your solution to this problem better be, how shall I put it? Oh, I know! Fucking bulletproof."

Blake turned red. "Right, okay. Here's what I think we can do. The problem I'm having in coming up with a structure that will soak up your troubled mortgage assets and make them salable is that the assets are so weak; the performance is bad; they've been put on CreditWatch by the rating agencies like Moody's and S&P; they've collapsed in value; and you owe more on the loan than they are worth. To use an overused phrase, even I can't put lipstick on this pig."

"Blake, don't tell me what I already know. Get to the point before I pick up the phone to call the SEC on you, and then shove the same phone up your fat ass."

Blake swallowed hard. "I'm getting there. The problem is that the assets aren't worth enough. In order to create a new CDO out of your assets, we'd have to sell them for a lot less than you paid for them, which doesn't help you at all. So what we need to do is change the assets."

John repeated the phrase several times for sarcastic effect. "Change the assets? How the fuck do we just change the assets? Wave a magic wand? I can't sell them. I can't swap them. I can't hedge them at this point. And they're fucking held in fucking custody at your fucking firm!"

"Precisely," Blake said with a smile.

John's eyes narrowed to slits. "Talk."

Blake proceeded to outline what he called a "switcheroo"—swapping the account number of John's trashy assets for the account number of a body of assets belonging to someone else that was worth far more—in fact, worth almost the face amount of John's mortgage-related assets.

"You've got about five billion dollars face amount of various mortgage-related assets that together are now worth about one billion. I have examined the accounts of a few of my other clients and have identified about five billion face amount of mortgage-related assets in there that together are now worth about four and a half billion. What I think I can do is simply a little bookkeeping switcheroo—swap your assets for their assets.

"I will just change the CUSIP numbers in all the accounts to make the switch," Blake explained, referring to the universal code used to identify securities. "You know no one ever really checks these anyway. All of the accounts I'm thinking of are very large banks and funds with hundreds of billions in assets. The difference won't even be noticed until the next audit cycle at the end of the quarter in December, and even then it will just be chalked up to a clerical error. Oh, and you will need to fire your auditors."

"Fire my auditors? That is a huge red flag for all of my investors."

"John, fuck that. Fire them, blame your problems on their hard-line ways and inattention to detail. I've seen it done before. Hire new auditors—I know just who you should use—who won't ask to see your historical portfolio records until you've had time to alter them with the new CUSIP numbers."

So there it was. John took a deep breath, knowing that he was about to make the biggest decision of his life. He could kick Blake the fuck out of his office. That would be the right thing to do, but it meant that he would go under. Or he could accept Blake's scheme. He would be committing a crime, but maybe things would turn around before it was discovered and he would live to fight another day. And guys like John always lived to fight another day.

As John pondered, Blake stood there with a shit-eating grin. "John, it's bulletproof."

"Bullshit," John hissed. Then he made up his mind. "It better be, otherwise you will be getting fucked in the ass at Rikers . . . and I will be the one selling tickets."

Blake called John later that day and said he had already identified all the securities. Given how many of them and to be sure that it was all done correctly, not to mention that Blake did have a day job, it would take about a week to complete. By Thursday, September 11, "Bulletproof" was a done deal. As it turned out, there was barely a minute to spare, with the Lehman bankruptcy about to occur that weekend. As John followed the turn of events, he was desperate for Blake to get the records of all the securities out of there. Who knew what would happen if he couldn't get access to them? For now, at least, he was still in the game.

CHAPTER FIFTEEN

Children Should Be Seen and Not Heard

On Saturday morning, Renee woke up early to get a few things done before her 9:00 a.m. breakfast with Bitten and Grigsby. She couldn't wait to see if Grigsby had imparted her social graces to her daughter, not to mention if she embodied the values about which Grigsby had waxed prolific.

She decided to go for a run before breakfast so she wouldn't feel too bad about having the Goldie Lox scrambled eggs with sausage and a pumpkin muffin. Dollops of cream cheese and lox in her eggs along with gobs of butter and jam on her muffin were worth an hour of running.

Central Park was glorious in the fall. The colors of the trees were starting to change from yellow to orange to red. The air was crisp, and runners and bikers were taking advantage of the park and everything it had to offer, knowing that bitter winds and chills would soon set in. She decided to run the full six-mile loop and was struck by how particularly beautiful the north end of the park was, even though the hills were killer up there.

When she got back to her apartment, she took a quick shower and took the subway to 96th and Lex and walked to Sarabeth's on 92nd and Madison. During the weekdays, Sarabeth's was fairly quiet. Mothers planning school benefits met there and a few low-key business meetings took place, but it was on the weekends that it came alive as a well-known brunch spot. From 9:00 a.m. when it opened until midafternoon, a steady stream of people made their way there for its well-known menu. Renee knew if they went anytime after 9:30, there would undoubtedly be a wait because of the no reservations policy. It wasn't unusual later in the day for there to be a forty-five-minute wait, but at 9:00 they could sit right down.

She arrived at the restaurant exactly at 9:00 and, not seeing Grigsby there yet, went up to the hostess to say they would be three. The woman at the desk said, "Is your entire party here?" and Renee responded, "Not yet."

"Okay, well, let me know when they are and we will seat you."

Renee sat down in the waiting area, a narrow pathway in front of the bakery case. Muffins, cookies, and brownies stared at her plaintively, saying, "Eat me!" She assumed that Grigsby would be there in a minute or two since they lived only around the corner. Even though Renee didn't have kids, she knew it must be difficult getting out the door first thing on Saturday morning. She looked at her watch and realized it was almost 9:10. She noticed a few more people coming into the restaurant, but no Grigsby. Tables started filling up. At 9:17, she thought maybe Grigsby had gotten the day wrong and thought they were meeting Sunday, not Saturday. She thought maybe she should call her but realized she hadn't gotten Grigsby's cell phone or home phone. When Renee called her mother at work, she always called Donita's cell phone. She certainly didn't want to call her mother, who probably would have been very uncomfortable to know that Renee was meeting with her. By this time, it seemed that almost all the free tables were gone and people were starting to wait around her to be seated. Finally, at 9:27 Grigsby and Bitten walked in, a full twenty-seven minutes past the time they'd agreed upon.

Renee expected that Grigsby would apologize profusely, but instead all she said was, "Hi! How are you? So glad we were able to arrange this time. Bitten, please say hello to Mrs. Parker."

Renee was a little taken aback that Grigsby didn't even apologize, and at the same time she was bemused that she was introduced as Mrs. rather than Ms., as if any woman over the age of twenty-five would automatically be married. At this point, however, she wanted to at least get them seated. First she put out her hand and said to Bitten, a pretty little girl with blond hair held back with an oversize pink bow on the side, "Hi there! It's so nice to meet you. Please call me Renee."

Bitten looked at her, put her head in her mother's legs, and said, "I don't like that lady. She looks mean."

Grigsby said, "Oh, dear, she is a very nice person, and we are going to have a fun breakfast."

"No!" Bitten said defiantly, and stuck her tongue out at Renee.

Renee silently said a prayer, then replied, "Oh, kids! Why don't I tell them we are here so we can sit down."

She made her way back down the narrow aisle to the desk, which was by now three deep with people waiting to give their names.

"Um, yes. We are all here now. Parker. Party of three."

The woman behind the desk looked at Renee as if she'd never seen her before and said, "Yes, that's probably going to be about fifteen to twenty minutes."

"But I was here before," Renee pointed out. "We are with a little child. Isn't there anything you can do?"

The woman looked at her with neither emotion nor understanding of her plight. "I'm sorry, it's our policy not to seat guests until the whole party has arrived."

"Well, if there is a small table, that would be fine."

"Yes. What is the name again?"

"Parker. P-A-R-K-E-R."

Renee made her way back to Grigsby and said, "It looks like there is going to be a little bit of a wait for them to seat us."

"Oh, dear. This place does fill up with every person on the Upper East Side. We probably should have picked a different place."

No, Renee thought, you probably should have come at the time we agreed on, and we would already be well into our second cup of coffee and food would be arriving at our table by now.

The next fifteen to twenty minutes turned out to be twenty-three minutes and was pure agony. Bitten was in no mood to be waiting in a crowded area, whined to Grigsby persistently about how she was hungry, and wasn't any nicer to Renee than she had been when they'd walked in. Grigsby chatted incessantly about God knows what—parties, dresses, vacations, the usual laundry list, Renee supposed, of things stay-at-home, wealthy mothers talked about. Renee tried to break the agony by getting up several times to check on the table list.

Finally, the hostess called their name, and they were led up the stairs to one of the tables on the balcony. At least they were finally seated. Within a minute, however, Bitten had managed to drop her Barbie doll over the balcony, narrowly missing a tray of four flowers juice that was being delivered to a table below. She emitted a loud wail before Renee, in an effort to keep the imminent tantrum at a minimum, jumped up to go downstairs and get it, in large part so she could have thirty seconds to regroup before what she knew was going to be as miserable as the first twenty-three minutes—well, fifty, counting the time she had been waiting for Grigsby.

She came back to the table and resolved to try to extract something from this child, because she was going to have to write a letter of recommendation, given the agreement she had made with Grigsby.

"Bitten, I want to hear about the things you like to do!" she said in a cheerful voice.

Bitten didn't respond.

Grigsby, at least, interjected. "Sweet-pea, please answer Mrs. Parker's question. She wants to know what you like to do."

"Princesses," Bitten said in a pouty voice.

Finally, one word. Renee could do something with this.

"Princesses! I love princesses! Who is your favorite? Sleeping Beauty, Snow White, or Cinderella?"

No response.

"My favorite is Cinderella, especially when she goes to the ball and loses the glass slipper," Renee offered, hoping this would get Bitten talking more.

"I don't like that part."

"Sweetie, please don't be rude, and don't make Mommy upset. Mrs. Parker has been very nice to spend some time with us today and wants to talk to us about the school she went to, which you might go to next year."

Renee thought to herself that if she had ever done this as a child, she would have been hauled out by her mother or father by her ear and spanked, hard. She knew people now considered that to be a barbaric act that could create deep, long-lasting scars, but she couldn't imagine how this child was going to end up with sweet cooing in lieu of discipline.

She had never been as relieved to get a check as when it arrived, and she had her credit card ready to hand to the waitress right away. Technically, Grigsby should have picked up the check or at least offered to pay, but Renee just wanted to get out of there as soon as humanly possible, and Grigsby did not make even a halfhearted attempt to pay. Renee assumed it was a combination of both entitlement and her current financial condition.

As they came out onto the street, it was now littered with people waiting for their names to be called. Grigsby did say to Renee, "I really appreciate your doing this, and I will tell your mother on Monday that she will be back on full-time starting immediately. I'm so pleased you have had a chance to meet Bitten. As you can see, she is a very spirited little child, so I am sure you will have plenty to say about her."

"Oh, yes, indeed I will," Renee answered, baffled at how blind Grigsby was to her child's bad manners. But she continued, "I really appreciate what you are doing for my mother. I will send a letter to the school next week." She felt a knot in her stomach as she said it and wondered how she would manage to write a letter that wouldn't be a bald-faced lie.

As she watched them walk down the street toward their building on Park Avenue, she could tell that no matter how blind Grigsby might be about her daughter's personality, she loved her little girl a great deal. Renee could see her periodically hug her as they walked, swinging her hand as she held it. She wondered what would happen to Blake and Grigsby in the coming months and whether little Bitten would ever have any idea how bad things had gotten for her parents. More important, she wondered and worried how things would work out for them and what that would mean for her mother. She had saved Donita's job, for now.

On Monday morning when Donita came in to work, Grigsby pulled her aside and said, "I wanted to let you know that I will be able to keep you at the same schedule that you have been on after all. Just please don't say anything to Mr. Somerset. He isn't aware of this."

Donita smiled broadly. "Oh, thank you so much, Mrs. Grigsby. I really appreciate it. Today I'm going to polish all the silver."

"Wonderful, dear. It certainly needs it. I was going to mention it to you."

Grigsby went into her bedroom and went through her jewelry collection. She spent a fair amount of time examining every piece, figuring out which ones she would want to keep and which ones she might get the most for. This would not be a permanent situation. She took several pieces, placed them in satin pouches, and put them in her purse.

Normally, Sheldon would be waiting downstairs to take her wherever she needed to go and wait as long as she needed him to, but now that he was gone she was on her own. It was a nice morning, so Grigsby decided to walk the twenty blocks down to 72nd. She always enjoyed

Park Avenue during the day. It was actually quite busy. Doormen were helping mothers in and out of the buildings with strollers, people were going to doctor and dentist appointments. One could always tell when there was a luncheon for ladies going on, as several black town cars, Mercedes, and black SUVs would be idling outside. She loved her neighborhood.

When Grigsby got to 72nd Street, she turned left and walked past Lexington to a small Greek temple–style building nestled between two apartment buildings close to Third Avenue. "The Provident Loan Society" was etched on the front. If one had not known what it was, it probably would have been overlooked. She quickly glanced at both sides of the street to make sure she didn't see anyone she knew. She paused for a second and pushed open the door. She had never visited one of these places... and never thought that she would have to.

The Provident Loan Society had been created during long-forgotten economic crisis. In 1893, when the federal government had yet to think of itself as a source of social and economic support, pawnshops thrived but were not the sort of place people of a "certain class" would go to. A handful of prominent businessmen with names like Schiff, Loeb, and Vanderbilt created the Provident Loan Society as a source of short-term funding. While in the ensuing years credit became much more widely available, Provident remained as a discreet source of cash, particularly for women who needed money but didn't want their husbands to know. Many a fine piece of jewelry was hocked while temporary funds were obtained. Should all work out, the Harry Winston diamond ear clips, or Schlumberger bracelets, or Cartier trinity ring would be returned to their rightful owners. If not, they would appear for sale sometime later at Doyle New York, an Upper East Side auction house that periodically sold "abandoned collateral" for Provident.

Grigsby felt as if she had just stepped back in time. There was a poorly decorated room with a few benches and chairs. Clearly the décor hadn't been redone in many, many years. A large bulletproof divider separated the office area from the customer section. One or two tellers and a few other people were sitting at desks behind the Plexiglas. There were a few people waiting in line ahead of her. She went over to the waiting area and saw that there was a selection of magazines, *Town & Country*, *Vogue*, *Allure*, and *W.* The Provident Loan Society knew its customers.

Grigsby could see various signs on the wall that had information about loan terms. Most of it didn't make sense to her. She went and sat down with *Town & Country*, noting that it was the issue with her picture from last year's New York Botanical Garden Gala, not realizing that she had actually sat in front of a woman rather than behind her.

"Excuse me! I am ahead of you," the woman said angrily.

"Oh, I'm so sorry. I had no idea," Grigsby said apologetically.

She had kept her sunglasses on lest anyone recognize her, and they afforded her a good look at the other people waiting there. They all looked vaguely similar to her, well dressed with expensive handbags and shoes. They all still retained that rich, relaxed look but like her were holding up under the same pretense, so that others would not see how far they had fallen.

She waited for what seemed like aeons. In fact, it was close to twenty minutes. Finally, it was her turn. She went up to the counter and said, "Yes, I have these pieces I would like money for."

"Let me see them, please," said the man on the other side of the partition.

Grigsby took her satin pouches out of her purse and slid them through the window.

She felt like weeping as he roughly, at least to her, took out the Cartier française gold-and-diamond watch, her two-carat diamond studs, and the Elsa Peretti "diamonds by the yard" necklace. Even though she didn't wear these pieces often, it pained her to see a part of her identity get passed through the window.

"I'll give you three thousand for the watch, two thousand for the earrings, and seven hundred and fifty for the necklace," he said.

"That's all? The watch sells for ten thousand dollars alone!" She was aghast.

"Ma'am, this is not a jewelry store. This is a place where we lend money based on the collateral you post."

"Well, it's just that I thought it would be a lot more."

"I'm sorry. Look, you aren't alone. There are a lot of people coming to us to, ah, 'pay the rent' right now. Do you want it or not?"

Nearly $6,000 would be more than enough to pay Donita's extra wages for quite some time, as well as give Grigsby some badly needed spending money. Besides, this was bound to be only temporary. Things would get better pretty soon. They had to.

"Okay, I guess it will have to do," she responded.

"Fine, so the rate currently is two percent monthly, which works out to twenty-four percent annual percentage rate. It's a six-month loan. If you extend after that, the rate doubles. There's a two percent vault fee, and if you don't pay the interest, then the collateral will be put up for sale at auction."

This man could just as likely have spoken to her in Greek. She had no idea what he was talking about.

"Excuse me. Could you please explain that? I thought you were going to give me the money for the jewelry."

The man rolled his eyes. "Oh, boy. They're coming out of the woodwork today. Look, let me explain this to you slowly. We will give you a loan, but it has something called *interest*. All loans have interest. That means we charge you every month a rate of interest. It's currently two percent a month. So let's say I was going to be giving you ten thousand dollars. That means every month you would pay two hundred dollars in interest. The loan has a term of six months—so you have to pay us back in six months. If you want to renew for another six months, then you have to pay twice that amount, approximately four hundred dollars every month. If you don't pay the interest, or if you don't have the money to pay back the loan, then we sell your things at auction so we have a way to get paid back."

Grigsby looked at him, trying to absorb what he was saying. She would need to have a calculator to figure out how much 2 percent would be on $6,000. Obviously less than the example he gave her, but her head was spinning too much right now.

"Oh, dear. Well, I guess I don't have any other choice, then."

He gave her some forms to fill out and took the pieces away in paper envelopes. He came back a few minutes later with a check. She quickly put it in her purse and left. She couldn't breathe and was glad to be out of there.

She wasn't looking and bumped into someone outside on the street. "Grigsby! What are you doing here!"

She looked up in horror. Who of all people should it be but Thruce Cogson. She froze in utter panic.

"Oh, Thruce. Hi. How are you?"

"I'm fine, dear, but what the devil are you doing at this place?"

"I, ah. Well, I actually did not mean to come in here at all. I thought it was JPMorgan Chase. The branch moved, and this seemed like it was it."

"Oh, I see. Well, you'd better pay more attention next time. You don't want people thinking you're coming here!"

"I don't even know what that place is," she said, not sure if Thruce had bought her story or not.

"Oh, my dear. It is the Provident Loan Society. Every girl knows it's the place to get a little extra cash when the bank account is low."

"Oh, Thruce. Leave it to you to know these things. I had no idea. I'm just all over the place today. I've got all sorts of appointments, and I have a few minutes to spare right now, so I think I'll head over to Payard for a cappuccino. Would you like to come?" She was now fully out of her panic and back in the carefree swing of making it seem as if her life were one big playdate.

"Oh, darling, I wish I could. I'm going to Gracious Home for light-bulbs and then have to go down to the Village of all places, to look at some pieces of furniture for Bitsy. She asked if I'd give her my opinion."

"I forgot Bitsy is doing that renovation. I'm sure you will know what chairs she should have more than she would! Well, have a nice time. Will I see you next week at Jenny's luncheon?"

"Yes, of course. Wouldn't miss it. Surrounded by all you glam and gorg girls. Darling, where else would I be?"

"Thruce, you do know how to flatter all of us, don't you! Well, be sure to call me first and perhaps we can head over there together. I'd love you to see my suit. It's one of those new designers I can never remember... Lim, no, Lam. Oh dear, something like that. Whatever it is, it's divine. Plus we haven't had time to gossip lately. I haven't even seen you since New Yorkers for Children."

"I know, and there is some really good stuff going on. Winnie and Les Smith are getting a divorce."

"No, they are not! I can't believe it! Where did you hear that?"

"Not heard, *overheard*, darling. I was having cocktails at Doubles with Vladimir last week and Winnie was at a table nearby talking to a friend. She's going to have a tough time since they lost so much of their net worth in Bear Stearns stock. Apparently she is using Roland Deitrich, and couldn't be happier. He is *the* lawyer to use, you know. Everyone who is anyone goes to him."

Grigsby took note of that. Their conversation went on for a bit longer, and then she realized she was, in fact, going to be late, so she air-kissed Thruce and made her way toward Park Avenue.

As Grigsby walked away from him, she breathed a deep sigh of relief. It was a close call. She was pretty sure that she had gotten by Thruce, but one couldn't be too sure. As far as she was concerned, she was never going back to the Provident Loan Society, except to pay off the loan and get her jewelry back. But when she did she would have to be much more careful. She just couldn't risk being found out. It was too dangerous for her social standing. She wondered what was going to happen to her friend Winnie but didn't think that she should call her since Thruce had only overheard it. She wondered if the decline in their net worth had led to the divorce and wondered if that was in the cards for her as well.

Had Grigsby turned around, however, she would have seen Thruce Cogson looking very carefully in both directions before opening the door of the Provident Loan Society and stepping inside.

CHAPTER SIXTEEN

Family Party

Sasha had a mix of dread and resignation about Tuesday evening, October 21. It wasn't a difficult business meeting. She didn't have to fire anyone. She didn't have a meeting to review a portfolio with an unhappy client. It was worse. It was the annual American Museum of Natural History Family Party.

To raise money, and to teach children at an early age that philanthropy can be fun, many institutions held annual parties for the entire family. It was an opportunity to see an institution in all its glory, while getting up close to some of the most remarkable scientific discoveries, artwork, and cultural institutions in the world. The events were smorgasbords of games, clowns, and food. Kids were dressed to the nines, and their mothers weren't so bad themselves. It wasn't unusual for a four-year-old girl to be wearing a $600 dress from Bonpoint on Madison Avenue, and it also wasn't unusual for a mother to be wearing a $6,000 suit from Chanel on 57th Street. Fathers usually looked lost and out of place, coming straight from the office in whatever they had put on that morning. Sasha often thought there should be a corralled area where fathers could be picked up or dropped off by their wives so they could make calls and check their BlackBerrys.

Before she left for work that morning, Sasha gave Maura specific instructions about what time to meet her, who was to wear what, and exactly where she would meet them. "Remember, I will meet you at the front entrance on the right, by the coat check. We will meet there at five thirty. Samantha should wear her red taffeta dress. It is hanging on the door of her closet. Put Josh in a pair of khakis and the blue gingham button-down shirt with his little green tie. Oh, also his blazer. No, never mind. I'll just end up carrying it around all night. And girls"—she turned to Coco and Lily—"I want you both to wear the Bonnie Young dresses I got you last year." Sasha paused, waiting for the inevitable complaints that would come from them as to why they couldn't possibly wear the outfits they had begged her to buy seven months earlier on spring vacation.

"But we don't like those anymore," Lily whined.

"Lily, remember when we were buying them in Aspen, and you were desperate for me to do so. I said, 'These are very expensive. I'm going to want to see you wearing these to several events.' And you said, 'Okay, Mommy. We love them so much, we will wear them to every party next year.' Well, here we are at 'every party next year,' so you are wearing them this evening. No ifs, ands, or buts."

"But—" Coco started to say.

"And that would be the but. No ifs, ands, or buts. They are adorable dresses, and you will be the two best-dressed twelve-year-olds there!" Then, for good measure Sasha threw in a little guilt-inducing comment. "You know, girls, I work so hard, and it makes me so happy to buy you special things that are as beautiful as you are. Please don't make me so sad that I don't want to buy those things for you again."

She knew she had gotten to them and felt slightly guilty looking at their sad faces. They glanced at each other with resignation as well as distress that they had made their mommy upset, then said in unison, "Okay, Mama. We will."

"Those are my special girls. Okay, so I will see everyone later, then! Daddy will meet us there. We hope. Maura, you have money for the cab. Call me if there are any problems."

"Okay, no problem," Maura said dependably.

Sasha left for work with a feeling that something was bound to go wrong with this plan. It usually did.

Getting out of the office at 5:00 is easy for people with trains and buses to catch or jobs that can be neatly packed away until 9:00 the next day. Sasha did not have one of those jobs. When her phone rang at 4:55, it was a client calling who needed some handholding, given the markets. She couldn't quite say, "Sorry, I can't talk now. I need to take my children to a party." So when she left the office at 5:20, she knew "the plan" was already in severe jeopardy. It could take ten minutes to go three blocks in rush hour, let alone the forty or so up to the museum. She dialed Maura's cell phone to warn her that she was going to be late, but her voice mail picked up. Why did her voice mail always have to pick up when she needed to get in touch with her? She didn't leave a message but immediately called again, in the unrealistic hope that it would be answered this time. Voice mail again.

"Maura, it's me. I'm in the cab. I'm going to be late. I should be there by five forty-five, but call me so I know you have gotten this message."

She sent Adam an e-mail saying she was running late. He responded with, "K. In Mtg." Great. The part of the plan where Adam was to meet them was never one she depended on anyway.

As she sat in traffic, she became more and more anxious and found herself cursing everything while rocking back and forth in an unsuccessful effort to help the cab move forward. She tried Maura's cell again. Voice mail again.

"Maura, I'm really concerned I haven't heard from you. Please call me right away. I'm in traffic and going to be a little late. I'm at Sixth Avenue and Fifty-fourth—no, Fifty-fifth Street right now. Call me back. Okay?"

At 5:47, the cab finally approached the museum steps and she practically threw the money at the driver as she ran out of the cab and up the steps. She rushed to the appointed meeting place expecting to see all five of them looking lost and upset. What she saw, however, was no Maura, no Samantha, no Josh, no Lily, and no Coco. She looked all over the area, which by this time was full of screaming children, clowns on stilts, museum staff, and photographers. Maybe they were looking for her in another place. She saw no sign of them. Maybe they'd checked in and left a message with the staff for her. That must be it.

"Hi, I'm wondering if my nanny and children have already checked in—Silver? It would be under Sasha Silver?"

"Oh, hello, Mrs. Silver. No, I'm sorry, we don't see that they have. Let us know when they're here. We have their explorer's bags and maps ready for them!"

She tried to call Adam, in the highly unlikely if not ridiculous chance they'd called him or he was on his way, but she got his voice mail, too. "Adam, as usual, I can't find anyone. They're not where I told them to meet me. Did they call you? Have you left yet? Remember, we are meeting in the Hall of Mammals, by the elephants. I hate when this happens. I really can't manage to handle all of this. Why isn't anyone ever where they're supposed to be? When are you coming? Maybe you're almost here. Okay, bye."

She saw a few people she knew who looked like happy, calm, complete mother-and-child units. She feigned cheeriness, waving. "Hi! See you in there. Just waiting for the kids. They're on their way." She really felt like screaming, "Where the fuck are my kids and nanny? Why can't they ever be here when they're supposed to be? Wipe that smug look off your face, since you know I have no idea where they are."

At 6:17, she was practically in tears when all of a sudden she heard, "Mommy!" and saw Samantha running toward her with the other kids right behind her, followed by Maura, looking as if she had not a care in the world.

"Hi! I have been trying to reach you. Didn't you get my voice mails?"

"Oh, I forgot my phone at the apartment," Maura responded.

Sasha was speechless, but this wasn't the time and she was already too aggravated to get angry with Maura. She just wanted to get them inside. All of a sudden, she noticed the kids. Samantha had a huge stain on the front of her dress and was wearing sandals with socks instead of party shoes, which made her look completely bizarre. The twins had not worn their dresses but instead were in some glittery sequined outfits she did not recall buying for them. Then she looked at Josh and immediately gasped as she noticed he was missing a large chunk of hair.

"WHAT HAPPENED TO YOUR HAIR?"

The twins shouted out gleefully, "He cut it! He took a pair of scissors and cut it!"

"Oh, my God! Josh! Why did you do that?"

"I wanted to see what it would look like," came the very obvious response from a seven-year-old.

"Maura, when did this happen?" Sasha asked.

"I was in the kitchen, and I didn't know he had scissors. He doesn't listen to me," came her less-than-appreciated response.

"I cannot even speak. Okay, Maura, you can go. I'll see you tomorrow. Kids, let's go into the party and try to have some fun."

As they checked in and entered the party, a photographer came up and asked if he could get a shot. Sasha said yes but could not imagine what this ragtag group was going to look like: one mother, completely bedraggled by this point, a three-year-old looking like a refugee, a boy with part of his hair missing, and the twins, who looked as if they had just stepped out of Princessville-meets-Hookertown.

Once inside, every child wanted to do something completely different, and thus all sorts of whining ensued. Sasha was hoping against hope that Adam was almost there, but she'd yet to hear back from her last call, so she sent him an e-mail: "Found evry1. Pls let me know where u r asap."

In case Adam was nearly there, they went to the appointed meeting place for him. The Hall of Mammals was lined with dioramas of gazelles, water buffalo, and other animals in perfect replicas of their natural settings. There was a herd of elephants in the center of the room that looked so lifelike, they seemed impervious to the fact that they were neither in the African plains nor alive. As soon as Sasha and the kids walked in, though, Samantha took one look at them and, clearly terrified, said in her three-year-old voice, "I dink I beder get out of here right now. Say whaa?!" adding in a classic Hannah Montana line for good measure.

"Lily and Coco, please wait right outside with Samantha while Josh and I look for Daddy, okay?"

She took Josh by the hand and did a quick lap, knowing as she searched that Adam was as likely to be there as Harry Mullaugh!

"Okay, guys," she said, coming out of the hall, "no Daddy. Let's go see what else we can find that's interesting."

After twenty minutes of running around and not really seeing much, Sasha remembered that she'd come to the realization last year that four-inch heels were not the best shoe choice for an event of this nature, nor was carrying a Hermès Birkin bag that couldn't be slung over one's shoulder. She rubbed the ugly red mark where it was digging into her wrist, weighed down by what seemed like five pounds of leather and brass, and suggested to the kids they go eat.

The refreshment area was set up in the Milstein Hall of Ocean Life, a truly incredible room made all the more memorable by the ninety-four-foot giant blue whale that hung from the ceiling. It had been the centerpiece of the museum since 1969. Whenever she came to the museum, Sasha couldn't help but look up in awe and gasp at its magnificence, along with no small amount of terror, wondering if it could fall. On the two floors surrounding the whale were displays of every kind of marine life known, some in dioramas and some hanging from the ceiling. There were swordfish, sharks, and creepy terrifying creatures with long snaggly teeth and bulging eyes, found only in the darkest depths of the ocean. It was truly spectacular. However crazy these parties were, seeing how much the museum had made Sasha feel glad that she was able to expose the kids to this and hopefully start to teach them that giving money meant that places like this could exist. This room, more than any, made her pause. It was truly the world's best source of natural science from dinosaurs to space. Funny to think when President Teddy Roosevelt's father started the museum in 1869 along with others, natural history meant taxidermy displays of animals that man had killed. Now it was a testament to how vital the world was. Once, Sasha had taken a special tour and was able to go into the rooms where they stored fossils that had yet to be categorized or identified, even some that were still wrapped in the same newspaper they were in when they were found and shipped. The *Salt Lake City Gazette* 1910, read one. That was history in and of itself!

They made their way down to the tables set up on the main floor and managed to find five free seats, which was a miracle all by itself. They put their things on the table and flipped over the chairs to indicate they were taken. The twins went off on their own to get some food, and Sasha took Josh and Samantha to get theirs.

There were long serving tables with chafing dishes and platters overflowing with food. There were chicken nuggets shaped like dinosaurs, peanut-butter-and-jelly sandwiches shaped like stars, giant bowls of mac and cheese, hot dogs from a real hot dog cart, French fries, pizza, and a tower of different cookies. A full bar sat next to giant tubs bursting with juice and chocolate-milk boxes.

"Guys, this looks so yummy! What should we get?"

Samantha said, "Juice," and Josh said, "Cookies." Great, remind me never to ask an opinion, Sasha said to herself, and instead filled up a plate with assorted items, assuming that she would end up eating most of it herself.

They made their way back to the table and, to Sasha's dismay, saw that someone was sitting at four of the five chairs they had saved. Their belongings had been thrown on the floor, and the chairs that she had leaned carefully against the tables were now being used. She felt like one of the three bears.

"Um, excuse me. These were our seats. We had saved them and placed our things here," she said to the two women who were sitting there with two small girls.

The women basically ignored her. Sasha felt her blood start to boil.

"Excuse me. I said that we had saved these seats. These are my children's things here, which you've obviously thrown on the floor!"

One of the women looked at her. "I'm sorry, but there is no saving. We did not see anyone sitting here, and we have very small children who need to eat at exactly six forty-five. My daughter is hypoglycemic."

Sasha stared dumbfounded at these two women, so oblivious to common courtesy and manners. She looked them up and down. Both were dressed as if they were going to the Winter Antiques Show benefactors' party rather than a children's event. One was wearing an Oscar de la Renta green silk taffeta cocktail dress, while the other had on the Prada lace outfit from head to toe that had been in every magazine that fall. As Sasha recalled, the top and skirt retailed for something like $4,300. She couldn't see the woman's feet but was almost positive they were encased in five-inch Brian Atwood platform pumps. What's more, her feet probably didn't even hurt.

Sasha realized she had seen these women before at Yura, in the mornings as she was dropping off the girls at school. They took up the whole sidewalk, meaning others literally had to step onto the street to get by them. She also remembered seeing them one day in tennis dresses, sauntering down the street with racket bags slung casually over their shoulders. She almost laughed. That would be nice, she thought, just to go off for the morning and play tennis without a care in the world. That was the same day she had forgotten about Josh's doctor's appointment, and it came up on her BlackBerry calendar as she was in the middle of a meeting with a new pension fund they were pitching for business. Amazingly, Adam had been free that day and managed to rush up and get him there.

Sasha knew it was a losing battle to try to fight these women without truly causing a scene and embarrassing the kids. So she muttered, "Typical stay-at-home bitches. Hope your husband's hedge funds blow up," just loudly enough that they could hear only part of what she said, while she angrily grabbed her things. She knew it was absolutely terrible, not to mention unlike her, as soon as it came out of her mouth, but it still felt good to say it.

"Excuse me!" said the one with the hypoglycemic child, but by that point Sasha had managed to spirit herself, the kids, their things, and two overloaded plates of food across the room.

After a solid five minutes of walking around the room, she finally found three seats. She had Samantha sit on her lap, while Josh wanted to go over to where there was a band playing, and each of the twins had her own seat. She kicked off her shoes under the table and wiggled her toes, hoping to get some feeling back into them. Her wrist was basically numb by this time, and she rubbed it in an attempt to get it back to normal.

"Sasha! Hello, dear. How nice to see you."

She looked up to see Grigsby Somerset standing across from her.

"Hi, Grigsby. How are you?" She cringed over her word choice, as Sasha had found that asking people how they were these days could be a loaded question. Someone might have lost a job or a lot of money, and in some cases both.

"Oh, well, you know. Very busy. Still running around to school interviews and tours and trying to get everything done."

Sasha knew this was somewhat of a bullshit answer, meaning Grigsby probably didn't want to say more than that.

"Oh, right. Did you and Renee ever connect on Spence?" she asked.

"Yes, as a matter of fact, we did. She was actually most helpful and is writing a letter for Bitten."

"I 'm so glad to hear that. I think she has a fair amount of influence there. By the way, where is Bitten, and where are the boys?" Sasha said, realizing none of the children were near her.

"The boys didn't want to come, so they're at home, and Bitten is with her friend and their sitter right now upstairs in the Digging for Dinos exhibit. They're supposed to meet me in a few minutes down here."

Sasha wondered how to get that gig. Grigsby had actually come to the party yet didn't have to be running all over the place with kids. It sounded pretty good. At that moment, two other seats at their table opened up, so Sasha said, "Why don't you sit down and join us. I'm waiting for Adam, but I don't think he's even here yet."

"Certainly. I'd love to." Sasha could see Josh was still jumping up and down to the band, and now there was an extra seat for Samantha, so she wouldn't have to be on her lap any longer. Samantha, however, had no intention of being removed from Sasha's lap, so one chair remained empty.

Grigsby sat down, placing her Chanel bag on the table in front of her. Sasha noticed that it looked rather worn. She'd always known Grigsby to have the latest model of every "it" bag reported on by all the magazines.

There was an awkward moment. Sasha felt as if Grigsby wanted to ask her something. "Grigsby, is everything all right? I know we only know one another from social events, but you seem a little, ah, distracted."

"Oh no. Everything is fine. I just have a lot going on with the school search and everything."

Sasha noticed that while Grigsby had managed to evoke her usual cheery tone, it seemed a bit flat, and she thought she noticed her eyes watering just the slightest.

"Yes, that can be overwhelming," Sasha responded. "And obviously this year there is so much else on everyone's mind with the state of the economy and the markets. Of course, you probably know that more than I do because of Blake. If you don't mind my asking, how is he doing? I assume he is at Barclays now, right?" she asked a little tentatively.

Grigsby looked down. Sasha had a feeling that she was about to let her "not a care in the world" guard down.

"Sasha, I don't know what to do. Promise me you won't say anything to anyone. I don't understand anything that is happening right now. But things are really quite bad. We had a great deal of money in Lehman stock, which we borrowed against to buy our houses and things. Now Blake says that we don't have anything left. He won't let me spend, and I don't know when or if things will change. We might have to sell our house in Southampton. I just can't believe it. My life wasn't supposed to go down at all. I know you understand more about these things than I do, and certainly more than any of my friends, and I can't tell them anyway. My whole position will be in danger. Do you have any idea of how long it took me to get where I am?"

Sasha was stunned, but not because the Somersets were in this situation. Stories like this were becoming commonplace across the city right now, and they had started the previous spring with Bear Stearns. At least Bear shareholders were bought out of their stock at $10 per share. Lehman stock was zero. What Sasha was surprised at was how up front Grigsby was with her. Exposing weakness could be social death. If word got out, it wouldn't be long before the whole city knew.

"Of course I won't say anything. But what does Blake say? Is he at Barclays now? From what I hear, they are paying them well so they won't lose them."

"Really? I didn't even know that. Yes, he has been kept on at Barclays, though he barely talks to me, except to wave a bill in my face or tell me I can't do something. We aren't even going to Palm Beach at Christmas! How can I not go to Palm Beach at Christmas? Everyone is there. What will people say?"

"Well, I think there are a lot of people that will be staying home or are already cutting things out. I'm sure you can think of a way to make it sound like it was your decision not to go to Palm Beach," Sasha suggested, while thinking to herself that this ranked as one of the stranger conversations she had ever had at an event like this.

"Yes, I suppose I could. But everything else is so confusing and upsetting. I don't know what is going on with Blake. I am totally in the dark."

"Mama, I want more juice," Samantha whined, interrupting them.

"Okay, sweetie, just a minute. Let me finish talking with Mrs. Somerset."

"Mama, nowwww."

Sasha was about to say something to Samantha when all of a sudden she heard a shriek and looked in horror to see the two women who had taken her seats at her original table approach Grigsby. Sasha's back was to them, so they didn't seem to notice her, thank God. "I'm just going to get Samantha some juice. Be right back," she said quickly to Grigsby as she swiveled around so the women wouldn't see her. "Come on, sweetie."

Sasha walked only a few steps away, though, as she wanted to hear the conversation.

"Grigsby! It's so good to see you," said the woman who was wearing the Prada lace outfit. Sasha decided she was going to call her Lacey. "I just got back from the Ashram this morning. I was there for two glorious weeks. You have got to go there. It's divinely fabulous!"

"Darling, it sounds wonderful," Grigsby responded. "I have been so busy at home, I don't know when I can get away with everything going on."

Then green Oscar dress piped up. Sasha nicknamed her Kermit. "Bill and I thought we would see you and Blake last week at the Ackermans' hoedown party. Where were you?"

"Oh, I was stuck at home with the worst flu. I was so disappointed to miss it. I'm sure it was wonderful as always."

Sasha wondered how long she would have before Samantha would demand juice again. She was dying to hear the rest. "Samantha, want to play the fun game on Mommy's BlackBerry?" Samantha was always a sucker for Brickbreaker, even if she couldn't really play it. She just moved the cursor back and forth, once in a while randomly hitting a ball. She would yell, "Yay, me!" Samantha seemed amenable to this idea, enabling Sasha to continue listening.

"Well, you were missed. Anyway, can*not* wait till Christmas. Steffi's party will be a blast as always. I hope her lawn will be done," Lacey said. "What a drag. You'll be at the Breakers as always, I assume."

"Oh, I cannot believe I didn't tell you when I saw you Monday at Yura. Blake and I have decided that we are going to have an old-fashioned northern Christmas. We are going to Southampton and having Christmas dinner at the house. We are going to pop corn in the fireplace, string cranberries, and go for sleigh rides. The children are so excited, and I can't wait myself. It will be so nice to give Palm Beach a break for a year."

Sasha smiled overhearing this. Grigsby could handle this. Kermit and Lacey seemed quite surprised, but the more Grigsby made the old-fashioned Christmas seem so like Currier & Ives, the more they appeared to have bought it and almost appeared to be jealous that they weren't doing the same thing. Sasha chuckled at how malleable these women were, imagining them all renting a sleigh to take them on the Long Island Expressway the following year. They'd probably pay to have snow made to whisk them straight to Southampton! Then, with a whirl of air kisses and shrieks, they were gone.

Sasha ran to get Samantha's juice. When she came back, she said to Grigsby, "Not bad. I think you got them with the winter wonderland thing. Look, Grigsby, I hope that things work out. Just try to hang in there. Let me know if there's anything I can do to help you. And remember, there are a lot of people who have it worse than us."

Sasha noticed that Grigsby looked at her with a mixture of pleasure that she had gotten Kermit and Lacey to buy her story, and complete confusion that anyone could have it worse than she did right now.

At that moment, Sasha's cell phone rang. Praise the Lord! Could it be? It was Adam! The party was going to be over in fifteen minutes, but at least he had made it. She told him where they were, and within a few minutes he was coming toward them, looking smooth and unfrazzled, unlike the vast majority of the fathers who had been there since 5:30.

"Daddy!!" screamed Samantha and the twins as if they hadn't seen their father in weeks. Sasha went to pick up Josh, who was rolling on the floor to the Sugar Beats' rendition of Rihanna's "Disturbia." His khakis had a large splotch of brownie ground into them, and his tie was around his head like a bandanna, thankfully covering his "haircut" quite nicely. She carried him over to Adam, now holding Samantha. They traded children, since Samantha weighed about twenty pounds less than Josh. It was just at that moment that Samantha turned toward her and promptly threw up juice all over Sasha's Alexander McQueen suit.

CHAPTER SEVENTEEN

Grigsby Makes a Decision

Normally, Grigsby loved the late fall. Her furs were out of storage, and she was looking forward to the galas that took place between Thanksgiving and Christmas: the New York Botanical Garden Winter Wonderland Ball; the New York City Ballet Fall Gala; the Rita Hayworth Alzheimer's Association Gala; and the UNICEF Snowflake Ball. Then it would be off to Palm Beach for Christmas vacation in their regular suite at the Breakers. It really made things so much easier with the children to have the extra space.

But things had been unusual since the day after Labor Day and showed no signs of returning to normal anytime soon. Grigsby struggled to understand what was going on in the outside world, because it certainly was affecting her world. After the Provident Loan, she did her best not to buy anything, but it was nearly impossible to be out with a group of her friends and not pick up something, even a D.L. candle; or to be at an event and not bid on something from the silent auction. Her life until this point was all about getting whatever she wanted. It was too much to ask her to turn on a dime and not spend one.

What's more, she and Blake were barely speaking with each other. On top of the money situation, he was acting so odd. He was in and out at all sorts of hours, flying into a rage if she asked him anything. He had basically missed every school interview, and she could use the Lehman excuse just so many times. She hoped that with Renee's letter, their chances at Spence were good, but she wouldn't know for sure until February, which seemed a million years away.

Things came to a head one evening. Blake came in at 9:30. He hadn't even called to say that he was going to be late. He walked past her without saying anything and went straight to the liquor cabinet, poured himself a glass of Scotch, took one sip, and then threw it against the wall. Pieces of glass flew everywhere; a brown trickle of alcohol dribbled down the Quadrille wallpaper, and a few large spots appeared on the Scalamandré silk pillows on the sofa nearby.

"What is wrong with you?!" Grigsby screamed.

Blake turned and looked at her with a glare that scared her. He turned back around and got another glass and poured himself another drink.

"Blake, I said what is wrong with you!? Look what you just did to the wallpaper and my Scalamandré pillows!"

This time, he turned and started to speak. "You know what, Grigsby? I don't give a shit about your goddamn pillows or your fucking wallpaper."

"Blake, I won't have you speaking to me like that," she said. "You walk in here hours past when you should, you don't call, and then you have a temper tantrum. And you certainly don't need to curse at me. Now please explain to me what is going on."

"Read the fucking papers, Grigs. Just read the fucking papers. I'm tired of trying to explain."

With that, he turned and walked out of the apartment, not returning until well past midnight. At least she thought she heard the door open. He slept in the guest room.

She was done. This was not what she had signed up for. When they were married ten years ago, it was an idyllic wedding, a portent of the life that was to follow. Blake had proposed with a ring in a Tiffany blue box. Their wedding picture had been in *Town & Country*. The cake was by Sylvia Weinstock, and her dress was the most simple yet elegant white Carolina Herrera. They had honeymooned at the Four

Seasons on Nevis for two perfect weeks. Everything in their lives was supposed to be wonderful from that day forward. And it had been, at least until now.

If Blake couldn't provide her with what she needed, she would have to find someone who could. So she decided she had finally had enough. It was time to get a divorce lawyer.

Roland Deitrich was the one everyone knew, and of course Thruce had told her that Winnie Smith was using him. But her friend Nini, who had just gone through her second divorce, swore by Lucille Smith, so Grigsby made an appointment to meet with her.

Lucille Smith, known as "Lucifer" by opposing counsel, had been in the matrimonial law profession for close to forty years and was legendary in the business. She was the only attorney to have scored a divorce hat trick, representing a Perelman, a Trump, and a Bronfman in one each of their assorted divorces. She dressed impeccably and had a youthful, beautiful face framed by short silver hair, making her look similar to Meryl Streep's characterization of Miranda Priestly in *The Devil Wears Prada*. She was brash, smart, and a mother hen who could turn into a mother bear when it came to protecting her clients. She played hard but not dirty, and when another attorney leaked something to "Page Six" or any other papers, she sprang into action.

Lucille had little patience for the entitled or weak, and had a little test of potential clients in order to see what type of stamina they would have when it came time to deal with the inevitable punches above and below the belt. She would arrange the first meeting with a potential client for late afternoon and then suggest they go out for a drink. If the woman ordered a glass of wine, a gin and tonic, or a martini, she would pass the test, and Lucille would stick with her. But if the woman ordered a Diet Coke, wine spritzer, Cosmopolitan, or, worse, plain water, she would be gently passed off to Lucille's elder, "gentlemanly" partner, Irving Dylan, who knew the law but was hardly the tiger she was. The client would still get the best legal representation but would not deal directly with Lucille. It was just her way of sorting out the fittest, for divorce is hardly for the weak-minded.

Grigsby wasn't sure what to wear to meet a divorce attorney, so she pulled out the camel's hair Michael Kors suit from last fall's collection. It had a crisp and conservative look. She imagined it was what she might wear if she went to an office every day. Yet at the same time, it had an edge to it, especially with the matching mink scarf. She grabbed the brown Birkin she'd gotten as her "prize" for having Bitten. As a last minute thought, before she left she went back to the bedroom and took out her contacts to put on her glasses so she would look smarter.

The offices of Smith & Dylan were located in midtown, in the GM building on 58th and Fifth. There were spectacular views of Central Park, not to mention Bergdorf Goodman.

"Mrs. Somerset, it's a pleasure to meet you. Lucille Smith," said Lucille as she walked into the conference room, her hand outstretched.

"Thank you for seeing me."

"Yes, I'm sorry that four thirty today was all I had available, but let's talk for a while and then perhaps we can go out for a cocktail. I have an appointment to meet someone a bit later."

"Oh, um, certainly. Well, that would be lovely."

"So, why don't you tell me a little about yourself, your husband, and what has brought you here today."

"Well, I'm afraid things just don't show any signs of changing for the better. You see, my husband, Blake, has been at Lehman Brothers, and ever since the bankruptcy... well, before that, really, he began acting oddly. I can hardly communicate with him at all now, and he isn't going to be able to pay for anything that I need."

Lucille thought the last comment a bit odd, but she'd heard worse over the years and simply said, "Ah, I see. Has there been any affair that has gone on? Now or in the past?"

"Oh no. Well, at least I don't think so. I mean, Blake has been too wrapped up in things with work. He is good-looking and all, but it is hard to imagine he would be interested in anyone but me."

Lucille didn't comment on that, though she thought of the supermodel she represented whose husband was having multiple affairs, so she found it unlikely that any man didn't have at least one wandering eye. In any case, there would be time to figure that out later.

"When you say acting oddly, what do you mean by that?"

"Well, starting last summer, he was very distant and distracted, even on vacation, and didn't spend enough time with me and the children. Then he didn't make any calls for ongoing schools and wouldn't go to the Spence interview or any others, and I've had to make excuses for him, and now he says that I can't spend anything."

Lucille was wondering if she even would make it to the cocktail hour. She imagined Grigsby ordering a Shirley Temple. But she patiently proceeded with her questioning.

"Would you say the marital problems are the same from his perspective?"

"Excuse me?"

"I mean, is he having issues with you? Has he met with a matrimonial attorney?"

"Oh, well, I hadn't quite thought about that. I'm, ah, I don't think he necessarily feels as strongly as I do, but I can't imagine that he is happy. He gets very angry with me. I don't think he has been to see anyone yet. We haven't talked about it."

"What would you estimate the net worth of you and your husband is?"

"Well, I really don't know. It used to be a lot more, certainly. I think at some point it was probably about fifty million, but I am not sure."

"And do you have access to any financial information? Brokerage and bank statements?"

"No, I don't think they come to the house. Since he worked at Lehman, most of our money was there through the private bank. I haven't ever really paid attention to it."

"I see. Do you have any idea of what your financial costs are each year? How much you spend on your homes, vacations, clothing, school, and so on?"

Grigsby was confounded. She had never thought about these things. It was Blake's job. "Well, it's probably easiest to start with the things I do know, like clothing. Let's see, I guess on clothes, is it seven, no, maybe nine. I'd say nine a month."

"Nine? Nine what?" Lucille asked, fairly certain of the answer.

"Oh, nine thousand."

Lucille had seen this movie many times before. "Okay, what about personal trainers or the gym, hair, things like that?"

"Well, Gerardo comes four times a week and that's a hundred and fifty each time. He's my trainer. We have the gym in the building, so I don't belong to one. Except in Southampton, where I go to spin class. That's maybe three thousand during the summer. Hair, I go to Blandi every two months. I think that's usually five hundred each time for cut and highlights. Of course, when I go to parties I get hair and makeup done, so that's about five hundred each time."

"How often is that?"

"Oh, probably once or twice a month."

"What about vacations?"

"I'm really not too sure. We go to Aspen and Palm Beach, usually."

"And where do you stay?"

"Little Nell's and the Breakers."

"Do you think that fifty thousand is a good enough number?"

"I guess so. I'm not sure."

They continued going through items, from nannies, to drivers, to the diamond necklace that Blake had gotten her on her fortieth birthday, to their tenth-anniversary trip with four couples where they rented a villa in St. John's. If Grigsby didn't know the costs, Lucille was able to estimate. Their annual expenses were probably in the $1.5 million range. Of course, this was before their change in fortunes over the last few months. Lucille had enough information at this point.

"Well, my dear, my advice to you is to keep spending. You need to maintain the lifestyle so that we can prove that you have a standard of support that you will need once you are divorced. Of course, should you file for divorce, we will need to document all of these expenses and make sure that all of the assets have been kept within the marriage, and that nothing has been sent or slipped out to other parties."

Grigsby looked confused. "I'm not sure what you mean by that."

"Well, we would have to determine if Blake has hidden any assets from you. It's quite common, I'm afraid, especially by men on Wall Street. They control the funds and usually are the ones that have the relationship with the financial advisor. Or—and I'm not saying this is the case—if there have been any extramarital affairs, we will need to find out if he bought jewelry, furs, things of that nature."

Grigsby was aghast. As much as she knew she had little choice other than to be here, it was so sordid and dreadful to think of. Blake with a girlfriend? Buying jewelry for someone else? The thought was inconceivable, especially because he wouldn't even know what to buy her if she didn't put an ad from Cartier or Tiffany on his nightstand. But if it was true, she was going to get everything she could from him.

"Well, how does it get decided? Do you just tell him this is what I should get?"

Lucille looked at Grigsby long and hard and then looked at her computer. "Oh dear," she said, "I've just gotten an e-mail from a client. It's an emergency I must deal with. I am going to ask my partner, Irving Dylan, to step in and handle things. He will be able to take it from here. Mrs. Somerset, it's been wonderful meeting you."

And with that, Lucille left, asking her assistant to please find Irving right away, knowing that she wouldn't have made it through a single sip of a cocktail with Grigsby.

CHAPTER EIGHTEEN

Lunch at Fred's

Sasha was more miserable than ever.

Her cell phone rang, and she saw that it was Renee calling.

"Hey, how are you?" she said, trying to sound cheerful.

"I'm okay. Thought I'd see if you wanted to have lunch Wednesday or Thursday. John isn't going to be here, so I have a little more flexibility than I usually do."

Sasha looked at her schedule. "Yes, I would love to. Let's meet at Fred's at Barneys. Twelve thirty on Wednesday good for you? I've been desperately craving their Belgian fries."

"Twelve thirty it is. I'll make a reservation."

Sasha usually went to restaurants in midtown, closer to her office, selecting them based on whom she was meeting. Lever House was for the fun, younger people she knew, but she reserved San Pietro or the 21 Club for the more conservative or older businessmen she met. It was important to tailor the location to the person. It could make all the difference in the outcome of a meeting or the cementing of a relationship. But being able to slip uptown for lunch at Bergdorf's or Barneys was a luxury for her. Plus, after lunch she could take the escalator down and do some shopping, which she never had a chance to do. She still felt like a guilty teenager, and although it was ridiculous, she imagined herself running into someone she knew who would say, "Sasha Silver. What are you doing here? Shouldn't you be at work?" Somehow she felt like she would be in trouble.

There were few meals as simple yet decadent to her as lunch at Fred's. From the towering tray of French country bread, delicately served with silver tongs, along with extra-virgin olive oil for dipping, to the paper cone of Belgian *pommes frites* placed in front of her like a fresh-cut flower arrangement along with three different dipping sauces, ketchup, mayonnaise, and a Russian dressing, each in its own ramekin. It was all mouthwatering. Sasha almost always had Fred's chopped chicken salad with extra balsamic vinaigrette. She usually took the rest home with her, it was so large. At Fred's, everything tasted that much more luxurious; even the Diet Coke with lemon somehow tasted better.

She arrived at the ninth floor and gave her name at the desk, happy that on weekdays (unlike on weekends) they took reservations. The receptionist said she was the first to arrive and told Sasha she would seat them when her guest was there. As she was about to sit on the banquette in the hallway, she saw a tall blond woman sitting inside at a nearby table, in perfectly faded Levi's, a crisp white shirt, and brown cowboy boots. Sasha went over to her and said, "Jessica! Oh, my God, how are you? I haven't seen you in forever!"

"Sasha! Hi, it has been a long time. I think at least a year. Life is crazy! Do you want to sit for a minute?"

"Sure, I'm just waiting for my guest. I would love to."

Sasha had gone to the Wharton School with Jessica Stark, and they had been great friends and confidantes for many years. They both understood what it was like dealing with the pressures of work, followed by the pressures of work once they had children. Jessica, however, had decided she wanted to get off the ride three years ago, just before Sasha had Samantha, and she'd stopped working. Their friendship wasn't the same after that. Sasha found it became harder for her to connect with Jessica when her life was consumed only by her husband and kids. Thus, their great friendship quickly became a casual one. Jessica's husband had been at Merrill Lynch for years, always on a plane or train to somewhere, leaving Jessica to keep things battened down at home.

Sasha had very mixed feelings about Jessica's move. It was terrible, but Sasha had felt abandoned by someone she'd thought was a kindred spirit. She missed the old Jessica and perhaps begrudged her slightly the life she had now. At the same time, she was also confused at why Jessica would have wanted to give up the identity that she had worked so hard to get.

"So what have you been up to, Jess? How is Guy?"

"Well, I'm truly exhausted and stressed beyond belief," she started to say. Sasha held her breath, expecting Jessica to go through the familiar laundry list of domestic complaints that would seem easy compared with Sasha's life, but instead Jessica said, "It's been so long since we've talked, so I'm not sure if you knew that Guy decided to start a new company about eighteen months ago, in the middle of everything going on in the world. It's been incredibly difficult. It's been nothing but almosts and if onlys. If he had started three years ago, you know how many private equity firms would have thrown money at him? There would have been giant piggy banks with the stoppers out dropping dough on him! The same business plan he has now would have probably gotten to term sheet within a few weeks, and they would have said his projections for an exit in five years would happen in three. But I don't need to tell you that institutional wallets have shut tight."

"Yes," Sasha said, wondering who the heck was going to buy BridgeVest right now, not that she would know, since she still was in the dark about what was happening.

"We are still trying to sustain ourselves with what the potential valuations will be *if* we raise the money, and *if* the business plan is executed, and *if* we still can exit in five to seven years, but the reality is that *if* we continue supporting the business out of our savings with no funding in sight, I don't know if we will have anything left."

Sasha was shocked. "Oh, my gosh, Jessica, I had no idea. It is really tough out there right now. Private equity firms are terrified to do anything. Is there anything that looks promising at all?"

"I really can't say. I think Guy has met with every firm named after every street or rock in Greenwich, and every word in the Latin and Greek language. God, they're all so uncreative in their names, it makes me laugh, although he did meet with a company called Scorpion Capital. That one actually cracked me up. I keep asking if there isn't a Goldilocks Capital, or a Cherub Capital, but so far they have yet to appear. I'll tell you, if I were him, I think I'd probably get up in the middle of a meeting and tell these guys to go fuck themselves. Actually, I think it might make them want to do the deal. You know, show that he has balls and all. That's how Wall Street is, right?

"Anyway, I'm on eggshells. It seems like I always ask him the wrong questions at the wrong times. I am exhausted from getting my hopes up whenever he says he met with someone who said something like 'You have the right business at the right time.' The worst of it is, with our money situation, I'm going to have to go back to work, and I don't know how the hell I can get a job right now with all the layoffs going on. I mean, you have how many Bear Stearns people out there, not to mention Lehman and then everyone else? I can't imagine someone saying, 'Oh, yes, let's hire a woman who left the industry three years ago to go live a life of leisure.' It's really bad, Sasha. I never in a million years could have thought this would happen. I wouldn't have quit."

Sasha was sobered. She felt really bad for Jessica. It was yet another example of how the world in which she lived was disintegrating. Above all, she was staggered at the stupidity and hubris of the people who ran the financial system. What were any of them thinking? Didn't everyone realize the bubble *always* bursts, and the bigger it gets, the more people it destroys? Why didn't any of them stop and say "Enough is enough" or admit they didn't understand what their own companies were doing?

"Jessica, I wish I could think of some way to help you," Sasha said, and she honestly did. "We are going through some changes in our business right now as well, so I understand how unsettled the markets are.

If I hear of any positions that would be good for you, I will definitely let you know. I'll try to think if there are any off-the-beaten-track firms that Guy might not have been to yet. Oh, I know, what about Old Line Capital in Fairfield?" she asked.

"Seen 'em. Passed."

"Friedman, McCann and Herremer?" Sasha asked hopefully.

"Ugh. Total assholes, gave a letter of intent and then passed at the eleventh hour. They said they 'weren't the right investor.' Like they shouldn't have known that before the LOI?"

"Oh no. TF Ventures?"

"Don't do early stage. Oh, except two years ago they backed a company exactly like Guy's, only it was earlier stage than he is now."

"Geez, Jessica, it does sound like Guy has seen everyone. I'll keep thinking. Hang in there." Just then, Sasha saw Renee come in the restaurant, so she said good-bye and went to give Renee a hug.

"Hey, sweetie, how's it going?"

"Things are pretty good, actually. I just want to run something by you. But tell me how things are with you. Anything further on this sale?"

Sasha took a deep breath and responded, "Not really. I'm so upset, I just don't know what to do. It's all really distressing. Clearly, there have to be things going on, but I feel like I'm going to read about this in the paper when it happens. I don't understand why Harry told me about the deal if he doesn't want me to be involved. I feel like crying, to be honest."

"It is odd. Maybe you should just come right out and ask him," Renee said, trying to be helpful.

"That won't do any good. He'll just stonewall me like he always does or end up snapping at me and questioning my loyalty as a 'team player.'" She made air quotes with her hands.

"Well, what about going to see the head guy at the parent company. What's his name again?"

"Kirk? I don't know. I'm not even sure if he will see me. He'll probably blow me off, too. It's just a lost cause, and I probably should just wait around to see what happens. I don't know, maybe I should just quit. It's not like everyone wouldn't be thrilled up in Springfield, and I could spend more time with the kids, and you know, just hang out and shop." Sasha was trying to sound amused by it, but Renee could see that her eyes were starting to water and her voice was cracking a little.

"Well, it seems like you need a plan at least to move forward."

"No, there's no point in doing anything. I really might as well just give up."

Renee paused for a second and then said, "Sasha, I'm gonna say one word to you right now. Stop! For as long as I've known you, I have always been awed by your ability. You have moments of being down, but then you get right back up again. Frankly, every time I have seen or talked to you recently, you are always complaining about what's happening, but don't seem interested in moving toward possible solutions. You let these guys up there, notably Harry, treat you like crap. You gotta suck it up, girl, and decide what you want the rest of your life to be like. Do you want to spend the next however many years, or even months, letting assholes like Harry keep you out of things? Or do you want to take charge of your life and make your own decisions? And forgive me for saying it, but you'd go nuts about two days into not working. You need to be out there doing things."

Sasha was a little taken aback. Leave it to Renee to speak her mind. Part of her wanted to get mad and defend herself, but part of her knew that Renee was speaking the truth. Sasha had spent so much of the last several weeks pouting about being left out that she was more focused on what she could not control than what she could.

"Wow, Renee, I guess I didn't realize I was sounding like that."

"Well, you have been. Look, I love you, and my gosh, you are older than me and so much more successful, but you know how I am. If I see something going on that doesn't seem right to me, I'm going to say something about it. Besides, everything bad that is happening to you is actually an opportunity to look for something positive."

"Yes, you're right. I need to start looking at things that way. So, what would you do if you were me?"

"Well, first I'd sit down and decide what it is that I want. Do I want to confront Harry and tell him that I'm on board with whatever the sale brings, or do I want SAMCO to be sold separately, or do I want to leave altogether? Then I'd sit down and figure out the strategy to accomplish that. If Harry is going to play his usual mind games, then you have to call Kirk. Harry isn't going to change, so you need to."

Sasha thought about that. She knew it was time for her to take control, which meant she was going to have to stop being reactive. She also was thinking of her meeting with James Ullman, who had said some similar things to what Renee had. Maybe she was finally realizing she had nothing left to lose.

"Renee, I am going to call Kirk and find out what is going on. When something does finally happen, someone will have to let me in on it, but I'm ready to find out now. Leave it to you to set me straight."

"Of course. If not me, then who else?"

Sasha again thought of James Ullman. She really needed to introduce the two of them. "Okay, well, now that my problems are solved," she said, grinning, "can we change subjects? What did you want to talk to me about?"

"Well..." Renee took a deep breath. "As you know, John is certainly the way everyone describes him. He can be such an asshole, it's unbelievable. Needless to say, the way the markets have been, he's always in the worst mood, and the fund is not doing well at all. But it is truly flabbergasting the way he treats people. Sometimes he walks up to the trading desk, or even an assistant, and says, 'Who pays you?' and the person just has to respond, 'You do, John. Thanks.' The guy is truly insane."

"Wow. That is nutty! It's amazing what money and power can do. Then add stress and meltdown and it makes jerks even jerkier," Sasha said.

"You're telling me!" Renee responded. "I cannot believe it, but at the same time, everyone who works there makes a ton of money, and they have for a long time, so they're used to it. No one's going anywhere—certainly not right now."

"How is he with you? I know you said he had yelled at you that first day."

"Actually, not too terrible, only once a day or so," Renee said with a smile. "He yells, but then he gets over it in a few minutes. Never says sorry, of course. It's usually just a stream of curses, and I've learned to kind of pretend it's not happening. It's really awful when I see other people in the office totally devastated by it. I think what has saved me, frankly, is that I've followed a long line of complete incompetents, so he is thankful to have someone who knows what they're doing. Not that he would ever say that directly to me, but I can tell."

Sasha shook her head. "He really sounds like such a butthole! I would not last two minutes without telling him to go screw himself. He is lucky to have you."

"Well, I guess I am like everyone else who's happy to take the money. My salary increased by nearly fifty percent, and I am so grateful for that. It helps with Dad's medical bills a lot right now, and God knows what will happen with Mama's job." She had told Sasha about what happened.

"Is everything okay with that? Is she still full-time? No changes?"

"For now, things seem to be all right. But I worry every day about her. Listen, what I wanted to talk to you about are some things that aren't adding up. Maybe you can help me figure out what's going on."

"Sure thing, if I can. Is it market related?"

"No, it's other stuff. Part of it goes back to the first morning I was there. Actually, that whole first morning all sorts of weird stuff happened."

"Really? Tell me."

"Okay. So, remember I'd told you about that horrible Amanda Belden from Spence who actually was getting fired as I was coming in that morning?" It still upset Renee to think of seeing her and to remember what Amanda had said.

"Yes, I know her older sister, Theresa. The whole family is unbearably awful. One day they'll get what's coming to them."

"Well, I probably would have chalked up her comments to just being Amanda, and her need to belittle me in any situation, even though she hadn't seen me in years. But as she was leaving, she said something about how John and I would be perfect together, because of how I lied through high school. Of course, that is totally not true. Right after that, she said something to Richie, who runs the office, about how John had better be careful because she knew what had been going on there. It was really weird, because I did feel like she was actually serious. Also, I am almost certain that she and John were having an affair. John clearly gets around, and enough comments have been made in the office. It wouldn't be too outlandish that she might know things that others wouldn't have. Pillow talk and all that."

"Hmm. Does sound strange. Tell me more."

"Okay, leave that aside for the time being. So then, after I've gotten to my desk, someone called three times, very agitated, looking for John. I kept trying to see if I could help him or take a message, but he said no. I wrote the number down and saw it was a Lehman exchange, called a friend, and got the person's name."

Sasha laughed. "Only you would immediately recognize the number and trace it, Renee."

"Well, yeah," she said, smiling. "So you will not believe who it was. Blake Somerset."

"Blake Somerset!? Are you kidding?"

"No! Of course, I'm totally staggered when I find out it's him because of my mom's job. But aside from that, he was so odd and secretive on the phone. Then John has me call him right away, and Blake scurries over to the office looking really scared. They proceed to have a meeting that lasts about two hours. I'm told not to interrupt at all. Pain of death type of thing. I hear a lot of yelling. In the middle of this, something else really strange happens."

"I'm listening! What?"

"Well, it's about ten twenty. This foofy English guy calls from some bank in the Cayman Islands and tells me he needs some wiring instructions pronto or this wire isn't going to happen. That's why John yelled at me, because I figured it was better to interrupt him than get this wire screwed up. John takes the call in a private conference room off his office. What do you think? Does this all make sense?"

Sasha scrunched up her forehead and said, "I have to say a lot of this is odd. Okay, so maybe the Amanda thing is a scorned girlfriend, but with the other things it sounds like it could be connected. It is strange that he and Blake would have this exchange and a long private meeting. Usually investment bankers like to travel in packs with the alpha dog in front, and all the other ones come along to sniff butts so someone can act submissive. And Blake is so NOT an alpha dog. He is definite butt sniffer material. Did you hear any details of the conversation?"

"Just this one part about Blake creating this crap and John having to deal with his investors because of it. Oh, and that he better remember 'bulletproof'!"

"Bulletproof! Hmm. That is an odd word for a conversation about investments. Sounds like John probably bought some financial products, CDOs or something, from Lehman that blew up. Not that that's a unique story right now. Every fund manager who acted like he's smarter than anyone else bought that crap. I would love to get some more information on this, but I have to think about where. So now this island guy. That's offshore banking stuff, which could be totally legit. Has the guy called since then?"

"Yes, every day. John always wants to take the calls, though. He won't let me help with anything related to it at all. Gets very nervous about it, from what I can tell."

Sasha tried to think of what this could mean. Everyone on the Street knew of John Cutter's reputation. He was brilliant. Being smart in a relatively unregulated world, though, could be a lethal combination. Skirting whatever rules do exist becomes a way of regular business. The Cayman Islands had long been known as a place where money could be hidden and banking rules were pretty loose. John could be up to anything.

"Renee, I think you definitely are on to something, but you're going to have to see what else you can find out."

Just as she finished saying that, though, she noticed Jessica's lunch partner had come in to join her, and something clicked. It was Mimi Cutter, of all people! Of course, the Cayman Islands had to be connected to the divorce! The question was whether it was connected to anything else. How interesting that Mimi was having lunch with Jessica. Sasha didn't know her, but if there was something here, it could come in handy for Jessica to be a connection to Mimi.

"Renee, what is the status of John's divorce right now?"

"From what I can overhear or documents I've seen, not much. John doesn't want to give up a lot, and Mimi's lawyer is busting his balls. I saw one settlement offer. John offered twenty million plus other support that, I think, was around thirty thousand a month."

"You have to be kidding me! With what he must be worth? That's insane. Flying Point must have generated a few billion dollars over the last few years, and I'd guess that John took most of it home. They've been married forever. I would think she would get a larger chunk than that! And by the way, I think Mimi Cutter must spend thirty thousand a month on shoes alone."

"Hah. Well, I've never met her, but I've seen pictures."

"Well, turn around. She's over there eating lunch with my old 'B' school classmate Jessica Stark."

Renee turned around and gasped. It was hard not to tell who Mimi was. The room seemed to buzz around her like bugs at an outside light in the summer. She could see Mimi was wearing a pair of pink-and-yellow Vivier pumps that looked like a Monet painting. They had an enormous pink rhinestone buckle. However, she had inexplicably matched them with a pair of neon yellow ankle socks. She was wearing a Giambattista Valli dress that probably retailed for $2,800, with a bright yellow T-shirt underneath. Renee also noticed a giant gumball-sized pink-and-yellow pearl necklace with a medallion hanging from it. She couldn't tell what it was, though.

She started to laugh. "Okay, please, seriously. Yellow ankle socks! That is the most ridiculous outfit I've ever seen. She looks like a modern-day interpretation of the Wham video 'Wake Me Up Before You Go-Go.' And what is that big necklace she has on?"

"That's her MedicAlert. She has a cortisone deficiency. I'm surprised you don't know about that. She has a whole series of custom-made ones. It's been profiled more times than I care to think of. I'm just waiting for *W* to do an in-out list that says, 'In, custom-made MedicAlert medallions. Out, brooches.'"

"Cortisone deficiency?! How random is that? It's not like peanuts or epilepsy! I mean, how often are you in danger of that? How ridiculous! And I'm sorry, but the rest of the outfit is just plain stupid, girl! If I were John, I'd agree to give her whatever she wanted but mandate that a fashion stylist go along with it. Although between you and me, if the shoes were worn with the right outfit, they are hot! I haven't seen those in any stores."

"Vivier, spring 2009. Of course, she would have them before anyone else. I'd guess they'll probably sell for over two thousand dollars. But believe me, it's no shortage of stylists. Unfortunately, what Mimi suffers from is a shortage of stylists *with style,* not to mention people who will tell her when she doesn't look good. That can come along with obscene amounts of money. It's really sad, though. She used to be a very pretty woman, and from what I hear, a long time ago she actually had a great sense of style. She was known for it. In those days, she would have had just the shoes with black pants, a black tailored shirt, and maybe some canary diamond ear clips. The shoes would have stood out perfectly. But I think she just lost herself along the way. Being married to a rich jerk doesn't do wonders for your self-esteem. It's really sad when you think about it. But more important, I think that the Cayman Islands thing could definitely be an attempt to hide money from Mimi."

"Oh, my God! That sounds like it could make sense. I haven't ever had that much to do with banking or offshore banking. So what do you think is going on?"

"I'm not totally sure, but it could be that John sends money to hide it from Mimi. I wonder how long it's been going on. But that may be just one part of it. The Blake thing still doesn't add up. You know, Renee, I hate to tell you, but your old 'friend' Amanda probably holds the clues."

"Umm, news flash, Sash—not sure she's waiting for me to call and ask what's up."

"That's true, but just remember, a woman scorned is the best place to find the truth. I have to say, my dear old pal, you certainly have an interesting situation going on there. I'd love to help figure out what the whole story is. It's gotta be really juicy!"

"Well, I would totally love your help in figuring it out. It's driving me nuts. But listen, my friend, you also have a job on your hands right now. Promise me the 'whiny, woe is me Sasha' is not coming back. You have to get your act together with Kirk, Harry, and the whole crew up there and tell them who's driving the bus, as my daddy would say."

"Yes, I know. Renee, you've given me a new outlook. I'm actually excited for the first time in a while. I'll keep you posted on what's going on. And I'll also think of whatever else I can do on your end. By the way, do NOT e-mail me from your work account, and do NOT use my work e-mail. You never know who is reading things."

"Oh, absolutely."

Just then Renee's cell phone rang. "Oh, shit, it's John. I gotta take this." She picked up. "Yes, John?" Sasha could hear yelling coming out of the phone and cringed. Renee whispered with her hand over the phone, "I'm gonna run. Call you later. Kiss kiss."

Sasha said, "Okay, bye."

As Sasha left the restaurant, she stopped by Jessica's table again to say good-bye. Jessica said, "Sasha Silver, do you know Mimi Cutter?"

Sasha put out her hand and said, "No, we've never met. So nice to meet you."

"You likewise," Mimi said.

Sasha was really trying hard not to laugh at Mimi's outfit and what appeared to be lip injections gone awry. When Mimi said, "Likewise," one side of her mouth dropped down and it came out as "Likewyshze."

Jessica said, "Mimi has graciously agreed to chair the winter museum gala, so we're just going over some things for the benefit. Are you coming?"

"I think so, but I haven't told Adam yet. We have two other events that week, and I have to break it to him that he's going to have to wear his tux three nights in a row. He just lives for those—not." Sasha also wondered how Jessica and Guy would have the money for the tickets, which as she recalled were $2,500, when things were so tight. Well, she figured, what was another $5,000 on top of a few million in debt? Anyway, giving money to charity might be good karma for his funding to come through.

Just then Mimi said, "Jessica is also helping me try to figure out some of the financial aspects of my divorce."

Sasha was stunned that Mimi would suddenly share personal information with a woman she hardly knew, but she was thrilled that it had come up.

"Oh, Jessica certainly is a great person to do that. She and I went to business school together, and I know how smart she is when it comes to understanding investments. And she also knows how to explain things very clearly."

"Yes, well, my husband has a fund, and it can be pretty hard to figure out what everything is and where all the money is held."

"I'm sure that must be the case," Sasha responded, but knew she shouldn't say anything since it was all conjecture at this point. As she and Renee figured things out, she would decide how and if she should share anything with Jessica. Anyway, as she looked at her watch, she saw it was now 2:30. She needed to get back to the office, figure out what her next steps would be with work and how she could help Renee with this developing puzzle.

CHAPTER NINETEEN

The Big McCheese

Sasha called Kirk McNeal's office. She usually didn't have Fern make calls for her, so as a result, she got to see firsthand how assistants treated people they didn't know or who they thought weren't important enough. A great executive assistant managed to be cordial, get necessary information for their boss, keep the wrong people from getting through, and do it all without being rude. A bad assistant could be just plain nasty. Empire Bank was a big company, but Sasha assumed Kirk's assistant would know who she was and be familiar with SAMCO.

"Good afternoon. Mr. McNeal's office. This is Muriel, may I help you?" The voice sounded pleasant enough.

"Oh, good afternoon. This is Sasha Silver, is he in?"

"I'm sorry, who is this?"

Sasha groaned. It was going to be one of those calls. "This is Sasha Silver. I am CEO of Silver Asset Management Partners, SAMCO. We are a subsidiary of BridgeVest."

"Oh, and what is this in reference to?" she said in a curt way, making Sasha feel as if she were some cold-calling interloper who had managed to sneak through the main reception desk.

Sasha thought about what she would really like to say to her, but instead she said, "I was hoping to schedule some time on Kirk's calendar to speak with him regarding the transaction. That is, regarding BridgeVest."

She heard silence on the other end of the line. "Hello? Are you there?"

"Yes. I am here. What specifically would you like to discuss with him?"

Man, this lady wasn't going to give her a break, was she? Sasha could bear it no longer.

"Excuse me. What is your name?"

"Muriel."

"Well, Muriel. I'm sorry to have interrupted your clearly important day, but I am the chief executive officer of a company that generates revenue that, in part, pays your salary. What is more, I am one of the more respected and successful women on Wall Street, so rather than treating me as someone the cat dragged in, I would appreciate you either getting Mr. McNeal on the line or scheduling time with me. In case you need to know, I do know him. What you don't need to know is anything more than I have just told you."

She definitely heard silence on the other end of the line.

"I see. He is in a meeting right now. I will have him call you back later."

"Well, why don't we just schedule some time later today. I'm free at three or four thirty."

"Ah, um... three is good."

"Thank you."

As Sasha hung up the phone, Fern came in shaking her head. "Sasha, have you been making your own calls again? I've told you not to do that. All you do is get yourself agitated. We assistants know the language by which we communicate with one another. You don't."

"I can't help it, Fern. These assistants make me so mad sometimes. I just want results."

"Well, next time, let me make the call, okay?"

"All right. I'm sorry, Fern." Sasha gave her a chagrined look.

Fern walked away muttering, "These superwomen think they need to do everything themselves. Don't they know even Batman had Robin? I tell ya, she will be the death of me."

Sasha was lucky to have Fern. She would try to remember next time.

Sure enough, at 3:00 the phone rang. Fern picked it up before Sasha had a chance to do so. More than likely it would be Muriel putting Kirk McNeal through.

"Okay, Sasha, there's your call. Be nice, all right?"

"I promise, Fern. Hello," Sasha said definitively into the phone.

"Sasha. Hello, Kirk McNeal here!"

"Hi, Kirk," she said, relieved that he was in fact on the line.

"What can I do for you?"

"Well, I wanted to talk to you about the BridgeVest transaction."

"All right. I assume that Harry has kept you apprised, but what can I tell you?"

Regardless of her decision to go to Kirk, Sasha still wanted to handle this professionally. "Yes, of course. But since I wasn't at the meeting when you met with the BridgeVest team in August, I wanted to get your thoughts on potential buyers."

"Oh, well, you know, Sasha, I was a little disappointed that you didn't make it to that meeting. Harry said that he had asked you but you were busy. It seemed to me that you would make time to attend an important meeting like that, as it had been planned for several weeks."

She could hear Renee's stern admonishment to her as he said that. So she *was* supposed to have been at that meeting. What a complete and utter asshole Harry was.

"Kirk, I wasn't asked to that meeting by Harry. I found out about it when he asked me to meet with him the day after Labor Day. I suspected something wasn't right when I heard. I would absolutely have done whatever I needed to in order to be there. Unfortunately, I have not been involved in details since that day, nor have I been to any meetings of potential buyers."

"You know, Sasha, when I asked some time ago that you be promoted, it was with the idea that you ultimately would take over the company. I did that also because I knew you have not only the talent, but the strength of character to manage things in a tough environment. But at that point, you were on your own to sink or swim. I cannot, nor did I intend to, be a parent making sure that Harry was playing nice, even though he clearly appears to have not been. I will add that I am not surprised that he has acted this way.

"Sasha, let me tell you something. Once this deal has occurred, at that point BridgeVest and SAMCO will be out of my life. I have a lot of serious issues going on right now, not the least of which is making sure we pay back the TARP money the bank has received, and still find a way to pay the people that have worked twenty-four/seven to keep the bank solvent, let alone profitable. On top of that, I have to make sure the FDIC is confident that our capital base is well protected. And then, of course, there is our stock price, which as you know, these days can be taken down in an instant. All of these things relate directly to my own tenure as CEO here. I don't want to be the one on whose watch the ship went down and who is blamed for driving it into the iceberg. I have worked too many years to end up like those guys. Continually babysitting BridgeVest is completely irrelevant to me."

As he said that, Sasha got it, along with his reasons for wanting to sell the company. A bank's survival depends on the confidence that people have in it. In normal times, most people didn't give that a second thought, but in the last few months, there had been a dramatic change. Now, rumors started one day were accepted as reality the next. The FDIC had overseen and regulated commercial banks since the 1970s, and had now become a very active regulator. They were actively pushing for changes in the way banks made loans, not to mention in the management of the institutions themselves. The CEOs of Bank of America and CitiGroup were already in the FDIC crosshairs. She could understand why Kirk had no desire to be added to that list.

What's more, like the French nobility who had been taken on tumbrels to the guillotines, executives at banks that had been given TARP money, even banks that didn't really need the money to begin with, were the new scourge of a populist focus. Calls for the return of bonuses, even ones that had to be paid contractually, were becoming louder and louder. Sasha and Adam's dear friend William "Billy D." Donigan, a senior executive at AIG, had received one of the infamous bonuses, and had to move his family out of their mansion in Connecticut when protesters picketed outside his home. It was terrifying for them.

What seemed to be getting lost in the fray was that the same compensation the protesters wanted to be given back would normally go into the economy, which desperately needed restarting. That money would go to taxes; be deposited into banks and be used to make loans; get invested in the stock market, giving capital to companies; and generate revenues for companies that made cars, suits, washing machines, and jewelry. In turn, that would mean that other, less fortunate people got paid. It was sad to see how screwed up capitalism itself had become.

With everything he had to deal with, BridgeVest and Harry did sound like a waste of Kirk's time. In a way, it was actually refreshing to hear.

"Kirk, I understand what you are saying."

"I'm glad, Sasha. I am happy that you reached out to me, but you are on your own. In this world, no one is going to take care of you. If you aren't happy with what Harry is doing, then I'm afraid you're going to have to deal with him directly."

"Right. Well, I appreciate your time nonetheless."

After she hung up the phone, she remembered that she had said she was going to lay her cards on the table to Kirk. The problem was, he wasn't at the table. She said to Fern, "I'm leaving for the day. E-mail me if you need anything,"

And she went right back up to Barneys and spent the rest of the afternoon shopping, picking up a dress for Samantha at Chelsea Passage on nine, a pair of Prada boots, and a Lanvin pearl-and-ribbon necklace.

CHAPTER TWENTY

Sasha's Revenge

"Sasha, Harry Mullaugh is on the phone for you."

Sasha hadn't heard from Harry in days, so she was surprised to hear her assistant say that he was calling. Her stomach did its usual little flip as she wondered what piece of bad news was going to come.

"Hi, Harry," she said as cheerfully as possible. "To what do I owe the pleasure of this call?"

"Sasha. How are you? It's been too long. I've really missed talking to you, partner."

Usually, Sasha would have agreed with him while thinking sarcastically to herself that Harry could have picked up the phone and called her; but this time she realized she was hearing the words actually come out of her mouth.

"Harry, if you missed talking to me so much, there is this piece of technology on your desk called a phone. You can pick it up and call me. I'm right there on the other end. Yet you never seem to do that, do you?"

"Excuse me, Sasha?"

"Yes, Harry, you heard me right. You always say you've missed talking to me, but you usually don't call me. Why is that?"

"Sasha, I'm not really sure I like your tone or implication. I called you because I want to give you an update on what is happening with the business transaction our company is going through."

"Oh, news! By all means, go ahead! Need me for a meeting

tomorrow morning? Need me to jump whenever you say to?"

Sasha could not believe what was coming out of her mouth, but she was loving it. She felt a sense of lightness that was intoxicating. She also knew that she needed to stick with it, for if she came down to earth, she would probably be very sorry for what she was saying.

"Okay. I wanted to see if we could meet in person, but maybe it's best that we just discuss this over the phone right now. We have been given an offer by Flembrose Partners. It's very attractive relative to what has been going on in the world right now, and we are prepared to accept the deal provided that due diligence meets with their approval."

Whereas normally Sasha would be having a fit that clearly many meetings had gone on without her, to the extent that a deal had been agreed to, right now she didn't even care. However, she was even more surprised by what Harry said next.

"And there is one other thing. Apparently they don't want to agree to the terms and the deal until they have met you. They feel that you are important to the transaction, which of course you are," he added quickly. "But George Fleming wants to see you tomorrow morning first thing. I've already told them a lot of great things about you and how meaningful you have been to our organization, of course."

She couldn't believe what she was hearing on the other end of the phone. She wanted to laugh. Yes, all along Harry had kept her out of it because of his stupid insecurities and need to promote himself. He had shoved her off in the corner. Now she was hearing that a transaction couldn't move forward without her, and Harry was doing everything he could to suddenly act as though he had been on her side all along.

"Oh, wow. That's interesting. I'm so flattered. Gee, tomorrow morning, I'm not sure that I can, Harry. I have some personal things that I was planning on dealing with."

"Sasha, this is very important. I'm sure I don't need to tell you that all of our futures are dependent on this transaction."

"All of our futures?"

"Yes, of course, all of our futures."

"Really? So my future was on your mind when you went off and did this deal without me? When you purposefully set up meetings from the very beginning and didn't include me? Even the first time when Kirk came up to meet with you? Now, Harry, you know if I'm anything, I'm not stupid. And now all of a sudden you need me. Okay, I'll come tomorrow, but you better understand that whatever is going to happen going forward is on my terms. The way I see it and the way you are communicating it to me, you need me. This transaction doesn't get done without me. Ha. How hysterical."

"Well, now that you put it that way, yes, Sasha, I need you, okay? Name your terms and your price. I'll do what you want."

"Okay, where is the meeting? I'll let you know afterward what I want."

"Meet at the executive offices of Flembrose, 650 Madison Avenue, twentieth floor."

"Okay, I'll see you there."

When Sasha woke up the next morning, she felt vindicated beyond what she could have hoped for.

As she got to the lobby at 650 Madison, she went up to the security desk to get her pass, took the elevator up, and got off at the executive floor.

The young woman at the reception desk said, "Yes, may I help you?"

"Good morning. I am here to see George Fleming."

"Ah yes, Ms. Silver. Right this way, in dining room B."

It was certainly not the first time that Sasha had been in an executive dining room, but she always found the atmosphere and process slightly ridiculous. Rooms decorated with Chippendale chairs covered in French silks, antique maps on the wall, gargantuan views of the city, and waiters who probably had been given very clear training on how to be subservient, including not making eye contact with the important people who would be in the rooms, and of course the threat of having their tongues cut out if they revealed any of the sensitive information that might have been discussed. She knew there would be a printed daily menu inside a leather folder but that anything she might want to eat or drink would be readily available. She also had noted that men usually made a point of ordering off the menu as some strange show of power designed to top their dining partner with its complexity or show the waiters that they must always be on their toes with powerful men. Overall, there was a feeling that this was the Emerald City; anything she might want could be granted, and she should really feel lucky to be there, even if she left empty-handed.

She did love being there early, though. There was something wonderfully uplifting about looking out the window at the city. She could see all the way to Long Island this morning. It made her think of the summer and the happy times she'd had on vacation and with her family and friends. She wondered what was going on there right now and if any of them cared at all about comings and goings in the big city.

Just then, she heard steps coming down the hall and the door opened. It was George Fleming, the CEO of Flembrose, with Harry behind him.

George was a hearty, cheerful man in his mid-sixties with a shock of white hair and a ruddy face. "This must be the famous Sasha Silver! Sasha, good to meet you. I cannot believe it's taken so long to get this meeting."

Sasha gave him her warmest smile while deftly shooting Harry a threatening look. She put out her hand and reached with her other hand to grasp his arm. "It is indeed a pleasure to meet you. I have followed you for years, ever since you were head of corporate finance at Lessing, Blum, and Kertess. I started there as an assistant on the fixed income desk."

"Oh, my Lord, that was a hundred years ago. You couldn't have been working that long ago, could you?"

"Yes, I'm afraid I look a lot younger than I am."

"Well then, you must have worked for Doug Millet, didn't you? He was best man at my wedding."

"Yes, I did, as a matter of fact. I still remember the day he interviewed me."

"Well, I speak to him often. Shall I send your regards?"

"By all means. Ask him if his handicap is below fourteen yet."

"Ha ha ha! I don't need to ask him. It's been stuck at fifteen forever. We also have another friend in common, James Ullman. He and I chatted about you. Said he's a big fan. Told me, 'Sasha knows what she needs to do.' You have some very smart people behind you, Sasha." She couldn't resist glancing at Harry in the same way that Josh would look at Samantha when he took her doll. Harry looked as if he were having the worst day of his life. "Now, Sasha, let's sit down and order breakfast and talk about the future. Grant, what do we have on the menu this morning?"

As Grant stepped out of the shadows, Sasha smiled to herself. There was nothing like knowing you'd made a great first impression, and the fact that she had worked for George Fleming's best man was a cherry on top. She could see Harry was completely out of his element, and it thrilled her.

"Yes, sir. This morning we have some fine blackberries, fresh oatmeal, eggs Benedict, and a western omelet." Grant dutifully recited what was on the menu even though it was clearly spelled out in front of George.

"Hmm. Let me think. Let's let the lady order first."

"Thank you. The blackberries will be fine for me."

Next Grant turned toward Harry, who said, "I'll have the oatmeal and then the western omelet with some white toast."

Sasha almost snorted out loud. Not only was a business breakfast not a meal where you ordered an appetizer and entrée, but as usual Harry ordered way too much food, another taboo when it came to power meals. George looked at Harry a little oddly but then said to

Grant, "Hmm, blackberries, you say. Can you ask if he can find me some raspberries and some of that turkey bacon I like so much?"

"Why, certainly, sir."

Grant left the room, shutting the door quietly behind him.

"So, Sasha, I understand from my people that when you sold your company to BridgeVest, you single-handedly increased the profitability of the company and have added immeasurably in the time since. I'd like to get your thoughts on strategy as we look to complete this acquisition. After breakfast, I'd also like to introduce you to the rest of our team. Everyone is looking forward to meeting you."

Sasha felt an affinity toward George and needless to say was thrilled by how much he wanted to hear her opinions and introduce her to the team. As she spoke, she knew she had never been more articulate.

Toward the end of breakfast, George turned to Harry, who had participated little during the meal, though not for lack of trying to interject, especially to second how terrific Sasha was. "Harry," he said, "why don't you head down to the conference room and see if the rest of the team is there yet. I'd like to have a conversation with Sasha alone."

Harry looked disconcerted, but he had no choice other than to leave.

"Now, Sasha, I want you to know how important you are to this transaction. I was disturbed that it wasn't arranged for us to meet you up until now, but the announcement is going out later this afternoon and I wanted to be sure that you were on board and happy with everything. I also want to talk to you about what my thoughts are for the future."

"By all means. I too was sorry we didn't have the opportunity to meet." Sasha paused; as much as she had an opening to give George a sense of Harry's actions, she knew that it could also be a minefield. She'd only just met him. Clearly, whether she had met George and the team at this point or not, they wanted the company and her. If she gave the impression that she was a whiner and ready to trash Harry, who was her superior, that could be a negative. She would play it cool. "I'm most interested in hearing what your thoughts are regarding the future."

"Well, look. Harry has led the company this far, and he will be important in the transition. It's going to be a lot of work retaining the assets and employees. But I see you as the longer-term future of the company. My plan is that after the first year you be named the next CEO and have Harry transition to vice chairman of global client relations at the parent. That's my plan. Are you with me?"

Was she with him? She'd died and gone to heaven. Being named CEO of a $1 billion company and Harry marginalized in the nonstrategic position of global client relations, where he could do her little harm, sounded absolutely wonderful. She would just have to exist with him for one more year.

"Well, sir, I think that sounds like a plan. I'm looking forward to it."

"Terrific. Well, let's head down to meet the rest of the team, shall we?"

As they walked down the hall, Sasha felt like skipping. She knew she had a stupid, shit-eating smirk on her face but didn't really care. She shot the woman at the desk a huge smile. The woman, who wasn't used to having eye contact made with her, looked back oddly at first but then smiled.

They entered the boardroom, another ornately decorated room with a long board table. Plush leather chairs lined the table, and speakers with microphones were positioned strategically at each chair.

Sasha noticed the entire executive team of BridgeVest Financial was there, all looking nervous as well as slightly bothered to see her. She gave them all one of her best smiles with a look that said, "Eat me, suckers."

George took the time to introduce Sasha to every member of the Flembrose executive team. Each gave her a warm smile. One said, "I feel like I know you already. My wife is always showing me your picture in the paper. It is amazing that you have time to do everything." Another said, "You know my brother Bill from the ballet board." And still another said, "I was a year behind you at B school. If Professor Jones didn't mention you once a week, we wondered what was wrong!"

Everyone sat down at George's direction and went around the room introducing themselves and their role. When it came time for Harry to speak, he went into a long, rambling speech that made little sense. Most people looked uncomfortable as he talked. Finally George cut in and said, "Well, Harry, I'm sure we will have plenty of time in the future for philosophical conversations, but for now let's focus on the business, shall we? We have a lot of work to do to get ready, including laying out our initial team and transition plans. So I think it's time we get to work."

As Sasha started to leave, Harry pulled her aside and said, "I think we should have a conversation about what George said to you and make sure we both know what's going to happen."

Harry was obviously very nervous, which made Sasha obviously very pleased.

"Harry, as I told you on the phone last night, I will let you know what I want. Isn't it funny that George and I both worked at the same company and that I have so many connections to the team here? You know, Harry, one of the things that you never quite understood was that I was working my ass off down here to make sure that the company was successful and that I was at the same time. So now you need me. Isn't that interesting?"

"Sasha, just tell me what George said and how I can make it easier for you to be a part of this."

"Well, apparently, Harry, it's all been decided. You don't have to do anything. George sees me as CEO a year from now and you move out, oh, I mean, up to vice chairman."

Harry turned purple, and then he turned white. His mouth opened, but no words came out.

"Yes, isn't it wonderful?" Sasha said. "I know this is something you have been intending to do yourself all these years. The timing might be a little sooner than you planned on, but nonetheless all your dreams are coming true for me, and for you. Anyway, Harry, I must get to the office for some things that I need to take care of. I'll look forward to seeing the press release later. Here's to the future, *partner*!" And with that, she turned and walked out. When she got to the street, she put her hands up in the air and yelled, "Yes!" A few people looked at her strangely, but she didn't care. Just then a car drove by, and she could hear Lenny Kravitz singing, "It Ain't Over 'Til It's Over" at a high volume. That's right, she thought. Take that, Harry! And she sashayed down the street behind him, singing along: "So many tears I've cried / So much pain inside... / So many years we've tried... / But baby, it ain't over 'til it's ov-er."

CHAPTER TWENTY-ONE

It Ain't Over 'Til It's Over

Sasha called Adam. "You won't believe it! It could not have gone better. I am dancing and singing. George Fleming loved me, and told me that his plan is for me to become CEO in a year while Harry gets bumped up to never-never land as vice chairman of global client relations. I just could not have imagined it having gone any better."

"My God, Sasha. That is amazing. Congrats, honey. I knew that it would work out for you. You're too good for the powers that be not to have realized it. What happens next?"

"Well, they're working on the press release. The plan is for the announcement to happen this afternoon after the close. God, you should have seen the look on Harry's face when I told him what George's plans were. I thought he was going to spontaneously combust on the spot!"

"What do you mean? You were the one that told Harry that? George hadn't told him yet?"

"No. George clearly doesn't seem to think that Harry is any great shakes. He practically shooed him out of the dining room so we could have time alone and he could tell me."

"Sasha, I really don't think that was a good move. First of all, wasn't it private between you and George? Secondly, Harry has been a conniving asshole surrounded by other conniving assholes the entire time you've known him. Now he knows this pretty big piece of news. What makes you think he isn't going to do anything to try and put the kibosh on it?"

"Adam! I cannot believe you! What can he do at this point? Harry knows that for this deal to happen they need me, and he's not going to be able to go against the wishes of George Fleming. Everything is fine and going to be fine. I'm not worried at all. Can you please just be happy for me and not throw cold water on my moment?"

Sasha was irritated. Why did Adam always look for the negative? It was ridiculous. She wasn't worried at all about Harry doing anything. Yet at the same time, she suddenly felt a nagging worry inside.

"Okay, Sasha. You know I just want you to be happy and don't want any surprises for you, especially when this has been such a rough ride for so long. Send me the press release as soon as you see it, okay?"

"Sure thing, hon. Look, everything is going to be fine. I just know it."

"Babe, it is always fine as long as you realize it's whatever you choose it to be."

As the rest of the day wore on, Sasha was a combination of elation and nerves. She didn't want to tell anyone else on her team what was happening. Part of her didn't believe it herself. She really couldn't do much more than waste time and twiddle her thumbs waiting to see the release. She wasn't sure whether it was going to come from the offices of Flembrose or from BridgeVest.

By midafternoon, she had rearranged her desk files and gone through everything outstanding in her in-box, but she was able neither to focus on anything meaningful nor to work on even mindless tasks. She thought maybe she should take a walk outside but was too nervous to leave the office. Actually, it probably meant a call would come through the minute she walked out the door. She checked her BlackBerry separately from her computer just in case messages weren't getting through to one or the other.

She was getting this nagging feeling that something wasn't quite right, but she kept saying to herself that she was just nervous and relieved that everything had worked out so well.

Finally, she could bear it no longer. She knew that they must have heard something up in Springfield, but she didn't want them to realize that she didn't know what was going on. She had to be thoughtful about how she uncovered any information.

"Fern?" she called out to her assistant. "Can you come in for a second?"

"Sure thing, Sasha. What's up?"

Fern generally was someone who could be trusted to know how to find out what was going on.

"I need you to do me a favor. I want to see if they have the press release up at headquarters yet, but I don't want them to know I am being anxious about it. Can you see what they know?" Sasha asked.

"Of course. Those ding-dongs? They'll never even figure out what hit 'em. Wanna watch? I'll make the call from here."

Sasha handed her the phone. "Go right ahead. It's all yours."

Fern dialed Harry's office. "Jacqueline? It's Fern in Sasha's office... Hi. How are you? How was last weekend? Did you guys win a lot of money?" She looked at Sasha and whispered, "Slot machines," and rolled her eyes. "Yeah? I can't believe it was that much... That's great. Hey, listen, hon, I am so sorry, but I am all messed up here. Sasha forwarded the release to me, but I erased it and can't seem to get it back. I don't want to ask her for another copy. She will kill me. You know it's such a big deal and all. Can you just e-mail me yours?... Great. Thank you so much. I totally owe you one. You're the best."

She hung up the phone. "See? On its way. Let me go check my computer to see if it's here yet."

A minute later, she came in. "Here you go."

BRIDGEVEST TO BE ACQUIRED BY FLEMBROSE PARTNERS

Transaction highlights fixed income markets... Silver Asset management key element of focus... Sasha Silver, one of the high-profile women on Wall Street...

Sasha read on, and it was wonderful.

Then Fern called out to her, "Sasha, hold on. Jacqueline says that's the earlier one that she knew I already had. She is sending the second one. Apparently it's just been released."

Sasha was more than a little perplexed, so she went out to Fern's desk to read over her shoulder as she was printing it out.

BridgeVest to Be Acquired by Flembrose Partners

She could see immediately something was wrong.

A significant transaction in troubled times... George Fleming firm acquires assets in transaction with Springfield-based firm.

Somehow Sasha's name, any mention of her future role, and that of her firm had been minimized to a single line at the end of the release. "BridgeVest's assets include Silver Asset Management, a New York–based subsidiary."

What the hell had happened! How had he pulled it off? Was Adam right? Had something she said given Harry the ability to pull the last move? She heard that Lenny Kravitz song in her head again: "It ain't over 'til it's over..." She felt so stupid right now.

Fern could tell that she was upset. "Is there anything I can do, Sasha?"

"Um, no, I just have to think for a minute. I'm going to shut my door for a sec, okay? Everything's fine. Really."

There was this terrible feeling that Sasha felt when things were bad, really bad. It was as if someone had taken acid and poured it down her throat. Her whole stomach retched and turned, and she felt for a moment as if she were having an out-of-body experience.

Somehow, after the agony of the fall, with Renee's help and tough talk she had managed to realize that she didn't care, that she could set her own course. And then when everything seemed to be falling into her lap, she got sucked right back in again. She'd had barely twenty-four hours of grabbing the brass ring, only to have it yanked away again. Now what? Go along and hope that somehow she was given the opportunity? Wait for George Fleming to come through on his promise while being tortured by Harry? She was sure if she called him up now, he would tell her she was still going to be CEO but then explain why the press release had been changed. Some "good old boy" line about making sure assets were stable. And you know what? She hadn't played the game as well as Harry had. But now she had a decision to make. There was a floor full of people out there depending on her. They were going to have to have someone to lead them, to protect them, and to make sure their jobs were safe, their way of life protected. She knew exactly what she needed to do.

"Fern. I'm letting you make this call. Get me George Fleming on the phone, okay?"

"Sure thing! One sec..." she said. "Yes, I have Sasha Silver on the line for Mr. Fleming."

"Sasha, my dear. So wonderful to hear from you. Are you still looking forward to the future?"

"Yes. Yes, I am," she responded, and took a big breath.

"George, listen. I have given it a lot of thought, and I think it's time for me to move on. I spent a lot of time over the last three years bringing SAMCO to the next stage. My partners retired when that deal was done. Now it's time for me to do the same." As she said it, there was no regret and no misgivings.

"Why, I... I don't know what to say. This is so unexpected. The release has gone out. We had such a lovely talk this morning, and I was looking forward to the next year. Can I ask what happened to change your mind?"

"Let's call it a lot of soul-searching." There wasn't any sense in "telling on" Harry and whatever he had done to make the change. If it was meant to be, it would have come out the right way. George Fleming hadn't gotten to where he was without being astute with people, corporate politics, and the seemingly mundane wording of press releases that spoke volumes between the lines. She couldn't go through another meeting like that morning, where her hopes were raised and her talent acknowledged, only to be shoved aside by someone she despised and, worse, had absolutely no respect for. Maybe she would end up CEO in a year, but she really didn't feel like being miserable getting there constantly watching her back for whatever Harry was up to.

"George, I'd like to request that you communicate with the media and internally to say that I've decided to step down. It would mean a lot if it came from you. And please don't say that I've decided to spend time with family or pursue other interests. I never wanted to be one of those people who clearly are being fired or just aren't wanted."

"Yes. Yes, of course."

"Thanks. I will call Harry and let him know."

She hung up the phone. She could see that Fern had heard everything and was looking teary-eyed. "Fern, we all have our time to move on and grow up. I can't take care of everyone else any longer. I've got to focus on me."

To her surprise, Fern said, "Sasha, I'm not worried about me or the rest of us. *We* will be fine. We're all grown-ups. I'm just pissed off that that dick won in the end."

"No, actually he didn't. Let's get him on the phone, and then right after I need to speak with Raj."

In a few seconds, she heard Harry's gleeful voice on the other end of the line. "So, my dear, I assume you have seen the release. We should talk about next steps and tomorrow's plan for communication."

"Ah yeah, Harry, I called to let you know, I just spoke to George to tell him I've thought about everything and I decided I'm not going to be staying on. It's just not where I want to be. I'd love to quote from *Baby Boom,* 'I just think the rat race is gonna have to survive with one less rat,' but that sounds so contrived. So I'll leave it with this between us. I have always thought you were a complete jerk, incompetent, a bad dresser, unable to remotely hold your own in public, particularly in any kind of social atmosphere. Oh, and by the way, you usually have food on your mouth at a meeting that you never wipe away, and you don't even know how to order a respectable meal." She was about to stop when a thought occurred to her. "Oh, and when George calls you his partner, just remember you work for him. You aren't *his* partner. He is *your* boss."

"Sasha," Harry started to interrupt.

"Harry, just shut up. Truth be told, I have zero desire to be a part of this, and zero desire to ever speak to you again. If you and I ever see one another, let's just smile and move on. No need for words or false pretenses. George will communicate about my leaving. I don't really want to have you be the spokesperson for anything related to me ever. Listen, gotta run. My attorney is on the phone."

She could see Fern beaming outside her office, and that gave her a bit more strength on top of what she had done. She picked up the other line.

"Raj. Hey, how are you? I have some news. You sitting?"

"Yes, my dear. Please tell me. What has been going on?"

Raj Mehta had been Sasha's lawyer, protector, and part shrink for many years. He had emigrated from India as a teenager and fit right in with the American culture. Princeton '74 and Harvard Law '77 had given him the pedigree, but it was his personality that made him able to deal with many different corporate bigwigs. Sasha had kept Raj abreast of what was going on but actually hadn't spoken to him since a very brief exchange yesterday afternoon. As she related everything to him, she said, "I really don't even care that much about severance. I'm glad for the decision I made, and I'm just ready. I'll go be a mom and wife for a while and then figure out whether I belong in the working world again."

"But Sasha, don't you remember when I said when you first sold the firm that one day you would be very happy because of what I put in your contract?"

She was embarrassed to say she didn't. Doing that deal was a blur at this point. "Raj, I'm sorry, I don't remember. What was it?"

Raj chuckled. "Oh, my dear, you can certainly go be a mother and wife if you want to, and I'm sure that you will do a very fine job at it, just as you have with everything else. But you are going to be a very happy woman—or should I say, rich. As a matter of fact, very rich indeed."

"What are you talking about? I already got paid on the earn-out two years ago."

"I'm not talking about that. I remember that very well. I am talking about the provision I added to your contract right before the deal was signed that said if a sale were to occur before your contract was up, you would receive an additional cash payout of ten million dollars."

"*What?!*"

"Yes, my dear. They don't call me 'the Rajinator' for nothing. I always try to add something like this. I usually am not very successful, as my counterparts are smart enough to think about the potential liability and catch it, but these guys... Well, I don't need to tell you about these guys, right?"

Sasha's head was spinning. For a minute, she couldn't even speak.

"Sasha, are you there? What do you think?"

"AHHH!" she screamed. "Are you sure?"

"Sasha, how can you ask me that? Of course I am sure. I wish you had a little more confidence in my legal ability and memory than that!" he said playfully.

"Raj, do you think that they realize it, too?"

"I would think so, but again these people have shocked me all along, so it's likely that they don't remember."

"Well, someone has to have read the damn thing at BridgeVest. They've been doing due diligence. That means check every piece of paper that a company has—especially the legal ones and contracts! I mean, they couldn't have lost it, could they?"

Sasha was already wondering, though, if the sudden effort to bring her into the fold wasn't an effort to keep from paying her the money. It certainly could be. Nah, more likely that they lost it. But did it really matter? It felt like she had gotten her cake and eaten it, too.

As she hung up with Raj, she smiled. Maybe the song was the right one after all.

"It ain't over 'til it's over!"

CHAPTER TWENTY-TWO

Divorce Court

Just as Grigsby wondered what one wore to meet a divorce attorney, she spent a similar amount of time wondering what one wore to court. She opened her closet and walked inside. When they'd moved into the building and done extensive renovations, her closet had been the crowning achievement. Seven hundred square feet devoted entirely to Grigsby Somerset. There was a wall with all of her purses. She had four Hermès Birkin bags, including one crocodile one. There were probably a dozen classic Chanel quilted ones in various sizes, a Celine "bowling bag," numerous Prada bags from the last several collections, and assorted evening bags, mostly Judith Leiber minaudières. Her shoe collection was impressive. Floor to ceiling and five feet wide. Each pair was in its box with a Polaroid photo attached to the front of it for easy identification. Her suits and dresses were in their own section arranged by color and season. Jewelry—costume, of course, as the real pieces were locked away in the vault—was arranged on giant velvet open trays and looked like a pirate's treasure chest, gleaming and inviting.

And then there were her gowns, which had their own section. They were arranged by year and encased in stiff plastic, though clearly visible. She also had a dress form in the closet upon which hung the gown she had worn most recently. She hated putting it away, as it was a sign that the party was over. So she would keep each gown out for a week or two, touching the folds of the fabric every time she walked by. It reminded her of the wonderful evening she'd had, and of course the photographs that had been taken of her.

As she looked around, she felt that today called for somber chic. She pulled out two different Chanel suits, comparing them with each other. One was red wool bouclé. Too aggressive, she thought, and hung it up again. The other was navy blue with gold CC buttons. Yes, perfect, she thought.

As she collected her things, she checked the address. How in the world was one supposed to find or get to 60 Lafayette Street? She hoped the cabdriver would know. This couldn't possibly take all day. She was hoping to still get to meet Thruce at Bergdorf's for a late lunch. He certainly had been a good friend to her over this trying time. She would have to remember to get him a special thank-you gift.

Her doorman hailed her a taxi and she settled back, closing her eyes. The last few months had been dreadful. Part of her still couldn't believe that she was in this position. Right now, she just wanted it to be over.

When she arrived downtown, she wasn't sure which of all these formal-looking buildings she was supposed to go into, but finally she found it and walked up the steps.

She saw Irving waiting for her. His usually ruddy face looked a bit pale. "Grigsby, *where* have you been?"

"What do you mean?" she asked.

"It's ten fifteen. You were supposed to be here at nine forty-five!"

"Oh, dear. Well, I had a hard time getting down here. Anyway, is there a problem? I'm sure the judge had plenty of other issues he could deal with."

"It's she, and that's not the way it works. You show up when you are supposed to show up. Please try to remember that these judges sit here all day long, have a backed-up calendar, and make as much in a year as many women are asking for their monthly support, yourself included. They hold the keys to your getting what you want. Please try and respect that."

Grigsby looked at him and tried to absorb what he was saying. To her, there wasn't any question that she wasn't going to get exactly what she wanted or needed. Irving was silly to worry. Everything would be fine.

Just then, they were called into the courtroom.

Judge Michelle Sampson looked irritated the minute they walked in.

"Counselor, I am so glad your client has managed to make it here. Great news. I think we have enough time before my late morning nap. Can we please get started?"

Blake was there with his attorney, trying not to make eye contact with Grigsby. For all her usual bravado and ability to wave off the serious, she suddenly looked small and scared.

"Yes, I am so sorry, Your Honor. We had a, ahh, miscommunication this morning as to the time, and Mrs. Somerset isn't familiar with the area down here."

"Well, the rest of these grown-ups managed to make it on time. Let's just get going, shall we?"

"Thank you. Your Honor, my client, Mrs. Grigsby Somerset, is in a deplorable situation. She expected her husband to provide for her, and for her children, but has now been left in a position where he is unable to do that."

"And why is that?"

"Well, Mr. Somerset was an employee at Lehman Brothers, and the firm went bankrupt."

"Yes, I am aware of that. Your client is the fifth Lehman wife I have had this month. Is he working now?"

"Yes, he is currently employed by Barclays Capital, the firm that bought Lehman's assets out of bankruptcy."

"And what is the net worth of the couple now?"

"Well, we believe it is currently approximately fifteen million dollars."

"Your Honor, that is ridiculous," said Blake's attorney as Blake sat there shaking his head. "The Somersets not only lost all value of his stock, which at its high point was over fifty million, but they had margin loans, mortgages, and home equity loans on their Park Avenue apartment and Southampton homes. There is nothing close to that."

"Your Honor..." Irving continued.

"You know, I have had enough of these prima donnas," Judge Sampson said. "These women who don't get that the world has changed and think because they want it to be the same, it will. Mrs. Somerset, your husband has lost most of the money that you had. There isn't enough left for your fancy shoes or dresses or vacations. Don't you get that?"

At this point, Grigsby was looking quite perplexed. Judge Sampson continued, "Mr. Dylan, what was the amount of spousal support that you are requesting for Mrs. Somerset?"

"Seventy-five thousand dollars a month."

"Seventy-five thousand a month! She is getting fifteen thousand, and when both the apartment and the country house are sold, the proceeds will be split evenly, after loans have been paid—"

"Nooooo. You cannnnn't do that. I will not live on that!" Grigsby wailed. Irving tried to both console her and shush her, neither of which seemed to work.

"Ma'am, you are going to have to calm down." Judge Sampson said to her sternly.

"But that's not fair," she wailed.

"Grigsby, stop. Stop right now!" Irving was purple and yelling at her.

"Your Honor, please, I have to explain this to you." Grigsby began walking up to the judge, moving right past the bailiff. "This is just not right. You see, I have done all of the work in taking care of the apartment and the children and the house."

"Ma'am, stop. Right now! Mr. Dylan, you are going to have to take your client out of here. I will not speak to her."

"Yes, Your Honor."

But Grigsby kept going. "I will not live on that. I am not one of those people who should have to think about what they are spending money on. It's bad enough that I had to pawn my jewelry to pay for the maid." Blake perked up at this one. If he weren't so disgusted with his wife, he would have been enjoying this.

"I have had to do what no woman of my status should do. I have had to sell my clothes to *resale* stores for cash!!" And she collapsed on the floor in front of Judge Sampson, sobbing hysterically.

"Mr. Dylan!" Judge Sampson screamed. "Get this woman out of here NOW!"

Irving did his best to drag Grigsby out of the room, which he managed to do along with the help of Blake's attorney, who actually felt embarrassed for his colleague rather than victorious.

It was the first time in all the years they'd worked together that Irving resented Lucille for passing off her crap to him. To deal with the destruction of a marriage was one thing, to have a grown woman act like a child and embarrass him was the last straw.

After managing to get the still-sobbing Grigsby in a cab, Irving went back to the office and left Lucille a brief note that said: "Lucille, my dear, after all these years together, I am divorcing you—your (former) colleague Irving Dylan."

CHAPTER TWENTY-THREE

Amanda Belden's Karmic Reaction

Amanda Belden's world came crashing down.

The Belden family had been longtime fixtures on the social scene. For nearly forty years, they had been established firmly in New York, Palm Beach, and Southampton. They never quite recognized or appreciated that just as they had inserted themselves into society (or perhaps because they had), they did not welcome people they didn't already know well or want to know, mostly because they could do something for the Beldens.

The family did not subscribe to the adage that in life you meet the same people on the way up as on the way down. They didn't have to, since they assumed that theirs was a ride that went in only one direction: up. Fate, however, had other plans for them.

The party always continued when there was money, prestige, and access. Their Georgian town house on Beekman Place had been featured in *Architectural Digest*, decorated by only the best decorator available, and, with no small amount of help from their publicist, had made it onto the cover.

They had virtually everything anyone else could possibly covet, and there was an almost constant group of people around them who wanted to be with them. Everyone loved what they wore, the places to which they traveled, the benefits they attended, the restaurants they frequented, and generally marveled at how perfect their lives were.

But the fact was, they weren't particularly nice to their extensive staff, always caused a bit of difficulty in restaurants by asking for a different (better) table, didn't mentor people less successful than they, were a bit too front and center at every event, rarely bought more than two tickets at charity events, *even ones they were chairing*, were always trying to be the smartest people in the room, and always seemed to forget that they'd been introduced to you, as they oh so elegantly and cordially said, "Nice to meet you," for the umpty-umpth time while looking across the room for someone more notable to chat with.

With this background, it was no surprise that Amanda had been as snobbish and rude as she was to Renee at Spence. She had continued acting that way at Yale, where her father had attended also. As captain of the women's varsity squash team, Amanda instituted a rather mean-spirited hazing process for freshmen that persisted for several years after she graduated, creating such a bad feeling that other colleges dreaded playing them. For a time, Yale even considered ending its women's squash program, but there were too many protests from alumnae, and rumors were already starting to reach the ears of recruits, so the idea was put aside.

So when it came out in January 2009 that Amanda's father, Stuart "Skip" Belden, had been heavily involved for years, if not decades, in a scandal that included insider trading, which in turn involved an elaborate money-laundering scam for a certain group of influential South Americans, a shock wave rippled from New York City to Palm Beach. Skip was led out of the Belden town house in handcuffs.

With the Beldens' escalator now changing directions rather abruptly, there were more than a few people who weren't all that sad to hear that their fortunes had changed—in fact, many were rather gleeful. A number of "friends" stopped calling immediately. Even more shocking were the rumors that started flying that seemed almost to take on a life of their own. Invariably, whether at the Regency Hotel for breakfast or the Four Seasons for lunch, someone at a business meal would say to his or her companion, "Look who is over there. No!! Don't turn around so quickly!" "Page Six" items were devoured and then followed immediately with, "Well, that's not all. I heard…" At cocktail parties, the next statement after the inevitable weather conversation was, "So did you know the Beldens?"

The rumors and innuendos were not limited to Skip and his wife. Amanda, her sister, Theresa, and brother, Skippy, also became fodder for a vicious gossip mill. Anyone who had ever been mistreated by them came out of the woodwork.

Amanda, who had put her dismissal from Flying Point Capital into a neat little box where she rationalized things, had spent the fall traveling, "refocusing and cleansing" as she described it, so she could figure out what her next move would be. When the scandal hit, she was shocked, hurt, and terrified. Many of her best friends all of a sudden weren't returning her calls. She could not believe the things she was reading in the paper about herself. In a matter of two days, she was asked politely if she wouldn't mind resigning as chair of the committee for two benefits and asked to step down from the committee of several others. The worst moment of all happened when she called to make a 7:30 dinner reservation at Swifty's and was told that they had only a 5:00 p.m. or 9:45 p.m. available. She said, "But this is Amanda Belden," to the receptionist, and the response was, "Yes, I know. We only have those two times available. Would you like to book one of them? Oh dear, I am sorry, the nine forty-five is taken as well."

She spent several days in her bed crying, staining her Porthault sheets with Lancôme mascara and M·A·C Glitz and Glam eyeliner. Finally, she decided she'd better do something and got dressed to go outside. It was a rainy day, and as she wandered aimlessly down Madison Avenue with oversize black sunglasses on, she thought everyone who stared as they passed by her must know exactly who she was, forgetting that the more likely reason was that most people didn't wear sunglasses in the rain. When she got to 57th Street, she decided to turn west and get a cappuccino at Mangia. Just as she was about to take a sip, someone bumped into her. She erupted, "Hey! Why don't you watch the fuck where you are going?"

"Well. Amanda. What a surprise."

She couldn't believe her eyes. Who of all people should be standing in front of her but John Cutter.

"John. Oh, my God."

Even though he'd had her fired and had treated her terribly, he was still drop-dead good-looking. Her stomach and heart flipped.

"Yes, I am still a god, that's for sure. So, I have been reading about your family recently. I certainly wouldn't have pegged your dad to do that. How are you holding up?"

Amanda's eyes started to well up behind her glasses. John was the first person she had spoken to in three days. "It's been pretty rough. I'm in total shock. My sister, brother, and I don't know what to do or say to anyone."

"Well, why the hell are you drinking coffee? The only thing to do at a time like this is get drunk. Wanna go to the Ritz-Carlton? For old times' sake?"

As much as Amanda should have turned around and walked in the other direction, she found herself nodding as they started walking toward Central Park South. They sat at the bar for a while and within short order were heading upstairs to a room. Once inside, she felt as if she were back where she belonged. John hadn't really meant to treat her the way he had. It was the divorce and all the stress he had been under at Flying Point. They spent all afternoon in bed, and then John suggested they order dinner from room service along with a bottle of champagne.

"I'm going to take a quick shower while the food's on the way up. Have them set it up, okay?" John said.

"Okay, sure thing."

As she waited for him, Amanda looked out the window at Central Park. As terrible as things were with her family, maybe there was a silver lining. Getting back together with John was something she had been dreaming about for months, no matter how terrible he had been. She wouldn't have run into him had the scandal not occurred. Maybe she could leave her family behind. John didn't ever care what people thought of him anyway. All that mattered to him was how much money he had in the bank. And that was all that usually mattered to the people around him, too. She started daydreaming about what things would be like with the two of them.

Room service arrived, and she made sure it was set up the way John liked it. The waiter left and she called to John that dinner was ready.

John came out, freshly showered, wearing one of the hotel's terrycloth robes. "This looks fucking great. I'm starved."

"Yeah," Amanda agreed. "So, listen, I was thinking that maybe tomorrow we could—"

"Tomorrow?" John said, looking at her strangely.

"Yes," she said, a bit unsure about his look and tone. "That maybe we could try that new place in the meatpacking district."

John started to laugh. "You think I'm going to be doing anything with you tomorrow?"

"Well. Yes, I mean . . ." Amanda started to feel flushed, not to mention sick to her stomach and stupid.

"Oh, my fucking God, you are a bigger twit than I thought, Amanda. There's no way in hell I'm going to be seen with you. With what is going on with your family right now? Like I'd want to risk having my investors think that I was connected to *your* family? This was just a for old times' sake fuck, babe. End of story."

Amanda turned purple. She had never felt this betrayed and foolish. She started screaming at him. "You asshole! You fucking asshole! How could you do this to me? I never did anything to you. Do you have any idea what I could do to you?"

At this point, John was laughing hysterically. "What you could do to me? Oh, please, Amanda, you are a loser in this town now. You'll be lucky if you can get a rental in Hoboken."

Through her tears, Amanda somehow managed to put her things on and grab her purse. John was still laughing but at this point was already on his BlackBerry, typing an e-mail to someone.

"John Cutter, if it is the last thing I do, I will get you back. I may not be in the position I was, but you fucked with me for the last time."

She slammed the door behind her, still hearing John's cackles as she ran down the hall. When she got to the street, she sobbed even harder. The doorman asked if he could get her a cab, but she shook her head no and walked down the street. She walked up Fifth Avenue, lost in thoughts of revenge. What could she do to get him? There had to be some way. Then she remembered. By the time she had reached her apartment, she knew exactly what she could do. She went to sleep at least somewhat satisfied that she had a plan.

The next morning, Amanda waited until 8:15, then picked up the phone and dialed the number she knew so well.

"John Cutter's office. This is Renee, may I help you?"

"Renee, it's Amanda Belden."

"Amanda! Hello. Ah... um, are you calling for John? He isn't here right now."

"I'm not calling for John. I want to talk to you."

Renee, who needless to say had gobbled up every article on the Belden scandal, could not imagine what Amanda was going to say. She also couldn't believe the timing since she had been talking with Sasha only a week ago about what Amanda might know regarding John. Renee believed there were no coincidences in life, but as it turned out, she was still more than a little surprised.

"I want to talk to you about some of the things that were going on with John that I, ah, referred to in passing that morning I saw you, when I quit."

Renee couldn't help but smile. It certainly was typical for Amanda to describe it as quitting when they both knew she had been fired.

"Are you available, maybe later today, to meet for a drink?"

Renee wondered if this was a setup, but something in the way Amanda was talking made her feel that she was telling the truth.

"Yes, I'm free this evening. Shall we meet at La Goulue at six thirty?

Amanda paused. "If you don't mind, I'd rather go someplace, um, more off the beaten track. I'm having some issues being seen right now. Why don't we go to the Green Harp? Like the good old days in school."

Even though Renee had been raised to be charitable and forgiving, she couldn't help but feel a sense of schadenfreude at Amanda's plight. All those years of torment and that first day at the office. It was nice to know that at least one member of the Belden family was feeling the effects of their meanness. She also did not recall good old days with Amanda, anywhere.

The Green Harp was a pub on the Upper West Side frequented by legions of New York City private school students for decades. Its reputation for being generous with accepting IDs made it a popular hangout. While it might have been cool in high school, it certainly had no such glamour for someone like Amanda, whose usual haunts were Swifty's, Le Cirque, and Bice.

"Sure, that's fine."

"Okay, and ah, please don't mention this to John."

"No, of course I won't."

As soon as she hung up, Renee called Sasha on her cell phone. "Sash, you won't believe who just called me! Amanda Belden! I think her family scandal may have brought out whatever tiny scrap of a soul is inside her. She says she wants to talk to me about what's been going on here. I'm meeting her this evening at—you'll love this. The Green Harp!"

"The Green Harp? You mean the same place everyone goes to in high school?"

"Yes. I suggested La Goulue but she doesn't want to be in a place where people will recognize her."

"La Goulue? Isn't that place closing soon? Oh man, well, I cannot wait to hear what she has to say! Obviously, this could be the missing link to everything."

"Don't I know it. I'll call you right after."

When Renee got to the Green Harp, she felt many memories come flooding back. She walked by the bar and saw, way in the back, at the same table where she and Zach Kahn had kissed junior year, Amanda with dark glasses looking down at her iPhone.

"Hi, Amanda," Renee said as nicely as she could muster, although with no sense of false cheeriness.

"Hi. Thanks for agreeing to meet me. I know this is awkward, to say the least."

"Yes, you could certainly say that," Renee responded.

"Look, I am sure you know, since everyone else in the world does right now, about what has been happening with my family. It's pretty devastating, to say the least, and I'm just trying to put the pieces of my life back in some kind of way. It's not as if I had anything to do with what happened. My life is basically over because of something my dad did," Amanda said.

Renee could still detect a sense of entitlement in her voice but wasn't surprised. It probably wasn't all that easy to erase a lifetime of that, especially when her family had lived that way for many years before she was even born.

"Amanda, I'm sure it's been really tough the last few days. You know people love to tear the rich and powerful down. They also like to build people up again if they are good people... or change their spots."

"Hopefully, you are right—I just want to try and get through this time. I don't know if I am ever going to speak to my family again.

Anyway, it's given me a chance to think about my life and what my parents always taught me, and I'm not sure that I ever got a great sense of values. It was always about being in the right places with the right people, and how ironic that it turned out to be the exact opposite."

"It certainly did." Renee remembered back to when she and the other black girls were the only ones in the senior class who weren't invited to Amanda's graduation party weekend in Southampton. The school and other parents were upset about it, but the party was two weeks after commencement, so technically school was over and there wasn't anything the school could do about it. Most of Renee's good friends opted not to go, but it was a hard invitation to turn down. The Belden home was on Meadow Lane, and there was a clambake on the beach and swimming all day. Apparently, only the "right people" were invited.

"Look, Renee, I don't expect you to all of a sudden want to be my friend or help me, but maybe I can be helpful to other people now. I'm sure since you have been working for John you have realized certain things aren't quite right. John's downfall may be when he ended up finally getting an assistant who would be smart enough to figure out that some dishonest stuff has been going on at Flying Point Capital."

Renee decided to be cagey. "Maybe. What kinds of things do you think were happening?"

Amanda sensed that Renee was being guarded. She would have to tell her the whole thing.

"Well, let me go back to tell you how I know everything. I still can't believe how stupid I was to think that John was going to marry me." Amanda's eyes watered as she said that. She wasn't thinking just about their earlier relationship, she was thinking about last night's humiliation, too.

Ah, so that was part of it. Renee should have figured that. Not only was Amanda having an affair with John, but she expected that once the divorce was final, she would slip into the shoes (and ring) of

Mrs. Cutter. She also thought to herself that those were definitely *expensive* shoes to fill, not that the ring was going to come cheap, either.

"I started work there two years ago, right after Harvard Business School, as head of marketing. I was really excited about the job. It was a phenomenal opportunity. I was able to meet a lot of institutional investors, pension funds, endowments, people at all the big firms, while promoting Flying Point. John's strategy was hot and the assets were pouring in. I went to every great restaurant in the city, traveled around the world, stayed in the best hotels, and flew first class, sometimes even in private jets. It was amazing. The funny thing was, I didn't even realize at the time that girls like me were a dime a dozen. Every hot fund had an equally hot blonde as 'head of marketing.' In a way, I really was more like a hooker, or at least a blond American version of a geisha girl. My Harvard degree was meaningless, but I was too caught up in it to realize it at the time."

Amanda paused to take a sip of wine. She winced at the taste. This was definitely screw-top jug wine, no doubt about it.

"So, I'd been there about two months when John and I got together. He'd definitely been checking me out since day one. We'd been staying late to meet with some investors, and after they left I went back to the conference room to get my presentation book. All of a sudden, John was behind me kissing my neck. I still feel chills thinking about it."

Renee was praying Amanda wasn't going to go into more details than that.

"We did it right there on the conference room table." Okay, Renee hoped wrong. Ick! "From that point on, it was like we were *totally* connected," she said, emphasizing *to*-tally in her Upper East Side accent, which was part Valley Girl and part Locust Valley lockjaw. "I know John can be a bit overbearing, but he was great with me. God, we'd have sex at least once a day in his office, and usually try and get over to a hotel a few afternoons a week. I don't know when the marriage talk started. Maybe I did it all. I just assumed, especially since he was going through the divorce from 'The Thing,' that he would want someone *naturally* beautiful, wealthy, cultured, and connected like me."

As she said this, Renee could detect an odd faraway yet angry look in Amanda's eyes, as if she were reliving something that had happened yesterday, not a few months before. But Renee was more focused on getting the information Amanda was here to share with her.

"I even had a special ring tone for him," Amanda whispered. "Want to hear it? I still have it saved."

Before Renee could say anything, Amanda whipped out her phone. A long moan came out: "Oooooh! You are sooo good, babe. *YES!*"

"I recorded it one day when we were having sex. Isn't it the best?"

Renee wondered where culture met skank. Apparently somewhere on Park Avenue.

"That's certainly a ring tone I haven't heard before."

"I know, pretty hot," Amanda responded. "So one day I was waiting for John in his office with nothing on but a *Wall Street Journal* strategically placed and a pencil holding my hair in an updo."

Oh, please, God, no, Renee was thinking. Wasn't I tortured enough by this woman in school? Why do I need to hear this? The ring tone really was enough.

"John was running late. He'd just called to say he was leaving a meeting at his lawyers' in Times Square, so he was going to be at least fifteen minutes. So I'm bored and start looking through his desk. I find this file that says 'Cutter Out.' I start looking through it and I see all of these different bank accounts with a bank in the Cayman Islands."

Renee interrupted. "Right! My first day of work, Smythe called. I had to interrupt John in a meeting and got my head handed to me."

"Right. It was clear in the files that money basically got wired to offshore accounts in the Cayman Islands so that they weren't reflected in the regular fund's assets. It listed each partnership, each fund, and how much got sent on a weekly basis."

"So this money, which is John's own capital—and we are talking about hundreds of millions of dollars—is being siphoned off, but still kept in the fund," Renee said, then added, "of course, that makes total sense. He doesn't report those assets, doesn't pay taxes on them."

"And most important, Mimi doesn't know about it, nor does her divorce lawyer, especially not Roland Deitrich, who is only interested in something if it means his name will end up on 'Page Six.' Deitrich would love the title of the file, too, don't you?"

Renee was confused. "I'm not following you."

"Cutter Out? Don't you get it? 'Cut-Her-Out.' Mimi *Cutter*. Cut-Mimi-out!"

"Oh, my God! Of course. That is pretty clever," Renee said.

"Yeah. John really hated Mimi. He didn't want her to get anything. Too bad Deitrich is known for being more focused on his PR, because if he had brought in someone like my sister used when she got divorced to analyze all of John's finances, and do some forensic work, it would have been found. Roland still would have ended up in the paper—probably the cover story of the *Post*, for that matter—for being brilliant!"

"So did you ask John about it when he came in?"

"No, I figured he'd be pretty pissed at me for going through his stuff, and let's just say that when he did get back to the office, we were, ah, distracted by *The Wall Street Journal*—below the fold, if you get my drift."

Renee could not believe how truly disgusting she found hearing tales of Amanda's sexual exploits with the person she worked for, especially what seemed like her penchant for sexual office fantasies.

"And also, I thought that this information would come in useful one day," she added.

Ahh. There was the Amanda Renee knew.

"I'm not sure if, as things got worse with his divorce or the markets started falling apart, or both, I seemed to become expendable to John.

It's one thing to have a cute blonde marketing a hot hedge fund when times are good. As Flying Point started to blow up, and then when things got worse, all those institutional investors who wanted me all over the world only called up to yell and ask to speak to someone who was more than a hot chick. You know, after Spence, Yale, and a Harvard MBA, it's pretty tough to realize you are still just a piece of ass to a lot of people. It is, I mean was, pretty demeaning."

Renee imagined that would be very tough for someone with Amanda's background. Although she also remembered what it was like when Amanda made her feel she was just a color to her.

"So, John gets colder with me. We'd still have sex here and there, but that feeling like we were *totally* connected was *totally* gone." Again she emphasized *totally.* "He'd yell at me in front of the entire office, which was pretty hard to take, because he never did that to me before. I know people loved it, because pretty much everyone knew we were seeing each other, so clearly they knew things were not going well. Then, the day after Labor Day, Richie comes in and fires me. That's it. I got a nice severance, hush money, really, but John has never picked up the phone to apologize or say good-bye or anything at all. It makes me feel like such an idiot." Amanda chose to leave out yesterday's interaction with John. She was still humiliated and not about to share that with Renee. As far as she was concerned, that was not material for Renee's purposes, especially as it would be clear that Amanda wanted revenge not redemption.

"Wow, that is quite a story. I'm sorry it happened. It must have been humiliating."

"Yes, it was, although my mother said—and this seems funny now—that I should focus on the more important things, like finding the right husband. Who would consider me the right wife, especially now? Anyway, I traveled for a while and thought when I came back I'd try something new, like starting my own business. Maybe something in PR, since I know so many people. Yet, who knew this was going to happen? So right now that seems like a silly problem."

Renee still wasn't sure what to think about all of this. She still wasn't sure if she wanted to be friendly to Amanda or not.

"And so that was it? You haven't seen him since?"

"Ah, no. Of course not. Not at all," Amanda said rather too quickly.

"Amanda, I have a question for you. Why are you telling me all of this? From the way you've always treated me, I would think you'd assume I'm helping John or hiding his secrets or something. How do I know you aren't setting me up?"

Amanda took a deep breath. "Renee, I have always known that you are honest. I probably should have been more like you all this time. John needs to be stopped. His wife, whatever a freak she is, should be given her fair settlement from a guy that's been hiding money from her and cheating on her long before me. John shouldn't be able to treat women that way. It's demeaning and unfair. He needs to have his comeuppance. I know you will do the right thing with it, whatever that may be."

Renee was prepared to believe her, although she still wasn't sure why Amanda was coming to her now. It did make sense that her family scandal might have made her see the light, but something in her still said to be careful. At least she would try to find out more if she could. "I have one question, Amanda. How does Blake Somerset fit into all of this? He and John spend a lot of time behind closed doors together, and Blake is always nervous whenever he calls. He is connected somehow."

"Blake Somerset? That wuss! He isn't, as far as I know. Why?"

"I just can sense there's something going on with him."

"Maybe there is, but not as far as I know. I do know that Flying Point bought a lot of securities from Blake."

They both sat silently. Finally Amanda spoke.

"Look, Renee, I hope that you can forgive me for all the years when I was so terrible to you. Maybe at some point we could even be friends.

It would mean a lot to me. I've grown up a lot in the last week, and you are the type of person that I wish I was friends with. I just want to say I am sorry for everything." As she spoke, Amanda was telling the truth to some extent, but also ensuring that Renee would pursue this. She needed to be sure.

Renee paused. One doesn't often get opportunities to have payback with lifelong enemies. Here was her chance to go off on her. She took a deep breath.

"Amanda, I'm sure it wasn't easy calling me. I'm not sure if at some point a friendship might be possible, but I do know you have seen the side of a lot of people in the last week that you didn't expect to ever see."

Amanda blushed. She was thinking of the side she'd seen only last night. "Yes, I have. It's pretty rough when you have never been on the other side. Look, keep me posted on what you do, and if you need some help with any of this, let me know."

"Okay, I will. I really appreciate it."

As they left the Green Harp and Renee caught the M104 at 72nd Street traveling up Broadway to visit her parents, she was happy that Amanda had given her this insight into what was going on. But she wondered how she and Sasha could figure out what role Blake was playing in this. She also realized that even with all the money, power, and privilege that the Beldens had, there was no question she would rather be a Parker than anything else. Realizing that made her all the happier to walk into her parents' apartment, smell the chicken curry on the stove, and give Donita and William one of the biggest hugs they'd gotten in their lives.

CHAPTER TWENTY-FOUR

Getting Somewhere

Renee dialed Sasha's cell phone but got her voice mail.

"You will *not* believe it. Amanda just told me that John's been wiring money for years to a bank in the Cayman Islands. He's been hiding money from Mimi— and God knows who else. Call me ASAP, girl!"

Sasha was walking up Madison Avenue and hadn't heard her phone ring. She always loved looking at all the boutiques and their luxurious merchandise. Outside, the scene on the sidewalk was usually as elegant as inside. Women's hair was always blown out perfectly, skin was toned, bodies were muscular and lean from personal trainers. But she noticed a difference now. Stores were closed, a PRIME RETAIL SPACE AVAILABLE sign was in at least one window every other block. People still looked wealthy, but she suspected that blowouts were not happening as often, and highlighting appointments were probably being stretched to every three or four months, rather than two. Women were actually walking around with plain shopping bags rather than the brightly colored custom bags each store normally used. There was a wave of resentment and anger against the rich right now, and as a result, there was a reluctance on the part of the wealthy to spend. But as she saw this change on the street, she also thought about all the jobs that relied on people spending money. How long would it take to come back? And would it ever be as robust as it had been?

She looked down and saw she had a message. When she heard it, she immediately called Renee back.

"Oh my God!" she said. "Tell me more!"

They agreed to meet the next morning at Sant Ambroeus on Madison and 77th for breakfast.

Sasha saw Renee in the window and waved excitedly. They hurried to sit down and placed their order for fruit and lattes.

"Okay, so tell me everything she told you!" Sasha said.

"Amanda is totally shaken to the core given what has happened to her family. I have to say, I actually felt a little sorry for her."

"Oh, come on! She's been a 'beyotch' to you her whole life, and to everyone else, for that matter. They're all getting what they deserve, if you ask me. I saw her sister, Theresa, at Bergdorf's a few days ago, acting like she had not a care in the world and spending up a storm. I mean, come on!"

"I don't know. I think we all have goodness inside us, and as long as it comes out sometime, that's all that matters. I mean, to have gone from total privilege at the top to being at the bottom, and having everyone know it and laughing at you, and talking about you, *and* to have it all over the *New York Post* and *Daily News*, that's pretty bad."

"You are a better person than I, that's for sure. Anyway, fill me in."

"First, surprise of the century, she and John were having a raging affair. Seriously raging. I had to hear a few too many details. Why do some people think you want to picture them having sex?"

"Ew!"

"Yeah, double ew. Anyway, the story is that John wires money to the bank in the Caymans that Alistair Smythe calls from all the time. Literally hundreds of millions of dollars. Mimi has no idea, it just shows up as a reduction in the fund's assets, which no one would question right now anyway, nor will it show up on his net worth statements. They're secret accounts, so he won't have to pay her nearly as much in the divorce."

"Wow. Pretty smart. I wonder how many other hedge fund guys are doing that. Maybe we should start a service for all the wives out there!"

"Yes, we could charge a fee based on a percentage of assets recovered!"

"Sounds like a great business model to me," Sasha said, her mind already humming along with the idea. "Think about it! There are billions and billions in hedge funds, and I read a statistic somewhere that the divorce rate is over fifty percent for first marriages, I think even higher for the second. You'd have to figure the guy isn't going to be stupid enough to let it happen twice. Well, maybe half won't. If we charged one percent of assets recovered, we would be rolling in it!"

"I love it!" Renee said. "So Blake is a salesperson. He sells stuff to John. I don't know how he could be involved in hiding money."

"Right. Hmm. Maybe that's connected somehow. I don't know. Can you get a list of everything that is in Flying Point's assets?" Sasha asked. She wasn't quite sure where she was going with this.

"I don't have one myself, but I bet if I call Amanda, she can help."

"Great. Get it and let me take a look at it. In fact, I think I know someone else who can help us."

"Really? Who?"

"Remember the day that we were having lunch at Barneys and Mimi Cutter was there with a business school classmate of mine, Jessica Stark? She used to specialize in structuring and evaluating investments like these. And what's more, she's a friend of Mimi's through a charity, and she is helping Mimi try to value some of the assets for the settlement."

"No way. Oh, my God. That is perfect!"

"Well, it could definitely be a huge step in the right direction, if not right to the Emerald City."

"Okay, can you meet after work? I'll get the list and we can go through it together."

"Yes. Oh, shoot. I have to go to an event first. Come with me. It's at that new diamond store opening on Madison Avenue. Oh, my gosh, can you believe it? I cannot even remember what store. I mean, how many diamond stores do you need in a five-block stretch of Madison Avenue? And can you imagine a worse time to be opening a jewelry store? I won't be there long, and then we can go drink wine and pore over it. I'll see if Jessica is free, too."

"Sounds great," Renee said. "I'm always up for looking at diamonds anyway. Why don't I see if Amanda can join us. After the event, that is. She might know some additional things that would be useful."

"Amanda!" Sasha said. "Only if you're sure you want her there."

When Renee got to work, she had to figure out where she could get the portfolio listing without raising too much suspicion. She knew that Richie had it. She also knew that John had it in his computer. The question was, could she ask Richie for it without him wondering why, or could she find enough time in John's office when he wasn't in there?

She decided it was worth giving Amanda a call to see if she was as true to her word today as she had been last night at the bar. Renee actually wondered if she had dreamed that Amanda had apologized to her. After all those years of treating her like dirt because she was poor and black, it was truly amazing that the Beldens' turn in fortunes had changed her.

She dialed the number, careful to use her cell phone. Amanda's voice mail was on. Renee had seen that Gawker had printed Amanda's cell phone number and message this morning, so she assumed she wasn't picking up the calls. "Amanda, hi. It's Renee Parker. I need you for one more thing. Would really appreciate it if you could call me today."

A few minutes later, her cell phone rang. "Hi, it's Amanda. Sorry, I'm sure you saw the piece on me, so I'm not picking up calls. More fun persecution."

"Yes, I figured. Sorry. Listen, do you have any idea where I could get a copy of the investments that are in the fund without raising too much suspicion? I'm sure it's in John's computer, but I don't even know where to look."

"Oh, absolutely. Just go to the M drive. But you want both files in there, and they're password-protected."

"What is the password?"

"Bulletproof."

CHAPTER TWENTY-FIVE

Precious Gems

Only Renee and Sasha were able to make the diamond boutique opening, but the others agreed to meet them later. When Sasha got to the store, it was packed. So much for recession and holding back! Renee wasn't there yet, so after taking a glass of champagne, she posed for a few photographs and said hello to a few people she barely knew, including Selina Gilhart, who like Zelig managed to be at every event and in every photo yet half the time wasn't even invited. She decided to venture back and look at the jewels, which were arranged in huge glass cases.

Sasha never understood why stores didn't just put the price tags where people could see them. Well, she did. If you had to ask the price, you couldn't afford it. But wasn't curiosity a good thing? She hated trying to crane her neck to pretend she wasn't looking for the price. There were several salespeople behind the cases, anxiously awaiting a real buyer. Sasha tried not to make eye contact, but it was too late.

"It's lovely, isn't it? Seven carats," she a saleswoman, pointing to a canary yellow diamond ring. "Shall I take it out for you?"

Sasha wanted to say no, but it didn't really matter. The woman's key was already in the case and she was taking out the ring and placing it on a velvet tray on the counter.

Sasha went through the obligatory oohs and ahhs.

"Would you like to try it on?"

Sasha felt like saying, "Back off, lady," but instead said, "um, sure!"

It did look gorgeous, though Sasha also noted that she was desperately in need of a manicure.

"It was mined in South Africa. Only one other like it exists in the world," the saleswoman continued. Sasha really wanted nothing more than to get away from her.

Finally, she could bear the suspense no more. "How much is it?"

"This one is... let me see... Ah here it is. Two hundred and fifty thousand dollars. It's a wonderful value and an investment. It will perform better than the stock market, that's for sure. So many people are putting their liquid assets into precious gems right now."

"Really?" Sasha wondered if the New York Stock Exchange was thinking of moving its headquarters up to Madison Avenue. "Can you write the particulars on it? I'll give it to my husband to think about for my birthday gift." It was always the perfect excuse, the old "let me tell my husband" lie. The saleswoman probably knew it, too, but couldn't let on. It worked well for both of them.

Just then, there was a bit of a commotion at the front door. Sasha looked up, and who should she see but Mimi Cutter! What a freaky coincidence.

Mimi was surrounded by photographers, the owner of the store, and Selina Gilhart, who was already putting her arm around her for a shot. Sasha saw one of the PR people working the event ask Mimi who she was wearing, but from what Sasha could tell, it was really a matter of who she was not wearing! Amid her usual mishmash of designers and colors, she was wearing the most spectacular diamond necklace with a diamond pendant upon which was her MedicAlert. Holy moly. This woman was nuts!

Sasha thought that Mimi had had some additional facial work done since she'd last seen her, as her lips, which had been askew at Fred's, now seemed to be aligned, although much, much puffier.

The saleswoman who had been paying so much attention to Sasha now made a beeline for Mimi. "Hello, Mrs. Cutter. So nice to see you again! I would love to show you our new collection." Fantastic, the perfect way for Sasha to gracefully end her budding relationship with the saleswoman.

Sasha lingered at the case, though, to observe Mimi. She could see that even amid her freakish visage, there was something about her that seemed very sad.

At that moment, Mimi looked over at her. "Hi. Didn't we meet at Fred's? I was with Jessica Stark."

"Yes, we did. I'm Sasha Silver. Nice to see you again."

"Thanks, you, too. Boy, these events are insane, aren't they?"

"Yes, they certainly are. So how have you been?" Sasha asked.

"Oh, I'm all right. I have been trying to get this divorce stuff worked out, but sometimes it seems like it's never going to end. I used to be married. Now my status is getting divorced. I'd just like to have it be done and be divorced. Unfortunately, my husband is a pretty wily guy when it comes to getting what he wants. The fact that he screwed me during our marriage means that he thinks he can keep doing it."

"I'm sorry. That has to be tough. You're lucky to have Jessica helping, though. She is really smart and cares a lot."

"Yes, she has been fantastic, but I don't know if she is smart enough to get by John. I don't know how, but I know John, and if he can find a way to win, especially when it means hurting someone else, he will."

Sasha could see that Renee had just walked in and was looking for her. She worried that somehow Mimi might know Renee was connected to John, even though it was unlikely, to say the least. She wanted to try to extract herself from the conversation and get over to Renee.

"Well, look, you may not realize it, but you have a great team working for you. I mean, between your lawyer and Jessica, and I'm sure others, that is. I have to run, but I really hope everything works out for you. I have a feeling it will."

"Thank you, Sasha, I hope you're right, and I really appreciate it."

Sasha practically ran off to Renee. "Did you see who I was talking to?"

"Yes, I did! I figured I should stay over here in case she saw me. I'm sure she doesn't know who I am, but I'm just nervous."

"Me, too. Anyway, we should go. Why were you so late?"

Renee said, "Oh, I was having trouble getting the files organized and printed. It was weird. There were two files, but they didn't look that different to me, so for a while I thought I was printing the same thing. Anyway, I just brought it all."

"Oh, okay. Well, let's go, and quickly. I see Selina Gilhart making her way over."

They had all agreed to meet at 7:30. Jessica was picking them up in her car. Amanda didn't want to be seen anywhere public, and given that the work they were going to do was sensitive to say the least, they decided that meeting at someone's apartment would be best. But Sasha's was out, because the kids wouldn't give them a moment's peace; Jessica lived in Locust Valley; Renee's was a one-room studio; and Amanda...well, no one really wanted to go to her house. So they decided the best and most secretive place to meet was Renee's parents' home.

"Renee, are you sure you want to do that?" Sasha asked. "I mean, I know you and Amanda are now friendly, but do you really want her to be there?"

"Actually, I think it's kind of funny and ironic—she missed all the great parties I had in high school anyway. I'm totally fine with it," she responded.

As they got out of Jessica's car, each woman was clearly out of her element, except Renee, of course, who took out her keys, opened the lobby entrance, and led them all back to the elevator. Renee's parents lived in one of those huge redbrick complexes that dot the landscape up in Harlem and the Bronx. Literally hundreds of families lived there in apartments that were twenty-five to the floor, unlike the thirty apartments that made up an entire building on the Upper East Side.

Renee pressed 32, and the elevator door slowly closed and creaked its way up, jerking periodically. "Sorry, girls. Sometimes it can be a bit unpredictable," she said without seeming to be too embarrassed about it.

They all murmured that it was fine, while worrying that they might get stuck or suddenly start plummeting down.

Finally, after what seemed like fifteen minutes, the elevator stopped at their floor. They got out, and Renee led them down a dark hallway with stained carpeting. She stopped at 32W and opened the door.

"Mama? Daddy? It's me, Renee. I am here with some friends."

Donita emerged from the kitchen, wiping her hands. "Hello, cookie. What a pleasure to see you." She kissed her on the cheek.

"Mama, I'd like you to meet some friends." And she introduced each one. When she got to Amanda, if Donita remembered that this was the same person she had heard so many terrible things about during Renee's school days, she didn't let on. It wasn't Donita's way to be rude, especially to guests in her home.

"Welcome. I am honored to have so many special women in my home. I wish I'd had some more notice, though. I'm afraid it's a little messy. But I have been used to Renee bringing people home for a long, long time with little notice!"

The apartment could not have been neater, or cozier, for that matter. Family photos lined the shelves, including the nine children that Renee's older sisters had. There were blankets that Donita must have crocheted over the sofas and well-tended flowers in the windows. It all had a feeling of love, warmth, and happiness. There was also the most enticing smell coming from the galley kitchen.

"Mrs. Parker, what is that amazing aroma!" Sasha said.

"Oh, I just made some plantain chips and banana bread. I'll bring it out for you girls."

As they sat down, they all felt like happy kids being served a snack. Donita also brought out a pitcher of lemonade, to which she had added some mint and fresh lemon slices. She returned to the kitchen, leaving them alone.

"Ohh, this is so good. I'm going to gain ten pounds," Jessica said.

They all nodded in agreement while reaching for more.

In part because it was in her nature to lead things, and in part because working on this with Renee had given her a level of enthusiasm she hadn't felt in a while, Sasha naturally took over the discussion. "Okay, guys. We have got some serious work to do here," she said. "Let's lay out what we know so far. We have a bank in the Caymans that money's been sent to, thanks to Amanda for that tidbit. But we also have Blake Somerset." She said his name softly, in case Donita might hear. "He is all over Cutter, as we know. We also have the file of everything John owns, thanks to Amanda again," who by this point was looking quite pleased to be the connection for so much important information.

"So now. What we need to do, and hopefully can with Jessica's expertise, is figure out what these things are and whether anything seems amiss."

Jessica was already perusing the list of investments, which had names like Series G Banfield Trust, Vertical CDO IV, and Traverse Point Floater MBS. Most of it seemed like gibberish. Each one had the identifying CUSIP next to it.

"Gosh, guys, there's a lot of stuff in here. It's going to take me a few minutes to sort through some of these," Jessica said, her mouth full of banana bread. "It's like looking for a needle in a haystack."

"I'm just going to call home for a sec," Sasha said, and punched in the speed-dial number on her cell. "Hi, Maura, it's me. I'm going to be late. Did Adam come home yet? He said he would try to be home by seven." She paused to hear Maura say the inevitable, "Not yet." "Okay, can you please stay till he gets there? I'd really appreciate it... No problem? Great. Thanks!"

"Hey, this is weird," Jessica said all of a sudden.

"What?" they all said in unison.

"Well, I see two separate listings of a bunch of the same CDOs, but the CUSIPs are different on each list. That doesn't make sense. The CUSIP is like the Social Security number for a security. It doesn't change." They all knew that, of course.

"Gosh, I wish we had a Bloomberg here," Jessica said, looking around, as if somehow one of the machines that every Wall Street trader and salesman relies on, which cost over $20,000 per year, would appear from Donita's well-stocked kitchen.

All of a sudden, Sasha smiled. For once, Adam's lateness would come in handy. She dialed his office. "Trish, it's me, Sasha. How are you?" she asked. Trish was a lifesaver for Adam, and Sasha always tried to ask her how she was. "Is the master still around?" she said jokingly.

"Of course he is, Sasha. Do you really think he remembered that you asked him to go home first? I tried to get him out of here, but lost the battle. Let me get him for you."

Adam got on the phone. "I'm leaving right now. I promise!"

"Don't worry, hon. I need you to do something for me right now."

Adam, clearly relieved that he wasn't in trouble, said, "Sure! Anything."

"Can you look up some CUSIPs for me? The first one is 349AX49YL."

She heard him say the numbers and, "Enter, Go," which on Bloomberg meant the information had been sent and the answer would be forthcoming in an instant.

"Umm, let's see. It's Gerard Place III 2005."

Sasha repeated that to Jessica, who then said, "Okay, what about 349AX4Y9 L," reversing one of the digits and one of the letters.

"Gerard Place III B4 2005."

"That doesn't make sense," Jessica said again.

"Here, you talk to him," Sasha said, handing her phone to Jessica.

For the next five minutes, Jessica gave Adam numerous CUSIPs that all seemed to be very similar but were off slightly. The names of the investments were mostly gibberish to all of them, but at one point Jessica said, "Oh, my God. I worked on that deal. I thought that piece of crap cratered a long time ago. It was vacation condos in Panama City, Florida. It's listed here as being worth ninety. How could that be?"

All of a sudden, she turned white and handed the phone back to Sasha. "I think I know what he did! Oh, my God. That's brilliant!"

"Babe, you're the best," Sasha said. "Now get your butt home and make sure Josh hasn't put his frog in the tub again."

When she hung up, Jessica turned to all of them and said, "I don't know all of these products, remember I haven't been working for a few years. But I recognize some, and I can sort of tell by the year it was issued what was going on in the housing market at the time. One list has CUSIPs listed next to the investment and a low value, but the other list has a different CUSIP with a different investment with a high value. I think John Cutter switched CUSIPs to inflate the value of his funds. He's really got all crap in here, but it looks like he's got a bunch of high-quality-performing assets. The CUSIPs are almost the same, and so are the funds. He's switched the lowest-level crap he had for the better-rated tranches someone else had." She sat back with a look of exhausted satisfaction.

"How could he do that, though? He doesn't control the CUSIPs," Amanda said.

"I'm not sure," Jessica said.

"Wait! I think I have it," Renee said. "Blake!"

"Blake!" they all yelled in unison, then whispered, "Blake!" as if Donita wouldn't have heard the first time they'd said it.

"Blake must have been the one who sold him a lot of this stuff. Two things make me think that. First of all, Richie was giving me a tutorial one day, and he was going on and on about how there are all these guys on Wall Street who want to sell complicated fancy investments to them. Blake is one of those guys. Also, Sasha, remember when I told you at Fred's, that first morning at work I heard all this yelling and the word *bulletproof* used? That must have been when they cooked up the idea."

"Oh, my God. I think you could be right," Sasha said. "And the file is called 'Bulletproof,' too. It's staring us in the face. It totally makes sense. And when I saw Grigsby at the museum family party, she told me how Blake was acting odd and coming and going at odd hours, yelling at her all the time. I mean, I think the amount of money they lost was probably enough to make anyone nuts, but I know for a fact that Barclays has also tried to reach out to these guys and pay them pretty well. I actually heard that they gave them over one hundred percent of their prior year's compensation. So there must have been something else that caused him to act that way. Wow. So now what?"

"Well," Jessica said, "I need to get this information to Mimi ASAP. First of all, the fund is worth a lot less than she or her lawyer may realize, but the Securities and Exchange Commission is going to have a lot to say about this. For Mimi, the Cayman stuff is probably more important right now. They can subpoena the records from the bank down there. She may actually have more money coming to her than she ever dreamed."

"Plus the fact that her husband is a scum-bucket, cheating thief," said Amanda, her humiliation by John still fresh on her mind.

"Yes, that too."

"Excuse me, Renee, can I use the bathroom?" Amanda said.

"Yes. The door over there to the left."

"Well, Renee," Sasha said, "Amanda's turned out to be a great help after all. What a strange turn of events."

"I guess everyone has some good ins—"

Just then, a strange sound emanated from Amanda's purse: "*Oooooh! You are sooo good, babe. YES!*"

Renee froze.

"*Oooooh! You are sooo good, babe. YES!*"

"What is *that*?" said Jessica.

"*Oooooh! You are sooo good, babe. YES!*"

All of a sudden, Amanda came rushing out of the bathroom, bright red. "Renee, I don't know why he is calling. Really I..."

Renee stood up. She stood up tall. She seemed even taller than her five-foot-nine-inch frame. A look came across her face that was terrifying.

"You BITCH. You played me, didn't you? You are still with him. I don't know what the hell you think you are doing, but get the FUCK out of my apartment right now! Do you hear me? Right now!"

"Renee, it's not what you think. I haven't spoken to him since—"

"Since when, you cunt?" Sasha and Jessica gasped at Renee's language. "Since when?"

"Renee, what is going on? Who was that?" Sasha said.

"It's John. John fucking Cutter. That was Amanda's ring tone for him. And that was also the sound of John Cutter having an orgasm, as if that weren't evident. Amanda, you told me you hadn't spoken to him since before Richie fired you. So what the hell is he doing calling you now? You know what? I don't give a shit. Get your white ass out of my parents' house right now."

Amanda picked up her bag to leave.

"Wait," Sasha said. "I want to know what happened. Renee, can we at least find out the truth?"

"Honey, there ain't no way you finding out the truth from this bitch. I can almost promise you that."

"Well, I would at least like to try to find out. Amanda, tell us what the story really is. You owe us that much."

Amanda started to cry. "Okay, I'll tell you everything."

She sat down. "I wasn't completely truthful. I mean, everything I told you about John and me being together was the truth except one last encounter." She told them what happened with John the other night.

"So seeing the light about being a good person was a lie?" Renee said.

"I guess so. But I didn't mean to be dishonest."

"Yeah, right. So why is he calling you now, then? What's that all about?"

"Honestly, I don't have any idea. Really, I haven't spoken to him at all."

"Give me your phone," Renee said. "Now! I mean it."

Amanda handed her the phone.

"What is the PIN number?"

"It's 3291."

Renee dialed and placed it on hands-free. "Let's see what he has to say on his message."

"You have one new message. You have no saved messages. To listen to messages, press one."

They were all anxious as they waited. There was static and some noise in the background. It sounded like a bar. They could hear John talking in the background and some other voices. After about thirty seconds, it became obvious that John must have mistakenly pressed Amanda's number while his phone was in his pocket. He hadn't meant to call her at all.

"Well, isn't it funny how the truth just finds its way out?" Renee said.

"Look, Renee. I am sorry. I really am. If I told you the truth about why I was giving you the information, you never would have taken my call, would you? I don't know how to be anything other than what I have always been."

"No, I'm sure I wouldn't have, Amanda. Even though we got to the bottom of what has been going on, I am not sure I like you any better than I did all these years. I still think it's best if you leave."

Amanda looked downcast and seemed to truly show some real emotions. She started to gather her things.

Just then, William Parker, who had been in the bedroom napping, appeared. "What is all this racket out here? I feel like you're in school again," he said.

"Hi, Daddy. We've just been working on a project. But we're all done now." Renee glared at Amanda. "Some people are just leaving."

"Well, if it's not on my line, I'm afraid I can't help you. Did you all solve the world's problems?"

They all looked at one another. "Well," Renee began, "sort of, but it's a little more complicated than that."

"Well, whatever it is, I'm sure if you were involved, it was done with grace, smarts, and sweetness."

Donita came out of the kitchen with some extra food wrapped up for each of them. Amanda suddenly said, "Mr. and Mrs. Parker, I don't know if you remember my name from Renee's days at Spence. I was pretty terrible to her. I just want to apologize to you all for what an awful person I was. I only wish I'd grown up with a family like this, in an apartment like this. I think I would have been a much better person. I guess it took me until this very moment to realize that."

If William and Donita were surprised, they didn't let on. Donita said, "You don't always need the right parents or the right home. Sometimes it just comes along at the right time in the strangest of circumstances, or for the oddest of reasons."

"I guess so. Renee, I'm sorry. I hope you can find it in your heart to understand why I did what I did."

Amanda left, leaving the other three standing there awkwardly. "Renee, is something wrong?" Donita asked, feeling the tension in the air.

"Mama, it's a little hard to explain. I'll tell you later."

"Okay. Girls, or I guess I should say ladies, I am glad you were here this evening. It's been some time since Renee has had friends over. It seems like school days again. I am going to bed, as I have an early day. Renee, are you staying here or going to your apartment?"

"I think I will stay here, Mama. For some strange reason, I just feel like it would be good to be at home."

Renee said good night to Sasha and Jessica and gave them both big hugs.

"Well, it's been some evening. I am not quite sure what tomorrow will bring, but let's stay in touch over the next few days."

CHAPTER TWENTY-SIX

John's Point of No Return

Unbeknownst to John, because of four women, including his assistant and his ex-lover, his world was about to come crashing down.

Jessica called Mimi's house the next morning but got her answering machine and left a message. She had misplaced Mimi's cell phone number. Oh well, she thought, Mimi would call her back eventually, but she was anxious to share the news.

"Mimi, it's Jessica. Please call me as soon as possible. I have some really important news regarding John's assets. Call me immediately. Okay? Bye."

Unfortunately, Mimi didn't get the message right away. She had finally heard that her dermatologist had gotten Smoothshape, a revolutionary new system to eliminate cellulite. Mimi's recent obsession was what she viewed as veritable lumps of cottage cheese on her thighs and rear end. Ever since she read about this new, noninvasive system that used light and laser waves to eliminate fat cells, she had been dying to try it. She was there for several hours, as after her treatment she had a long conversation with the doctor about the virtues of Radiesse vs. hyaluronic acid as new fillers to try. She wasn't pleased with how Restylane was making her look. Given how much she spent there every year, Dr. Oren Exler wasn't about to rush Mimi out. Before she left, he gave her a little Botox pick-me-up. After her appointment, she felt better than she had in a while. It was always a relief to know she could make herself look just a little bit better and a little bit different. If she kept trying, she would eventually be perfect.

After her appointment, Mimi decided to stop at Bergdorf's for a little retail therapy. There was no better place to make that happen than the second-floor shoe boutique. She always felt calm when she was sitting on one of the plush sofas surrounded by shoes brought to her by favorite salesman Thomas Khadafy, the stylish man with the three-piece suits and Alfalfa-like Afro, who had an encyclopedic knowledge of all things footwear. In fact, he'd called her that morning to tell her that several of the fall collections had arrived and he'd taken the liberty of setting aside a number of pairs in her size. In addition to his selections, Mimi's routine was always the same. She would wander around the perimeter of the store from Vivier to Chanel to Manolo to Louboutin to Prada, working her way to the center table, selecting about a dozen pairs to try on. She would then visit the two side rooms for additional selections from Gucci and Miu Miu. Once she'd made her initial choices, Thomas would have the boxes brought out, along with another ten pairs or so. She rarely left without purchasing five or six of them. Recently, she'd become enamored with Giuseppe Zanotti and was particularly taken with the platform sandals that were embellished with spike, fringe, and strategically placed feathers. They looked like weapons, like spears, in fact. She called them "angry shoes," and when she put them on, she sometimes thought about what it would be like to step on John's face with them and grind into him. That was how angry he had made her with everything he had done to her. She really could picture killing him at times, and in worse ways than with her shoes.

The feeling was mutual.

While Mimi was fantasizing about gouging John's eyes out with a five-inch heel, John was looking at the latest bill from Lucille Smith. In the last year, he had spent $772,494 in legal bills and knew he would end up paying for Roland Deitrich as well. He could only imagine how much that would total. Roland probably used Mimi like a cash machine.

Just then, Renee told him that another angry client was on the phone, to which he responded, "Tell him to fuck off. I'm out of here."

Renee was used to John responding this way and instead said, "I'm so sorry, Mr. Curtis, he's just gone into a meeting. Let me take your number and I'll have him call you as soon as possible."

John grabbed his jacket and stormed out of the office and headed downstairs to Brasserie 8 ½, the restaurant located in the basement of 9 West 57th. He went to the bar and ordered a shot of Patrón, downed it, and then had another.

Everything was closing in on him, and at this point he was out of options. He'd never been like this. Things were always supposed to work out for him. That's why he was a brilliant trader, as he always knew when to take the loss or sensed the moment the market was about to turn. He was so deep in a losing position right now, he didn't know how he could climb out of it.

Man, he thought, how the fuck did I end up like this? I just wanted a simple life: to do decently, have a few kids and an attractive wife who loved me. I never asked for this huge success and equally bad flame-out. How did I get from being a college soccer star who planned on becoming a doctor, to this?

As his mind wandered, he blamed a lot of what happened on Mimi and her need to have more and more. Of course, it was completely ridiculous. Mimi had nothing to do with his situation. She wasn't with him at work every day. She hadn't even lived with him for the last year. But right now, she was the most convenient person against whom to project his anger and frustration. He started thinking about every ridiculous thing she wore and things she did to her face or body. If only she were out of the way, he could get back to focusing on his fund and improving his performance. But he had to deal with Mimi and this fucking divorce.

He hated her so much, he really could kill her.

He could kill her.

As soon as he thought of it, he couldn't get it out of his mind. *He could kill her.* Why not? He should. He could. But how, without getting caught?

Just then, the woman next to him sneezed. "Sorry," she said to her friend, "my allergies are driving me crazy."

Her allergies! How perfect. As soon as he heard the words, he knew he had the answer. Now he just had to think about how to make it happen.

John had actually been exceptional in chemistry at school. In fact, it was his brilliance in the subject, along with his soccer prowess and 790/800 score on his SATs, that had sealed his admission to Harvard, not to mention Johns Hopkins, MIT, and Stanford. He'd spent hours in the lab at college, which had also led to a huge fight with Mimi the day of "The Game," when Harvard played Yale in football. They were supposed to go to a formal party at his club that night, but John lost track of time on a chemistry problem set. Mimi waited for hours and then, in a huff, went to the Hong Kong with her roommates, in her formal dress, got wasted on scorpion bowls, and ended up going home with another guy. It took a good two weeks for them to get back together after that one.

John had spent time assisting a Harvard med student with work on adrenal insufficiency in lab rats, the exact problem that had plagued Mimi since childbirth. One day, he had erroneously mixed the wrong chemical in the solution that was injected into the rats. Within an hour, the rats had died. John was embarrassed, in fact devastated, by his error. He was supposed to be perfect in every way. He had never failed or even made a mistake. People counted on him to be perfect. He quickly put two other rats in the cage and disposed of the dead ones without telling anyone. It was a portent, perhaps, of things to come.

How ironic. That would now be what would save him, so to speak.

It actually wasn't that difficult to obtain. He left the bar and practically sprinted down the street to the Duane Reade on the corner of

Sixth Avenue and 57th Street. That same substance he used all those years ago at Harvard could easily be made by combining a few over-the-counter items. He grabbed what he needed and paid the two people on line ahead of him $100 each to pay first.

Once on the street, he dialed Mimi's cell. It went to voice mail. In his most charming voice, he said, "Mims, it's me. I've been thinking that maybe we could sit down and try to talk some of this stuff out. Call me. Please?"

Mimi had just paid for the $7,494.15 in shoes when she saw the missed call and John's number. She was staggered. Her heart pounded when she heard his message. As much as she hated him, she still loved him desperately. That was the way it had always been between them since they first met nearly twenty-five years ago.

She stood there for a minute, just staring at the phone. Then she dialed his number.

"Hi."

Perfect. John had her, and he knew it.

"Hi, babe. I wanted to see if we could get together for a little while. I've just been thinking about everything, about you and me. I don't know how we got here. I thought maybe it was time to talk, no lawyers, just us."

"Um, yeah. I'd like that, but our lawyers would have a fit. As long as you promise no funny stuff, I suppose it can't hurt. As long as it is in good faith. Is this in good faith, John?"

"Of course," he lied.

"Okay. Do you want to come over to the house?"

That would make it much easier for him. "Sure. How about in an hour?"

"Okay, I'll see you then."

John ran back to his office, much to Renee's surprise, went into his private bathroom, and mixed the items together. He found a half-empty travel-size mouthwash bottle, emptied it, and put the concoction into it, stuffed it in his blazer pocket, and ran back out of the office, telling Renee he wouldn't be back till later, if at all.

Ironically, John and Mimi were only half a block away from each other, as Bergdorf Goodman was just down the street from John's office building. In fact, they could have bumped into each other, but whereas Mimi's car was around the corner on 58th Street, John hopped into a cab at 57th. He didn't think it would be good to have his car take him and thus have a record of his whereabouts. As a result, he actually got to the loft before Mimi. As he waited outside, he felt surprisingly calm. His decision had brought him to the point of no return. He just wondered how this was all going to go down.

Her car pulled up to North Moore Street, and Mimi rushed out. "Oh, John, I'm so sorry. I got caught in traffic."

When he saw her face, he felt his stomach turn slightly. She clearly had had work done since he'd last seen her and in fact he could see she must have just had something done today, as there were still red marks on her face. He felt like puking. Nevertheless, he said, "No problem. I was only waiting for a few minutes. You look great."

"Really? Thanks. Let's go up."

Unfortunately, since she was so rushed, she didn't have a chance to check the blinking answering machine, which held Jessica's by-now several messages to call her.

"Would you like a glass of wine?"

"Sure. Why don't I get it for us? Still keep everything in the same place?"

"That would be great. Yes. All where it was. I'll have a Pinot."

As he grabbed two glasses and poured them each some wine, he reached into his pocket and pulled out the mouthwash bottle. He hoped that using it in this way would have the same effect as when he'd injected it into the rats all those years ago. To be safe, he added a bit more. If all went well, within a short period of time she should be on her way out, without realizing he had done anything.

"Here you go."

He wasn't sure how long it would be before it took effect, though, and he was nervous. Maybe it wouldn't work. The last time Mimi had an attack in college, she had a reaction within thirty minutes; nevertheless, he was going to have to try to wait it out to be certain it worked, which meant he would have to fake interest in trying to reconcile with her.

The next fifteen minutes were agony, but he did his best. He noticed Mimi started looking a little sweaty above her mouth and brow.

"It's a little hot in here, don't you think?" she asked.

"No, I'm fine. Do you want me to open the window?"

"No, that's all right. I'll do it."

As she got up, he saw her start to wobble. He wondered if he could leave, since clearly things were starting to work. He was about to say something about receiving an e-mail that he had to deal with when he noticed something he had completely forgotten about. Mimi's MedicAlert. How could he have missed it? Today she was wearing the hammered gold Elsa Peretti. He remembered when he'd bought the necklace at Tiffany's for her, dropping twenty grand after he'd cheated on her one Valentine's Day. He'd been extremely irritated when he got the bill for the matching MedicAlert she'd had made. It wasn't the cost. It was just her ridiculous need to show off with these silly medallions.

Shit. He was going to have to figure out what to do about that. It would be too obvious if anyone saw the necklace on her. Why hadn't he thought about it before? He needed to stay until she'd collapsed and get it off her neck.

He didn't have to wait too long. She said, "I'm really not feeling well. I think I need to lie—" And she collapsed on the floor. He ran over to her and checked her, slapping at her cheeks to see if she was going to come around. She didn't respond. He moved her head to the side and unfastened the hook of the necklace. He slipped it into his pocket and left the apartment.

He felt a sense of elation and adrenaline. It was like having sex on the board table of his office. Extreme power and control over anything and anyone he wanted. Except this was the ultimate power and the ultimate vanquishing of his enemy.

Back at Mimi's apartment, all was quiet. The two glasses of wine sat on the coffee table, Picassos on the walls looked down as if nothing had happened. The current issue of *Vogue* was on the counter, in which Mimi was featured in the "People Are Talking About" column. And Mimi lay there on the floor, as Jessica left one more message about the Cayman Islands and something about switched securities, oblivious to the fact that her husband, John, had apparently just killed her.

About thirty minutes later, Concetta, the maid, unlocked the door. She wasn't supposed to come until tomorrow morning, but she was in the neighborhood and needed to check on the cleaning supplies because she was going to clean the loft from head to toe. When she walked in and saw Mimi on the floor, she screamed, dropped her things, and yelled, "*Ay, Dios mío!* Meesus Mimi! Meesus Mimi! Wake up!" She was shaking her, but Mimi did not respond. Frantic, Concetta dialed 911. "You come quick. My boss, she is fainted on the floor."

The ambulance and EMT people arrived minutes later. Mimi was not dead, but they needed to get her to the emergency room immediately. Concetta went with them. She had her rosary beads in her hand and was so upset, she neglected to notice Mimi's missing necklace. Frankly, Concetta never actually knew what all those medallions were anyway, so she wouldn't have been able to help them if she had seen that it was missing.

As the emergency room staff worked on her, they were baffled. They did a battery of tests but couldn't figure out what would cause this seemingly healthy forty-three-year-old woman to be near death. It didn't make sense. Dr. Yanni Galifanakis, the chief ER resident, ran his hand through his hair in frustration. Doctors couldn't know everything, and sometimes the symptoms just didn't add up without additional information about the patient's medical history. He was worried that if he gave her the wrong treatment, it could make her worse. In a few minutes, he might not have a choice.

Just then, Annie Lee, the new nurse on duty, walked by and saw the commotion. Annie was twenty-six and came from Fort Lee, New Jersey. Working in a Manhattan hospital was a big step for her. She had lofty plans for herself, which mostly involved finding a doctor on staff to marry. She liked being a nurse, but she loved following the comings and goings of society and its players. She read *W* and *Vogue* and always checked NewYorkSocialDiary.com first thing in the morning so she could see who had been where the night before. She religiously studied the boldfaced names in the "Style" section every Sunday in *The New York Times*.

"Nurse, we need you right now." When Annie saw Mimi lying there, she said, "Oh, my God, that's Mimi Cutter! Wow!"

The ER staff looked at her and rolled their eyes. This wasn't the time to be pointing people out, but if she knew who she was, perhaps they might learn something about her that could be helpful.

"Do you know her? Is she a friend of yours?"

"Ha! A friend of mine! I wish. No, this is Mimi Cutter. Big society lady. She's getting divorced from her husband, you know, he runs Flying Point Capital? She was Bergdorf Goodman's biggest client last year. She's in the new issue of *Vogue*, too."

Dr. Galifanakis seemed disappointed that this was merely some society woman. That wasn't going to help figure out what was going on with her, and he needed answers fast. He turned away from Annie.

"Yeah, she's really superstylish. So many great clothes and jewelry. Oh, and *W* says her custom-made MedicAlert collection is probably worth close to two million dollars. When she first came on the scene in the—"

Dr. Galifanakis turned suddenly. "What did you say? Her MedicAlert collection!? What are you talking about? What is she allergic to?"

"Oh, she has Addison's disease, a cortisone deficiency. Had it since she was born. She's turned it into this fantastic fashion statement, though. She has over forty necklaces. At least that was what *W* said last year. Some are precious stones, exotic materials. She was presented with one by the Museum of Natural History as a gift after she walked up to the podium and announced a spontaneous five-million-dollar gift at their annual benefit. It had pieces of amber with a fossilized mosquito in it and—"

But Dr. Galifanakis was no longer listening to her. He knew what the problem was and how to deal with it.

The next few minutes were crucial. He would need to inject her with steroids immediately. She still wasn't out of the woods, but he had a good chance of saving her.

"Oh, Meesus Mimi, ees okay, I was so worry. I am so glad you are good to be now," Concetta said a few hours later when Mimi was sitting up in her bed. She still felt pretty woozy and was staying in the hospital overnight for observation. The doctor said she was very lucky to be alive.

"I don't understand why you weren't wearing your alert, Mrs. Cutter. From what I understand, you have quite a collection. Why would you go through all that trouble to have them made and then not wear it?"

"But Dr. Galifanakis, I did. I had on my gold Peretti. It's one of my favorites. It must have come off in the ambulance."

"No, the EMT staff is very careful to always check for those. It can save us time and make the difference in saving a life or not. In fact, if not for your maid coming in early and our nurse, who recognized you from party pictures and knew about your collection, we wouldn't be here having this conversation right now."

Mimi would have furrowed her brow, but Botox had long ago made that impossible. "Well, I'm baffled. Let's see, I know that—" She went pale. "Doctor, I know what happened."

"You do?"

"Yes. This was no mistake. This was attempted murder. By my husband, John. God, I'm so stupid not to have realized it all along! He wouldn't have called me to talk things out."

"Okay, Mrs. Cutter, I'm really not sure what you are talking about."

"No, listen to me. I have been going through a terrible divorce for over a year. My husband, John, runs a very large hedge fund and has been under a lot of pressure with the markets. John called me this afternoon and asked if we could talk. I'm such a stupid idiot that I still love him and would have taken him back. He came over and we had some wine. He got it for us. He must have put something in my drink and then taken off my necklace after I collapsed. He probably took it with him, knowing him, and will give it to a girlfriend."

Dr. Galifanakis was stunned. He had never heard anything like this in his career. "Mrs. Cutter, are you sure? I don't even know what he could have done to you. It's staggering. At the same time, I need to get the police involved right away. Let me go see the hospital administration. I guess all's well that ends well, for you, at least. Your husband is going to be facing some serious charges."

"Oh, that's not the least of it. I also assume my divorce proceedings will move along pretty smoothly at this point. Doctor, thank you again for everything you did. Can you ask that nurse to come by and see me? I'd like to give her a special thank-you."

When Annie left Mimi's room a little bit later, she was in complete shock. Mimi, in addition to thanking her, told Annie she would be getting a check for $1 million as thanks for saving her life. It wasn't the kind of first day Annie had expected to have at the hospital, and it also wasn't the last day she'd expected to have, either. She walked into her supervisor's office and immediately announced her resignation.

For her part, Mimi was stunned and speechless. She couldn't believe how foolish she'd been, but she was also devastated and embarrassed by what John had tried to do to her. As she lay in her hospital bed that night, tears streamed down her face. How did things ever get this far with John? For God's sake, they had a child together. How could John not have thought of her before he decided to do this?

When she arrived home the next morning and listened to her answering machine, Mimi heard message after message from Jessica. She couldn't believe that when she'd walked in only a day before with John, the information about the Cayman accounts was already on the machine. Thank God she still had a chance to hear it.

Mimi called her right away and related where she had been over the last twenty-four hours, and they exchanged what each had learned over the prior day. Mimi was shocked, although only to a point, given how well she knew John, to hear the extent of his duplicity. While she was overjoyed to realize that she would be getting a huge payout, she was also devastated by what John had done—to her, of course, but also to himself. The Mimi and John who had started in Harvard Yard all those years ago were really never coming back.

When the police arrived at John's apartment later that evening, he wasn't surprised. He assumed they were there to tell him that his wife had been found dead in her apartment. What did surprise him was when they said, "Mr. Cutter? You are under arrest for the attempted murder of your wife, Mimi Cutter." Before leaving, John grabbed the same jacket he'd worn the day before, and as they cuffed him, one of the officers felt a bulge in his jacket, and there in the pocket was Mimi's Elsa Peretti hammered gold MedicAlert necklace.

CHAPTER TWENTY-SEVEN

Cutter's Last Stand

The *New York Post* headline screamed, CUTTER'S LAST STAND— HEDGE FUND BIGWIG ACCUSED OF TRYING TO POISON WIFE TO KEEP MILLIONS.

It was all anyone could talk about over lattes at Sant Ambroeus, the seafood salad at San Pietro, the organic arugula omelet at the Regency, and the chicken hash at 21.

The offices of Flying Point Capital were grim. The employees came into work with the *Post* and the equally dramatic *Daily News* headline UNTIL DEATH DO US PART: FLORENCE NIGHTINGALE SAVES SOCIALITE WIFE FROM CERTAIN DEATH. A CNBC van was parked outside to report on the situation. At the office, no one knew what to do. Richie tried to handle the support staff, and the other senior partners tried to talk to investors when they weren't wondering themselves what was going to happen—with the fund, of course, but more important with themselves. A once-prestigious job would now be a résumé killer. Calls came in fast and furious, mostly with redemption requests. It didn't matter that the next redemption date wasn't for another two months. Fraud and attempted murder were two tickets that superseded the terms of the private placement memo. By the end of the day, requests totaled nearly 80 percent of the assets.

Renee wasn't sure what to do. She knew it was only a matter of time before John's securities fraud was added to the list of his other crimes. While attempted murder and hiding assets from a spouse didn't make one eligible for a Boy Scout badge, securities fraud would make both look like a walk in the park. Although it probably would have come out one day, that was going to be revealed now thanks to Renee.

What was more, Renee got more calls than anyone else, as she had to deal with all the requests for interviews that were coming in. With any scandal, getting the first interview was the hot ticket. The *Today* show, *Good Morning America*, *Anderson Cooper 360°*, even *Nancy Grace*. At the end of the day, she went to see Richie and said, "I am handing in my resignation." Word had yet not gotten out that she was involved, so Richie assumed it was because she didn't want to be associated with them and the fact that the fund would be closing soon anyway.

After spending the night in jail, John was arraigned and released on $2 million bail, which he obtained by pledging his apartment. He hired Dave Van Zandt, the noted criminal lawyer, to represent him. Van Zandt specialized in making a lot of grandiose (bordering on ridiculous) claims intended to throw suspicion into an airtight case. It mostly had the effect of providing more headlines for the daily tabloids:

HEDGING HIS BETS! HEDGE FUND BIGWIG CLAIMS ATTEMPT ON WIFE'S LIFE WAS REVENGE FOR GAMBLING DEBTS.

STOP WINING! CUTTER SAYS WINE HAD ALLERGIC INGREDIENT IN IT.

When the Cayman Islands activities were leaked to the press—by Amanda, of course, but followed within minutes by Roland Deitrich after Mimi told him what had happened—they had another field day with CUT HER OUT.

Of course, in addition to all this, a more frightening prosecutor appeared at Flying Point on the same day John was arrested. Sasha had called the Securities and Exchange Commission to report on the "Bulletproof scam." Already under fire for missing the Madoff scam, the SEC was ready to follow the trail of any financial crime, especially one that was all over the mainstream papers. But murder was relatively easy to prosecute compared with this complex fraud. The other investors who had been duped with the change were none too happy. At least a dozen SEC staffers were at the office, their jackets emblazoned with ENFORCEMENT on the back, poring over file after file. While it seemed as if no one else at Flying Point had been involved, the premise was that everyone was presumed guilty until proven innocent.

Blake Somerset, upon hearing of John's arrest, was not surprised when the doorman buzzed up at 7:00 a.m. to say that there were two detectives who wanted to come up. In fact, he was relieved. He wouldn't have to listen to John berate him, and he wouldn't have to keep up the charade of the switched securities any longer. When he opened the door, they showed their badges and informed him that he was under arrest.

Although Renee had missed seeing Blake on TV the night of the Lehman bankruptcy, this time she did see him on CNBC being led in handcuffs from his rental apartment on Third Avenue and 83rd Street. He'd had time to put on his blazer. But for having his hands behind his back, he cut a rather dashing figure in gray slacks, pinstriped shirt, and Paul Stuart blazer as he was led into the waiting car. Needless to say, he was quickly terminated from his position at Barclays, which issued a statement saying they had neither knowledge of nor involvement in his activities, also noting that these issues were part of the Lehman Brothers estate, the entity that was representing the bankrupt firm. The estate, for its part, girded itself for the inevitable lawsuits that would follow. The SEC too found reason to visit Barclays, as well as all the other major firms that might be liable for the same activity. Congress was already planning special hearings on the matter.

Grigsby was beyond horrified at the news. Dealing with her reduced economics had been bad enough, but the day after his arrest, Ms. Lennon from Spence called to say that under the circumstances, the school had no choice but to ask her to withdraw Bitten from next year's kindergarten class.

She couldn't, and wouldn't, sink any lower. It was time she took matters into her own hands.

Epilogue

Sasha opened the envelope that had her and Adam's names handwritten in calligraphy. The invitation was on creamy, thick Tiffany stock and read:

> *Mrs. Gwendolyn Rumson Cogson*
> *and*
> *Mr. and Mrs. London Havemeyer the Third*
> *Request the honor of your presence*
> *at the marriage of their children*
> *Grigsby Anne and Thruce S[illegible]son Junior*
> *on Saturday at six o'clo[illegible]*
> *August 22nd, 2009*
> *St. Andrews by the Sea*
> *Southampton*
> *Reception immediately to follow*
> *"Windward Dunes"*
> *Meadow Lane, Southampton, New York*
> *White Tie*

As for those who were surprised by the marriage of Grigsby and Thruce, given the general knowledge of his sexual preference, they underestimated both of them. For those who had always assumed Grigsby was weak, frivolous, and oblivious to world events, they couldn't have been more wrong. She was in fact quite pragmatic when it came to the very serious matter of maintaining her lifestyle in the manner to which she had become accustomed. After her embarrassing outburst in court, not to mention Blake's arrest, and Bitten's acceptance recision, which traveled through the social network like wildfire (aided by none other than Thruce himself), Grigsby realized that money from her ex-husband was unlikely to be forthcoming and she was falling faster and further than she could bear.

Grigsby was at Provident with more jewelry one day when her timing was either impeccably on or off target. She ran smack into Thruce while inside. It turned out that he had been pawning pieces from his failed cuff link collection to pay the rent and buy clothing that he couldn't afford on his meager allowance. When each confronted the other, their confessions flowed. Thruce told her that his mother's parsimony (and his subsequent cheapness) was tied directly to her son's apparent sexual preference. Gwendolyn felt that men and women should be married. It didn't matter what they did behind closed doors, or other people's closed doors, but the institution of marriage was one she expected for her children. Given her own marital situation, she had demanded her husband put in his will before he died that Thruce must be married to have access to his large trust fund. It was really a marriage made in heaven, if not in the Provident Loan Society.

When people wondered to each other, or on one or two occasions asked Grigsby directly, if Thruce was gay, Grigsby simply tossed it off and said, "Of course not. That was some silly rumor started by a jealous woman a long time ago. He couldn't be more of a man—if you know what I mean." This, in turn, made most of the gay men on the social circuit cackle hysterically with one another, given their "inside information" on the matter.

Though Grigsby had already acquired during her first wedding all the accoutrements she would need to start her new life with Thruce, she still insisted on registering at Tiffany's, Frette, and Bergdorf's home furnishings department. She'd seen that nifty silver-and-deer-antler magnifying glass for $775 while shopping for her wedding gown and had fallen in love with everything else on the eighth floor. It would go perfectly in Aspen. The couple already had their eye on a cute little five-thousand-square-foot log cabin nestled right in Aspen Highlands. Grigsby was baffled, though, as the gifts came in. She hardly got any of the more expensive things for which she'd registered. She was sure that the Llewellyns would have come through with at least one sterling silver place setting, but they sent only two wine goblets. She hinted strongly to her bridge partner, Ellie Benson, that the Olga cashmere blanket at Frette for $6,200 would be perfect for Southampton but received only one Moroccan beach towel for $295. Then Thruce's cousin Jeannie Duckworth actually asked her if she'd registered at Crate & Barrel, and her co-chair from last year's ballet gala, Emily Franklin, said they were going to leave after the reception on Saturday because they were renting out the house and didn't want to spend the money on a hotel!

Still, their wedding could not have been more perfect, held on a stunning August day at the Cogson family estate in Southampton. For the first time in two years, people were enjoying their end of the summer vacation without fear of another meltdown. All of their friends and family were there. However, to the dismay of both Thruce and his mother, his older brother came with his new girlfriend, none other than Renee Parker! Jay Cogson had none of the ill-placed social morals of his younger brother and had met Renee in the elevator of 9 West 57th Street, as his office was on the floor above Flying Point. They'd been dating for several months, appeared to be rather serious, and caused more than a few people that day to wonder how the family would feel should another engagement be announced. The will did not have a race clause.

All in all, Grigsby still ended up getting everything she wanted, because she and Thruce were able to buy it themselves. They had such similar tastes and enjoyed picking things out together. They found, however, that unless they did the entertaining, it was hard to get people to go out the way they used to. Thruce's tennis partner, Peter Cahill, had gone back into financials too early and lost (it was rumored) between $10 million and $20 million. Their friends Bill and Ellen Compton had both lost their jobs; ironically, he was in high-grade fixed income at Merrill, and she was in high-yield at Bank of America. Bill and Ellen had always joked that they were a well-hedged couple. That turned out not to be the case. Both were replaced by their counterparts at the opposite firms when the merger was completed. Subsequently, they decided to move to Washington, D.C., the new financial center of the country, to take jobs at the U.S. Treasury for a fraction of their prior compensation. Grigsby and Thruce had a going-away party for them at Swifty's, where Ellen talked about how wonderful the public school system was in Bethesda, Maryland, the town in which they'd decided to live. Grigsby remarked that they should definitely look at Landon and Sidwell Friends, since both had excellent reputations. After all, most of Washington's elite, even President Obama, sent their children there, although she whispered that fact when Thruce was not around.

It turned out some friends had already been encountering difficulties. Steffi never did have her Palm Beach party. Oh, the landscaping was completed on time, but it turned out that their landscaper wasn't the only one who had lost money investing in Madoff. While Steffi's husband would never invest with "someone like that," it turned out what money they had that wasn't in Lehman stock, which of course they'd lost, was in Madoff via the Fairfield Greenwich Group. Steffi tried to make up an excuse about why the party was canceled, but everyone knew what really had happened. Lacey and Kermit, the two hedge fund wives from the American Museum of Natural History party, went in differing directions. Once Lacey's husband was arrested in the Galleon insider trading scandal that broke late in the summer, Kermit was told in no uncertain terms by her husband that she and Lacey could no longer associate. It wouldn't look good to spend time with a felon's wife.

For Grigsby, though, all was well. After Bitten's Spence acceptance had been withdrawn, the school quickly found a place for her when the engagement was announced. Mrs. Cogson was a member of the class of 1942 and an honorary trustee. Grigsby now had everything she wanted. She had managed to maintain her lifestyle, and she rarely, if ever, looked back on her prior life with Blake. As far as she was concerned, those years had served their purpose and gotten her to this next stage. She was back on track for a life that would now continue to go only up.

Blake spent a lot of time wondering how he had gotten himself to this position. The trial was reported on by Bloomberg and a number of hedge fund media outlets but only marginally picked up in the mainstream media. When it ended with Blake being found guilty, a numbness set in that lasted until sentencing day. It was only upon learning that he was to be sentenced to three years at a minimum-security prison that it hit him. That was three Christmases, three summers, three Mets seasons (to be fair, he could have gotten life and they still wouldn't win the World Series), and three years of children's birthdays.

Blake didn't really expect Grigsby to bring the children to see him; she acted as if he'd never existed. But he did make arrangements for Chip and Chessy to bring them up. The visits were awkward, and he could see he was losing any sense of a relationship with them. It made him tremendously sad and was the most painful result of his actions. After each visit, he thanked Chip and Chessy profusely for bringing the kids and asked them to make sure to tell the four of them on the way back how much he loved them and deeply regretted what he had done. He loved seeing the closeness that his half brother and sister-in-law had with their twins and with each other. Blake couldn't even stomach the thought of talking to Grigsby, especially after she married that gay guy.

How stupid was she, anyway? At least his financial obligations to her stopped, not that he had any money to pay alimony anyway.

As it turned out, Blake's time in prison gave him a new perspective on life. He realized that chasing an ever-increasing standard of living had worn thin well before his fortunes changed. Compromising his principles and values to get money had gotten him nowhere but here. He truly felt sorry for his former colleagues who still slaved away during the day, their BlackBerrys never far from reach, always hoping to upsize to the next apartment, house, jewelry, and life, when the next annual bonus was paid out. He spent a lot of time in prison working in the carpentry department and realized he had quite a talent for it. Upon his release, he moved to Vermont and opened a store midway between Okemo and Stratton Mountain that sold hand-carved furniture for the ski houses that littered the area. Whereas Grigsby liked to say "I'd never" ski in the East, once she'd skied Ajax at Aspen, Blake actually preferred evading the blue sheets of ice and granular corn that passed for snow where he was. From time to time, people came in the store who looked like he used to look and acted like he used to act. With his torn jeans, bulky sweater, and the beard he had grown, no one ever guessed that he could once have been just like them. And deep down, he was glad that he wasn't.

John was tried separately. The charge of attempted murder in addition to the very serious list of securities violations was certainly tough to overcome. Lucille Smith didn't feel that sorry for John, for just as she didn't like it when other lawyers played dirty, she abhorred it even more when her own clients did so. While many had threatened vociferously over the years, this was the first time one had actually tried to kill his spouse. She called Roland Deitrich to apologize for her client's actions. No sense being on the bad side of an opposing attorney, no matter what she thought of him. Roland was gracious when she called and was thrilled with the turn of events anyway, because the Cutter case sealed the negotiations for his second book deal: *What's Love Got to Do with It?: Getting the Most Out of Your Divorce.* He also took full credit for uncovering the Cayman Islands account and even the switching of securities.

John was defiant and told anyone who would listen that he was completely innocent and would be exonerated. In the end, though, he agreed to plead guilty and was given a lesser sentence than he might have received, of twenty-four years in prison. He was released in twelve and a half years. Though now barred for life from the securities business, John was once and always a trader who would be on the prowl for the winning deal.

In June, Mimi's father passed away. She hadn't been back in Sayville in several years. Her parents' house seemed so tiny, and while the town had changed a great deal since she grew up, it seemed old and small. After the service, she decided to take the ferry over to the Pines on Fire Island to walk on the beach. That June was exceptionally cold and rainy, and the Dolce & Gabbana dress she'd worn to the funeral wasn't warm enough, so she grabbed her old Sayville High cheerleading jacket. She couldn't believe her mother still had that thing hanging on the hooks by the door as if it were only yesterday, not twenty-eight years ago, that she had worn it. It was so strange to be back in the Pines. Whereas once she had helped her mother clean houses and been in those homes only as the help, now she knew many of the designers and art dealers who summered there. She laughed to herself thinking about how imposing those homes had once been. It was also ironic to realize that it was these houses and this very beach that had led her to her current life. Thanks to losing her husband, nearly losing her life, and certainly losing herself along the way, she now had more money than she would ever be able to spend. As she walked on the beach, she realized that she didn't really know who she was now. For the first time in many years, she saw what she really looked like, and it wasn't pretty. She put her hands into the pockets of the jacket and felt something metal. She pulled it out and realized it was her old silver-plated MedicAlert bracelet she wore growing up. It was tarnished, and the red paint that spelled out the words was chipped, but there was actually something very substantial, and almost stylish, about it. She put her hand around her neck and fingered her custom necklace—it was the amber one that had been a gift from the museum. She unfastened it and threw it into the ocean. She knew it was a dramatic *Titanic* gesture, but it seemed appropriate given what she had been through. She watched it sink into the waves. Maybe it would wash back on shore within a day or two, or maybe it would end up at the bottom of the sea for as many millennia as it had taken originally to create it.

On the ferry back to the mainland, she realized she hadn't felt this good in a long time and decided she was ready to make some other decisions. She sold the loft and the house in Water Mill. She didn't care that there were dozens of houses on the market right now. The money wasn't going to make a difference to her. The art collection from their homes and the office was auctioned at a special sale at Christie's. Lynn Fenestre helped to arrange the sale, and given the notoriety of John's case, the auction drew a tremendous amount of interest. Some of the pieces even sold for record amounts amid the worst art market in years.

Mimi appreciated what everyone who worked at Flying Point had gone through having to deal with John all those years, and thus she paid them all extremely generous severance packages. For Renee's work in uncovering John's transgressions, Mimi also gave her a special bonus of $1 million, as well as one of the Jeff Koons dogs, as she knew how much Renee liked his work.

Mimi bought herself a little cottage on the Great South Bay in Sayville. It wasn't much to speak of. Her old New York friends would have thought a maid lived there. She enrolled Annabella in the same public school she had attended. Then she took the vast majority of the money she had received from John and set up a foundation to give it all away. As a result, she was invited to more events than ever. She turned down most of the invitations, although once or twice a year she would go to them, if only to remind herself of what she was missing. She didn't wear much makeup anymore and let her hair grow long and gray. One event she did attend was at the Fashion Institute of Technology, when they featured her dress collection (the one originally intended for Annabella), which she had donated to them. When she arrived, she looked so different from the Mimi people remembered that some of the photographers didn't recognize her. It was fine with her, and she enjoyed watching the new crop of darlings flirt and prance in front of the cameras.

When she wasn't handing away John's money, she opened an art gallery on West Main Street in Sayville. She had a rather good clientele during the summers, when people would come over from the Pines and Cherry Grove. She spent a lot of time with her mother and many of her former friends from high school, most of whom, unlike her, had never strayed that far from their roots.

It had been a long journey, and she was glad to be home.

Sasha spent the summer not dreading the arrival of Sunday night, not longing for vacation, and not weeping at its conclusion. She took the summer off for the first time in her life, which only confirmed what Renee had suggested to her all along. There are some people who like having long vacations but were never meant to be unemployed. Sasha was one of them. Sure, she was happy, but at the end of the summer she was antsy to get back to the world. She heard with some satisfaction that the majority of SAMCO assets had left BridgeVest after she retired. Harry had his hands full trying to deal with the defections and ultimately was terminated by Flembrose, although the release said he "resigned to pursue other interests." George Fleming begged her to come back, but Sasha graciously said that after an entire career on Wall Street dealing with fixed income securities, that same well-worn corporate euphemism notwithstanding, she really did have other interests to pursue.

Sasha knew that she wanted Renee to be with her in her next endeavor. Needless to say, Renee was only too happy to jump at the opportunity. Sasha also called Jessica and asked her to be a part of the new venture. So in October, the doors of FashionAble Capital opened for business. Its mission: to fund and assist in the growth of fashion companies. Because they did not have outside investors to whom they had to provide a specific return, they chose businesses they really wanted to invest in, nurture, and take to the next level. They also wanted to have fun doing it. There was an article about them in *Vogue*, and as a result, a number of other women wanted to become investors. They were very careful whom they selected. The first requirement was that it had to be *her* money and *her* decision. She had to have a love of fashion and an entrepreneurial spirit. They particularly loved when a newly divorced woman became an investor and did their best to give her investment management lessons as well.

Sasha and Renee had a wonderful time working together. A friendship that can withstand the transition to work is rare indeed, but they were honest and up front about their personality strengths and weaknesses, and if they ever got into a disagreement, they were careful to stop and discuss what was going on. Sasha was in awe of Renee's ability to see through to the essence of a person or a business and figure out what to do. Some business skills cannot be taught at business school, intuition being one of the most important. Renee, in turn, loved working with Sasha, one of the most accomplished women in the financial sector. It was the opportunity she had been searching for since graduating from Barnard. With the bonus she received from Mimi and working at the new company, Renee was able to take care of all her parents' needs. She bought them a condominium in Florida, which she was able to buy out of foreclosure for fifty cents on the dollar. She put the remainder in FashionAble.

The best day of FashionAble Capital was when they took That Old Black Magic public. Renee and Sasha stood proudly at the New York Stock Exchange podium to ring the opening bell with Bruce Smith. While he had turned down the original deal after that meeting with Sasha, the one that had contemplated mass-producing cheap versions of his designs, the company now was positioned as the next Kate Spade, stylish but not outrageously expensive. After the proceeds of the IPO, Bruce would probably net about $15 million and Sasha's original $150,000 stake would be worth $3 million. There weren't too many female-funded companies that made it to an IPO, so for Sasha, standing on the balcony and seeing the mostly male crowd of traders below poised to start the trading day, the scene was so emotional that her eyes welled with tears as she pressed the button that would signify the market opening. When the first trade of OBM went by on the ticker, her heart swelled with pride and excitement. She was so glad that she had counseled Bruce to do what was in *his* heart, not *her* wallet. After everything that Sasha had been through over the last several years, she knew she was standing exactly where she should be. It was no surprise to her that OBM closed at 20, up from its opening price of 18. What was more, the market ended up 189 points that day.

A Word from the Author

The main character that knit together the lives of Sasha, Grigsby, Mimi, and Renee over the last two years was the financial markets. Things had stabilized by August 2009 as Thruce and Grigsby celebrated their merger... um, wedding. Since the government and its public faces snapped into action in the fall of 2008, the economy, it appeared, finally found a bottom in March 2009, and thus the risk of a meltdown had seemingly gone away. It was still not a pretty picture, however. The debt bubble that had been created in home mortgages and banks and hedge funds was deflating; government, however, couldn't let that happen for fear of outright economic collapse, so it moved the debt bubble onto government balance sheets. Not much better.

The Department of the Treasury became the most activist in modern times. They seized those institutions deemed too big to fail (AIG, Fannie Mae, and Freddie Mac), let fail those that weren't (Lehman, General Motors, Chrysler), forced dispositions where they could (Bear Stearns, Merrill Lynch, Wachovia), put in billions of dollars to prop up the country's nineteen biggest banks (Citi, B of A, Goldman Sachs, JPMorgan Chase, and many others), put two of the largest on super-probation (Citi and Bank of America), and got a stimulus package passed by Congress (Hank Paulson on bended knee to Nancy Pelosi). The Federal Reserve, led by Ben Bernanke, pledged that it would do everything in its power to avoid another Great Depression, resulting in interest rates at zero, outright support of the bond market, and other unusual liquidity and lending programs. The executive branch—first Bush, then Obama—made supporting the housing market and staving off a foreclosure boom a cornerstone of its efforts and ran up budget deficits and government borrowing to new records. Banks large and small continued to fail under the weight of bad loans. State and local governments were in turmoil as tax receipts fell, but unlike the federal government, they couldn't print their own money, so budgets got slashed and services were cut. California resorted to issuing its own IOUs for state tax refunds and payroll. Over seven million jobs were lost, and across the economic spectrum rich and poor households alike increased their savings rate and cut their spending. The story in the United States was played out around the world, as foreign governments and central banks found themselves inextricably linked to the same problems. Welcome to the downside of globalization.

New York City itself had changed. Historically, Washington, D.C., had the power and New York had the money. Now Washington had it all, and "Wall Street," rightly or wrongly, was being vilified as the cause of the economic collapse. Public outrage at egregious bonuses and taxpayer-funded bailouts was palpable. The sense of primacy that all New Yorkers felt was slipping. Indeed, with the ever-growing dependence on foreign investors—primarily dollar-rich China—to fund the American recovery through the purchase of U.S. Treasury bonds, the primacy of America itself was slipping.

Stressful times test the strength of everything—the bigger the stress, the bigger the test. Some people rose to the top by sticking to their principles, while others tried to scrape by or, worse, cheat. Relationships always fail or get stronger through adversity. Business models adapt or get pushed aside. History may not repeat itself, but it does echo, time after time after time. The mistakes that led to the Great Recession of 2009 will no doubt be repeated as long as there is profit in it. That's the nature of markets and capitalism. But at the same time, entitlement and quick-rich schemes become a thing of the past, replaced by the hard work and street smarts of entrepreneurs, inventors, and producers.

That's the nature of people.

As Sasha, Grigsby, Mimi, Renee, and millions of others pulled themselves out of the rubble, this was enough to give each of them hope.

Update to the Author's Note

When *The Recessionistas* concluded with Thruce and Grigsby's wedding in August 2009, the citizens of New York and the rest of the world were still picking themselves out of the rubble of our economy and financial system. After hitting bottom in the fall of 2008, it seemed as if the worst had passed. Writing today from the vantage point of March 2011, even though there appears to be stability in market conditions, there is still a lot of rubble.

It's just a different kind of rubble: banks, financial institutions, and other companies are perhaps no longer in danger of going out of business, but now it is the countries and governments that bailed them out that are suffering. Government policymakers in the United States and around the world have gone to extraordinary lengths to bring about this illusion of stability. The Federal Reserve injected massive amounts of money into the markets through purchases of over $1.5 trillion of bonds and when the economy continued to weaken through 2010, committed to buying another $600 billion. The European Central Bank did likewise as it contended with the struggles of many of its member states, including Greece, Ireland, Portugal, and Spain.

While policymakers have staved off collapse through their actions—for now—the legacy of the credit crisis still remains. Unemployment in the United States still hovers above 9%, and the housing market is still reeling, with foreclosures rampant and a huge oversupply of homes for sale. Households have been reducing debt and increasing savings;

while these actions are admirable, they nevertheless slow down our consumer-based economy, which needs spending to thrive. Budgets at the local, state, and federal levels—American and European—remain out of balance as expense burdens inexorably rise, thanks in large part to the growth of entitlements, causing a new round of fear about the stability of the Municipal Bond market in early 2011. It is perhaps no surprise that Americans followed the traditional course and voted with their wallets in the 2010 elections, but it still remains to be seen whether a new cast of characters in Washington will have any better ideas.

Another American tradition followed the credit crisis—setting up a committee to lay blame. The Financial Crisis Inquiry Commission was created in May 2009 to "examine the causes, domestic and global, of the current financial and economic crisis in the United States." The Commission held hearings, took depositions, and did loads of research to try to get to the bottom of the problem, but it was hard to pin it on any one thing.

For their part, Wall Street chieftains did admit that mistakes were made, but they didn't apologize. Goldman Sachs CEO Lloyd Blankfein told the Commission, "We talked ourselves into a complacency which we should not have gotten ourselves into, and which, after these events, will not happen again in my lifetime." Others expressed that they had lacked the foresight to tighten up their risk management. Morgan Stanley's John Mack said, "On some of the product in mortgages, we did our own cooking and we choked on it. We kept positions and it did not work out."

Almost two years later, the FCIC issued its report and concluded with the obvious: The crisis was avoidable—the result of human actions, inactions, misjudgments, and ignored warnings. The report stated: "The greatest tragedy would be to accept the refrain that no one could have seen this coming and thus nothing could have been done. If we accept this notion, it will happen again."

So will anything like this ever happen again? Policymakers think they found a legislative solution in something called the Dodd-Frank Wall Street Reform and Consumer Protection Act, which President Obama signed into law on July 21, 2010. The Dodd-Frank Act provides for new regulations on financial institutions and creates new supervisory and advisory bodies, including the new Consumer Financial Protection Bureau, and it tasks many agencies with issuing a variety of new regulations, including rules intended to oversee the areas that caused the issues to begin with. It will take years for many of the regulations to be completely written and most companies will find themselves overburdened with new costs to manage the rules.

If, as the FCIC concluded, what caused the crisis was human nature, then the Dodd-Frank Act will likely neither reform Wall Street nor protect consumers. For all the new rules, there will always be a Bernie Madoff. After all, human beings will always believe what is too good to be true, exhibit bad judgment, and ignore bad news. Some, however, will work diligently, focus, and lead their employees to great success. It is these people who are truly the fabric that makes Wall Street, New York City, and our country great.

Turn the page for everything
you need to be a

RECESSIONISTA.

Places to See and Be "Scene"

All the characters in *The Recessionistas* know the right designers to wear, places to eat, and parties they need to attend. Here are a few details for any budding Recessionista ready to make her (or his) mark in New York City:

- **Fred's at Barneys on Madison Avenue and 61st Street:** Lunch on the ninth floor provides nourishment for the grueling shopping on the floors below. The Belgian fries served with ketchup, garlic mayonnaise, and Russian dressing in small ramekins are not to be missed. Fred's is chic and delicious, and reservations are a must, especially on a weekend when Bill Cunningham, attired in his jaunty blue jacket, is often perched, waiting to snap shots of those who embody the theme of his "On The Street" column for the following Sunday *New York Times* Styles section. In the old days, Mimi Cutter was there every weekend with her stylist Flamenco. Ahh, those were indeed the days. Barney's lost a lot of money when she moved.
- **Bergdorf Goodman on Fifth Avenue and 57th Street:** If Barney's is the Dalton—the uber-cool, coed, private school of shopping—then Bergdorf Goodman is surely Spence. Old money and breeding ooze from its walls and even on the street outside. The shoe department on the second floor, one of Mimi Cutter's favorite places, is a veritable museum of shoes. Don't miss the home

department on seven, although this is the wrong place to buy a blender. Grigsby Somerset registered there and has declared the Gotham Salad at "BG," which overlooks Central Park, to be *divine.* Much to her dismay, however, she still hasn't received that silver and deer antler magnifying glass for $775.

- **Yura On Madison located on Madison and 92nd Street:** Ground Zero for Upper East Side private schools, this airy gourmet shop and cafe is one of the most popular locations in the Carnegie Hill neighborhood. Whatever you do, don't sit in Grigsby's corner, and beware of other mothers and meandering toddlers trailing muffin crumbs after school drop-off in the morning. Seventh- and eighth-grade girls from Sacred Heart, Nightingale-Bamford, and Spence rule the roost after dismissal, eating "pinwheels" while on the lookout for St. David's and St. Bernard's boys before the girls from the other schools get to them.
- **Monkey Bar on 54th Street between Madison and Park Avenue:** If it's owned by Graydon Carter, it's got to be hip. When the restaurant reopened in the spring of 2009, anyone who was anyone wanted to book parties and get in for the scene, the after-premiere dinners, not to mention the buttery monkey bread and chocolate mint malt balls that are served with the bill. The Monkey Bar is a regular spot for several of *The Recessionistas'* cast of characters. Art consultant Lynn Fenestre is often dining with a new client discussing what they saw at the Winter Antiques Show or Henry Street Art Show. John Cutter used to go there with Amanda Belden when they were together. Amanda still shows up at the noisy bar in the evenings with her friends. Annie Lee is now a regular too, following the turn of events that led to her financial boon and subsequent "fifteen minutes" that followed.
- **Sarabeth's Kitchen on 92nd Street and Madison Avenue:** Trying to get in on a weekend after 9:15 a.m. means a wait of well over an hour as people clamor for pumpkin muffins, "Goldilocks" eggs,

and Four Flowers juice. Infinitely quieter on weekdays, the topic du jour at the tables is usually planning for school auctions, while other tables are occupied by nervous parents eating prior to an interview at Sacred Heart, Brick Church, or St. David's, a few of the nearby schools. Renee Parker has not been back since the breakfast with Grigsby and Bitten. She'd like to forget that it ever happened.

- **Regency Hotel:** The address is 540 Park, and 540 Park is also the name of the restaurant where the power breakfast originated in the 1970s. It is also the place Sasha Silver has called home for the last fifteen years. Sasha's world changed when she met her Neanderthal boss Harry Mullaugh for breakfast the day after Labor Day in 2008. Today, she and partner Renee Parker are likely to be meeting with a potential investor in their fund, "Fashion-Able Capital." Harry has never set foot back in the place, which is just fine with Sasha. He'd be too scared to see her on her turf now.
- **Frederick Law Olmstead Luncheon:** Better known as "The Hat Lunch," this must-attend event is held in early May, at the spectacular, formal Conservancy Garden on 105th Street and Fifth Avenue. This is New York Society's version of the Kentucky Derby—only without the race, at least when it comes to horses. The benefit, hosted by the Women's Committee of the Central Park Conservancy, has raised millions of dollars for the upkeep of Central Park. Tickets cost $1,000, while hats can easily cost well over $1,000, and the Oscar de la Renta floral dress purchased especially for this event can cost $4,000. That adds up to a nice and tidy $6,000 afternoon. If you haven't bought a ticket before the invitations come out, chances are you won't be able to. The lunch sells out almost instantaneously and some women have been known to burst into tears when they learn they can't get in. One year, Mimi Cutter attached a $750,000 antique emerald-and-diamond floral clip she'd bought at Fred Leighton that morning to her hat.

- **Couture Council of FIT Fashion Lunch:** Started only a few years ago, this is now a not-to-be-missed lunch held in early September at Lincoln Center at the start of Fashion Week. Fashionistas and socialites alike come to honor a fashion designer, the list of whom includes Ralph Rucci, Alber Elbaz of Lanvin, Dries Van Noten, Isobel and Ruben Toledo, Karl Lagerfeld, and Valentino. Mimi bought four tables the year Alber Elbaz was honored and gave all her guests gift bags featuring Lanvin pearl and ribbon necklaces. At $875 each, with tax, that was *only* another $37,000.
- **New York City Ballet Nutcracker "Family Benefit":** Held on a Saturday in early December, this event starts with the matinee performance of the classic ballet and then moves upstairs to the Promenade where kids go wild. The cast of the show, which includes soloists from the Company and students from The School of American Ballet, joins everyone on the dance floor autographing programs for the children. A few high-profile fathers even make it to the event. John Cutter suffered through it once and tried to make a move on the Sugarplum Fairy.
- **Botanical Garden "Winter Wonderland Ball":** One of the few events held on a Friday night, this gala in early December attracts people in their mid-twenties to early fifties who are ready to dance the night away. Since they don't have to worry about getting up the next morning, they are happy to drive up to this gorgeous location in the Bronx. Cocktails begin in the Enid A. Haupt Conservatory, amid romantic, majestic palms and the holiday train show, which depicts an entire cityscape fashioned from wood and plants. Dinner is held in a tent decorated like a white winter scene. Women dress in gowns of silver, white, or black to complete the look. Sasha Silver loves this event, especially when the Nutcracker benefit is the next day, although by Saturday evening she is ready to drop!

- **San Pietro Restaurant on 54th just off Madison:** Walking into this restaurant means the smell of sautéed pears hits your nose first, followed by the stronger aroma of alpha male power. The Bruno brothers who have owned San Pietro, Sistina, and now Caravaggio for years treat the men (and a few women) who come here like kings. Whether it's Gerardo Bruno who greets you or head waiter Manolo, who can recite the southern Italian specials to you frontwards and backwards, there is no other bastion of alpha male power that is stronger. On any given day, Larry Fink, Joe Perella, David Komansky, and Marty Lipton are likely to be seated in window tables. It was said to be the one place at which John Cutter felt intimidated.
- **Cinema Society:** When a new film comes out, those in the know uptown and downtown want to be invited to a screening by the Cinema Society. Started by Andrew Saffir in 2005, a few hundred celebs and socialites alike attend these events and dinners that follow at a hip restaurant (see Monkey Bar above). Recently the *New York Post* reported in the "We Hear" section of Page 6 that they have supposedly nabbed the screening for the documentary about John Cutter due out in 2012, entitled *Clipped Wings: The Story of Flying Point Capital.*

Top Ten Signs of a Recessionista

Definition: A Recessionista is someone who made it through the recession and is coming out a stronger woman—especially when it comes to money. Here are a few ways to recognize one:

1. She rents ball gowns at Albright Fashion Library and pays 10 percent of the retail price. What's more, she doesn't have to pay to have them dry-cleaned after.
2. If she doesn't rent ball gowns she waits for Hallak Cleaners' "Penny Sale." If she brings in three of the same item to this high-end cleaner of wedding and party gowns, the cheapest one is only one cent.
3. She makes sure to be free and at her computer at noon every day so she can be online at Gilt.com, which features deeply discounted designer clothing and accessories from Alexander McQueen to Kenneth Jay Lane to Carlos Falchi.
4. Her favorite colors of nail polish are Essie "Ballet Slippers" and OPI "It's A Girl" because they last four days longer than darker polish. Over the course of a year that's $322 saved!
5. She is on the mailing list for Soiffer Haskin sample sales featuring Carolina Herrera, Dennis Basso, and Pratesi Linens.
6. She recycles her hat every year for the hat lunch by removing the old flowers and adding new ones purchased at MJ Trimmings in the Garment District.

7. She loves being a working woman because if she goes out to breakfast or lunch with a man he usually pays.
8. She buys her Prada bags and Manolo shoes "New in Box" (NIB) on eBay for half price.
9. She wears vintage costume jewelry instead of the real stuff to black-tie galas.
10. She takes home her salad from lunches at Fred's at Barneys and eats the rest for dinner.

Saving and Investing Tips

From investments to shopping there are so many ways to save money. Some large, some small, but all add up. A good Recessionista knows that no matter how much money she has, saving is always chic. Here are a few tips to bring out the Recessionista in you:

- Bring your own cup to Starbucks. You save eleven cents off the price (and what's more, you can help save the environment as well). That translates into $40.04 per year. If you did that every year, invested the money you saved, and earned 8 percent, at the end of ten years you would have $709.48. At 10 percent the total amount you would have is $804.50.
- Save money on gas. Don't leave your car running! If you need to pick someone or something up, turn your car off and get out. Leaving the car idling is sending money (not to mention fumes) into the air and that's not good for anyone.
- While you're at it, save on gas by checking the various gas stations in your neighborhood. You may find that you can save several cents per gallon by going a few blocks away.
- Water, water everywhere! And it's expensive as well. Buy a water filter or drink straight from the tap—especially if you live in New York City, which has some of the finest water around. What's more, as with many of these tips, you can help the environment by using your own glass and skipping the plastic!

- Take advantage of any tax-deferred saving plans such as Individual Retirement Accounts (IRA) and 401ks offered by your employer. If you earn $48,000 annually and have 3 percent of your salary contributed to your 401k with a 3 percent match by your company, an 8 percent return after thirty-five years would mean you end up with $550,531.80! What's more, consider the match by your company as additional salary.
- Buy in bulk. Most people know it costs more to buy a single can of soda than a six-pack and it costs even less to buy a case. Make all your nonperishable purchases in bulk.
- Watch personal debt, especially credit cards. It's hard to do when credit cards give us the ability to buy things out of our reach. The interest rates charged for unpaid balances are easily in the double digits and exceed 20 percent in many cases. That means that $1,000 can mean $200 in interest (and actually more since interest is compounded, building on itself each month). It's easy to see how balances can spiral out of control. Make sure you have a plan to pay off balances as quickly as possible.
- Try to only withdraw cash from your own bank's ATM. Sometimes it's not possible, but each time you use another bank you pay anywhere from 1 ½ to 3 percent in fees. If you withdraw $100 each week that could be as much as $156 per year.
- Refinance your mortgage to lower interest charges. Consider refinancing your mortgage to lower the rate and term. On a fifteen-year $100,000 fixed-rate mortgage, lowering the rate from 7 percent to 6.5 percent can save you more than $5,000 in interest charges over the life of the loan. For each $100,000 you borrow at a 7 percent rate, you will pay over $75,000 less in interest on a fifteen-year than a thirty-year fixed rate mortgage. And you will accumulate home equity more rapidly, thus increasing your ability to cover large emergency expenditures.

Discussion Questions

- The book illustrates two sides of New York life: society and the financial services industry. Which side "runs the city"?
- What do you think of Grigsby? Do you like to hate her, or do you think she is misunderstood? Have you ever come across women like this before?
- The character of Mimi has an expansive narrative arc. You see where she began and where she ends up in high society. Would you agree that she turned herself into a clown? Do you think that it was a stretch for her to realize on the beach what she had become after her father's funeral?
- How do you see Renee Parker fitting in this group of women? Do you think her family, while not from wealth, helped make her grounded in dealing with high society and the financial world? Did it give her an advantage? Do you know any "Renee"s? What drives them?
- Do you think men and women react differently under stress?
- What have you learned about the financial crisis upon reading this novel?

- Do you think the wealthy should pay more in taxes than they do now?

- Do you think there has been reform on Wall Street?

- Did Sasha make the right choice to leave after the press release changes?

- Contrast Blake and John. Both are bad characters, but how do they differ? Is one more or less admirable?

- If you had to make changes in your lifestyle (a la Grigsby and Thruce selling jewelry), what would you do? Could you do it?

- The characters in the book have neatly tied-up conclusions. Do you think the average American feels things ended that way for them?

- Do you think if there were more women in senior positions on Wall Street, the financial crisis would have been as bad as it was?

About the Author

Alexandra Lebenthal is the president and CEO of Lebenthal & Company and its multifamily office, Alexandra & James. She comes from a storied Wall Street family. Her grandparents Louis and Sayra Lebenthal founded Lebenthal & Co., Inc., a municipal bond specialist, in 1925. Her grandmother worked until age ninety-three. Alexandra followed her father, James Lebenthal, as the company spokesperson, and became president and CEO in 1995 at the age of thirty-one.

As a recognizable woman on Wall Street, Ms. Lebenthal is a frequent commentator on television and makes regular appearances in the media.

She is an active member of New York society, serving on several boards and as chair or committee member of several galas.

A passionate supporter of women in business, Ms. Lebenthal was named one of New York's one hundred most influential women in 1999 by *Crain's New York Business* and one of the top fifty women in wealth management in 2009 by *Wealth Manager* magazine.

A graduate of Princeton University in 1986 with a bachelor of arts degree in history, Ms. Lebenthal began her career in the municipal bond department at Kidder, Peabody & Co.

Ms. Lebenthal lives in New York City with her husband, Jay Diamond, and their children, Benjamin, Charlotte, and Eleanor.